Raoul de Navery, Anna Theresa Sadlier

The Monk's Pardon

A historical romance of the time of Philip IV. of Spain

Raoul de Navery, Anna Theresa Sadlier

The Monk's Pardon
A historical romance of the time of Philip IV. of Spain

ISBN/EAN: 9783337246242

Printed in Europe, USA, Canada, Australia, Japan

Cover: Foto ©Andreas Hilbeck / pixelio.de

More available books at **www.hansebooks.com**

THE MONK'S PARDON.

A HISTORICAL ROMANCE OF THE TIME OF PHILIP IV. OF SPAIN.

𝔉𝔯𝔬𝔪 𝔱𝔥𝔢 𝔉𝔯𝔢𝔫𝔠𝔥 𝔬𝔣 𝔯𝔞𝔬𝔲𝔩 𝔇𝔢 𝔑𝔞𝔟𝔢𝔯𝔶.

BY

ANNA T. SADLIER,

Author of " Names that Live in Catholic Hearts."

FOURTH EDITION.

NEW YORK, CINCINNATI, AND CHICAGO:

BENZIGER BROTHERS,

Printers to the Holy Apostolic See.

TO M. ZACHARIE ASTRUE.

You brought from Spain a copy of one of those works, which reflect the greatest honor upon the genius of that immortal galaxy of great men, whose glory reached its culminating point in the reign of Philip IV.

I first thought of writing the dramatic story of Alonso Cano when I saw and admired his wonderful statue of St. Francis, which it is impossible to contemplate without respect and emotion.

The book therefore belongs of right to him who first made this statue known in France, and who, like the Spanish master, wields alternately the pen of the author, the pencil of the painter, and the chisel of the sculptor.

RAOUL DE NAVÉREY.

CONTENTS.

THE MONK'S PARDON.

CHAPTER I.

THE STUDIO.

THE sun of a warm, glowing noontide fell in rich streams upon one of the finest studios in Madrid, and brought out its every detail in the fullest perfection. Students crowded eagerly to the luxurious dwelling of Alonso Cano, anxious to study and to perfect themselves in the various departments of art, all of which the great artist cultivated with equal success.

It was because of the versatility of his talents that the studio of Alonso Cano presented an aspect so different from those of his rivals in genius and in fame, Estaban Murillo and Velasquez. One end of the large room, well lighted from above, was entirely occupied by the *retablo** of an altar. Truly a magnificent one, such as is rarely seen outside of Spain or Flanders. Colossal in its proportions, it was executed with wonderful precision as to its merest details. The wood in the skilful hands of the artist formed an elaborate floral ornamentation, and, in an architectural point of view, the decorations were so exquisite that nothing of its kind had hitherto surpassed this work of Alonso Cano. Among floral

* Altar screen.

bowers, graceful arcades, and groups of light, elegant
pillars, statues of saints, figures of angels or processions
of virgins seemed to wander, pausing to pray in Gothic
chapels. Like the crown or complement of it all was
the Madonna, with a face so living yet so divine in its
expression, that the beholder felt inspired at once to
pray. Painting had combined with sculpture to give
life to these beautiful creations, and the warm sunlight
of a spring day striking full upon this grand conception reflected thence a double radiance upon the studio.
The walls were covered with holy epics rudely sketched.
Easels displayed great unfinished canvases, awaiting the
artist's hand. One of these represented Balaam's ass.
It was a picture wonderful in the richness of its coloring, the exquisite grace of the angel, and the expression
of the prophet's face. Alternating with these canvases
were statues of marble, which, in their faultless precision
of design, stood upon pedestals in all the perfection of
that ideal life, with which the art of the sculptor had endowed them.

Near these finished works were vague, half-defined
forms of terra-cotta, wrapped in damp cloths, and images
of wax ready for the final touches. The chisel, the pencil,
the brush, and the mallet fraternized in the studio of
Alonso Cano. Comparing the marble statues from his
hand with his paintings, one might vainly ask in which
of these arts, both of which he so successfully cultivated,
did the genius of Alonso Cano most appear!

Great vases of flowers seemed to display their grace
and beauty, as it were in contrast to the grandeur of all
else around them. For this studio, in its sublimity, was
like a temple. Here art heard as it were no sound but
the light step of the Spanish Muse passing hither and
thither among the disciples of the great master, encouraging them with merited praise, or dealing out needed

correction. The young men, all busy at their various tasks, usually worked with unflagging ardor, till the bell of a neighboring monastery warned them that the hour of rest had come. The silence which had hitherto reigned among them was then broken by a joyful movement. Each student put aside his palette, with a long-drawn sigh as of relief. He arose, shook hands with the others, and cordially, without the slightest jealousy, each inspected the other's work. One alone remained at his place. He was an Italian named Lello Lelli. He was apparently some twenty-five years of age, but in his face or manner there was none of that noble enthusiasm so delightful to behold in youth. The very suffering which was the predominant expression of his countenance had nothing noble or resigned about it; there was ill-concealed envy in his furtive glance, sarcasm in the corners of his thin lips, and a suggestion of torturing jealousy and ill-repressed rage in his deadly pallor. Fierce cupidity often shone in his eyes, which were yellow like those of a beast of prey, as he gazed upon purses filled with golden ducats, or the rich jewels of the court ladies who sat to his master. His mean, contracted forehead was surmounted by bristling red hair, whilst his dark brows, forming a straight black line over his eyes, lent a peculiar hardness to his expression. His long, nervous hands would have been beautiful, were it not for the form of the nails, and a habitual movement of the fingers, which constantly reminded one of the claws of a panther. His lithe, supple, willowy figure had something of the fatal attraction of the serpent in it. He stooped too low. In fact, he never seemed to confront any one boldly, but rather to glide, to insinuate himself into one's presence. He scarcely ever allowed his face to be seen. The daylight appeared to hurt his eyes. His voice sometimes changed from its habitual low.

morose sound to a shrill, piercing treble when he was excited. This peculiarity of voice had the same effect as
his look; it gave one an uneasy feeling, for it too was
treacherous. Certainly Lello Lelli seemed aware of his
defects, for he avoided as much as possible all inter-
course with his comrades, and if any of them forced him
to speak, they usually regretted a conversation, which
nearly always ended in bitter taunts or biting sarcasms.
Too proud to admit his comparative failure as an artist,
Lelli avenged himself by cordially hating all that was
great and beautiful and pure. He never discovered the
ideal side of a work, but quickly pointed out its defective
one. His bitter sarcasms were translated by strokes of
his pencil more cruel than any words. In this way he
certainly had talent—nay, as a caricaturist, in making
travesties of the thoughts of others, he had genius.

The poverty of his appearance formed a complete
contrast to the elegance displayed in the costumes of his
companions. Whilst they set off their handsome faces
by doublets of rich stuffs, embroideries, Spanish laces, or
ruffles edged with costly guipure, and arranged their
hair with a careless and becoming grace, Lelli wore a
thin reddish coat and a sober-colored, short cloak. A
leathern belt encircled his waist, whence hung a stiletto
with a very plain hilt, but a finely tempered blade, which
had no doubt given many a cruel wound. The motives
which had brought Lelli from Italy to Spain always remained a mystery. He himself maintained the deepest
silence upon this subject. It seemed not improbable
that it was an affair in which the poniard had played
an important part.

Hearing Lelli extol the Count de Ribera in the gran-
diloquent terms peculiar to him, and dwell upon his
talents and his munificence, the thought naturally occurred to one that he had belonged to the band of

ruffians and cut-throats that Lo Spagnoletto kept in his pay. One thing which undoubtedly contributed to sour Lelli's disposition was his want of artistic power.

Placed among a number of ardent young men, who were one and all fanatics in art and devoted to its highest cultivation, Lelli, limited to mere copying, felt it a double humiliation. But if creative genius were denied him, if his talent consisted in a purely mechanical reproduction of the work which he was set to copy, he was gifted as a compensation with a critical sense which none ever ventured to dispute. This being his only incontestable superiority, he never lost an opportunity of displaying it and making it a means of revenge. What wrong did he want to avenge? He could scarcely have defined it himself. His ugliness, his deficiencies as to talent, his own vicious nature, perhaps remorse and the hidden crimes of his past life, were all so many grievances, for which he would fain have held his companions responsible—those companions whose noble pride and unblemished honor involuntarily exacted his respect.

In spite of themselves, the latter often allowed their dislike of Lelli to appear. Their master vainly tried to overcome this dislike, and to smooth away the frequent difficulties which arose from the disposition of the copyist. Not that he felt any personal attachment for this enigmatical being, whose antecedents no less than his future plans remained a mystery, but he gave Lelli credit for the scrupulous fidelity with which he performed the task allotted him. Besides, at this period everything Italian was held in the highest esteem. Artistic Spain, not having yet reached her culminating point, openly admitted that all her sympathies were with Rome, Naples, or Florence.

Of all the painters of Spain, Alonso Cano was certainly the least Spanish, and his canvases belong rather to the

Lombard school than to that severer one, so full of austerity and of archaism, which owes its origin to Sanchez de Castro,* who painted at Seville in 1454. This style of art continued until Vargas † found himself beaten in the breach by those ardent young spirits, who sought to overthrow that tradition of coldness. Juan de las Roelas,‡ Herrera el Viejo § Pacheco,‖ who in this new path surpassed even Velasquez, Zurbaran,¶ and at length, Alonso Cano, who was, so to say, the last expression of the artistic genius of Spain.

Now Lello Lelli was an Italian, and was thoroughly versed in all the Italian schools: in the greatest as in the least studios he had painted and copied, becoming initiated into a style of composition of which he had mastered the theory.

---

* In or about 1450 Juan Sanchez de Castro founded the earliest school at Seville, whence came some of the most renowned artists of Spain. The style of his art has been intimated above.

† Luis de Vargas, studied at Rome, and brought into his own country the true method of oil and fresco painting. It was he who substituted the Renaissance art for the Gothic. One of his greatest pictures is the famous *Calle de Amargura* (" Way of Bitterness"). He died about 1568.

‡ Juan de las Roelas made himself famous for his use of the rich Venetian coloring which he studied under Titian, and afterwards brought into Spain.

§ Herrera el Viejo was among the first and most noted of the Andalusian school. He is said to have possessed " the true science of art besides correctness of drawing, profound and varied expression, and grandeur in strength." His style was fiery, with a certain coarseness and harshness, yet breadth and freedom of expression.

‖ Pacheco, another light of the Andalusian school, and one of the masters of Velasquez, was distinguished, on the contrary, by a cold correctness without passion or life.

¶ Zurbaran has been called the Spanish Caravaggio, not because he resembled him in fire or passion, for his works are colder, more reserved, nobler, but from the bluish tint which both so much employed. His greatest work is a St. Thomas Aquinas.

A fluent talker, and possessed of a rich store of curious facts and interesting anecdotes, his society was often beneficial to Alonso Cano, whose disposition tended somewhat towards melancholy. So quick was he to seize upon and comprehend his master's thoughts that it almost seemed as if he spied upon him for the purpose of being able to anticipate them. Poor and wretched in appearance though he was he was naturally arrogant and even insolent; yet he was always ready to gratify Alonso's slightest wish, or the merest caprice of Mercedes, the artist's wife. He played very well upon the viol, declaimed Tasso with great facility and considerable taste, and improvised verses at will. Without actually descending to the rôle of a buffoon, he was always ready to lend himself to the amusement of others. Friends, and amongst them Velasquez himself, often asked Alonso why he kept about him this repulsive stranger, who inspired such antipathy in every one.

"He copies with wonderful precision," would Alonso reply, "and in his interpretation of my work puts a certain suggestion of the Grecian which pleases me mightily. His poverty is made a reproach against him, but I do not see how he can help it, nor I either, since he earns so little. He works very slowly. He is, besides, very amusing, and then people hate him so cordially that I feel myself bound to take his part."

As the subject seemed displeasing to Alonso no one ever went farther than this, yet every one agreed in distrusting Lelli.

On the day upon which our story opens, when the bell of the neighboring monastery had sounded noon, the pupils threw aside their brushes, and after indulging in a prolonged stretching of their limbs, they rose and formed into friendly groups, or went about looking at each other's work. Lelli, as usual, was the last to leave his

place. But when he had left it, he strolled over carelessly to a picture just sketched by Pedro Castello, and representing Prometheus chained to the rock. Pedro had
certainly put considerable power into the composition;
the figure of the conquered one was at once pathetic and
terrible.

"Well," cried Castello to Lelli, "art thou about to
sharpen thy wit on my Prometheus?"

"Heaven forbid," answered the copyist; "thou knowest
my contempt for insipid pictures; thine is glorious as a
specimen of the terrible. Every one follows his own
bent. It would be impossible for thee to create the
lovely faces, which come quite naturally from the master's pencil. Thou shouldst study at Naples, Pedro, and
not at Madrid."

"Wherefore?"

"Because there is but one master who would understand thee."

"What master dost thou mean?"

"A man so pale, emaciated, and miserable looking, so
unprepossessing altogether in appearance, that out of
respect for Spain, the first nation of the world, they do
not call him the Spaniard, but Lo Spagnoletto, the little
Spaniard. I myself have seen him going about in his
misery from place to place, scarcely earning bread to
keep himself alive, and yet already dreaming of wonderful works, the realization of which was to make known to
the world all the sufferings and the agony of Ribera,
poor. Now that he is rich as a duke and powerful as a
king, having about him his train of poets, flatterers, and
train-bearers, he does not forget those evil days when he
wandered about the streets of Naples. His painting is
the reflex of his life. He lays bare his lacerated heart
upon his canvases. Gall is mingled with the colors,
which give so wonderful a life to his pictures; having

suffered in body and mind, and heart perhaps, he has made himself, and must remain, the painter of interior anguish and of physical torture. He reveals the secret of his character in his startling effects of darkness and sudden light. He can neither create a head of Christ nor paint a divine Madonna. He must needs astonish, strike, overcome, terrify, by a sanguinary spectacle of torn and palpitating flesh. He is only himself when he represents the struggles of Ixion upon the eternal wheel, Hunger preying upon the vitals of Tantalus, the Martyrdom of St. Lawrence on the gridiron, or of St. Bartholomew, where morsels of jagged flesh show that he was flayed alive. Thou art of his school; why dost thou stay with Alonso Cano?"

"Because I admire his genius."

"Yes, but so did Lo Spagnoletto admire Correggio.* Canst comprehend that? Correggio, the painter of Angels and of Virgins. Ribera, however, understood the character and scope of his own genius too well to follow Correggio. He felt that such an influence must destroy

---

* Josef de Ribera, surnamed " Lo Spagnoletto," the little Spaniard, was born at Hativa, near Valencia. He made his way to Rome, where he at first led a life of great poverty, though he afterwards became rich, honored, and independent. His first step in life was owing to the charity of a cardinal, who gave him the means of pursuing his art. His works, as intimated above, belong to the rude, savage, yet fiery and powerful school of Caravaggio. Led astray for a time by his admiration for Correggio, he attempted some imitations of his softness and delicacy, which did not, however, succeed. Ribera is purely Spanish in his style, despite his Italian training, and may be said to be among the first of realistic painters. He is noted for his exaggerated contrasts of light and shade, and for his frequent selection of wild, terrible, or hideous subjects. His jealousy of others amounted to ferocity, and led him, together with his faction, to drive from Naples all artists not of his school, such as Guido, Carracci, and others.

him irrevocably, and he soon returned to the rude school ot Caravaggio."*

"God preserve me from being like Lo Spagnoletto," cried Castello, "even while I might well envy him his fame."

"Art sure he has not been calumniated?" asked Lelli.

"It is certain that he embittered the life of Domenichi-no," said Castello.

"He did not prevent him from painting," said Lelli.

"He caused an attempt to be made upon the life of Guido Reni," continued Pedro.

Here Lelli visibly shuddered.

"That accusation was never proved," he said hoarse-ly.

"Was not Guido so terrified as to be obliged to leave Naples?" questioned Pedro.

"He might safely have remained there," said Lelli.

"No, no," cried Pedro. "Never will I follow the school of such a master. He takes no pupils, for he will tolerate no rivals. Death and terror forever surround him. He can count more bravoes than friends, and all the admiration which he excites is not worth the least part of the esteem which our kings and our people give to our own great men. Ribera would have done well to have remained in his birthplace, Spain, which he renounced, as he did her school when he became a Neapolitan."

"And yet," cried Lelli, "thy work is after the manner of Ribera. Oh, thou needst not turn pale with anger, thou hast the same elements of success, thou art fantas-tic, impetuous, violent, yet with an indisputable power

*Correggio, mentioned in a former paragraph, whose real name was Antonio Allegri, was among the first of Italian painters. His works are remarkable for their wonderful chiaro-oscuro, for a movement, variety, grace, and delicacy peculiar to himself.

in the greater effects of light and shadow. Thy figures cannot be very well distinguished from the darkness whence they emerge. There is something unreal and visionary mingling with reality upon thy canvases. Thy Prometheus is superb, and yet he is like one seen in a dream. This reproach in part at least is often addressed to Ribera himself; certain parts of the work are magnificent, for thy power approaches the power of the scalpel."

"That is to say," cried Pedro, "that what I do is not original."

"It is borrowed from Lo Spagnoletto, that is all. Thou needst not blush for the nature of thy talent, and God grant that thou attainest either the fortune or the reputation of that great master. He who, once half starved and ragged in the streets of Naples, has now lackeys in magnificent liveries, and the costliest equipages in the town. An ensign-bearer to hold his brushes and let him know the hour stands like a living clock forever at his side. His studio is the resort of painters, poets, and great lords. Consider my criticism therefore as the highest praise, and persevere in thine own way till thou hast given a second Ribera to Spain."

Pedro sat down discontentedly before his easel.

"The master will not be pleased," thought he.

"Ho, ho!" cried Lelli, stopping before a nearly finished picture of Bartholomeo Roman, "here we have, by our Lady del Pilar, a Saint Catherine dressed in brocade like an infanta. Were it not for the wheel peeping out from behind the folds of her dress, or the golden circlet which forms her aureola, one would have mistaken her for a great Spanish lady just putting the last touches to her toilette. God be praised, these are rare stuffs, heavy as Hungarian leather, and bravely loaded over with gold. Where didst find these Moorish-skinned angels, Bartholomeo, and with such haughty mien? I could fancy them grandees from Paradise."

"Always mocking, Lello," cried Bartholomeo.

"Mocking? I? Where dost thou find any mockery in my words? Has not the same been said of Zurbaran himself, and the Saint Cecilias, Saint Lucys, and Saint Ursulas which he exposes in our churches are as haughty as Castilian dames?"

"That does not prevent—"

"Does not prevent Philip IV. from calling Zurbaran 'the painter of kings and the king of painters.' I am of his opinion, but thou wilt permit me to prefer Zurbaran's monks to his figures of martyrs."

"Ah!" cried Pablo as Lelli approached him, "it is my turn now."

"Not yet," said Lelli, with a sardonic smile, "it would be very hard to praise or blame what does not yet exist."

"But the sketch?"

"Reminds me of the anecdote told of Herrera el Viejo."

"What was that?" asked Pablo.

"To economize his time, which had become very precious, when orders were pouring in to his studio, he had his canvases prepared by his old servant. She covered the ground with colors, haphazard, rubbed them in with a tow-brush, and out of this horrible chaos Herrera brought forth figures and draperies."*

"What then?" asked Pablo.

"Thou art still at the tow-brush stage of the work," said Lelli.

Pablo bit his lips till the blood came.

As the Neapolitan was about to approach a canvas representing an Ascension, the pupil who was working thereupon promptly threw a curtain over it.

---

* Such an anecdote is really told of this great painter, Herrera.

"Ah," cried Lelli, "thou wilt not let me see it."

"No," said Miguel, in a voice so cold that it was almost hard.

"May I know why?"

"Because, even if thy criticism is just, its effect is bad. Thy very praise leaves an involuntary discouragement behind it. There is something perfidious in thy counsel. Poor Roman is quite disturbed, and yet his composition is good, well posed, and the heads superb. Pedro Castello, whom thou didst honor by comparing him to Ribera, is not charmed by the comparison. And I, who carry my devotion to art to the length of fanaticism, fear a word of severe blame or of exaggerated praise. Thou, who art content to copy the works of our master, canst never understand what quiet of mind, what inspiration, and what fervor it needs to create and invent. Let me have Alonso alone for my guide, and I will gladly give thee all the merit due thee of being a skilful critic."

"Oh, thou never failest to taunt me with my mediocrity," cried Lelli bitterly, "and the little that I am, a copyist. Do ye not all among yourselves call me 'the beggar'? What harm does that do me? dost think that thy contempt humiliates me, Miguel? Thou art mistaken; and I would rather know at once that thou hatest me."

"I do not hate, I distrust thee," answered Miguel.

"Did I ever do harm to any one here?" asked Lelli.

"Yes," replied Miguel, "and what at first seemed to me unjust on my own part is yet as certain as the existence of the sun. Thou seemest to be surrounded by a fatal atmosphere and bringest misfortune whether thou wilt or no. One proof of this is that thou never excitest in us one elevated sentiment; discouragement is sure to follow from contact with thee, just as certain poisons flow from certain barks. Thou seemest to wither and dry up all that approaches thee. But if thou wert not what I have described, thou wouldst be an artist, and a true artist. It simply is, that God has refused thee the two mainsprings of genius, faith and kindness. Thou must be sterile, because thou hast never loved anything in the world. Many people's punishment lies in their impotence to create, and this impotence is infectious. The manchineel tree kills all plants that grow in its shadow. Thou killest inspiration and faith in the souls of all who hear and are tempted to believe thee."

"Proud and arrogant being that thou art," cried Lello."

"Proud," cried Miguel, "I cannot be proud as yet of what I am, for I am nothing. I am proud perhaps of the possibilities within me, my pure and noble aims, proud of having Spain for my country, Heaven for my hope, and Philip IV. for my master; proud that I study under Alonso Cano; proud in the hope that my name may one day be associated with those, who are the glory of our country. If such pride and such hope seem paltry to thee thou alone art to be pitied, and the blame is not mine."

"Miguel," said Lelli, in a tone of intense bitterness, "what thou now sayest aloud thou hast, I doubt me, long thought."

"Perchance," said Miguel.

"Why didst thou wait so long to let me know it?"

"Because thou didst never before undertake to mock at me and my companions. Because I never so well understood the fatal influence that thou wieldst upon us."

"It would have been more frank to speak out at once," said Lelli.

"But more respectful to be silent," answered Miguel.

"Why?" asked Lelli.

"Because thou art under our master's protection," said Miguel.

"Dost insinuate that I screen myself behind him?" cried Lelli.

"I state facts, I do not assign motives," said Miguel.

"And if it depended upon thee?" asked Lelli.

"Thou wouldst not remain an hour longer in the studio," replied Miguel.

"So at last thou hast thrown off the mask," cried Lelli.

"To be silent is not hypocrisy," responded Miguel.

"After what thou hast just said," cried Lelli, "friendship or communication of any sort is impossible between us. I am a restraint upon thee, and know once for all that I hate thee."

"What follows?" said Miguel.

"That both of us are too many here."

Miguel turned pale.

"Go on," he said, "what wouldst thou suggest?"

"That thou givest place to me or that thou takest thy chance of being killed."

"A duel!" cried Miguel.

"Yes, a duel here and at once," cried Lello.

"After the Italian fashion?" said Miguel, with bitter irony.

"Italian or Spanish," cried Lelli, furiously, "provided that it end in the death of one of us."

"Miguel! Miguel!" cried Bartholomeo Roman, "what wouldst thou do?"

"Rid you of this man, who has been too great a friend of Ribera not to have used his sword in his service."

Lelli in a fury snatched the stiletto from his belt.

"When I cry ready!" said Miguel.

Pedro Castello threw himself between them.

"Away!" cried Lelli, "I must kill him."

"Fairly, at least," cried Bartholomeo.

He took down, as he spoke, two swords from the panoply which decorated one of the panels of the studio, and offered one to each of the adversaries.

Miguel rested his hand upon the hilt of one, the while Lelli tried the metal of the other, making the fine blade hiss like a snake.

"On guard!" cried Miguel.

Lelli threw himself on the defensive, the swords clashed. Just then the door of the studio opened.

"The master!" cried Bartholomeo in a stiffled voice. Alonso Cano stood upon the threshold! *

---

* Alonso Cano is usually termed the Spanish Michael Angelo, partly because he practised the three arts of painting, sculpture, and architecture. He was even more of a sculptor than painter. As an architect he principally devoted himself to *retablos*, for which he made all the ornaments himself. The principal character of his works is softness and gentleness. He was remarkable for his execution of hands and feet, and distinguished in that way above all the painters of his country. His style is correct, elegant, and full of grace, and he undoubtedly ranks with Velasquez and Murillo among the first of Spanish artists. Of these latter we shall give an account farther on.

CHAPTER II.

THE MASTER.

AT sight of Alonso Cano the combatants hastily sepa rated. Miguel looked at his master with an expression of sorrowful respect, whilst Lello muttered an imprecation.

Alonso advanced towards them, as pale as a corpse. "Unhappy that ye are," cried he, "what could have led you to attempt each other's life? Is not human existence a sacred thing? How dare ye for a word or gesture spill the blood of a fellow being like miserable assassins? Yes, I repeat the word, assassins! Every skilful duelist is a murderer, and believe me sooner or later the curse of Heaven must fall upon his head."

Miguel bowed his head, but Lello stood looking the artist straight in the face with a mocking intensity.

"Who began the quarrel?" asked Alonso, abruptly. All the pupils at once cried:

"Lello, Lello!"

The Italian started as if stung by a viper.

"No," cried he, "ye lie, all of you! I never insulted any one. Ye hate me here in this studio, and ye rejoice in the thought that the severity of the master will rid you forever of a disagreeable companion."

"Silence," said Alonso, sternly. "I have pardoned thee a great deal, Lello, and my indulgence has often, I fear, been misplaced. This time I will be deaf to thy entreaties, I will hear no excuse, for nothing can lessen my horror of what thou hast done. I will have no brawlers in my house. Thou, Miguel, must find another studio wherein to study art. I shall regret thee, for thou hast been as dear to me as my own son.   And thou, Lello, must leave here in three days."

Miguel, approaching Alonso, said in a supplicating tone: " Do not drive me hence, master, do not drive me hence. Thou knowest my respect for thy character, and my admiration for thy genius. Who will make me such an artist as I hope to become if I am deprived of thy lessons? I know I was in the wrong, and that is why I humble myself now before thee. But could I hear my companions, my brothers, scoffed at so cruelly? My Spanish pride revolted under the constant sneers of this cursed Italian, who seemed to take a special pleasure in disparaging all that we hold as our greatest glories, and whose perfidious counsels discouraged my comrades. Master, thou must make some allowance for the ardor and impetuosity of youth. This severe lesson will, I swear to thee, be of service to me. So, forgive me, master."

" Yes, yes!" cried all the young men, "forgive Miguel."

"If it were a personal offence merely I should indeed forgive it, but I have, as you know, so terrible a horror of bloodshed that I cannot tolerate a readiness to quarrel which makes men mere bullies. No, Miguel, I cannot take back what I have said; but, while refusing to keep thee as a pupil, I confess that I will regret thee sincerely."

"I ask no pardon nor forgiveness," cried Lello, fiercely. " I know too well why Alonso Cano has this secret horror of dueling."

The artist changed color and leaned heavily upon the back of a chair. The Neapolitan regarded him fixedly.

" A singular incident occurred," said he, "in Granada somewhere about 1637, I believe."

At the mention of this date Alonso grew still paler and unable to stand sank into a chair. His pupils sur rounded him anxiously, but the artist waving them aside said gently:

"Thou art right, Lello, it was in 1637."

"About that time," resumed the Italian, "a young man, Sebastian de Llano y Valdez, was studying paint·ing with the first artist of the town, whilst the master executed wonderful *retablos*, such as we see here now. Sebastian was gentle, modest, and good—yet, one day, in a fit of rage he fought with swords, and was left for dead by his adversary."

Grasping the arm of the chair with one hand, and extending the other towards Lello, Alonso arose:

"I killed him!" cried he, "I killed him! but none will ever know the tears that his death has cost me. Yes, thou art right, Lello, and thy malice, in which I have hitherto refused to believe, has found its aim in the most vulnerable point in my heart. Well, it is because I have suffered such anguish, the remorse which follows upon such a crime, that makes me now so anxious to spare you. I wish that your hands be not like mine stained with human blood. I would not that your young lives be darkened by a calamity such as has overshadowed mine. Thou hast made known the crime and the sorrow of my past life, Lello, I accept the punishment; but I wish you all to know that since the hour when Sebastian fell pierced by my sword I have scarcely known sleep. Ye often see me oppressed with sadness, weighed down by an unconquerable dejection. It is because I am thinking of a young life gone out in darkness. I shudder at a recollection, at a chance resemblance, the sound of a voice disturbs me, the sight of a knife turns me pale, and I avert my head from a spot of blood. The phantom of death pursues me; forever before my eyes is that red gaping wound; among the voices of my friends, through the music of court orchestras, comes the cry which Sebastian gave in falling. I hear it even in the joyous laughter of youth. Ye have often, no doubt, wondered why I seemed weighed down by the burden of some sorrow when everything was smiling around me. Ye know why now. Lello has told you. I fought a duel and killed my adversary." The artist stopped, a sob arising in his throat choked his utterance.

"Pardon, master, pardon," said Miguel, softly.

Bartholomeo Roman advanced to Lello.

"Shame upon thee," cried he, "to awaken such painful memories. If thou hadst an atom of feeling thou wouldst not stay here three days, but would depart to-morrow, now, on the instant, for henceforth thou canst inspire only horror and disgust."

"I said three days," exclaimed Alonso; "till then he is free to continue his work and to keep the room which he occupies in my house."

"I would rather go at once," said Lello.

As he spoke he returned his stiletto to its place in his belt, then, looking slowly round at those who had so lately been his fellow-students, he said:

"Farewell! pray Heaven that I never cross your path again. I will now rejoin Lo Spagnoletto."

Not a single hand was outstretched to him, as pale and trembling with rage Lelli quitted the studio which he was nevermore to re-enter.

When the door closed with a loud bang after him Alonso looked sadly at Miguel.

"I will regret thee!" he said, "for I loved thee very much!- but do not fear, I will take care of thee. Thank God, there is more than one master in Spain, and to-morrow I shall recommend thee to the King."

"To the King?" cried Miguel.

"Yes," said Alonso, speaking with effort, "to Philip himself. I returned here full of joy and natural pride.

This morning, when the Infante Balthazar was taking his drawing lesson, his Majesty came to inquire about the progress of my royal pupil. He seemed much pleased thereat, and promised to pay me a visit to-morrow."

"The King coming to the studio?" cried Bartholomeo.

"Will he have his portrait taken?" asked Pedro.

"I hope so," answered Alonso.

"Ah, thou hast well deserved such an honor," said Miguel, "and severe though thou art to me now, I rejoice, master, in whatever good befalls thee. Hitherto, thy kindness to me has been more than paternal, and if ever, which Heaven prevent, thou hast need of young Miguel's aid, be assured that he will gladly die for thee."

The artist held out his hand to him.

"Thou wilt be here for the King's visit," he said.

The young man raised Alonso's hand to his lips; then he turned away to hide the tears which gathered in his eyes.

But the scene which had just occurred did not pass out of the young men's minds; the thought of the great honor which Philip IV. was conferring upon their master did not suffice to obliterate the painful impression produced by Miguel's dismissal and Alonso's confidence. Hitherto his pupils had supposed that his constant depression arose from too close application to his art; now they knew the cause thereof, and felt so much the more affection for him because he was really unhappy. How often they had envied him. And now, which of them would have been willing to exchange his youth and poverty and uncertain prospects for Alonso's princely fortune, high renown, and hopes of royal favor?

Perhaps they had too lightly regarded the regret en-

gendered by past faults, and the remorse which makes a
crime in some sort everlasting. To teach them this bitter lesson, remorse itself had taken a voice, a bodily
form, and appeared before them living and palpable, and
the story of Alonso's suffering was so much the more
salutary and impressive because they respected him so
highly. Sorrow had then its share in a life apparently so
cloudless. The triumphs of Alonso were, after all, expiated by secret tears. When the artist saw the impression which his sad recital had made upon his pupils he
endeavored to dispel it somewhat by speaking some
words of encouragement to each. It was not hard to
stimulate their zeal; each of them hoped one day to hold
a place in the history of art. They listened to their
master's lessons with deference, and painted with enthusiasm. The moral influence which Alonso exercised
upon them was only equalled by their devotion to him.
Alonso made his teachings wonderfully clear, illustrating them by demonstrations of which he had the proofs
at hand. He made sculpture for them the complement
of drawing; like himself, he accustomed them to give
their attention to various branches of art, so that their
artistic education was as universal as their talents permitted. A calm and recollected silence was the ordinary
atmosphere of the studio. If the silence was broken
from time to time, it was usually by the voice of one of
the students reciting strophes from Lopez de Vega or
Calderon.

Occasionally the regular routine was broken in upon
by the visit of some important personage. Sometimes
it was a rich merchant, desirous of bringing some costly
pictures with him to the East Indies, or again it was
monks, attracted by Cano's double reputation, who came
to ask him to undertake the decoration of their chapel.
His wonderful facility enabled him to fulfil all the de-

mands of his admirers. He labored indefatigably, some said for fame, others for money, and others again to gratify the whims of Mercedes, his wife. The truth was that Alonso worked in order to forget. Whilst he painted his exquisite Madonnas he lost sight for the time being of the blood-stained corpse of Sebastian Llano y Valdez. The young men resumed their various tasks, and it was only when nightfall darkened the studio that they put aside their brushes, and left one by one.

When Alonso found himself alone he passed his hand wearily over his face.

"My God!" cried he, "have I not wept enough, have I not bitterly expiated my fault? I hoped that Thou hadst accepted favorably and as the ransom for my crime, not only my secret tears, and my sleepless nights, but that long succession of pictures and statues which men call masterpieces, and upon which I have tried to imprint ardent sentiments of faith and love, so that the prayers which are said before these creations of my hands may rise to Thee, and perpetually plead my cause. I sought to calm the agitation of my heart and the anguish of my mind, that a divine peace might shine upon the faces of my Virgins and martyrs. I thought that each would become my advocate, and implore of Thee some quiet for my soul delivered unto torments of unrest. I deceived myself. The expiation was not sufficient, and the rod with which Thou hast chastised me grows more terrible than ever. Ah, how the memory of my crime was recalled to me just now. Another moment, and I should have found a corpse here in my studio." Shuddering Alonso Cano hid his face in his hands.

The door of the studio opened softly, a light step crossed the floor, and Mercedes bent over the armchair in which her husband sat. She was a charming young creature, but nervous and delicate looking; her mobile face reflected with rare vivacity the impressions of an ardent but fickle nature. There was a good deal of the child about her still. Perhaps this was partly Cano's fault, for finding her charming and attractive, he asked nothing more of her than her beauty and her high spirits. Mercedes was, in fact, frivolous, and her vanity, besides a strong tinge of levity made her character peculiarly unstable. As she did not occupy her mind with serious things it naturally became filled with frivolous ones. Heart and head were alike inconsiderate. Her young ill-regulated mind was ever on the alert for excitement. She loved her husband, but her affection did not inspire that security which is the charm of tenderness. A thousand things diverted her mind from her duties, which she skimmed over without fully comprehending them. In carrying out her caprices she displayed the temper and stubbornness of a child. Alonso usually yielded to her desires, at first through love for her, and at last for the sake of peace; for if he refused her anything, she always declared that the daughter of Frances-co Pacheco, Alonso's old master, and the wife of Diego Velasquez, was far more beloved than she, because her husband always gave her magnificent toilets. Mercedes' great fault was that she narrowed her husband's life by constantly keeping before him the frivolous side of existence, and tormented him by her never-ending whims, as if his only occupation were to order belts of gold, pendants, or agrafes for her. She would calculate as closely as a Jew the value of a picture, and spend the price of it for a bauble which delighted her for an hour, and was forgotten next day. Certainly, she was far from reaching the high level of the husband whom Heaven had given her; her levity and coquetry sometimes annoyed Alonso, but she rallied him so prettily upon his jealousy and soothed him with so much grace, that he always ended by acknowledging himself in the wrong, and promising her whatever she asked. If it chanced that Alonso refused her anything, she made great parade of her grief, and throwing herself into the arms of her old nurse, cried out that she was the most unhappy of women. The servants were of course not altogether of this opinion; but Alonso's melancholy contrasted so strongly with his wife's gayety, his frequent absences at the court, whither his duties called him, probably served as a basis for lying accusations. Hence, in her own household it was not generally believed that Mercedes was happy with Alonso.

Yet the artist was a model husband to her, and his only fault lay in that he was too indulgent and lacked the necessary firmness to deny her anything she asked.

However, such scenes were not of daily occurrence. Sometimes a whole week would pass without a single unreasonable demand from Mercedes. At such times, this light, capricious, ardent nature was really attractive to Alonso. Mercedes could always bring a smile to his lips; and her light, harmonious singing often chased away his gloomy thoughts. He forgave her childishness for the sake of her beauty, her grace, and her innocent prattle. If she were wanting in the dignity of a companion, she had all the charm of a child. When his dejection bordered upon despair, Alonso could console himself by the companionship of this young heart so full of illusions and so powerful in dispelling his dark visions. At the moment when she entered the studio Alonso had great need indeed of her smile. Seeing that he was not aware of her presence, Mercedes laid her little hand upon his shoulder. Alonso shuddered, then looking up cried:

"Thou ! it is thou !"

"It would seem I am not overwelcome," she said.

"Thou art ever welcome," answered Alonso.

"Oh, ever is an exaggeration," said Mercedes.

"No, I swear to thee," he cried, "only thou must remember my anxieties and cares, and sometimes— "

"Sometimes," said Mercedes, softly, "I do thee the injustice of dividing thy life into two parts."

"How ?"

"I leave thee the bad, Alonso, and I take the good. Oh, I know it is wicked and selfish. I know there are no words strong enough to condemn such conduct. But what is to be done ? It is not in my nature to suffer. I am weak, light, and so childish. Tears would dim my eyes, and I want to keep them for a long, long time to admire thy masterpieces."

"Art proud of them, Mercedes ?"

"Ay, that I am. I will be the happiest woman in Madrid when thou hast made as much money as thy friend, Velasquez."

"Ah, thou art growing avaricious."

"On the contrary, thou wilt make the money, I will spend it. Now, the day before yesterday Pacheco's daughter—"

"Say no more, Mercedes, I can guess the end of the sentence."

"Nay, I think not."

"Thou hast repeated it a hundred times. I can finish it from memory."

"Let us see if thou canst."

"Pacheco's daughter wore a brocade gown."

"Yes, that is it, that is really it, Alonso, a brocade gown, and a necklace, a royal necklace."

"Then thou didst envy her this dress ?"

"Naturally." ·

"And wert jealous of her necklace ?"

" As thou sayest."

" But thou art wrong Mercedes," cried Alonso, "thou art very wrong to attempt to vie with the wife of Velasquez, the friend and companion, rather than the painter and chamberlain to the king. I do not earn as much as he."

" It is thine own fault."

" I think not."

" Thy talent is equal to his, Alonso, nay, it surpasseth it. Velasquez only paints pictures, and thou makest statues of marble, and buildest altars, and causest churches to spring up out of the ground. Sell thy pic tures and statues and plans for a higher price."

" Art is not a question of money, Mercedes."

" For thee, evidently not, but—"

" But my fame should pay for thy toilets. Is that what thou wouldst say ?"

" In all truth, yes."

" Well, rest content, thou shalt have thy brocade gown and thy necklace."

" When ?"

" Very soon."

" Thou dost expect a large sum of money then ?"

" A very large sum."

" From whom ?"

" From the King, whose portrait I am to take, and who is coming here to-morrow."

" His majesty Philip IV. coming to thy studio ?"

" Yes, Mercedes. Therefore, as the King's liberality is well known, I can promise thee in advance that thy wishes will be gratified."

" But I did not tell thee all, Alonso."

" Go on then, what more wilt thou have ?"

" I want thee to take me to the ball given the day after to-morrow by the Count d'Olivarez, thy patron."

"Is that all now?

"Yes, but I want that very particularly. Wilt thou pledge thine honor to take me?"

"Most solemnly," said Alonso, laughing, "so thou canst begin to-morrow to prepare thy toilet, which I suppose will take two whole days."

"At least," said his wife gravely.

"Child," said Alonso, "thou art very fortunate, when it requires nothing more than a gown and a necklace to make thee glad. There are times when I could wish thee more serious, and again I envy thee, I who but for thee would never, never smile again."

"Wherefore?" asked Mercedes.

"Ask me not! A young memory should never burden itself with painful thoughts. All I can tell thee is that a moment ago, one of my fits of dark despondency was upon me, and I suffered bitter anguish, but thy presence has dispelled somewhat the burden which weighed upon my heart. I believe, that if thou wouldst thou couldst cure me completely."

"How could I do that?"

"By pitying me sometimes. I often fear that my gloom may be oppressive to thy twenty years, and that it is because thou art indifferent that thou refusest to take even the slightest part in that other portion of my life to which thou art a stranger."

"Well," said Mercedes, "I will try to overcome my selfishness some time. Meanwhile, come away from the studio and rest; I want thee to talk to me about this royal visit that thou dost expect, and to give me thy counsel as to the costume I ought to wear."

"God preserve thee from every sorrow," said Alonso, kissing her forehead, "for thou wouldst not have the strength to suffer; while to me it has been given."

Together they left the studio, and repaired to their own apartments.*

---

* Diego Velasquez de Silva, or more properly Diego Rodriguez de Silva y Velasquez, for Velasquez was really his mother's name, often mentioned in the foregoing chapter, was born at Seville in 1599. His masters were Pacheco and Herrera el Viejo. Studying from nature he, however, gained the wonderful truthfulness which is the chief characteristic of his style. Velasquez, undoubtedly the greatest painter of Spain, "has tried various styles, and succeeded in all," history, portraits, landscapes, animals, interiors, flowers and fruit. His skill in painting the human form was wonderful. Rousseau calls him "the man of nature and of truth." "His coloring was firm, sure, and perfectly natural." In the distribution of light and shade Velasquez excels. Velasquez enjoyed the constant favor and support of his sovereign, Philip IV. He studied in Italy for many years. In personal character he was austerely virtuous, benevolent, and devoted to his art.

CHAPTER III.

THE KING'S VISIT.

IT would be impossible to give an adequate idea of the bustle of preparation in Alonso Cano's house that day. Rich Oriental carpets were thrown over the marble vestibules, the staircases were adorned with a double balustrade of flowers and fragrant plants. All the servants were at work under Alonso's direction. Juana, Mercedes' nurse, superintended all the interior arrangements, whilst the petulant Jacintha, half-crazed with delight at the honor conferred on her master, put the last touches to her young mistress's toilet.

The pupils arranged the studio, placing the great canvases in the best light, and turning the statues upon their pedestals to form the most harmonious outlines. Marble busts were enshrouded in dark red draperies, while from a grove of flowering shrubs a wooden statue of the Virgin, painted with exquisite delicacy, seemed about to ascend into Heaven in a new and brilliant Assumption.

A single cloud threw its shadow over the festivities. Cano's pupils loved Miguel so much that they could not help lamenting his approaching departure. But, having once heard their master's terrible secret, they knew that it would be useless and even indiscreet to solicit Miguel's pardon farther. His presence would perpetually remind the artist of the scene of violence which had met him on his entrance to the studio, and thus revive his own sorrow.

The generosity of Miguel's character led him to acknowledge his punishment as just.

"I am indeed unfortunate," said he to his comrade "but I do you a parting service in ridding you of that viper Lello."

"Has he left the house?"

"Yesterday evening, Juana tells me," answered Miguel.

"Good riddance," cried they all. "But what wilt thou do, Miguel?"

"Try my wings and seek a new path for myself," he answered cheerfully. "I admire Velasquez, but I will not enter a studio which is in rivalry with that of my master. So discourteous a proceeding would almost seem like revenge. Alonso Cano has promised to present me to the King. With some encouragement from his majesty, I hope to find a place under the sun of Spain. And when, after your day's work, ye bethink yourselves of your old comrade come to his modest studio; together we will empty a glass to Spanish art, the most spiritual of all schools, and we will form a phalanx ready for the combat and worthy of victory."

"Yes, Miguel," answered all the young men, cordially offering him their hand.

Just then the distant sound of carriage wheels was heard. Alonso Cano came hastily down the stairs, while the gracious Mércedes, dazzling in her youth and beauty, well set off by her robe of black brocade embroidered with gold, lightly crossed the vestibule, which was as fragrant as a flower garden. Ranged in two lines were Alonso's pupils, with uncovered head and one arm akimbo, waiting grave and respectful. The mules halted at the door, and the King alighted from the carriage. The door was thrown wide open, and Alonso Cano, kneeling on one knee, took the King's offered hand. Philip IV. saluted Mercedes with his habitual courtesy. Few women even

at the court could rival the painter's wife in beauty;
therefore the King paid her a compliment which made
her blush with delight.

"We must see thee full soon at court, Doña Mer·
cedes," he said graciously.

Mercedes smiled and curtsied, replying to the King
with perfect ease and grace.   Then Alonso successively
presented his pupils to the King.   He began by saying
with a just pride:

"Pedro Castello, sire, a name which I trust your
majesty will remember, for if he follows somewhat in his
style the abrupt and fiery method of Ribera, he at
least will never abandon a country where thou deignest to
patronize art in so royal a manner."

"Pedro Castello," repeated the King, "thou art right.
I will remember."

"This is Bartholomeo Roman," said Alonso, "who
studied with Herrera before coming here; I mention this,
sire, to prove that he hath been trained in the highest
and truest principles of art."

"And this mere stripling," said his majesty pausing
before Pablo.

"Sire," cried Pablo answering for himself, "a pupil
and admirer of Alonso Cano, who, proud of the teachings
of such a master, will never cross the threshold of an·
other studio, for nowhere else would he obtain so perfect an artistic education, nor be taught so fully to
appreciate and to be grateful for the happiness of living
in the reign of Philip IV."

"Already flattering," said the king smiling.

"Only grateful, Sire," said Pablo.

Alonso Cano now took Miguel's hand.

"This one," said he, "is about to quit my studio; not·
in truth because of his unworthiness, sire.   He is of
noble heart and lofty mind.   He must succeed.   I ask

thee to grant him the execution of the first Sargas, which thou wilt have painted for the procession of the *Corpus Christi.*"

"He is but a mere youth," said the King kindly.

"Yet his style as a painter is broad," continued Alonso, "and his grouping of figures skilful. One day your majesty may deign to thank me for having made known Miguel to thee."

"Thy request is granted," said Philip.

Alonso Cano then presented his other pupils each in turn, after which they departed leaving the King alone with the artist in the studio. Mercedes herself had withdrawn, and radiant with delight was declaring to Juana and Jacintha that she would be sure to go to the first ball given at the court, and eclipse by her toilet the beautiful and haughty wife of Velasquez. Meanwhile the King passed slowly round Alonso's studio. Philip IV., the most artistic of kings, and the intimate friend of Velasquez, whose studio communicated with the palace, though accustomed to all the excellence of Spanish painting, which under his reign reached its zenith, was far from anticipating all that awaited him in Alonso's studio, or rather series of studios. All at once he perceived at the further end, erected into a chapel, the grand *retablo*, peopled with a whole world of saints, virgins, and angels. He could not repress a cry of admiration. He had never seen anything so beautiful before.

"And thou shouldst demand of me half a province for it," cried Philip. "I must have this *retablo*. To give it a case worthy of its perfection, I shall build a church grander and more beautiful than any in Spain. The palaces of Granada and the beauties of Seville shall pale before this new creation, which must give to the faithful an idea of the heavenly Jerusalem described by the apostle. Gold shall flow in rivers there; the walls shall be covered with gorgeous frescoes. If possible, Michael Angelo's St. Peter's shall be surpassed. Make thy mind easy, Alonso, the shrine shall be worthy of its jewel." The artist opened a portfolio and showed the King, who was wonder-stricken, the plans for a cathedral, saying in a tone of noble confidence:

"Wilt thou permit me sire, to carve out myself the shrine for this *retablo*, which thou deignest to call a jewel? Behold, sire, these majestic doors, the carving of which gains life from being peopled. Far from us be the Grenadine architecture, which recalls times of oppression; the house of God must not be built on the plan of Generalife. Since the Creator has lavished upon us exquisite beauties in nature, it is but just that we should use them in the ornamentation of His temples; as they enchant us in the panorama of the universe, so must they add unto edifices the charm of a new grace. I would fain combine with the magnificence of forests the elegance of plants, the grace of flowers, and the supreme beauty of the human figure. Creation should in some sort concur to realize the ideal of the Christian architect. To give, according to my view, a complete idea of how nature should be used in the decoration of churches, I believe that the artist should employ therein these three elements of ornamentation mingled in a harmonious whole; first, unintelligent but animate beings, serving to vary the carvings in the chapels, the capitals of pillars, or portions of the façade; second, man represented by saints and heroes, sombre statues shrouded in armor, monks ravished in ecstasy, young virgins crowned with roses, martyrs bearing palms; and third, to crown the work, the Immaculate Virgin smiling down upon the earth redeemed by her Son, Christ the Conqueror of Death, and highest above all, the divine figure of the Almighty Father."

Philip IV. seized Cano's hand.

"This church," he cried, "which thou describest with an enthusiasm so rare that I seem to see it rise out of the ground at thine invocation, thou shalt erect in Madrid, Alonso, and to-morrow, if so thou wilt, thou canst begin thy labor. Greek and Italian marbles shall come hither upon laden vessels ·for thee, and gold from the East Indies to realize thy dreams."

"Sire," cried Alonso, "thou hast realized my most ardent wish." Philip IV. turned again to examine the magnificent *retablo*, passing in review the statues of marble against their sombre backgrounds.

"Did not the Doña Mercedes sit for this figure?" he asked:

"She did, sire."

"An expressive countenance, a charming figure, a childish grace. Thou art fortunate, Alonso."

"Yes sire, most fortunate," answered the artist.

"Few men appreciate what they possess," said the King.

"It is but little merit to be grateful, sire."

"Yet gratitude in man is a noble quality."

"Sire, the first favor for which I had to thank Heaven was that I had a good and accomplished woman for my mother. Her lips taught me my first prayer; pure and saintly was she as the doctrine which she implanted in my youthful breast. She imposed naught of hard or difficult upon me, but inspired me with the desire of imitating her. Thus did my childhood speed on like a cloudless day. Goodness seemed indeed the natural atmosphere of the domestic hearth, and the air of piety there inhaled made body and soul at once robust."

"Proceed," cried the King, "thou dost interest me deeply."

"Pardon, sire, but dost thou ask from me my story?"

"Yea, and most completely," said the King.

Alonso's face darkened with its shadow of unrest, and he continued with some effort:

"Sire, if thou wilt deign at first to examine these pictures, after which, the while thou dost rest, I shall endeavor to gratify thy desire."

Philip admired each wonderful canvas in turn; the Virgin and Child; that masterpiece of tender and ingenuous grace kept him long spellbound. When he beheld the picture of Balaam's Ass, he cried:

"That angel is living and breathing! Ah, what drawing, what coloring! I thought I knew thy works, Alonso. To-day alone do I realize their full value. Therefore, it seemeth to me that the story of thy life should be one indeed of enthralling interest. Interest, in truth, there must be in the story of one who, in his full strength and power, scarce yet bordering upon maturity, has in fashion so wonderfully mastered the three arts."

Alonso bowed deeply, while Philip seated himself in a great arm-chair.

"Since I am here," said the King, "begin my portrait Alonso, it will be an excuse for me to come thither again."

"Sire, thou art generous," said Alonso, "generous as a king, a king of Spain, upon whose vast dominions the sun never sets."

Alonso placed his easel in the proper position, and hastily preparing his other materials, began to sketch his august model.

"Is it thy wont to paint standing?" asked the King.

"Nay sire, but respect—"

"Take thy artist's stool, Alonso," said the King; "the Grandees of Spain are permitted to cover in my presence, and yet of them who can equal thee? Truly, in beholding all that meets my eye here, I fain would con-fer nobility upon thee."

"Thou wouldst thus humilate many a proud gentle-man," said Alonso.

"Without elevating thee; I understand," said the King.

"Thou wilt deem me over-proud, sire."

"Nay, but of greater sense than vanity, which is rare," said the King. "Now am I ready to hear thy story, and thou knowest already with what interest."

Alonso began as follows:

"I have told thee, sire, that my father's house was one of benediction. Never did the day's work begin before we had all heard Mass. When we returned thence my mother applied herself to the cares of her household, whilst my father and I went to our places in the studio. Perchance, to flatter my pride, my father is usually de-scribed as an architect, but it was not the case. He mounted and arranged *retablos*, such sire as that thou seest here. I did, in fact, devote myself with passionate love to the study of sculpture and decoration. In the details of a tabernacle I attempted what I have since dreamed of doing upon a mighty scale. So rapid was my progress, and such hopes did my father conceive of me, that it presently entered into his mind to de-spatch me to Seville. My mother wept, but I, with the carelessness and ardent curiosity of youth, rejoiced at my father's resolution. My promises and caresses con-soled my mother somewhat, and the period of my de-parture was fixed. My father did himself accompany me. He desired to present me to my master, Francesco Pacheco, who had even then opened a studio in that city, which has been entitled the wonder of Spain. Need I, sire, make Pacheco's panegyric to thee? Will it not

suffice to say that Velasquez was his pupil, and Murillo *
and Zurbaran were likewise indebted to him for lessons. But Pacheco was not only a master in the art of
painting, his dwelling was in truth an academy. Science
and letters flourished there side by side. Hard indeed
would it be to picture to thee, sire, those assemblies of
eminent men who came thither to seek new inspiration,
or to brighten the spark of the artist's genius by their
own."

"That which is most worthy of remark in the master
whom thou praisest," said the King, " is that he hath in
a manner so absolute departed from recognized tradition. Wherein have his pictures of the depressing gloom
which marks those of Morales ? His personages are real,
they seem in truth to move under their draperies, and
from his school hath proceeded all of whom Spain is
justly proud."

"That which your majesty doth observe in Pacheco's

---

* Bartholemé Estaban Murillo, one of the greatest painters that
Spain or any other country has produced, began life in very humble
circumstances, but became, by force of genius, the first, perhaps, of
Spanish painters. "In scenes of human life," it is said, " he rivals
the greatest masters, in the imaginary scenes of eternal life he is
alone." It has been said of the two great Spaniards, " that Velasquez
is the painter of earth, Murillo of heaven." In religious subjects, a
writer on art says, Murillo comes up in every respect to what our
imagination could hope or conceive. His earthly daylight is perfectly
natural and true, his heavenly day is a wonderful radiant light. "In
the attitudes of the saints, and the expressions of their features, is all
that the most ardent piety and the most passionate exaltation could
feel or express." "In such scenes of supernatural poetry the pencil
of Murillo, like the wand of an enchanter, produces marvels." He had
three styles of painting, the cold, the warm, and the aerial. The
first for human subjects, the ecstasies of saints in the warm, and the
annunciations, assumptions, etc., in the aerial. He painted more
pictures than almost any other artist. He belonged to the Andalusian
school.

pictures comes from this," said Alonso, "that he was himself capable of discerning such beauties of ancient art
as were unnoticed by his predecessors. In the Casa de
Pilatos, richly stored with treasures of art by the Duca
d'Acola, Pacheco saw and comprehended at once, in
studying busts and statues brought thither at enormous
cost from Italy, what were real grandeur of style and
propriety of drapery. He abjured the Gothic in favor of
what he found in the most brilliant epochs of antiquity."

"But," asked the King, "have I not heard that thou
also didst enjoy the lessons of Herrera el Viejo ?"

"Yea, sire, and it is, true. But I passed hastily, as it
were through the studio of Herrera and did not linger
there. His own sons perforce abandoned him. His
nature is rough, powerful, ay, and terrible. His habit
of mind at once grand and cruel is reflected upon his
canvases. He paints with a something which approach-
eth frenzy, but the inequalities of his character take
from his pictures the sovereign calm of art at its highest. Never was man less fitted to gather students about
him. He is unsociable to the verge of savagery. In his
painting he disdains the art of pleasing. For him it
sufficeth to strike and to strike hard. Verily none can
deny him genius, but it is an almost brutal genius, and
better fitted to the vast dimensions and startling effects
of fresco than to the delicacy of pictures. His violent
school has produced in truth a schism in Andalusia.
Great was his renown, ay, and his influence, even Velasquez hath felt it, but he like myself cast it aside; we cannot forget the brutality of the man in the power of the
artist."

"I saw Herrera," said the King "not indeed at the
period of which thou speakest, when his studio was the
resort of numerous young men, but at that time when his
researches for the purpose of making medals of perfect

beauty caused him to be accused of the crime of counter,
feiting. When I beheld and admired his Triumph
of St. Hermengilde, I declared him innocent, for this
reason alone, that an artist like to him, who might demand what money he desired for a picture, would never
descend to the baseness of coining it. When one can
obtain so many golden ducats wherefore counterfeit
them ?"

"Oh, sire, thou wert right," cried Alonzo; "a Herrera's
violence never stooped to any baseness. He was too
great not to have enemies. But happy the artist who,
weighed down by so grave an accusation, finds a king
for his advocate !"

"Far have we strayed from the studio of Francesco
Pacheco," said Philip.

"To return thither," resumed Alonso. "Ah, what sweet
memories those days of study leave within my mind.
What a charm still lingereth around that dwelling, which
we were wont to call, 'the golden prison of art.' There
did we read book by book that wonderful satire of 'Don
Quixote;' there did we encounter sacred orators, princes
of science, poets and prelates. Pacheco, at once man
of letters, poet and painter, attracted a triple Pleiades
around him. And the teaching ! Pacheco perchance
exaggerated his opposition to Herrera. · It might in truth
be declared of him that he dreamed of the orthodoxy of
painting, and would fain give fixed rules to those who
followed inspiration alone. His school, full as it was of
ardent mysticism, had its infallible dogmas. Pacheco
permitted not that his pupils should dream as he himself had dreamt. He discussed in all sobriety the color
and form of the denizens of heaven ; he allowed us
neither to suppress an ornament nor invent a new
one. But this exaggeration apart, he gave soul unto
his figures, he disposed his light and shade with marvel-

lous skill, and his groups in relievo or to life were impressed with most rare grace and truthfulness. If he
hath much taken from the Grecian, revealed to him
by the splendors of the Venetian school, he hath likewise
profited rarely by such lessons to create a Spanish school
in Andalusia."

"Thy recollection of Pacheco is indeed of good sa-
vor," said the King.

"All who studied with him, will support me in my
utterance," answered Alonso. "Velasquez hath taken his
daughter to wife; among his friends are, Lopez de Vega,
Calderon, the glory of the Spanish drama, Villegas, the
ingenious poet, Luiz de Gangoras, Miguel Cervantes.*
The models used by this latter, in creating his wandering knights, likewise posed before us. In Seville was I
initiated into the grandeur of the true artist life, and there
sounded I its depths. Pacheco's dwelling resembled
indeed a palace, where flowed freely the gold of the New
World, and which was enriched with the rarest masterpieces of art. Furthermore, in that city, the greatest
commercial mart of the world, a painter's success was
not confined to his studio. A multitude, an eager, enthusiastic multitude, gave verdict upon his work. On the
Feast of Corpus Christi the streets through which passed
the procession were one vast exposition; even upon the
steps of the cathedral were displayed all the glories of
art; poets sang them, and the people greeted them with
acclamation. A young artist unknown on the eve of
that day might be famous on the one which followed.
This was a tempting prospect for a young ambition."

---

* Miguel Cervantes, the author of "Don Quixote." Calderon, who
has been called the poet of the Blessed Sacrament, is the greatest
dramatic writer of Spain; his dramas are marvellous; Lope de
Vega is, perhaps, her greatest poet. Villegas and Luiz de Gangoras
are pleasing and agreeable versifiers.

"Thy first triumphs date then from that epoch," said the King.

"Yea, sire, my first triumphs as a painter; but they did not long suffice for me. I yearned to model in clay or in wax, and to sculpture in marble. Hence, without completely deserting the 'golden prison of art,' I studied sculpture under Martinez Mantanez, the first sculptor of Spain."

"He who studied with Michael Angelo?"

"Yea, sire."

"But how, since thou wert a pupil of that great but fiery master, couldst thou have learned the secret of that supreme calm, which is the highest rendering of the word great?"

"Because, like Pacheco, I strove to follow the antique."

"Thy progress was no doubt rapid?"

"So rapid or judged with so much indulgence, sire," said Alonso, "that I was presently commissioned to execute three *retablos* for the College of Saint Albert, where I was then painting with Zurbaran and Pacheco, and two for the monastery of Saint Paula. These *retablos* were solely my own work. Modelling, architecture, and painting!"

"Were they as beautiful as this?" asked the King.

"They were much praised, sire!" said Alonso, "but at this period I lost my father. He was then at the Convent of Lebrija, where he was putting the final touches to the *retablo* of the main altar. He died before he had time to finish his work, and I was called to complete it. I did so with sentiments of twofold respect and profound sorrow. When this monument of mourning and of prayer was done it seemed to me that the happiest phase of my life was over, and that a funeral veil was stretched before the future. In good sooth there was naught to justify these apprehensions, yet did they never leave me. Glory could not compensate me for affection, and the joy which I might have felt on seeing the Flemish artists crowding to Seville to copy my work perished in the thought that henceforth I was alone, alone in the world."

"Fame cannot then console us for everything, Alonso," said the King.

"It hath not even the power to make us forget," answered Alonso.

He was silent after that. He laid down his pencils and palette and drew back to judge the effect of his first rough sketcn. But the pause seemed more for the purpose of mastering his emotion than of observing his work.

"Well?" said the King.

"I trust your majesty is satisfied. But I fear that my story—"

"Resume it, I pray thee, Alonso. Fear not, it cannot seem long to me."

"Henceforth it is sad, sire."

"But all the more human for that," said the King.

The artist snook his head, seized his palette, and resumed in an agitated voice:

"I was right in saying, sire, that I was henceforth done with happiness. My youth lies buried with my father."

"I can image well the poignancy of thy grief," said the King, "but at thine age sorrow is speedily consoled, and so many new emotions must have seized upon thy mind, and thy heart too, perhaps."

"I promised to tell thee all, sire. The more so that thou knowest half that secret, the memory of which still overwhelms me."

"Ah," said the King, "thou speakest now of that misfortunate duel?"

"Yea, sire. The cause was futile, merely a question of

art. Sebastian Llano was gentle, timid, and pious, comprehending no other school than that of Morales * the
Divine. He painted like him, not only with the inspiration of talent, but with piety, Virgins with the sword-
pierced heart, or Christ dying in the arms of angels.
His work was only less estimable than his character.
One day, in the course of a discussion on painting, he
upheld Morales, whilst I extolled Herrera el Viejo. This
question became the occasion of a direct and personal
quarrel. We fought with swords, and Sebastian fell.
Grief-stricken I rushed towards him, shedding tears of
sincere sorrow, and imploring him to pardon me his
death. He forgave me with angelic sweetness, repeat-
ing only:

"'I leave Inez without a protector, bereft of all means
of support. Let my sister find a brother in thee.'

"I swore to take his place in her regard, and Sebastian
forgetting himself once more, cried out:

"'Now, lose not a moment in leaving Seville. Thou
knowest the severity of the law against dueling. If I
survive, forget me; if I die, remember Inez.'

"I had my poor comrade brought to his lodgings,
where I entreated his sister to pardon me my crime,
and to remember that, whensoever and howsoever,
Alonso Cano would hold himself bound by his honor and
his hopes of salvation to respond to her appeal. Then
I left Seville and came to Madrid.

"Velasquez was here. I knew his generous and chiv-

---

* Luis de Morales, a painter of the Castilian school, was surnamed
the Divine, principally from his great fastidiousness in the choice of
subjects, which bore the imprint of an ardent piety. He drew with
care and correctness, always faithful in anatomical details. He ex-
celled in the expression of religious grief, especially in such subjects
as the Ecce Homo, Mater Dolorosa, or the like. He is somewhat
hard in his outlines, and has other defects common to his period.

arrous character, and felt certain he would not refuse me his support. I did not conceal anything from him. He reassured me, commended me to the Count d'Olivarez, and thou, sire, didst deign to take under thy protection a man more unhappy even than culpable. I say unhappy, for never, never can I forget the dying glance of Llano y Valdez, and I know that one day I must dearly expiate this crime of my youth. Whatever misfortune strikes me, and strike me it will and must, I am convinced it will be the punishment of this fratricidal duel. Often hath my uncertain temper been objected to me, for none can see a reason to justify it; my friends have reproached me for sudden and unto them unreasonable fits of despondency, but they cannot divine that at such times I am thinking of Sebastian, dead at the point of my sword, and of that weeping orphan-girl whose voice I have never since heard."

"Velasquez," said the King, in a tone almost affectionate, "is a dear friend of mine, but he hath rendered me no service so great as that of keeping thee at Madrid. I was not slow to appreciate the value of thy work. Once I had beheld the monument for Holy Week, executed by thee for the Convent of Saint Gil, and thy marvellous triumphal arch erected at the gate of Guadalaxara for the entry of Queen Mary Anne of Austria, I discerned that vigor tempered by grace which renders thy works so different from those of any other painter. I confided to thee the artistic education of the Infante, Don Balthazar, and—"

"Ah, sire," cried Alonso, "in coming to-day to the artist's studio, and commissioning him to paint thy portrait, thou hast done more than he would ever have dared to expect."

Philip rose.

"I know thy worth, Alonso," he said; "thy style is

thine own, it differs from that of any other artist; in th /
paintings one perceives the sculptor, and it is to thy pro-
ficiency in these various arts that thou owest thine indisputable superiority over all thy rivals."

Then regarding the sketch just made by Alonso, he
added:

"It is true to the life."

"Thou dost overpower me with kindness, sire," said
Alonso.

"Do not forget my cathedral," continued the King.
"I would that it be worthy the King of Spain who erects
it, since whatever thou dost it can never be worthy the
King of Heaven. So courage, Alonso. Strive to cast
aside thy painful memories. Remember that thy master
esteems thee and thy sovereign loves thee. Henceforth
Spain need not envy Italy, for she hath her Michael
Angelo."

And Philip IV., accompanying this royal flattery with
a smile quitted the artist's studio, leaving Alonso radiant
with joy and gratified pride.

CHAPTER IV.

A LETTER.

THAT evening Mercedes was in one of her gayest and most charming moods. Her dream was more than realized. The day before, the prospect of a ball at the Count d'Olivarez was sufficient for her happiness, and now the King had himself invited her to balls at the court. What a glorious occasion to display the toilet promised her by Alonso. She could think of nothing else. Whilst Philip IV. sitting to her husband in the studio conversed on art, Mercedes planned her costume and all its various embellishments with Jacintha. It never once occurred to her that this ball would be a great expense to Alonso; she knew he was generous, and besides, she must at any price eclipse the wife of Velasquez, famous throughout Madrid for the elegance of her costumes.

Alonso, more deeply touched than he could express by the kindness of the king, forgot for the time being the fatal shadow which darkened his life, and listened smilingly to Mercedes' chatter.

"Come," cried she, "thou wilt give me four hundred ducats for my costume?"

"Oh," cried Alonso, "that is a large sum."

"Thou dost make so much money."

"I lead the life of a prince, Mercedes."

"I am going for the first time to the court."

"Which is in truth a great misfortune."

"Wherefore?"

"Because thou wilt desire to return thither."

"The better for thee; thine influence there will increase."

"Yea, but, and thou askest of me each time four hundred ducats—"

"Nay, nay," cried she, "I promise henceforth to be sensible."

"It is I who am lacking in sense when I yield to thee," said Alonso.

"How dost thou make that appear?"

"These four hundred ducats are in truth all that I hold in reserve. Thou knowest me well enough to be assured that I would never ask a favor of Velasquez or of any other friend. Now in life we must needs consider the unforeseen."

"The unforeseen is the court ball," said Mercedes.

"I am very weak, Mercedes."

"Only kind," said she. "Wilt thou promise?"

"Yea, and yet—"

"Oh, I know what thou would'st say: Wait until the morrow. The night bringeth counsel. Thou hast given thy word. As a noble Spaniard and a good husband thou art bound to keep it. To-night, even now, thou must give me the four hundred ducats."

"Tyrant!"

"Dost agree?"

"I must."

Mercedes held out both hands to her husband.

"I was never so happy in my life," she said impulsively.

"So much the worse," said Alonso gravely.

"Wherefore?" asked his frivolous young wife.

"Because, my child," he answered, "one runneth great risk who placeth her happiness in things so futile as a festal robe and a ball, even at the court. Thy twenty years, Mercedes, have brought thee but small experience."

"And thy wisdom repels me at times," cried his wife. "I shall have my twenty years but once, permit then that I enjoy them. Whilst I am young leave me to my mirth, and go not hence to-night. We shall converse, thou shalt read to me the poesy of Soto Rioja, and I will sing to thee the airs in which thou dost most delight. Frivolous though I be I love thee dearly, Alonso, more dearly far than thou knowest, for did I not know that I possess thy whole heart I should be jealous, yea, I should die of jealousy."

"Are there who seek to instill doubts into thy mind?" said Alonso gently. "Ah, child, have a care. To profit little by the good we possess is ingratitude. Beware that thou comprehendest thine."

"Thou art right," cried Mercedes, "ever right."

Alonso and his young wife then repaired to a little boudoir oddly yet beautifully furnished, and Mercedes taking down a guitar from the wall began to play with delightful animation. She was beginning to sing in a voice clear and thrilling as a nightingale, when a lackey appeared, and offered Alonso a letter. As he read he grew deadly pale and seemed overcome by some strange emotion.

Mercedes perceiving her husband's agitation asked uneasily:

"Are thy tidings evil?"

"Not so," he answered; "yet it is an urgent matter, and I must even quit thee forthwith."

"Forthwith and thus, when thou hast pledged me this evening?"

"I would fain have spent it with thee," he said; "but I must perforce depart."

"Perforce!" said Mercedes, with peculiar emphasis.

"At the call of an unforeseen yet imperious duty," he answered.

"May I not at least learn what it is?" asked Mercedes.

"Thou mayest not. The duty includes a secret."

"It is passing strange to deny me this knowledge," said she, somewhat bitterly. "The perfume of that letter, the quality of the paper, all, all fill me with a strange misgiving. In fine, I would know from whom this letter cometh."

"Be generous, and ask me not," said Alonso. "It is an appeal to my honor, to my friendship, to a memory."

"This letter is from a woman," said Mercedes, coldly.

"It is," said Alonso; "I cannot stoop to falsehood."

"And I may not read it?"

"Nay," said Alonso, "my honor is concerned therein."

"But our honor is one and the same," said Mercedes.

"Dear child," said her husband, tenderly, "I will tell thee later. Do not voluntarily mar thy joy."

"I will no longer be held for naught," cried the young wife, angrily.

"Enough, Mercedes! enough!" said Alonso, imperiously; "seest thou not that I suffer? Add not then to this bitterness. If the secret herein contained could have been confided to thee, that would I have already done."

So saying, he rose to depart.

"Leave me not," cried Mercedes with a strange passion, which impressed the artist in his own despite, "leave me not! for and thou departest to-night there whither thou art going, I have a presentiment that evil will come of it."

The injustice of his wife so irritated Alonso that the veins of his forehead swelled, his nostrils quivered, his teeth were clenched, till Mercedes, starting back in horror, recalled him more quickly to himself than anything could have done. This involuntary movement of hers humiliated him profoundly.

"What," thought he, "when I have scarce finished reciting to the King the terrible consequences of my quarrel with Sebastian, I am again the sport of this blind rage which I had supposed forever overcome. I deemed not that the evil lay so deep; and, withal, this poor young creature must not be held responsible for my faults."

Thinking thus, he approached Mercedes gently.

"Have confidence in me," he said. "Perchance, later it may be within my power to tell thee where I go tonight. That hitherto I have tried to make thee happy even thou must admit. A moment since I promised thee in all sincerity to do everything to please thee, and gratify thy caprice. What has now occurred neither thou nor I could foresee. Providence wills it so, do thou submit to its decrees. I ask of thee a great sacrifice, if I judge by the ardor of thy entreaties. I must go, and I know not when I will return."

"Thou hast then a journey to take?"

"Perchance."

"What! Thou knowst not?"

"In all sincerity, I know not."

"But she who thus commands thy presence—"

"Hath a claim upon me which I may not overlook."

"She hath this claim upon thee, how?"

"Through a death," said Alonso, in a low, agitated voice.

Mercedes, with an effort at self-control, continued:

"Hence, if thou dost not return to-night—"

"Await me not," said Alonso, "and before sleeping pray to God for thy husband."

"But if thou goest," cried Mercedes, "I can neither go

to the ball of the Count d'Olivarez nor to that of the King."

"No, Mercedes, but rest assured, I will compensate thee later for such privation."

With an effort Alonso proceeded:

"Renounce, I implore thee, Mercedes, all thought of these pleasures; it is wiser. An imperious reason compelleth me to dispose this very night of the sum which I had so joyfully placed at thy command."

"Thou mayest go, Alonso," said Mercedes, in an icy tone; "but on thy return thou wilt not find me here."

"Great God! what wouldst thou do?"

"Seek another refuge till such time as thou shalt hold me in esteem sufficient to make me a sharer in thy secrets."

"Ah, thou art cruel, cruel," cried Alonso, in a tone of mingled grief and tenderness. "Thou torturest me with thy woman's whims and thy childish jealousy; thou wouldst lead me to betray my faith, my conscience, and to confide to thee a secret which is not mine. Thou wouldst make me in very truth the Judas of beings who have placed their trust in me. One day thou wilt regret what thou hast made me suffer. God grant that it be not too late."

"Stay," cried his wife.

"Farewell," said Alonso.

And without looking back lest the tears of his wife might weaken his resolution, he quitted the room.

He rushed into a plainly-furnished apartment, drew out a key from his pocket, and opened a cabinet, richly inlaid with amber and ivory. In one of the numerous drawers of this cabinet were ducats, with which he hastily filled his pockets, and closing the cabinet again went out. In the vestibule he met a lackey, who rose respectfully, and to whom he said:

"Thou needst not await me, Juan. If I return to-
night at all it will be late. Moreover, I have the little
key."

A moment later Alonso was walking rapidly down the
street. Meanwhile. Mercedes remained alone, a prey to
a twofold despair at not having learned Alonso's secret,
and at the thought of missing the King's ball.

As we have said Mercedes was of a weak and frivolous
nature. Educated by a mother who thought more of
her toilet than of her duties, she had not learned to find
a consolation for all the troubles of life in religion.
The least grief swept over her like a storm wind.
Doña Soledad, her mother, had frequently impressed
upon her that a woman should be absolute mistress of
the house; she had invariably quoted her own example,
and as Mercedes' father was a model of conjugal docility,
the illustration had some weight. Doña Soledad's second maxim was that a woman's beauty was a power
without appeal, and that everything must give place to
exterior graces.

From this false education it followed that Mercedes,
while making every effort to heighten and preserve the
physical charms with which Heaven had endowed her,
totally neglected the study of those things that give an
enduring charm to life, and the practice of virtue which
is its consolation. Her selfishness became immeasura-
bly developed, a selfishness more childish than deliberate,
but often dangerous, and sometimes cruel. Alonso
Cano, too busy with higher things to attend to the details of their household, usually accepted upon all such
points the opinion of Mercedes, whose whims were its
moving levers. Instead of being the tender master, the
educator of this light and thoughtless creature, he left
her in her ignorance, and forgot in the distractions of
his art and the urgency of his work that this soul was

placed in his hands as a precious deposit for which God would hold him accountable. He regarded the storms which obscure the domestic atmosphere as those summer showers which arise and pass away between two rays of sunshine. Had he not found by experience that Mercedes' hottest wrath was calmed by the promise of some new ornament? It never occurred to him that by acting in such a manner and encouraging Mercedes in her levity he was lowering the dignity of marriage as well as his own authority. Thus, when he left the house, Alonso knew that his wife was annoyed, but was far from comprehending the depth of her indignation. A fit of jealous fury had, in fact, seized upon Mercedes. For the first time in her life she was capable of a shameful action, and unhesitatingly and remorselessly sought means to accomplish her end. She knew that Alonso usually placed his important papers and his money in an Italian cabinet, which stood in an adjoining room. The key of this had never been in Mercedes' possession. But now in her anger she resolved to discover its secrets. Without stopping to consider the consequences of her act, she took a finely-tempered steel dagger and introduced the point of it into the lock. She was small and delicate, but at this moment she seemed possessed of a strange nervous force. The lock gave way, and Mercedes' little hands were soon busy in the drawers.

A few hours before Alonso had told her that he had four hundred ducats in ready money; again he had declared that he must apply them to a mysterious use, and he spoke the truth, for the sum had disappeared. Except some few insignificant papers Mercedes found nothing which could enlighten her upon what she wished to know, or reveal to her the secrets of that evening. She was about to close the cabinet, when a crumpled and torn letter met her eye, stowed away in one corner of a drawer. Mercedes took it and recognized it at once. She saw that the writing was that of a woman, and with dry and feverish eyes read this missive:

"Thou didst once swear to grant me at any time so-ever the service I might ask, did this service even cost thee life and fortune. I need thee now. Come to-night. A hundred paces from the palace gate thou shalt find a guide who will conduct thee to me. Bring with thee all the gold that is at thy disposal. My welfare depends wholly on thee.   INEZ."

Having read this letter Mercedes fell like one stricken. The sound of her fall and her piercing screams brought old Juana, her nurse, to her side. She raised her in her arms like a child and laid her on the bed, where she sought to bring her back to consciousness by softly bathing her temples and applying restoratives. Slowly Mercedes opened her eyes. A flood of tears gushed forth, and she hid her face in her hands without reply-ing to the questions of Juana, who, distressed beyond measure, could not divine the cause of this violent out-burst of grief. In vain did the devoted creature call upon Mercedes with maternal tenderness. Her young mistress made no answer, but continued to sob more and more bitterly.

At length, exhausted by her very grief, Mercedes grew calm, or at least her despairing sobs ceased; she sud-denly dried her eyes, and sitting up in bed took Juana's hands in both her own.

"Thou lovest me?" she asked, excitedly.

"Ah, dear child, canst thou ask?"

"Thou hast pledged thyself to forsake me never?"

"Ay; and that pledge will be kept sacred, Mercedes."

"Thanks, oh thanks!" cried Mercedes; "for weighed down by my burden of grief and my wretched memories I shall have thee at least to console me."

So saying the young woman threw her arms round Juana's neck, and remained thus silent a moment. Then she arose, and with a tranquillity which surprised the nurse opened her wardrobe and began to take out her brocade dresses and her lace mantillas, throwing them upon the chairs. She next seized a jewel-case and spread the contents upon the table.

"Help me, Juana," she said.

"To do what?" cried the nurse, more alarmed by her mistress's calm than she had been by her tears.

"Dost not comprehend that I am going hence?" said Mercedes.

"Away from this house?" said the nurse, aghast.

"Where I have been insulted? Yea!" cried Mercedes.

"Thou wouldst abandon thy husband?"

"Who has ceased to love me," said Mercedes icily.

"Oh, but it would be folly, ay, and shame, Mercedes. Thou wilt never do that, my beloved mistress, thou wilt never do that; and thou wouldst not see thy faithful Juana die of grief. With what canst thou reproach Señor Alonso? Never was husband more kind. He yields to all thy whims. For thee he is more indulgent than a father, and as affectionate as a lover. His genius has made thee the envy of all other women."

"His genius!" said Mercedes with deep bitterness. "Ah, perchance it is to that I owe my present anguish. Were I but the wife of some obscure artisan, none would envy me what thou callest my happiness. Yea, I was happy, or so I deemed, for my happiness was but a mockery, a delusion. Whilst I congratulated myself upon my choice, I was an object of contempt and derision. But, if hitherto I have been blind and senseless I will no longer tamely submit to insult; but, defied to my face, I will fly, cursing him who has descended to such perfidy."

"Señor Alonso capable of perfidy?" cried Juana; "impossible!"

"Wouldst thou have proofs?" said Mercedes.

"Yea, and strong proofs," said Juana; "plain must they be indeed before I could doubt the honor of a master whom I esteem as much as I love thee."

Mercedes took the letter, which was lying upon the bed, and read it aloud to Juana, in a voice trembling with anger.

"Well?" she asked, with a sort of fierce joy.

"Appearances are no doubt against Señor Alonso," said Juana; "but I declare to thee—"

"Is not that letter proof sufficient!" cried Mercedes.

"Nay," said the old woman, gravely; "that letter concealeth, perchance, some mystery. Recall all the proofs Señor Alonso hath given thee of his affection. Before thou allowest thyself to condemn him as base and perfidious reflect upon the nobility and generosity of his character."

"Hypocrisy is his crowning sin," said Mercedes, bitterly.

"No, Mercedes," said Juana, warmly, "no. If Señor Alonso were not a Catholic I might, perchance, suspect him. But he is a Christian, a sincere and fervent Christian. His genius even is inspired by his faith, and kneeling before his Madonnas I pray with new fervor. Child, thou must not go till thou hast questioned him; thou must not accuse him without hearing his story. It would be cruel and unjust, and yet thou art by nature kind and equitable. When he returns open thy heart to him with its doubts and its anguish."

"Have I not already questioned him?" asked Mercedes.

"The secret is not his," said Juana. "Do not torture thyself needlessly. A few hours' reflection can do no harm. Let Señor Alonso return thither. Be not rash. Lay aside till to-morrow thy project of a flight, which must ruin two lives. And kneel, Mercedes, now, asking courage to drink this bitter chalice."

Mercedes made no answer, but still crumpled in her hand the accusing note. With affectionate violence Juana took the letter, and throwing it to the other side of the room, joined Mercedes' hands.

"When thou wert little," she said, "I joined thy hands thus; and thou didst repeat after me the prayers which I loved to teach thee. Once more, Mercedes, and perchance for the last time, follow the counsels of thy old nurse. Call upon Heaven, which heals all wounds and dries all tears. Have recourse to Mary, whose heart was pierced with seven swords, and ask her for courage to bear this trial. I dare assure thee it will be short. My mind is not prejudiced like thine. I reason, when thou dost abandon thyself to the violence of jealousy. Shouldst thou, alas! be right, examine thy conscience before God, who sends thee this trial, perchance, to bring thee back to Him and to thy most serious duties. For hast thou not been light and childish beside thy husband, who is so great in power and talent?"

Mercedes stood silent and grave.

"Pray," said Juana, "pray to-night, and to-morrow thou wilt be consoled."

"But should I still persist in my design, wilt thou promise to accompany me?" asked Mercedes.

"I promise," said Juana.

The old woman then began to repeat aloud a prayer, in which Mercedes did not at first join. But soon, with some recollection, no doubt, of childish piety, and induced by her imperious need of some support, she repeated the holy words. True, she did not put therein the fervor of her childhood, but slowly the sentiments of faith, hope, and love expressed in the prayer entered into her soul. Her heart grew softer, her mind more calm, and when the last words were said she kissed the crucifix which her nurse held out to her. She accepted her trial as a Christian at last.

Then gently Juana undressed her, unbraided her long tresses, and saw her safely in bed. She lit a night-light before the statue of Mary, and Mercedes, consoled by the words of hope which her nurse had whispered, fell peacefully asleep. Then Juana crept out of the room on tiptoe, closing the door softly lest the sound might awaken her young mistress.

CHAPTER V.

THE CONSPIRATORS

A HIGH, narrow house, dark and sombre, with crumbling, mouldy walls, and odd, irregular casements, presented a curious and unprepossessing aspect to the passers-by. It would seem as if the architect had made a wager to crowd as much disorder as possible into the smallest space. A few rickety steps led up to the door which, with its great protruding nails and rusty grating, gave promise how dismally the hinges would creak when it was opened, or rather held slightly ajar, to admit the visitor.

It was in every point of view, and notably amongst all the others in the street, a suspicious-looking house. It might have been a den of thieves, a haunt of the lowest characters, or the meeting-place of conspirators.

Some sinister association connected with the place had beyond all doubt, brought it to its present dilapidated condition. For ten years at least it had been left to cobwebs, mildew, and memory. Scarcely ever was a light seen shining through those dusty panes; and when, perchance, the feeble glimmer of a lamp came thence, the passer-by could fancy an assemblage of ghosts holding solemn conclave in those dim, deserted rooms.

Yet upon the night of the 14th of June, 1644, a young man and woman poorly clad, and bearing about them the impress of untoward fortune, sat in one of the bare and almost unfurnished rooms of the house.

The man seemed engrossed by some painful and all-absorbing thought, whilst his companion eagerly watched the changing expressions play over his proud and strongly-marked face. Despair was in every line thereof.

"Inez," cried he, "thou must in thy heart hold me guilty of cruel want of foresight. Wherefore did I associate thy youth and inexperience with the desperate chances of a life like mine? My very love for thee should have been the strongest motive which forbade me to unite thy existence with mine own. Thou hast thy youth, and whosoever hath youth hath hope. A peaceful and retired home would have best beseemed thy tastes and inclinations. Yet I have brought thee into the midst of tumult and adventure which menaces our very lives."

"José," said his wife, gently, "when I took thy name, and pledged my faith to thee before God's altar, I swore to bear my part in all thine evil fortune. Yet even that thou dost exaggerate. Hitherto there hath been naught of hard or painful in it but, should it so become, even then would I gladly share it with thee. Perchance thou art right in saying that a retired life would best beseem me, but thou knowest full well how little hath this desire of mine been gratified. When I had reached the age of twelve my mother died, and my father followed her within three years to the grave. I was left alone with my brother, who did all that human soul could do to console me by his brotherly devotion. He was my guardian, protector, and friend. But God snatched him from me, and in a terrible manner. It was in my utter desolation that thou didst offer me thy whole devotion. Was not such an offer beyond my dearest hopes? In giving thee my hand I followed the spontaneous impulse of my heart, and I have never for an instant repented."

"Thou art generous, Inez," said José, "yet I behold thee now hiding like a criminal. From town to town hast thou fled, proscribed, thy life perchance threatened, for my fault. Heaven grant that I bring not new and more formidable dangers upon thee. I tremble lest at any moment they track us hither. If we are discovered they will hold thee as mine accomplice, and thou wilt suffer for my offence."

"This house is our best protection, José," said Inez, "and the messenger whom thou hast despatched is a trusty one who will never betray us."

"But will the succor thou expectest be given us?"

"Yea, José, for I have appealed to a sacred promise."

"Men forget speedily," said José.

"This man hath a noble heart, José," said Inez; "he is of violent disposition, indeed; but above all baseness. His sorrow for Sebastian's death was too deep and sincere for him now to disregard my appeal."

"God grant that thou art right, Inez, for without his aid, I know not what will become of us."

Just then a sound was heard without in the street. José y Florès, taking the lamp, prepared to open the door, but his young wife sprang forward to prevent him.

"Nay," said José, "let me descend first."

"Alonso Cano knows thee not," said Inez; "the house is of ill-repute. Seeing a stranger first he might suspect some snare."

Inez descended the spiral staircase with a light quick step, and reached the foot of it just as Alonso Cano stood upon the threshold. She raised the lamp which she held in her hand, so that the artist could see her face distinctly. Alonso bowed respectfully.

"Come," said she, "and thanks for thy presence here."

"No thanks dost thou owe me, Inez Valdez," said Alonso. "I would fain acquit myself of my debt to thee, and I will bless God if He permits me to be of service to thee."

Inez led the way into the wretched room where José was sitting, saying,

"This is my husband, José y Florès."

"Accept my hand," said Alonso; "a brother's hand, for I have sworn to be a brother to thy wife."

The two men clasped each other's hands, and Inez giving Alonso a seat began thus:

"Thou saidst a moment since that thou wouldst bless Heaven for an occasion to do me service. I believe thee, and to show my faith have brought thee hither. We two are in peril."

"In peril!" repeated Alonso.

"Before I proceed," said Inez, "I must warn thee that wert thou discovered here in this house, with us, thy good name would be much endangered."

"Doña Inez," said Alonso, "has an absolute claim even upon my life. On that day when I so unhappily killed her brother in a duel, I swore to hold myself at her discretion. Speak not then of dangers to be met in sharing thy evil fortune, and tell me without delay all that I can do for thee."

"One more word," said José. "What thou art about to hear may wound perchance thy deepest feelings, jar upon thy opinions and belief."

"Yet the expiation of my crime is above and beyond all other duties," said Alonso firmly.

"Thou wilt swear secrecy?"

"As though my own life depended thereupon."

"Thou art brave, as we know. But there are sacrifices more cruel than that of life itself."

"Thou art right," cried Alonso; "a moment since before coming here I deeply grieved my wife in refusing, Doña Inez, to show her thy letter. I left her in tears."

"Oh," cried Inez, "I will write her the whole truth later on so that she may never doubt thee."

José resumed.

"Therefore, if thine honor, honesty, all that is dearest

to thee on earth be compromised by thine interview with
us to-night thou will still guard our secret ?"

"I will."

"The lives of several men and Inez' own life are con,
cerned therein,"

"I pledge myself upon oath, then, that come what may
I shall be silent upon whatsoever I may learn and whatsoever I may do for your safety.   This do I swear by
the memory of Sebastian Llano y Valdez, whom I saw
stretched lifeless at my feet."

Inez overcome by this terrible memory hid her face in
her hands, and Alonso himself turned deadly pale. José
looked the artist steadily in the face.

"We have conspired," he said.

"Thou ?"

"Yea, and many others !"

"Against his most Christian majesty ?"

"Philip IV. is a great prince, loyal and true, a friend
of art, the helper of the needy, just and of fervent piety."

"Yet ye hate the government of such a prince ?"

"There is only one thing against Philip IV."

"What is that ?"

"His minister."

"The Count d'Olivarez ?"

"Precisely."

"The Count d'Olivarez, Marquis de San Lucar, is my
patron," said Alonso Cano gravely.

"We do not ask thee to become his enemy. He hath
rendered services to the kingdom, and for some years his
influence was salutary over king and country. Unhappily it hath so come about that Philip sees all things
through the eyes of his favorite; since the latter has
grown harsh, exacting, tyrannical, the King becomes involuntarily the accomplice of his faults. Olivarez is a
man of great cunning, versed in all the intricacies of

statecraft, intimately acquainted with public affairs. His crime at present is that he says, '*I and the King.*' I know him well. My father's experience hath more fully enlightened me upon his character than my own entire life. Whilst the father of the minister occupied the important position of ambassador to the Holy See my father was resting after the fatigues of many wars, and watching with an interested eye the events which so swiftly succeeded each other in Europe."

"The King's favorite was born in Rome, and there my father watched him grow up. Then he had defects which power has changed into vices."

"Enough, enough, and it please thee," said Alonso Cano. "What thou tellest me now I would fain forget to-morrow. Thou dost place me in a terrible position. I am deeply grateful to the Count. The crime of which I was guilty, in taking Sebastian's life, had placed me under the ban of the law, and would have brought about my ruin but for the man whom thou dost accuse of cruelty and despotism. He came to my aid; to him I owe my liberty. He hath been the architect of my fortunes, and even the visit of his Catholic majesty to my studio to-day is owing to the Count d'Olivarez. I cannot, therefore, listen to the accusations which thou dost bring against him."

"Let it suffice that thou dost not share our opinions," said José, "and permit me to continue and explain, that if I am Olivarez' enemy it is less through a spirit of intrigue or personal hatred than for the welfare of the King and the glory of Spain."

"A country's glory," said Cano, "never proceedeth from party strife."

José resumed:

"As a man, Gaspardo de Guzman, Count d'Olivarez, has some fine qualities, of which thou thyself hast given a proof since thou declarest thyself his friend; for one can feel friendship only for a man who is of some worth either in mind or heart. Yet thy gratitude should not carry thee so far as utter blindness. Olivarez is in a fair way to ruin the monarchy. If we leave him in power, soon shall Spain pronounce the downfall of a monarch too feeble to resist the will of his minister."

"These accusations are most vague."

"Shall I enter more into details?"

"Hope not to convince me."

"It will suffice that I justify myself in thine eyes."

"I will hear thee," said Alonso with more resignation than curiosity in his manner.

Inez, resting her arms upon the wooden table, kept her eyes fixed upon José with a curiously sustained attention. One could see from her attitude and the expression of her face that her husband's soul had passed into her own.

Alonso was deeply distressed. When answering to the appeal of Sebastian's sister he thought simply of acquitting, at the cost of some service rendered, the debt so long since contracted. But now he was not only called upon to risk his life and empty his coffers, but to become, in his own despite, an accomplice in a conspiracy against the repose, the power, the very life of a man to whom he owed everything. On one side was his oath to Sebastian dying, by which he pledged himself to protect his sister, on the other was the prospect of injuring a minister to whom he owed his reputation, his fortune, and the favor of the King. A sinister presentiment seized upon Alonso. The darkness of the night, the gloom of the house, the remembrance of Mercedes' tears, all combined to fill him with strange forebodings. With an effort he tried to follow José in what he was saying.

José began slowly:

" The Olivarez family was poor. Now there are two means of success in the world: one man begins by being rich, and through his fortune wins his way to honors; another commences by ambition, and proceedz thence to wealth. This was the path marked out by Olivarez; but once he became prime minister and Marquis de San Lucar, and in full possession of the confidence of his sovereign, he began to reflect that if through some evil chance the most Catholic Monarch of all Spain chanced to die, his son might not confirm the minister in his present degree of power. A fallen minister who has not at least the prestige of wealth in place of his vanished power is sure to pass into oblivion and to meet perchance with contempt. Olivarez was determined to be rich. Therefore, without consulting the King, or at least without fully explaining to him his motives in so doing, he doubled the public taxes in Spain. At first nothing was said. Respect for the King was deep and widespread, but at length the most humble complaints were sent up to the throne, or at least efforts were made to send them there. The count intercepted all such petitions. The King knows or hears nothing of all this, and the revolution will break out before there is even a suspicion of danger."

" The revolution, didst thou say ?"

" Yes. Beginning in Andalusia it will soon spread over Catalonia, and God knows where it will end. But this is not all. I could almost forgive Olivarez his tyranny did he not also aim a blow at the King his master."

" Olivarez betray the King ?"

" He hath betrayed him. At this very moment Portugal is ready to rise against Spain."

" And this rebellion ?"

" Is the work of the prime minister himself. Its object is to place the crown of Lusitania upon the Duke de

Braganza's head. Philip IV., unable to prevent such a step, can only, in return, seize upon the duke's Spanish possessions."

"But what can Olivarez hope to gain by thus impoverishing the kingdom ?"

"A personal fortune."

"How ?"

"The possessions of the Duke de Braganza are enormous. In recompense for his numerous services Olivarez will ask them of the King, who can never refuse anything to his favorite. Hence Olivarez will be the richest lord in Spain."

"Thou believest then—"

"That the count will be instrumental in losing Portugal to the King, that he himself may gain the castles and lands of Braganza. The bargain is concluded, and Judas awaits his thirty pieces of silver."

"It is monstrous," cried Alonso.

"All that is cowardly and ungrateful is monstrous," said José.

"But to accuse a man of such infamy doth not suffice The infamy must be proven."

"Just now it would be impossible for me to give thee absolute proofs. The future will prove it far better than I. I am at the head of a plot to nullify the prime minister's treason in favor of the King. But hitherto fortune hath shown herself hostile to us. A traitor hath sold us. We know him not, but Olivarez' police are in pursuit of us now, and we were obliged to separate lest the secret of our meetings be revealed. I came hither with Inez to watch the last operations of my friends, and was warned this very evening that I was sought for in the town. We must depart without delay, God knows whither. I have exhausted my resources, most willingly it is true, to succor some more needy than myself, but now we need horses and money. In our distress Inez bethought herself of thee."

"A thousand thanks, Doña Inez," said Alonso. "I begin to comprehend my task. As a conspirator, José, I promise thee secrecy upon my honor, and as a friend, a brother, the husband of Inez Llano y Valdez, I implore thee to accept my good offices."

The artist then drew forth the heavy purse with which he had provided himself before leaving home and went on:

"The wisest thing ye can do is to quit the city without delay. I will accompany you. Doña Inez will lean upon my arm; a mantilla concealing her face, she will be mistaken for Mercedes my wife. Thou, José, wilt follow us, closely wrapped in thy cloak. Should any curious *alguazil** interrogate us let me answer and say all."

"Oh, thanks, thanks!" cried Inez. "Thou wilt save us both."

"Whatsoever I do, my debt must still remain unpaid," said Alonso.

The young woman then wrapped herself in a mantilla, which completely obscured her face, and José enveloped himself in a dark cloak.

Soon after the deserted house had become more desolate than ever, and three people, conversing in a low voice, were gliding through the streets of Madrid. Ever and anon the snatch of a serenade reached their ears, or the heavy tread of the *alguazils* going their rounds filled them with sudden affright.

"José," said Alonso, "I will accompany you without the walls, and in truth I shall not feel at ease till I have procured you the means wherewith to fly hence with all speed. Hearken to me, José, I pray thee, and renounce a work which, despite all the accusations thou bringest

---

*A species of military police like the gens d'armes of France.

against the Count d'Olivarez, can only result to thine
own prejudice.   When thou art in safety apprise me of
thy place of refuge, that I may write to thee and keep
myself in thy memory."

As they passed a species of hostelry they heard the
pawing of horses in the court.

"God comes to our aid perchance," said Alonso.

He knocked at the inn-door.   A boy, half asleep,
opened it.

"What would your lordships?" said he.

"Two horses," said Alonso.

"For a long journey?"

"So long that thy beasts will not return."

"Then, thou wouldst not hire them?"

"Nay, I would purchase them."

"They are swift coursers," said the boy; "my master
will sell them dearly."

"And thou wouldst some *maravedis* for having aided
in the traffic.   Take this ducat and make haste."

"Generous as a king," cried the boy, "they will be
dear, my lord, especially at this hour.   But, for thy generosity, I will hasten to discover."

The lackey mounted hastily to his master's room.
"Here is a brave affair, " said he, "if thou wouldst sell
two horses.   Two cavaliers, and a lady; there is a mystery afoot.   To buy horses at four in the morning without proclaiming whither they go."

"They will pay me double," cried the innkeeper,
dressing hastily.   "A hundred ducats, not one less."

"And my share, master?"

"A new coat for the feast of *Corpus Christi.*"

The innkeeper descended hastily to the court, but in
spite of all his efforts could not recognize the purchasers
of his horses, so completely were their faces enshrouded
by the folds of their cloaks.

The bargain was soon completed, and José mounted one horse, taking Inez on the crupper, while Alonso rode the other. When the first streaks of dawn appeared in the east the three travellers were outside the walls. Alonso then alighted, and Inez having done likewise, he assisted her to remount the most gentle of the two steeds. This done the artist uncovered his head.

"God guard you," he cried. "*Vaga con Dios.*" *

"We shall never forget thee," cried the young couple, simultaneously.

The fugitives set spurs to their horses, and Alonso, thus left alone, followed them with his eyes till they had passed out of sight. Then, worn out by his long vigil, and by the varied emotions through which he had passed, he sat down upon the stone steps of a colossal calvary, and fell into a profound reverie. The rays of the early sun made him shiver, he sprung up and began to walk slowly towards the city. The duty which had just devolved upon him had been indeed an imperious one; but Alonso felt sad misgivings as to how he should calm Mercedes' wrath and dispel her jealousy of the previous evening. What reason could he assign that would put her suspicions at rest? How excuse himself? Could he once more employ the vulgar but often happy expedient of overcoming her resentment by gratifying some costly whim? No, for he had given to José all the savings originally intended to purchase for Mercedes the robe and jewels she craved. She would accuse him of treachery, indifference and avarice all at once; and he knew that it was impossible for him to tell her what he had done, or explain that it was absolutely necessary he should dispose of the four hundred ducats upon which she had counted for her costume at the ball.

---

* A Spanish saying, literally " Go with God."

On the other hand, Alonso felt relieved that he had in some measure paid to Inez the terrible debt contracted through Sebastian. Meanwhile, he slowly pursued his way, pausing to contemplate every familiar detail of the common peasant life, as though he saw them for the first time. Thus do cowards hesitate when they are about to enter upon a perilous way.

Venders of fruits and herbs began to open their shops, and fresh rosy faces to appear through the *miradores.** There was a stir of life in the streets. Monks in their long and sombre garb, women on their way to church, water-carriers with their pails, and flower-sellers with baskets garlanded with pomegranate leaves, offered their bouquets to the passers-by. Whilst the artist seemed to be completely absorbed in the living panorama passing before his eyes, he never lost sight for a moment of the face of his young wife whom he had left in tears.

At last he was in his own neighborhood. He drew near his own street. He heard as he approached a dull murmur which increased till it assumed the proportions of a tumult of voices. Some extraordinary event seemed to have transpired. Alonso quickened his steps. He was astonished to behold an excited throng gathered before his door. Every one was talking loud, and he could distinguish cries of horror and compassion. When they recognized Alonso Cano the groups of curious people separated, making way for the friend of the Count d'Olivarez.

But it was not only in token of respect that the people thus drew aside, and the artist felt his heart sicken as at the approach of some terrible calamity. He advanced, pale and haggard, and with parched and trembling lips. He caught as he went these few words:

"It is an awful, an inconceivable occurrence."

---

* A screen used in connection with the balconies which are inseparable from all Spanish houses.

CHAPTER VI.

THE CRIME.

WHEN Alonso appeared upon the threshold, Miguel detached himself from the group of pupils collected around the studio door and ran to meet his master.

"Courage!" said he, "courage!"

The artist's face blanched.

"It is true then that some terrible misfortune has happened here."

"A most terrible misfortune," said Bartholomeo Roman.

Alonso Cano passed his hand across his forehead, upon which stood great drops of sweat, and cried out in a tone of agony:

"Mercedes!"

He would have rushed up the stairs when Miguel seized him by the arm.

"Go not up," cried he, "for the love of God go not up, it is too horrible."

"Horrible!" repeated Alonso, half dazed, "Mercedes !"

He stood still supporting himself against the balustrade, for his brain seemed paralyzed, and his thoughts wandering. A terrible misfortune mingled in his mind with the name of his wife.

"Come into the studio," said Miguel, gently insisting; "later on, in a moment, when thou art stronger."

Bartholomeo joined his entreaties to those of Miguel, but Alonso, pushing them both aside with tremendous violence, rushed up the stairs and into Mercedes' room with the fury of a madman.

A horrible spectacle met him.

Upon the crumpled and disordered bed covered with blood lay the body of his young wife. Gaping wounds in the chest met his view; it was clear that the murderer had accomplished his horrible task with even unnecessary cruelty. Mercedes' countenance, which had grown fixed in death amid the convulsions of fearful agony, wore a look of awful horror. One arm was extended as if to push away the murderer, the other was upon her breast, as though she would fain staunch the blood flowing thence. Various indications went to prove that there had been a struggle. Around the room upon chairs and sofas lay robes of velvet and brocade; upon a table were open jewel-cases; some furs and a few pieces of gold had fallen upon the ground, and the red carpet was dyed a deeper red by the blood of Mercedes. A small safe lay open close to an Italian cabinet, the drawers of which had evidently been forced. The windows of the room, with their panes of tinted glass, threw a soft light upon this horrible picture. Never did sunlight shed its golden rays upon a sight more pitiable. Alonso Cano stood upon the threshold, and in an instant saw it all. He leaned against the door-post for a moment motionless in his anguish. At length he crept over towards the bed, tottering, shivering, grasping at the furniture which came in his way, and there fell upon his knees. He neither wept nor moaned, but he gazed upon his wife. The agony of his heart did not find relief in a single utterance. It seemed to him he was going mad.

All at once the sound of sobbing aroused him. Juana crouching in a corner, with her face hidden in her black apron, was weeping with a bitterness impossible to describe. Near by was Jacintha, with a rosary in her hand saying her beads.

" Mercedes! my Mercedes!" cried Alonso all at once

in a voice of terrible anguish, " is it thus I see thee again ? Thou beautiful and blithesome child, whom I left so full of life, and return to find thee stiff, motionless, and bloody. To behold thee dead, and know naught of the secret of thy death. Oh God, my God, I made her suffer, and left her in tears, and I shall never see her again. And thou, who wert so eager about the King's ball, wilt never, never open thy lovely eyes again. Oh, I am fatal to all whom I approach. I am accursed. There is blood upon my hands."

He started back with a sort of frenzy.

"Blood!" cried he, "blood everywhere, always! Sebastian's blood, the blood of—"

The words were lost in a deep groan, then he rose suddenly, crying:

"Thou shalt be avenged, avenged, avenged!"

"Yea, the victim shall be avenged," said a grave voice, as a man of austere visage entered the room. It was justice that, in his person, appeared upon the theatre of the crime.

Gaspardo del Roca was followed by four other men, as grave and silent as he. One of them carried a writing desk and a roll of parchment. The nearest police magistrate had just been apprised of the murder, and came thither to accomplish his mission.

He had often met Alonso Cano in the salons of the Count d'Olivarez, and had felt as strong an attraction for his personal character as admiration for his genius. He therefore came to the dwelling of the prime minister's favorite, with a feeling of profound compassion for the awful blow which had fallen upon him. He resolved to perform his task with all possible diligence, and to show by every means his sincere sympathy for the Michael Angelo of Spain. He held out his hand to the artist, saying:

"Courage! thou hast need of all fortitude and presence of mind to aid us in what we seek."

These words had an indescribable effect upon Alonso. He drew himself up, his eyes lost their wandering expression, and he answered:

"Thou art right; since I cannot bring her back, even at the price of my own life, I must, at least, aid thee in thy work of justice."

Whilst the judge and the artist thus exchanged a few friendly words, one of the men accompanying the chief magistrate went round the room, examining its details with an inquisitorial eye. He observed the position of the furniture, the disorder which reigned in the room, and seemed as if beginning on his own responsibility the inquest about to take place.

"Hast thou enemies?" asked Gaspardo del Roea of the artist.

"I know of none."

"To judge from the breaking open of the safe and these empty jewel-cases theft must have been the motive for the crime."

"It must have been that," cried Alonso. "Mercedes was a perfect child, kind and gentle to every one; none could have hated her."

Just then Juan Rosalés, who was Gaspardo's principal assistant, leaned over and said a few words to his chief in a low voice. The latter nodded in token of assent, and taking Alonso by the hand, said:

"Leave this room, my friend; contemplate no longer, I implore thee, this mournful spectacle. When we have need of thee for necessary information we shall send for thee."

Alonso would fain have stayed, but Gaspardo was inflexible. Bartholomeo and Miguel brought their master into the studio, where the portrait of Philip IV. seemed

to stare them blankly in the face, reminding the artist of
a so different scene which had lately passed there. Whilst
Alonso, completely absorbed in the one terrible thought,
remained fixed and motionless amidst a group of his
silent but sympathizing pupils, the officers of justice pursued their work.

"A theft has been committed," said Gaspardo, regarding the empty jewel-cases and the safe.

"But your excellency may remark," said Juan Rosalés,
"that there is no appearance of any one having effected
an entrance to the house."

"True," said Gaspardo; "which proves that the guilty
person must be well acquainted with the premises."

"Are not these two women in our way?" asked Rosalés.

And the magistrate gave orders that Jacintha and
Juana should be taken from the room.

"Cano seemeth certain of his own household," said
Gaspardo; "we must seek for the guilty elsewhere."

"Fifteen wounds," pronounced the doctor, "of which
three are mortal. He who dealt them must have been
not only a strong man, but accustomed, I dare swear, to
the use of the poniard."

Rosalés bent down and drew up his arm covered with
blood.

"This was the weapon used," he said.

The doctor took the poniard from him and compared it
with the wounds.

"Thou art right," he said, "that was the weapon."

"To whom doth this poniard belong?" asked Gaspardo.

"There is an initial upon the handle," said the doctor,
"but it is so coated over with blood that I cannot de-
cipher it."

"Leave the blood where it is," said Gaspardo quickly,
"and let us go on."

The doctor now made an effort to bend back the stiffened arm of the dead, and as he did so uttered an exclamation.

"What now?" cried Gaspardo, who was the presiding magistrate.

"This," said the physician, "a clue!"

And raising Mercedes' arm the doctor showed a tuft of red hair in her stiffened fingers.

"Evidently," said the physician, "she seized the assassin by the hair in the final struggle."

"This," said the judge, "is indeed a clue, and it seemeth to us of grave import. We are now upon the track. Little as this is, it is something. Before examining Cano, who is still totally overcome, we can proceed with the matter by questioning his pupils. Some of them may, perchance, furnish us with important details. An entrance effected without force; this tuft of peculiar-colored hair. Rosalés, have Cano's pupils brought one by one into the adjoining room."

Miguel was the first called into the little room where the Señor Gaspardo del Roca sat surrounded by the doctor and his assistants.

"Thy name?" asked the judge.

"Miguel."

"How long hast thou been the pupil of Alonso Cano?"

"About three years."

"Canst thou give us any information which may throw light upon this crime?"

"None," said Miguel; "I came here this morning by mere chance. I am no longer a pupil of Alonso Cano."

"Thou hast left Cano's studio?"

"Yea, but at the master's desire."

"Hast thou then offended him?"

"Grieved him rather. I can fearlessly speak of my fault to your excellencies, for if it be grave, it is not disgraceful. Two days ago I quarrelled with an Italian copyist."

"Did he inhabit the house?"

"Yes, your excellency."

"What was the cause of this quarrel?"

"A question of art. I acknowledge that Lello Lelli's opinions if held by any other would rather have led me to oppose them by arguments than by the sword. But, quite instinctively, we hated Lelli in the studio. The master's kindness to him never helped us to overcome our repugnance towards him; his captious, critical, malevolent spirit irritated us anew every day. He was known among us as *le pobre*, or the beggar. He had little talent, but much mechanical skill, and the master tolerated him for many reasons. Some malicious words of his envenomed my old antipathy to him, and in a moment of anger I accused him of being a hanger-on of Lo Spagnoletto at Naples, and of using the stiletto in his service much more than the brush."

"What led thee to form such opinion of him?"

"It seemed merely an intuition, founded upon the details of our daily life, and one which it would have been impossible to prove."

"Thou didst, then, provoke this Lelli?"

"Yea, Señor; but just as we crossed swords the master entered. I shall never forget his look and the sound of his voice. He condemned duels and duelists in scathing terms, and dismissed us both, Lelli and me, from his studio."

"Thou hast not since renewed the quarrel?"

"No, your excellency. Lelli quitted the studio immediately, and the house two hours after."

"Ah," said the magistrate, "then thou knowest no more of him?"

"No more."

"Canst describe Lelli to us?"

"Readily, my lord. His face is pale, with a look of suppressed passion in it. Hatred and envy seem to have marked his thin lips with their fatal seal. His forehead is low, furtive, and cunning, his nostrils thin and dilating when he is roused to anger. His red hair bristles upon a head where I would wager there are more evil designs than good thoughts."

The magistrate took the tuft of hair which the doctor had extricated from the stiffened fingers of the corpse.

"Was Lelli's hair of some such color as this?" he asked.

"It was precisely of that color," cried Miguel.

"Lelli inhabited this house, thou sayest, for some time," said the magistrate, "and would doubtless have been well advised as to the Señora Mercedes' habits?"

"Most certainly."

The judge then held up the poniard with which the crime had been committed, and said:

"Knowest thou that weapon?"

Miguel regarded it attentively.

"I know it," he said. "It belongs to the master."

"Thou art sure?"

"Very sure; and despite the blood upon the handle I can perceive an A and a C engraved upon a silver plate."

"Was this poniard part of a panoply?"

"Nay; it most frequently lay upon a table in the studio."

"Thou mayest retire," said the judge. "If thou art needed further I will recall thee; meantime remain in the house."

Alonso's pupils, summoned one by one, gave a precisely similar account of the quarrel, and threw all the blame upon Lelli.

"Knowest thou what hath become of him ?" asked the judge of Pedro Castello.

"That very evening he quitted Madrid," said Pedro, "mounted upon a sorry steed. I met him whilst in company with some friends."

"At what time ?"

"About eight in the evening."

"The crime was committed that same night," said the judge.

"And it is easy to guess at what hour," said Rosalés, placing Mercedes' watch upon the table before the judge.

The glass of it was broken and the hands had stopped at half-past two in the morning. It had been found close to the bed, near a small table which had been overturned.

"Thou art right, Rosalés."

Gaspardo del Roca was silent a moment; then he said:

"This tuft of hair is almost a proof."

"Yet the hour at which Señor Castello met the Italian offers an alibi," said Rosalés.

Juana was next introduced.

She was almost unrecognizable; her eyes, red and swollen, testified to the tears she had shed; her cheeks still bore their traces; her pale lips worked in a nervous mechanical fashion, whilst her fingers opened and closed and her whole body trembled.

"Thou wert," said Gaspardo kindly, "Doña Mercedes' nurse, and thy present sorrow proves how sincerely thou wert attached to thy young mistress."

"To my child; say rather, my child," cried Juana, with a fresh burst of sobs.

"Despite thy very natural grief canst thou answer my questions, and keep thy mind upon the point at issue ?" asked the judge.

' Your excellency may interrogate me," answered Juana, "and I will strive to collect my thoughts and keep up my courage to reply to thee."

Gaspardo then made a sign to the others to take down her evidence, and thus began the examination:

"At what hour didst thou leave the Señora Mercedes ?"

"At midnight," answered Juana.

"Was thy mistress wont to remain up so late ?"

A troubled look passed over Juana's face and she seemed to hesitate.

"Remember," said the judge, "that thou art addressing the representative of justice, and that every word has the value of an oath."

Juana crossed herself.

"I ask pardon of your excellency," she said, "but there are things which do not appear to have any bearing upon this matter."

"Let the law decide," said the judge.

Juana sighed.

"I will speak then," said she, "whatsoever it may cost me. But beware, Señor, lest thou shouldst gather from my words one thought of blame against my beloved Doña Mercedes or my venerated master, Señor Alonso. Heaven knows that I love them both. God knows, too, the secrets of hearts, and that their quarrel was no proof that they did not love each other."

"Quarrel!" interposed Rosalés hastily, "thy master and mistress quarrelled ?"

"I know not wherefore; but Doña Mercedes oftentimes deceived herself. Thou knowest, Señor, she was a child, loving flowers and trinkets. Accustomed to be obeyed, the slightest refusal or the least contradiction grieved her. I know, for I nursed her in my arms, and would fain have given her the stars of heaven when she reached forth her little hands for them. His majesty, Philip IV., to whom Heaven grant a long reign, came yesterday to the studio. This was a great honor for my master, yea, a very great honor. I know not how to proceed with my recital; old women wander, and grief hath turned my head. My poor, beautiful Mercedes! If thou couldst know, Señor, how much I loved her."

Rosalés' piercing glance passed from the judge to Juana, and patting the latter upon the shoulder, he said:

"Courage; thou wert speaking of the quarrel."

"Did I say quarrel, Señor?" said Juana: "the word was too strong, much too strong; dispute at the most. They loved each other so dearly, but poor Doña Mercedes was jealous. A child, a perfect child was she. She knoweth now how ill-grounded were her suspicions, but at eighteen one is quick and ardent, and one never reasons. I was at the King's visit. Well, he deigned to invite my young mistress to the court balls, and when I saw her after his majesty had been most royally gracious to her, she spoke of naught but her costume, her ornaments, the gala dress she would wear and the jewels she was to purchase. As I have said she loved flowers and trinkets. This was childish, very childish. Jacintha discussed with her the color of her new gown, and I smiled at thought of seeing her so fair and beautiful departing for the ball. Ah, how she chattered during dinner. Señor Alonso seemed grave, and we all knew wherefore. He had driven away Lello Lelli, that wicked Italian. When I wanted to picture the devil to myself I always thought of Lelli."

"Did he do thee any personal injury?"

"Nay, but we all felt him to be a miscreant."

"So thy master seemed less gay than Señora Mercedes?"

"Just then a messenger brought a letter."

"Didst know this messenger?"

"No, Señor, he left his missive, and departed without awaiting a response. My master went out in about an hour. Then I sought Doña Mercedes, whom I found in tears. She did not reason, but spoke as one in a dream: 'Alonso loves me no more,' she said, 'he never loved me.' I sought to calm her, but could not overcome her resentment. She emptied wardrobes and coffers, and taking out everything, declared that she would leave Señor Alonso forever."

"To what didst thou attribute this sudden resolve?"

"To the letter."

"Her husband then showed it to her?"

"What does that import? She had read it, and became half-crazed as I tell thee. I persuaded her with much difficulty to postpone until to-day her foolish departure. I felt sure that my master would explain that fatal letter; that he would tell his wife the secret. She loved me well, and had great confidence in me. I advised her to pray, and soon she grew calm. I left her sleeping."

"Knowest thou from whom came this letter?"

"Thou wilt find it no doubt in my master's apartments."

"We shall seek it hereafter. Proceed."

"What I have now to say is uncertain, so that I hesitate."

"Speak," said Gaspardo, "in the name of truth."

"I could not sleep at first," said Juana, "the memory of my mistress's tears troubled me still. Though Señor Alonso had not yet revealed the secret, I sought the key to this mystery. I was falling asleep, when I heard a step upon the first floor."

"Art sure that thou wert not dreaming?"

"Sure, for in my affection for my mistress I sought to

picture what was going on. My God, my God! why
did no fear or doubt cross my mind? Wherefore did I
remain in my room? But, alas, no warning presentiment came to me. I knew Señor Alonso had a key. I
heard some one come upstairs. Who but my master
could come thither at such an hour? Hence it is I who
have killed Mercedes. If, on hearing the footstep on the
stairs I had gone out to be certain that I was right I
would have seen the robber, the murderer, and Mercedes
would have been saved."

Juana broke into sobs once more.

".Be calm," said Gaspardo, gently; " we have greater
need than ever of what thou hast to tell."

"Then," asked Rosalés, "thou art convinced that it
was not Alonso Cano who entered the house at two in
the morning?"

"Why," cried Juana, "my master came in but a moment before your excellencies."

Gaspardo looked at Rosalés in surprise, and said;
"What dost thou mean?"

"Nothing, oh nothing," said Rosalés, "only that the
affair is more complicated than it seemed at first." The
judge resumed, addressing Juana:

"Didst hear any noise in the apartment of thy mistress?"

"A sound like the falling of some piece of furniture,
that was all. I explained this noise to myself most
readily. I supposed that my master had come up without a light."

"Didst hear aught else?"

"In about a quarter of an hour I heard the sound of
some one descending the stairs; the awful deed was accomplished, and the wretched murderer was escaping
from the house. And I, pursuing my thought, and
connecting everything with the master, said to myself,

Señor Alonso is obliged to go upon some journey, and has come to reassure my poor child, and inform her of his reasons for going. Thinking this I went to sleep at last."

Here Juana burst into tears again.

"To sleep," she cried, "and at that very moment Mercedes was dying alone and unaided, having but the statue of the Blessed Virgin upon whom her dying eyes were fixed."

"At what hour wert thou in the habit of entering thy mistress's room?"

"About seven. This morning I went as usual, and oh, my lords, what a horrible sight met my eyes."

"Thou knowest nothing more?" asked the judge.

"Nothing more."

"Did Lelli possess a key to the house?"

"Yes, Señor, but he returned it to me in departing."

"Then to your knowledge," said Rosalés, "Señor Alonso and thou alone possessed the keys of the house?"

"Yes, your excellency," said Juana, wiping her eyes.

"During his stay in the house," said Gaspardo, "Lelli may have had a second key made."

"Before proceeding farther," said Rosalés, "and if it so please your excellency, it seemeth that we should recall Señor Castello and question him farther. His evidence will tend to prove an alibi for this Lelli, or to disprove it entirely."

Again Gaspardo looked at Rosalés in surprise, yet his suggestion was but just, and the judge proceeded to act thereupon.

In a few minutes Juana had disappeared, and Castello was again in presence of the judge.

"Remember, Señor," said the judge, "that the slightest details are of importance, and answer with all possible deliberation and sincerity."

"I will try, your excellency," said Castello.

"Thou wert present at the quarrel between Miguel and Lelli; dost thou know, exactly, at what hour the latter quitted the studio ?"

"It might have been about five. I left, myself, soon after. I went to a *posada* situated on the road towards France, where I had promised to meet a friend. There I saw Lelli mounted on a sorry horse, and clad in his everlasting red doublet. He called for a glass of wine, drank it without stopping, and pursued his way. I recognized him, but he did not see me. And I am convinced he did not know of my presence there; had he seen me he would most certainly have addressed some opprobrious language to me."

Castello then gave the name of the keeper of the *posada* where Lelli had stopped. As the examination of this latter was not just then necessary, the other servants of the house were called. Jacintha knew nothing, except that the evening before she had left her mistress radiant and laughing with glee at the thought of the ball, and in the morning found her dead. Juan, the valet, deposed that his master had told him not to wait up, saying, "Do not wait, I have the key."

As no light seemed thrown upon this mysterious case Gaspardo was quite cast down. Rosalés on the contrary rubbed his hands with an air of satisfaction.

"This Lelli is a clever ruffian," said the judge; "all these precautions were no doubt taken to defeat the ends of justice."

"But what proof is there of Lelli's guilt ?"

"Every proof; the hatred he bore to Cano, especially after his dismissal; the theft of the jewels, a motive for which is found in the poverty of a man called by his fellow-pupils 'the beggar.' Art thou not of my opinion, Señor Rosalés ?"

"No," said he; "we must not stoop so low if we would discover the real criminal."

"What dost thou mean?"

"That we have not sufficiently examined these apartments, and that in seeking farther we may find new sources of information."

There was a peculiar light in Rosalés' eyes as he rose, and again the representatives of justice passed into the chamber of death.

CHAPTER VII.

SUSPICION.

THIS time the premises were much more minutely examined. Every corner of the chamber of death was inspected, and in fact every place where the slightest clue might lie concealed. Rosalés, in foraging about the room upon which death had left its awful horror, picked up a crumpled, torn, soiled paper, which had been reduced to its present state evidently neither by negligence nor indifference, but by an impulse of violent anger. An exclamation of surprise, and one would have almost said joy, escaped his lips, and going over to Gaspardo he said, with ill-concealed satisfaction:

"I thought I was upon the right track; now I am certain."

"What hast thou found?" asked the judge.

"Three lines which are quite sufficient to hang a man."

"Show them to me."

"Let the others," said Rosalés, "continue making an inventory of the remaining furniture in the mortuary room. What I have to say must be heard by thee alone."

"Thou dost frighten me," said the judge.

"I knew not thy friendship for Alonso was so great."

"Say sympathy rather; had I known him better I doubt not this sentiment would have warmed into friendship. But, as thou knowest well, I will suffer no private feeling to interfere with the course of justice."

"I know it not without proofs," said Rosalés, "for thou didst begin by denying my assertions, but now thou wilt soon be convinced by undeniable evidence."

"Come to the point," said the judge sharply.

"Thou believest, Señor, in Lelli's guilt ?"

"I do."

"Whereas I am certain that he is innocent."

"But the ease with which the murderer effected his entrance into the house ?"

"Is explained by the fact that the murderer possessed the key."

"What, thou believest —"

"Thou dost not dare to utter the name of the criminal."

"The criminal ? Say not that, Rosalés, it is impossible. Alonso loved his wife, and thou thyself hast witnessed the depth of his grief."

"Hypocrisy," said Rosalés coldly.

"How provest thou that ?"

"By this letter."

Rosalés handed Gaspardo the letter which had been brought to Cano during the unfortunate evening upon which he had visited the hapless sister of Sebastian Llano y Valdez. Gaspardo read it attentively, and passed his hand repeatedly across his forehead, asking Rosalés in a trembling voice:

"What dost thou, what canst thou, conclude from this ?"

"That which follows: Mercedes' jealousy and other defects of character had irritated Cano against her. Juana herself admitted that a somewhat violent scene occurred between them yesterday evening. Mercedes took it so much to heart that she thought of leaving her husband. Cano returned home, say about two in the morning. The explanation with his wife which ensued threw him into a violent rage. Cano struck her. Probably the first stroke was fatal, and hence Juana heard no noise proceeding from their room. Terrified at what he had done, and fully comprehending its awful consequen-

ces, Cano seized upon his wife's diamonds to divert suspicion from himself and make it appear that the murder
was committed with a view to robbery. When all was
over he fled, and probably wandered about half the night
in the country outside the walls; this is sufficiently at-
tested by the dust upon his clothing and boots. Having
somewhat recovered his composure he came hither
where everything accuses him, from the letter signed
Inez, which I have just found, to the dagger with which
Mercedes was assassinated."

"Horrible, horrible!" cried the judge; "thou dost
accumulate details, carefully chosen, and which, combined, form—"

"Proofs," said Rosalés, in an icy tone.

"Well," cried Gaspardo, "though it is true that certain indications form a chain against Alonso—I will not
say of proofs, for God forbid that I accuse any one rash-
ly, but of circumstances—my whole being from my heart
as a man to my conscience as a judge protests against
the accusation thou bringest against him. Nay, there
are crimes so impossible, perversity so revolting, I rejoice at being unable to comprehend them; and therefore shrink from them with all my strength. Alonso a
traitor and a murderer? Nay; so much perfidy and so
much cruelty crowded into one day are incredible.
Thou dost not know Cano as an artist, Rosalés; thou
hast never, perchance, even entered his studio. Otherwise thou wouldst divine the man's character from his
works. Grave, thoughtful, devout, he finds his loftiest
inspirations in faith. His architectural plans are always
for churches, his finest pieces of sculpture, *retablos* or
tabernacles; his mother was a saint, and I am only surprised that Alonso did not become a monk."

Rosalés listened quietly to all Gaspardo said, but
when he had finished he raised his head and said calmly:

"Thou vauntest the gentleness of this man; yet his hands are already stained with blood."

The judge was disconcerted. Rosalés' persistency irritated him, and this recollection of an old affair seemed to strike him like a blow.

"That was a duel, not a murder," he said.

"Surely, Señor del Roca, it is not for thee to excuse a duel, since dueling is condemned by the laws of God and man."

"Something may be forgiven to the effervescence of youth."

"Perchance, had Cano been insulted; but he was the aggressor."

"He hath been cruelly punished for it."

"No doubt, though at least thou wilt allow that he is not more to be pitied than his adversary."

"It would seem that thou hatest Cano," said Gaspardo, looking Rosalés steadfastly in the face.

"And it would seem that thou, Señor, wouldst impede, or at least retard the cause of justice," answered Rosalés.

Gaspardo's face glowed with noble indignation.

"On the contrary," he said warmly, "I would but wish that justice be free from all prejudice or prepossession. Thou art but a novice in a difficult career, Rosalés, and perchance thine ambition may lead thee to rejoice in having the direction of an affair wherein thou mayest display thy perspicacity and indisputable skill. But, believe me, there comes a time when the strictest judge questions his own conscience, asking: 'Have I sufficiently protected the innocent? Have I placed my personal ambition above my duty?' Bitter regrets and unavailing remorse must assail the unhappy magistrate who, neither criminal nor false, has not yet pursued the way of justice with energy mingled with compassion, with courage and honesty. I would spare myself such anguish. I seek truth always and everywhere, but such truth as I describe. I seek her that she may enlighten, not blind me."

"Rest content," said Rosalés, "light shall be thrown upon this darkness."

This interview was held in a corner of the room, and in a voice so low that the assistants could not catch a word. But what they did remark was the paleness that overspread Gaspardo's face, and the triumphant expression of Rosalés.

The latter, now advancing to the table, said coldly:

"Thinkest thou not it is time to examine Alonso Cano?"

"Yes," answered Gaspardo, "it is time."

And turning to one of the secretaries, he said:

"Ask Señor Cano to come hither."

Alonso came. He could scarcely stand; he seemed exhausted; sorrow had already done its work in every feature of that noble and expressive face. His eyes were red with weeping and his lips trembled nervously. As the judge had declared, there was no trace of a criminal about him. Gaspardo's first impulse was to receive him as a dear brother, and strive, if not to console him, at least to soften his grief. But the presence of Rosalés and the remembrance of the duty he had to perform kept him within the limits of a certain reserve.

Alonso looked from one to the other, saying:

"Have ye as yet any clue to the criminal?"

"We are still seeking," said Gaspardo, in a tremulous voice. "Oh, collect thy thoughts; forget if thou canst a moment the awful blow that hath stricken thee, and aid us."

"What can I tell thee?" he said; "my head is dazed, and my heart broken."

Rosalés took the fatal poniard from the table.

"Knowest thou this weapon?" he said.

Alonso regarded it with horror. The blood upon it was that of Mercedes.

"That weapon is mine," he cried in amaze. "It was carved by Balthasar Gonsalvez. How comes it here? Where did the assassin find it? It was always upon the table in the studio."

"Art sure," said Gaspardo, "that it has not since changed place?"

"Most sure."

"This weapon is finely tempered," said Rosalés; "the *alguazils* give us all an occasion of doing police duty for ourselves, or at least being on our guard. It would not, therefore, have been surprising hadst thou, in going out yesterday evening for a long walk, stuck this dagger in thy belt or concealed it in thy breast."

"I have always regarded that dagger," said Alonso, "which is a marvel of carving, as an object of art, and not at all a weapon of defence. When, Señor Judge, I find it necessary to take such precautions as thou suggestest, I will make use of a dagger at once plainer in the handle and readier to the hand."

Gaspardo replied gently:

"Thou didst leave the house early yesterday?"

"Yes, quite early in the evening."

"And," continued the judge, "I crave thy pardon if I must inquire into certain details of thy private life. But justice is slow in her progress, and nothing is too slight to be of importance. Thou didst apprise Señora Mercedes that thy absence would be long."

Alonso covered his eyes for a moment with his hand.

"Poor child," said he, "poor, dear child. It is not only her death which breaks my heart, it is to think of her state of mind at the moment when death overtook her. In the bed beside her was found her handkerchief wet with tears."

Unable to say more, Alonso, half choked by sobs, hid his face in his hands.

"I take thy sorrow as a proof that thou didst really love thy wife," said Gaspardo.

"God knows how well," said Alonso; "that was our first serious disagreement, and ah, about how trifling a matter!"

Rosalés had for some moments turned over and over in his hands the letter found in the chamber of death. He spread it out upon the table, where Alonso could see it, and fixing his piercing eyes upon him, said:

"Was not the disagreement whereof you speak caused by the reception of this letter?"

Alonso instantly recognized Inez' writing, and said calmly though sorrowfully:

"Yes, it was in truth caused by that letter."

"It compelled thee to go out," continued Rosalés; "thy young wife implored thee to remain with her; hence her anguish and her tears."

"I would have dried them this morning," said Alonso.

"Didst thou go with this mysterious messenger who waited for thee at a short distance from the house?"

"I did."

"Whither did he lead thee?"

Alonso's face flushed, and he answered faintly:

"I cannot say."

"I implore thee," cried Gaspardo vehemently, "no reticence, no fear, nor concealment. The hour is solemn, the questions are exact, thou must answer them with perfect frankness. Speak, speak, Alonso, how didst thou spend the night?"

"I repeat," said the artist, "that I may not reveal my

whereabouts. An oath, a sacred oath seals my lips, and even though it should concern—"

"Thy honor," interrupted Gaspardo, rising.

"It may concern thy life," added Rosalés.

The artist clutched the seat on which he sat with both hands, and livid with horror, his eyes bloodshot, cried out:

"I must have misunderstood. It concerns *my* honor, *my* life! What do ye mean to say? What do ye dare to suspect? Because I may not inform thee of my whereabouts last night, do ye conclude that I am guilty? I must be silent, because two lives depend upon it. I have sworn to keep their secret, and I will. I have sworn, even though it leads me to torture or to death, and never yet has Alonso Cano broken his word. Dishonor would be in perjuring myself, and perjury I will not commit."

"But, hapless man," cried Gaspardo, "seest thou not that thy silence will condemn thee?"

"Of what?" said Alonso in a voice the very calmness of which was terrible.

The judge turned away and could not answer, but Rosalés said, laying a stress upon every word:

"One thing thou didst forget to mention, that thou didst return to thy house at half-past two in the morning."

"I return thither?" cried Alonso; "but I have told thee that the whole night was devoted to the accomplishment of a sacred and delicate duty; and wherefore should I return thither, and at that hour precisely? Or rather, if I came in, wherefore did I go out again?"

Rosalés, still turning the letter over in his hands, said:

"Thou didst return because thou knewest Doña Mercedes to be troubled, anxious, and as thou hast thyself said so unhappy that she spoke of leaving thee. Thy explanation with her, far from appeasing her, led to a violent scene; thou wert armed with this dagger, and —"

"Stop!" cried Cano with a violence which almost terrified his hearers, "stop, thou art about to say, wretch, that I murdered my wife."

The rage depicted upon the artist's face was something indescribable; the horror, the agony in every line of it.

"Observe," said Rosalés coldly, "that thou wert the first to pronounce the word."

"Then it is true that thou darest to accuse me," cried Alonso.

Gaspardo grasped both his hands.

"Defend thyself, oh, I pray thee, defend thyself."

"Defend myself against such a crime as that—the crime of murder? No. God sees, and He will judge me."

"But men accuse thee," urged Gaspardo.

"That," said Alonso, "concerns but their own conscience."

"Oh, God is my witness," said Gaspardo, "that I believe fully in thine innocence, but it must be proven to men. Reveal but the secret of how the hours of the night between thy going and returning hence were spent, and thou art saved."

"Then I am lost, Señor Gaspardo, for that is impossible."

"Nothing is impossible in such a case," said Gaspardo. "We sometimes promise secrecy, and in ordinary cases honor compels us to keep our promise; but here, where there is question of a fearful accusation, aggravated by the suspicions which thy refusal may engender, and sustained by—"

Gaspardo stopped for the second time. He had not the courage to finish. Alonso himself finished the sentence:

"Sustained by this letter signed by Inez, and the poniard?"

"Yes," said Rosalés.

"But there has not only been murder but theft committed here," said Alonso.

Rosalés merely pointed to one sentence in the letter.

"Then I am not only capable of killing my wife, but of taking her diamonds to give them to—"

He stopped. Gaspardo seized his hands again.

"Go on," he said, "go on."

Alonso threw back his head proudly; there was a new dignity upon his face, a new light in his eyes.

"What art thou about to do with me?" he said.

Gaspardo answered gently:

"Our duty done, we will refer the matter to the judgment of the Supreme Court."

"Till then?"

"Thou wilt pledge thyself not to leave the house?"

"I pledge myself."

"Remain here then, Alonso Cano."

The judge and his assistants withdrew, and Alonso with a firm step passed into the chamber of death.

A great calm had succeeded to his horror and despair. The very extent of the double calamity that had befallen him endowed him, as often happens in a great crisis, with wonderful fortitude. He accepted the sacrifice, thinking of Sebastian Llano y Valdez.

"The stain of blood is not yet washed away," he thought; "it is the justice of Heaven which strikes me now. I will humble myself and accept it."

He entered the chamber of death as a criminal enters a church. He knelt down beside the bed, and after praying for some time rose and opened the door. Without he saw Miguel.

"Thou hast not abandoned me, Miguel," he said.

"Nay, master, nor the others either. The greater thy misfortune, the more faithful shall we be to thee."

"Then, Miguel, go down into the studio, and bring thence an easel, a canvas, and a box of colors."

"What wouldst thou with them, master?" asked Miguel in some alarm.

"I would take the portrait of Mercedes dead," answered Alonso.

The young man looked at his master in amazement.

"Be quick! be quick!" said Alonso. "I know not whether I shall have time to finish it."

Miguel went down, got what he was told, and brought them to Alonso. While left alone the artist had opened the window and let in air and sunshine. A ray, falling upon the bed, seemed to rest upon Mercedes' horror-stricken countenance, and, by a pious illusion, Alonso persuaded himself that the expression upon the face of the corpse had grown soft and peaceful.

"I would fain," said Alonso to Miguel, "whatever may befall me, keep this memory of Mercedes. If I die, I will leave it to thee. If I survive this horrible drama the tragic details of which are not yet ended, I will find in the constant contemplation of this portrait a reminder of the worthlessness of life. Remember that, Miguel, yesterday the King of Spain sat in my studio; to-day, to-morrow, at any hour, the judges may demand my head."

"Oh, master, canst thou speak of anything so horrible with calmness?"

"I have my conscience," said Alonso, "but if it is calm my heart revenges itself upon me. Would cries, or tears, or despair aid me? I will put all of them into this picture. My dead Mercedes will forever remind me not only of my present misfortune, but of the other, the other."

"What, the duel?"

"The duel which cost a human life, Miguel."

Alonso then seated himself at the easel, and for the

moment forgot, in the artist, the husband and the an under a terrible accusation. He began to draw Mercedes' features with a precision of touch and an inspiration before unknown to him. Miguel watched him with an admiration not unmingled with terror. The pallor of death overspreading the face of Mercedes, her disordered hair, the wounds in her throat, were all rendered with terrible reality. The resemblance was perfect. Never had Alonso Cano shown such power, and it was to the terrible excitement of that hour that he owed his most magnificent work. The day was waning into night when he laid aside the brush.

"Miguel," said he, "I know not what may befall me. Keep this canvas, guard it faithfully, until I ask for it again. Should I die it will be the legacy of my friendship to thee."

Miguel bathed his master's hand with his tears, as, taking the picture, he departed. For Alonso had said to him in a tone which admitted of no appeal:

"Now leave me, I would pray."

Miguel felt that he could not disobey, and at once left the room. At the foot of the stairs he met Juana, weeping as though her heart would break.

"Thou art going, Señor Miguel," she said, "thou wouldst desert thy hapless master. Can it be true what thy companions said? Yesterday Alonso forbade thee the house, and to-day—"

The young man took the nurse's withered hand in his.

"Had matters remained as they were yesterday, Juana," he said, "were Señor Alonso still professor to the Infante, a favorite of the King, I should long since have departed from a house whence I was dismissed. Severe or not my master's command was sacred to me. But a fearful misfortune has fallen on him, a misfortune greater even than thou canst conceive."

"Mercedes my child is dead," said the old woman. "What can be worse than that?"

"Señor Alonso being accused of the murder," answered Miguel.

"Our Lady of Mercy," cried Juana, raising her withered hands to Heaven, "that cannot be. It is too vile, too infamous, for it is a calumny, and a greater crime even than the murder of Mercedes."

"Yet it is true," said Miguel; "I have it from the master's own lips."

All at once Juana tapped her forehead with a sort of frenzy.

"Rosalés," she said, "Rosalés."

"He is the assessor to Gaspardo, who showed such compassion towards Señor Alonso."

"It is possible, quite possible," cried the old woman, as if talking to herself. "I alone know it, the master does not guess it. Rosalés will be his ruin. He has a motive for it."

"What motive?"

"He asked Doña Mercedes in marriage before Señor Alonso."

"She refused him?"

"Yes, yes! she confided it to me."

"You suppose him capable of—?"

"Of anything," said the old woman hoarsely, "of anything."

"What is to be done? what is to be done?" cried Miguel. Then he remembered his comrades, and hastily leaving Juana said to her kindly:

"Appearances, the law, are now against the Michael Angelo of Spain, but he still has the brave young men of his school to defend him, and all is not yet lost."

CHAPTER VIII.

MIGUEL'S ALGUAZILS.

THE judges, on leaving Cano's house, repaired to that of a judge of the Supreme Court. Having heard their report, and the evidence of the witnesses, and Alonso's own examination, he decided upon the arrest of Cano, against whom he declared there was strong circumstantial evidence. However, in consideration of the artist's high reputation in Madrid and his favor with the King, he decided to wait until night, so as to spare him being subjected to the humiliating curiosity of the crowd.

Gaspardo del Roca vainly sought to influence his superior and bring him to his own way of thinking. The latter, a veteran lawyer, applauded the keen perception displayed by Rosalés, and plainly told him that Cano's trial would lead to his own advancement.

" Dost apprehend any resistance on Cano's part to the law ?" asked the judge of Gaspardo.

"None whatever," said Gaspardo. "Strong in the acquittal of his conscience, for I persist in believing him innocent until his guilt is absolutely proved, Alonso will go quietly whither it pleases thee to send him."

The judge touched a gong. An officer appeared.

"Send a carriage to Señor Gaspardo's house at ten o'clock this evening."

The latter rose hastily.

"Your excellency will deign to excuse me from the performance of so painful a duty," said he.

"Rosalés will take thy place, Señor Gaspardo," said the judge; "but permit me to remind thee that such exaggerated sensibility is ill in accordance with the stern and impartial administration of justice."

"I am at thy service, my lord," said Rosalés.

The judge then turned altogether to Rosalés, as if he placed the matter wholly in his hands.

"The carriage will be at thy house at ten precisely,' he said; "thou wilt go in it to the dwelling of Alonso Cano, and ask him to accompany thee. If he assents no force is necessary. If he resists twelve *alguazils* and an *alferez* * will be there. Thou canst use them at need."

"Once in the carriage—"

"Thou wilt bring him to the prison, and leave him there."

"Your excellency may count on me."

Gaspardo rose.

"Does, then, the burden of this affair still rest with me?" he asked.

"It does," said his superior, "for whatsoever thy opinions may be, I know thy integrity."

Gaspardo then withdrew, leaving Rosalés and Manoël Lascazaros together. These men had each a very different interest in the affair. Manoël Lascazaros loved justice for its own sake, but he exaggerated alike its duties and its privileges. His desire was to make this "priesthood of the law," of which he was a member, the greatest power in Spain. With a clear, methodical, though somewhat biased mind, he was admirably fitted for the high dignity with which he was invested, so far as its principal obligations were concerned. But his unbounded self-esteem, and the importance which he attached to his own personality, often had a bad effect upon the administration of his office. In his judicial capacity he took only the most severe and implacable view of every case.

---

* An officer in command of the *alguazils* or military police.

Constant contact with criminals had so hardened \ s
heart that he did not believe in innocence. Every suspected man he held to be guilty. Pity had no place in
his heart. He felt that he soared above the common
herd in two ways, by his power and by his contempt of
them. Philip IV., who from the natural gentleness of
his disposition, was inclined to clemency, almost feared
Manoël Lascazaros. When he would fain have granted
a pardon, Manoël invariably represented the dangers
which menaced the state, showed Spain to be upon the
brink of ruin, and managed to associate with any crime
or misdeed whatsoever some suggestion of a Portuguese
rising.

This was Philip's susceptible point. All who showed
any sympathy with the house of Braganza were the
King's enemies. By means of some such subterfuge
Manoël hoped to surprise the King into signing Alonso
Cano's death-warrant. For, after an hour's conversation
with Rosalés, Manoël was perfectly convinced of the artist's guilt.

As for Rosalés, Juana was right when she told Miguel
that the lawyer had kept the old grudge of Mercedes'
refusal rankling at the bottom of his heart. Too hypocritical to show his hatred, he had waited with a sort of
fatalistic certainty till Alonso should fall into his hands.
Certain birds can foresee a storm; certain beasts can
scent a corpse from any distance, and certain men can
anticipate, almost to a nicety, the precise moment when
some one whom they hate will fall into their hands, and
his happiness, his honor, or his life be at their disposal.

Alonso Cano's life hitherto had given but little hope
of any such opportunity occurring. The impetuous
young man, once so skilful with the sword, whose duel
with Sebastian Llano y Valdez had had such disastrous
consequences, had grown since that event gentle and pa-

tient. His works all inspired the beholder with a tender piety as well as an ardent admiration. If artists are now permitted to expose publicly various works of art which cannot fail to offend every delicate feeling, it was not so in Spain, where the great respect for religion engendered also a reverence for art. No artist, sculptor, or painter was allowed the right of exhibiting indecent pictures, and just as there were tribunals of common law, or ecclesiastical courts for cases of conscience, so there existed a special tribunal, connected with the Inquisition, having absolute supervision over all works of painting or sculpture executed by Spanish artists.

Never had Alonso's pencil or brush lent themselves to any reprehensible work. His genius and his honor were upon the same high level. Hence Rosalés had had to wait years for an opportunity to wreak his spite. Eagerly now he sought the ruin of a man who was not aware of having even involuntarily offended him. It wanted but a few hours of the time- when he could, in the name of justice, lay his hand upon the shoulder of Alonso Cano. Yet short as the time was, he could scarcely restrain his fiery impatience. Once alone, he began to mutter hoarse imprecations mingled with a low, sardonic laughter, more frightful than the most awful outbursts of rage. To pass the time he questioned the *alferez* in command of the twelve *alguazils* who were to do escort duty.

"Thou didst understand me, Señor *alferez* ?" he asked.

"Perfectly," replied the officer.

"Let me hear thee, then, repeat my orders," he persisted.

"At ten o'clock precisely," began the officer, "a carriage is to be at Alonso Cano's door. My men are to surround it to keep back the crowd, and help thee in case of need."

"Very good. I trust that these precautions will be useless. Nevertheless, prepare yourselves well."

"We shall be prepared. Has your excellency any further orders to give?"

"None."

The *alferez* retired and Rosalés began to pace the room. At half-past nine he left the house. He might have had the carriage call for him, but he preferred to walk. His head was burning; he was feverish with the consuming fever of hatred impatient to gratify itself.

Whilst judges, officers and soldiers were taking precautions in case of resistance on his part, Alonso was quietly kneeling in Mercedes' room beside the bed of death.

Juana, knowing that the inquest was over, had, with the utmost care and maternal tenderness, sought to divest the room of a portion of its horror.

She drew the white coverlet over the body of her young mistress, concealing its ghastly wounds; she placed a crucifix in the stiffened hands; she arranged the curtains so as to cast a soft light upon the young face, pale with the awful pallor of death. Some fragrant pastilles burning in a brazier improved the air of the room, and Juana had besides sent to a neighboring *huertas* * for branches of flowering orange and pomegranate, which she disposed around the bed. All the while Alonso remained absorbed in prayer. The blow which had fallen upon him was so sudden and so terrible that he had no energy to defend himself from it.

Besides, as we have said, the recollection of his duel with Sebastian weighed so heavily upon his mind, and he had so long believed in the retributive justice which must come upon him, that he accepted this terrible trial

---

* Plantation.

as an expiation. He felt that any defence he might make would fail. He would be found guilty. If human justice were mistaken in accusing him of Mercedes' murder, Divine justice was but accomplishing its work, slowly but surely, in asking of him the price of Sebastian's blood, which had not ceased to cry to Heaven against him.

At ten o'clock the door of the house opened to admit two sets of men; the one came with the coffin for Mercedes, the other to arrest Alonso.

And from that desolate house the dead and the living were to go forth. Who could tell that they were not soon to meet? for the death of the one might but precede the execution of the other. Alonso Cano was to be taken first; the dead could wait. When Rosalés appeared upon the threshold of the door the artist rose. He bent over the bed, and his lips, almost as cold as those of the corpse, touched her forehead.

"Sleep in peace, poor murdered one," he said softly.

"Such hypocrisy cannot impose upon the law," said Rosalés.

"Señor," said Alonso, calmly, "thy duty, I believe, is to arrest me. I was not aware that the tribunal which has not yet pronounced upon my fate had given thee, in advance, a commission to insult me."

Alonso turned quietly from him to the *alferez*.

"I am thy prisoner," he said, "and place myself confidently in thy hands; a Spanish soldier never yet insulted the unfortunate."

Juana rushed over and kissed her master's hands.

"A parting word, Juana," said Alonso: "This house is mine. I leave it in thy charge. Remain here, whatsoever befalls. If I return, it will console me to find thee here. If I do not return, keep it in remembrance of the beloved dead, and as a token of my gratitude. In such case I will send thee all the necessary authorization. Weep not, this trial is from God; His adorable will be done."

With one last look of mingled reverence and affection at her master, Juana turned away and threw herself down at the foot of Mercedes' bed, sobbing as if her heart would break.

The *alferez*, Rosalés, and Alonso went downstairs together. Once there Alonso turned towards the studio door. He expected to see all, or at least some, of his pupils waiting for him. To bid them a last farewell would have consoled him. He had believed so firmly in their love for him.

But, alas! the studio was empty. Through its wide open doors came glimpses of statues, or the golden gleam of picture-frames, shining out in the glare of the torches which *alguazils* held upon the threshold. Without, the mules were pawing the ground and tossing their heads.

The *alferez* drew back to let Alonso pass first. The artist turned to Rosalés.

"Is it absolutely necessary," asked he, "that thou shouldst accompany me?"

"Yea, absolutely necessary," said Rosalés. "I fear that did I leave thee thou wouldst corrupt with thy gold the men charged to conduct thee."

The *alferez* hearing what passed, said:

"Remember, Señor, that a soldier esteems his honor as highly as a magistrate."

"I submit," said Alonso.

He entered the carriage, and Rosalés entered with him. The mules went at a moderate pace, so that the *alguazils* and the *alferez* who were on foot could keep up with the carriage. Alonso was silent, and Rosalés observed him curiously; this scrutiny from a man whom he knew to be hostile to his cause so wearied Alonso that he closed his eyes to escape the searching glance.

In the distance was heard the sound of guitars. Some *navios* serenading their sweethearts.

As the carriage passed through a street, so narrow that the word lane would have better described it, it was ob-structed by a group of young men. They were singing and shouting with an uproarious gayety, which proved that they had partaken freely of Spanish wines. All held instruments of one kind or another in their hands; drums, tambourines, violins, guitars; they played lively tunes, accompanying a dozen different songs set to differ-ent airs. As we have intimated, the street was so narrow that the first carriage could scarcely make its way; and now a second one, well-appointed and carefully driven, appeared from the opposite direction. The *alguasils* advanced and ordered the serenaders to retire.

They seemed too drunk to have the least respect for law or even armed force. They responded to warn-ings by a couplet, and to threats by a touch of the guitar. Yet despite their disobedience they seemed so merry, so light-hearted, so unconscious of offence, that the *alferes*, though understanding the awkwardness of the situation, hesitated to give an order which might have terrible consequences for some.

At that period every one carried a sword or a dagger, so that bloody combats were not infrequent. Never was human life held more cheaply, notwithstanding the severe laws made to protect it. Not a week passed but some one was found dead in the streets. The King dis-liked bloodshed above all things, and had given express orders to prevent quarrels between soldiers and citizens.

Besides, in this case the first sword drawn would be the signal for a general affray. These merry young blades, elated by wine, would certainly make a determined resistance, and many lives might be lost in this futile skirmish. The *alferez* came to the carriage door.

"I cannot take any responsibility upon myself," he said to Rosalés. "Your excellency must decide."

The judge was perplexed.

"The carriage which is blocking the way has not gone on?" he said.

"No! and even should it pass we still have to deal with this band of half-drunken students, whom, as it is, can scarcely be kept back by my men. They insist that there is a Señora hidden in this carriage, and they swear to protect her."

"Take the wisest course, then," said Rosalés; "have the carriage turned and let us go by the next street."

"But your excellency must be aware that the street is so narrow that it would be impossible to turn."

"Decide on something, Señor," said Rosalés sharply.

Just then the measured tread of a company of soldiers was heard at the other end of the street.

"Here are reinforcements!" cried the *alferez*.

The carriage in which Alonso and Rosalés were, was in this position: directly before them, to protect the mules, the vehicle and the coachman, were the *algua-sils*, who kept back, with ever-increasing difficulty, the advance of the disorderly revellers. Farther on was another carriage, whereof the mules kept up a great snorting and pawing whilst the drivers uttered ringing oaths, and a young man put his head out of the window, ever and anon, and ordered them imperiously to go on at all hazards. Behind were the detachment of men whom the *alferez* hailed as a reinforcement.

"Señor *alferez*," said Rosalés, "since it is impossible for us to advance, thanks to these insolent, drunken fools, and we cannot turn back, there is but one course open to us. Whilst thy men keep these drunken ruffians

at bay we shall alight, and, escorted by thee and these
new-comers, whose services I will demand in the name
of the law, we shall proceed on foot to the prison."

"It is the best thing that can be done," cried the *alferes*.

In a short time twenty additional *alguazils* surrounded
the carriage. They scarcely awaited their officer's orders.
They declared that Castilian honor forbade that they
should turn back. When they had put themselves on
guard around Alonso and Rosalés, and attempted to push
them forward, a terrible uproar occurred in the street;
the mules snorted, all the instruments began to play at
once, the students rushed to the mules' heads, and a
pistol-shot was heard.

This sound seemed to alarm the revellers, and they
began to disperse with great hue and cry and shouts of
murder. All at once Rosalés saw that the passage was
free, and even the carriage which had obstructed the way
was gone.

Beside Rosalés still sat the motionless figure, with
cloak drawn up round its throat and hat somewhat over
his eyes. In all the tumult Rosalés had never lost sight
of that a moment. It was his prey, his vengeance. The
judge then re-entered the carriage, and his silent companion took his place at his side; gradually the shouts
of the serenaders, the noise of the *alguazils* in pursuit of
them, and the rumble of the departing carriage died
away one by one.

The *alferes* was close at hand.

At last the great dark mass of the prison was outlined
in the gloom. The heavy knocker was sounded by one
of the escort; the door rolled upon its hinges, and the
carriage drove into the yard.

Then only did Rosalés breathe freely. Once behind
these gratings his prisoner could not escape him. The

prisoner seemed, indeed, to have little thought of escape just then. Wrapped in his own thoughts, he leaned back quietly in a corner of the carriage. He got out when he was told and followed the jailer unresistingly.

"Thou wilt answer for this man with thy life," said Rosalés to the head jailer.

"What is given into my charge I keep," said the jailer, curtly.

He opened a great book and said to the judge:

"I must inscribe the prisoner's name."

"Write," said Rosalés, slowly, as though pronouncing his enemy's name under such circumstances gave him a rare degree of satisfaction, "Alonso Cano, *painter to the King!*"

A shout of laughter echoed through the room.

The jailer, the *alferez*, and Rosalés all looked sternly at the soldiers, supposing that one of them had committed the unpardonable fault of forgetting that the head turnkey's room was, as it were, the vestibule of the court.

"Accused of what crime?" asked the jailer.

"The murder of his wife."

A louder and more unrestrained burst of laughter followed this statement.

"Who has been guilty of that indecorous laughter?" asked Rosalés looking around.

"I crave your excellency's pardon," said the prisoner, "but it was I. I am not laughing at the law, only I think it is sometimes deceived. I am not Alonso Cano, much to my regret, for the man who bears that name is the glory of Spain."

"Thou art not Alonso Cano," said Rosalés in a terrible voice, and thrusting his blanched face close to that of the prisoner. The prisoner for answer threw off his sombrero and showed a young and joyous face of twenty.

"My name is Elio," he said, "and I have just been

taken in *flagrante delicto* of nocturnal disturbance with the aggravating circumstances of guitar and castanets."

Elio threw off his cloak, and they saw that he actually had a pair of ebony castanets and a guitar slung over his shoulder by a blue ribbon.

"Wretch! wretch!" cried Rosalés.

"I crave a thousand pardons of your excellency," said Elio, "but one is not a wretch for having drunk a little too much Spanish wine and sung a couplet or two under a *mirador*. Perchance I esteem too highly the privileges of youth, but in any case I belong to a noble family who will willingly be my security and come to seek me in prison if your excellency thinks proper to detain me until to-morrow."

Rosalés stamped his foot with rage.

The *alferez* meanwhile stood by and regarded the scene without moving a muscle of his face. He was not altogether displeased at the turn affairs had taken and the deception practised upon a judge who had told him plainly that he would not trust him with so valuable a prisoner as Alonso Cano.

"As I said before," cried Rosalés, "thou art a wretch. I comprehend now the aim of thy devilish serenade and the carriage which barred the street; thou hast made a sport of legal power, laid a snare for the law, and helped a criminal to escape."

"Alonso Cano was not yet judged!"

"Ha! thou confessest then thy guilt?"

"How can I deny it in presence of the witnesses?"

"The *alferez* and his men?"

"No, my guitar and my castanets."

Rosalés bit his lip with rage.

"What is to be done?" thought he, "what is to be done? If such a scheme, so many subterfuges, were devised, a serenade, an *emeute*, a conspiracy improvised to deliver Mercedes' murderer, I can gain little by pursuing him. He has escaped me, and the vengeance which I hoped to enjoy bit by bit is lost to me forever. To detain this insolent young fool, who laughs and mocks at me to my face, would be only to expose myself to further ridicule. The very evidence of the *alferes* would tell against me. So, naught remains but to admit that the game is lost." He turned to Elio.

"Thou art free," said he.

"I thank your excellency all the more," said Elio, "that the night is not yet so far advanced but that I can continue my serenade."

So saying he threw his cloak over his shoulder, took his guitar in his hand, placed his hat jauntily upon one side and left the prison. Scarcely was he outside when he began to improvise, with no mean skill, a song with peculiar words which caused many a head to appear at the windows as he passed.

In about an hour he reached one of the *fondas* of Madrid. He gave some mysterious countersign at the door, and was immediately admitted to a room where Alonso Cano's pupils greeted him with the utmost enthusiasm.

CHAPTER IX.

THE RIDE.

AT the moment when the twenty newly arrived *algua-zils* surrounded the carriage containing Rosalés and his prisoner, and when the uproar in the street seemed at its height, Alonso Cano, alighting with his conductor from the carriage, felt himself suddenly jostled and pressed forward in the most unaccountable manner. He knew nothing more till he found himself again shut up in a close carriage. Putting his head out of the window he saw himself still punctilliously escorted by nine or ten *alguazils*. Ever and anon, at stated intervals, or in turning the corners of streets, the driver of the carriage pronounced some word which Alonso could not understand. Other *alguazils*, who seemed stationed at these posts, replied by some countersign, and the carriage went on.

The night was very dark, and but for the lamps burning in front of houses to honor the Madonna, there was no light in the streets. Occasionally the snatch of a serenade came with a sort of cruel irony as if to mock the artist's terrible situation.

To the episode of the disorderly students he owed his deliverance from Rosalés' presence, for the piercing gaze of those dark eyes had so unnerved him that he rejoiced at being left alone.

So many varied emotions had succeeded each other since the evening previous that the hapless artist was scarcely able to realize the terrible blow that had fallen upon him.

The whirlpool of sorrow had engulfed him. Heart and mind were weighed down with heavy grief. From the pinnacle of a much-envied prosperity he had rolled into an apparently fathomless abyss.

If Gaspardo del Roca's honor and integrity consoled him somewhat and gave him some hope, Rosalés' sinister looks, and the manner in which he had conducted the examination, convinced him, on the other hand, that he had a mortal enemy in a man whom he could not remember to have offended in any way. It is often thus in life; the wayfarer, heedlessly pursuing the aim of the moment, suddenly steps upon a nest of vipers, who rise, hissing at him, with venomous tongue and eyes of fire. So with the man who, disdaining all sordid cares, free alike from hatred and from jealousy, is guided solely by inspiration, and makes his life a carefully guarded sanctuary, till unconsciously he finds in his path a brood of traitors and slanderers whose tongues distill calumny, and who gloat over the wounds they make.

Though unaware of the cause of Rosalés' hatred, Alonso felt assured of the hatred itself. Moreover, he knew that his mysterious silence, as to his whereabouts during the fatal night, cast great suspicion upon him. His only consolation was the thought that he had done his duty and acquitted, as far as possible, his debt to Sebastian.

Alonso began also to wonder whither they were taking him. Evidently not to the common jail. The carriage had passed through the streets and suburbs of Madrid, and was without the walls in the country. Where could they be taking him? If he had conspired against the King, the state, or even the prime minister, he knew that his destination would be some remote fortress. But the crime of which he was accused came within the jurisdiction of the ordinary tribunals, and in the province of judges charged with the administration of common law.

Whilst the horses were being changed he opened the carriage window and called. An *alguazil* appeared.

"What wouldst thou, Señor Cano?" he said gently.

"Knowest thou whither they are taking me?" he asked.

"Thou wilt learn presently," answered the official. "Meanwhile, permit me to offer thee some refreshment; thou hast taken naught during the journey, and must be faint."

"Thanks," replied Alonso, "my heart is too full of emotion. I cannot eat."

"Courage, Señor," said the *alguazil;* "things may be better than thou thinkest."

He saluted and retired, but returned soon after with a glass of Malaga wine, which Alonso accepted. In a moment the carriage had started again. Involuntarily Alonso felt relieved. The voice of the man with whom he had spoken was full of sympathy. The unfortunate are more susceptible to pity than any others.

Letting down the window Alonso saw that they were passing through a fertile and beautiful country; plantations of maize, *huertas* of orange, lemon, and pomegranate succeeded each other, giving forth rich perfumes to the soft and balmy air of that glorious June night.

At length Alonso perceived a habitation on the roadside to his left. He heard a whistle, and the carriage stopped. Two *alguazils*, stationed on either side of the coach, and one riding behind, were now joined by five horsemen, who had formed part of the escort from Madrid. They were armed to the teeth, and it would have gone ill with any who dared to dispute their passage. The *alguazil* who had spoken to Alonso before now advanced again and said:

"Wilt thou alight, Señor Cano?"

The artist did as desired.

"Follow me," said the young man.

"Wilt thou not inform me at least whither I am go-ing?" said Alonso.

"Thou hast arrived at thy destination," replied the other.

The young man went first. Alonso followed him, whilst the horsemen and the other *alguazils* brought up the rear.

Two old servants, aroused by the knocking of one of the soldiers, appeared upon the threshold, bowed very low, and threw open the doors of a large *salon*, whither they brought two lamps.

This done they retired, much puzzled by the whole affair, and half alarmed at the uniforms of the *alguazils*. The manner of the latter, however, which was not very warlike, reassured them.

Alonso went first into the dimly lighted room. He was followed by eight men. Each of the eight now threw off his hat and cloak, and Alonso thought he must be dreaming, when he recognized Miguel, Pablo, Bartholomeo, Pedro Castello, and four others of his pupils.

"You here," he cried, "what means this?"

"It means, master," said Bartholomeo, "that we have carried thee off."

"Ah, hapless youths, what have you done?" cried Alonso.

"The only sensible thing," said Castello.

"It was Miguel's idea," said Pablo, "a splendid one, which we adopted with enthusiasm."

"But to fly from justice looks as if there were reason to fear it," said Alonso.

"And so there is, master," said Miguel.

"It matters not," said Alonso, "since I am accused I must appear before the tribunal of justice."

"Master," said Miguel, "wilt thou permit me to explain our idea to thee?"

"Speak, my boy, speak!"

And more touched than he cared to show, Alonso clasped Miguel's hands in both his own.

"I respect the law," said Miguel, "but it sometimes acts with dangerous haste, and like all things human is liable to error. Art not thou thyself a striking illustration of what I say, master? Thou art bound by an oath, its nature I know not, but it seals thy lips."

"True," murmured Alonso.

"Is it possible for thee to be released from this oath?"

"It is."

"May not the wretched murderer of Señora Mercedes be also discovered?"

"Undoubtedly."

"Reflect then, master, that placed between two favorable chances thou wouldst throw away the benefit of both. The haste with which Señor Rosalés is acting in this affair for motives of his own, will prevent thee from apprising those who hold thy life in their hands of thy danger, or of awaiting the arrest and conviction of the real criminal, who I am persuaded is Lelli."

"Yes, Lelli!" cried the others.

Miguel resumed:

"What we have done is not to defeat the ends of justice, but to preserve it from a rash act, the consequences of which would be irreparable. No one in Madrid suspects where thou now art. Rosalés took to prison a brave lad, disguised in thy coat and mantle, who bore his captivity with the best possible grace."

"But the serenade?" said Cano.

"Say rather the *charivari*, master," said Miguel. "But since it pleases thee to be indulgent, the serenade was organized by some good comrades of ours, pupils of Velasquez and Murillo."

"They awaited then the arrival of the carriage, wherein I was?" said Alonso.

"Yes; but well armed. Their drums and guitars were not their only weapons, swords and poniards were hidden beneath their cloaks."

"And the carriage obstructing the street?"

"Was that in which thou hast since made this journey."

"But the young man who stormed so at the driver?"

"That was I, Señor," said a good-looking young student, bowing respectfully to the artist.

The latter extended his hand to him with emotion.

"And the *alguazils?*" cried Alonso, more and more amazed.

"Were Miguel's alguazils," cried Bartholomeo.

"My friends, my children," cried Alonso deeply moved, "this is a miracle."

"A miracle of gratitude," cried they.

"But how could ye in so short a time conceive a plot so marvellous?"

"Oh, it did not take long, thanks to Miguel," said Castello.

"Always Miguel!" exclaimed Alonso. "Yet on the day before I—"

"Punished Miguel for a grave misdeed," interrupted Miguel; "that was thy right, and mine is to place myself between thee and misfortune."

"Tell me then all that transpired," cried Alonso; "I would hear every detail."

"When the judges left thy house," said Miguel, "Señor Gaspardo's despondency and the ugly smile of Rosalés revealed to us thy danger. Juana gave us some further information which decided us. I remained with thee in the chamber of death while thou didst sketch the portrait of thy lost one. When I left thee I met my comrades in a *fonda*, where sometimes at evening we are wont to sip our sherbet. We were all of one mind and one heart, we were determined to rescue thee from the hands of a man whose hatred and malice are justly to be apprehended. Had we consulted thee thou wouldst not have given thy consent."

"No," said Alonso.

"Thou wouldst have depended upon thine innocence before the bar of justice."

"Innocence is strength," said Alonso.

"Such strength as belongs to martyrs."

"There is grandeur in suffering."

"Yes, for a great cause, master, for king, for country, or for God. But to suffer for a crime of which one is innocent, to undergo undeserved shame and humiliation and death is terrible, not only for the victim but for those who have condemned him, and must sooner or later be consumed by unavailing remorse. If justice comes slowly, she comes none the less surely, and when she tears away the final veils and displays the real criminal, with what pity and horror must she not remember her innocent victim. That is what we were determined to prevent. We were obliged to act alone, for we knew full well thou wouldst not become our accomplice. In less than an hour the pupils of all the great studios of Madrid were assembled in the *fonda*. Each one swore solemnly to be silent as to all that took place. Whosoever betrayed this oath would be degraded forever in the eyes of all from that nobility of art of which we are so proud. We exacted an oath when indeed a promise would have sufficed. Castello was the spokesman. I assure thee he spoke eloquently, and pronounced not thy panegyric, it was a true description of thee. Not one of the valiant young men present refused his aid; the enthusiasm was unanimous; the pupils of Alonso Cano, Velasquez, and Murillo were brothers in that hour."

"Brave hearts!" cried the artist.

"Yes," said Miguel with growing emotion, "they were brave hearts indeed. We knew it would be useless to attempt a rescue once thou wert in prison. The drive from thy house thither was our only chance of success. But we were aware that the serenaders alone would be of little avail, any more than the carriage blocking the way. Nor could we dream of armed resistance; bloodshed in thy cause thou wouldst have regarded with horror. Moreover, in case of failure, for under such circumstances everything must be foreseen, such bloodshed would have doubled thy peril. We had to defeat justice with its own weapons, armed force by unarmed force, real *alguazils* by false ones. It is good to have friends everywhere. I had often made decorations for the theatre, where the dramas of Calderon and Lope de Vega are acted. I went to the manager of this theatre and told him that we were going to play a very amusing comedy, called "Le Corregidor," among ourselves; that twenty of us would represent *alguazils*. I hinted that if he were good enough to lend me the costumes I would be at his service for the first decorations he required. I gained my point. The costumes were at the *fonda* in an hour, and we soon transformed twenty of us into ridiculous looking *alguazils*, who would, however, each one have died for the good cause he had sworn to defend."

"Dear, dear boys," said Alonso in a broken voice.

"It was then about nine o'clock," continued Miguel,

"and it would have been imprudent for us to dress in the *fonda*, for the worthy innkeeper would have been rarely puzzled to know how his best apartment was suddenly changed into a guard-room. Each of us took our uniform under our arms, drew our cloaks about us, and arranged a meeting place near thy dwelling."

"Yet when I came downstairs and saw the studio empty," said Alonso, "I accused you in my heart of having deserted me."

"Our absence did seem like ingratitude," said Castello.

"We were sure of explaining it to thee later," said Pablo.

"Scarcely wert thou in the carriage," said Miguel, "when we formed ourselves into a battalion. We had to follow thee, remaining invisible. To have gone in advance would have been useless, for the way was blocked up by serenaders. We were to arrive in the thick of the uproar, appear to Rosalés as delivering angels in the uniform of *alguazils*, and deceive the *alferez* himself, thanks to the darkness of the streets. The rest thou knowest. Having made thee alight from the carriage, we wrapped thee up, hurried thee into the carriage, and whilst Elio, his guitar over his shoulder, went to prison in company with Rosalés, we brought thee here."

"Where am I then?" asked Cano.

"In my father's country house," said one of the young men present; "the keys were in my possession, and when he learns that thou hast deigned to stop here he will be proud and happy."

Alonso rose and stretched out his arms.

"Come all of you," he cried, "to this heart which ye have so much consoled. If I die, to you the task of clearing my memory."

"Thou shalt not die!" cried all present.

"Can I then lie under the ignominy of such an accusation, and fly from my judges?" said Alonso.

"Thou must, master," said Bartholomeo gravely; "thou didst not fly, but rather submitted to a stern necessity. If thou dost not leave Madrid, thou art lost. The death of Doña Mercedes has made a sensation; the inquest and thy departure will make another. It will surely reach the ears of those for whom thou art sacrificing thyself."

"Yes, perchance," said Alonso.

"Moreover," said Miguel, "one of us can go in pursuit of Lelli. I, if thou wilt. I will journey through Spain and France, and search Italy, town by town, till I find that cursed Italian. I will bring him to confession; I swear by our Lady of the Pillar. Oh, undo not what we have done with so much difficulty. Reject not the aid of thy pupils, thy friends, thy children. Enshroud thine existence with the deepest mystery till the secret of thine innocence and thy heroism be revealed to the nation. God has not favored thine almost miraculous escape that thou shouldst throw away the benefit thereof."

"Thou art right; it was a miracle," said Alonso.

"Accept it then from Heaven, master," said Pablo.

"Break not our hearts by a refusal," said Bartholomeo.

"In the name of thy dead Mercedes," said Miguel, with affectionate entreaty, "consent to let us save thee. She, whom thou didst love, and who didst suffer so cruel a death, has prayed to God and the Virgin for thy safety. Doubt not, master, that it was she who obtained from Heaven this favor, who inspired us to save thee, and procured us the means."

The artist let his head fall upon his hands. He did not speak, but his pupils saw that he was weeping. They respected his sorrow. Silent and deeply touched they stood upright, forming a compact group around him, and holding each other's hands like men bound by a common oath, and whom a common heroic action had united for evermore in an indissoluble friendship. For some time Alonso remained absorbed in the newly-aroused recollection of his wife. He also weighed carefully the reasons advanced by his pupils against his risking his life. His conscience seemed in harmony with the opinions of those around him. He raised his head. He dried his tears; a noble fire shone in his eyes.

"I accept," said he, "all that ye have done, and I bless you for your devotion. It will best prove any worth I may have, for it will prove how much I was loved."

"What wilt thou do next?" said Castello.

"Go straight before me seeking oblivion."

"Good," said Miguel; "meantime I will go to Italy. Do not pity me, master, nor yet applaud me too highly for what I do. If my purse be light, thou hast often told me I had talent. In the schools of Bologna, Venice, and Rome, I shall find work enough to keep me from starving. Be assured that I shall not forget Naples. I shall be glad of an opportunity to visit Ribera's studio, and compare his present luxury with his former poverty. Who knows but I may find Lelli there? Those two men are made for each other."

"Beware, Miguel," said Alonso; "be on thy guard against Lelli."

"I will, indeed, master," said Miguel; "though I am convinced that honest people always win at such games as this."

"Right, Miguel," cried Castello, "for Heaven is with them."

The young men now produced, each from the pocket of his doublet, some pieces of gold.

"Master," said Bartholomeo, "it is but little, the offering of pilgrims of art; but do not grieve us by refusing it."

"No," said Alonso. "I may well accept your gold, since I have accepted your lives."

Castello now approached, moved to tears.

"It remains but to say farewell, master," he said; "we must be in Madrid before dawn, and be assured we will assist at the Señora Mercedes' requiem."

"Farewell, noble hearts," cried Alonso; "God knows when we shall meet again. May ye be as happy as ye deserve; win fame and honor, and believe that while Alonso Cano draws the breath of life he will remember you."

They departed, and Alonso watched them; some entering the carriage, others mounting their steeds. Then gradually the noise of wheels and the gallop of horses were lost in the distance, and Alonso was alone. He threw himself into a chair, 'where, exhausted, he fell into a profound sleep. At dawn he took a slight repast, gave a piece of gold to the servant, and passing out through the little garden, reached the high road. The high road—whither did it lead? He knew not. But, as he said, he placed himself entirely in the hands of Providence, and determined to go straight before him till he found repose, solitude, oblivion.

CHAPTER X.

THE HAUNTED HOUSE.

A TRAVELLER, who showed his extreme fatigue by the manner in which he leaned upon his staff of orange wood, wended his way from the port of Grao to the village of *Las Cabañas*. Nothing could be more charming or more picturesque than these clusters of rustic dwellings, thatch-covered for the most part, surrounded by masses of flowers and foliage, and looking out upon the expanse of deep blue sea, the surface of which is rarely ruffled.

The traveller sat down a few paces from the shore, and his eyes looked out with a lingering wistfulness over the space which lay between him and the far-off horizon. After having observed the cabins, the fishing-boats, and the children picking up shells at the low-water mark, he began to wonder to whom he should address himself for needed information. The simplest course was to proceed to the *posada*,* before the door of which several muleteers were whiling away the time till supper in friendly chat.

The traveller entered the inn-parlor, which was permeated with a strong odor of garlic and allspice. He ordered a modest repast, and while it was being served, questioned the attendant.

" To whom must I apply concerning the hire of a little house which I saw upon the strand, and which appeared unoccupied ?"

---

* Inn.

"It is not to rent, Señor," said the young girl.

"For sale, then, perchance?"

"But, Holy Virgin of Saragossa, who would dream ot living there?"

"Is it unhealthy?"

"If that were all!"

"What then?"

"It is haunted."

"By thieves?"

"By ghosts."

"That would necessarily lower the rent."

"Thou wouldst still think of living there?"

"Why not?"

"Thou hast no fear of ghosts, Señor?"

"I fear men much more."

The young girl crossed herself devoutly, as she went on.

"There are spots of blood in the house."

The traveller shuddered, but nevertheless said:

"The situation of the house pleases me. Knowest thou to whom it belongs?"

"Oh, thou needst not disturb thyself. Thou art not from Valencia as one can see by thine accent. Otherwise thou wouldst know that the old fool Milagro comes every day through the great avenue of trees between Valencia and Grao. Milagro owns that dwelling. Thou needst not speak of hire to him, for he will rather pay thee to remain there. He will then believe that some one deems him innocent."

"Of what was he accused?"

"Of the murder of his wife!"

The traveller started to his feet.

"Ah," cried the young girl, "I knew I would fill thee, too, with horror. Stop, here is he whom thou seekest.

He is pale enough, as if the devil had breathed in his face. He has come, as he does each day, to know if I have found an inmate for his house. To-day I will let thee answer."

An old man, bowed down by age, was, in fact, just then advancing towards the *posada*. His hair was white, his form bent, his expression restless, piercing, and hard, his mouth, contracted, had bitter lines at its corners. A pointed beard terminated the strange, angular, fierce, and almost repulsive countenance. Seeing him, the traveller who desired to rent a dwelling at Las, Cabañas could not repress a shudder. An instinctive aversion caused him to shrink from contact with the new-comer; but, as if some thought of mercy had suddenly arisen within him, he advanced to where Milagro stood. The latter had been so long unaccustomed to be treated like other men, that observing this movement on the part of the traveller, his face lit up with something that was almost joy.

"Thou art not of Valencia?" said he, accepting the goblet which the traveller held out to him; "thou art from Grenada, as thy speech betrays. If thou wert of Valencia, —well, in short, I am Milagro. Thou dost not know that I am old Milagro."

"Thou art wrong, I do know!" said the traveller.

Milagro timidly resumed his seat. This humble movement touched the traveller. He took the flagon of Alicante, which stood before him, and refilling Milagro's goblet, said:

"After we have drunk, we will come to business."

"Business!" repeated Milagro, "what wouldst thou of me?"

"I want to rent thy house at a modest rate."

"Rent the haunted house," said Milagro, trembling in every limb. "Art thou serious in thine offer? Thou art not of Valencia, otherwise— To live in that house!

The people hereabouts declare that never, never shall those stains be washed away!"

"Name thy price," said the traveller.

"Twenty ducats a year, Señor. If that is too much, say so. Twenty ducats; or nineteen, if thou thinkest twenty too much. I am not rich! My goods were confiscated. A trial costs money!"

"Be it so," said the traveller. "I will pay thee twenty ducats."

"Twenty ducats without making any repairs," cried the old man in delight. "Thou art a true *caballero.* When wouldst thou take possession?"

"This very day!"

"There is nothing easier, nothing easier. If thou art not fastidious there is some furniture in the house."

"I am not fastidious," said the traveller.

He took out his purse as he spoke and gave Milagro twenty golden ducats.

"I can trust thee!" said Milagro, "thy face inspires confidence. I will sign thee a receipt for a year's rent. In whose name shall I make it out?"

A cloud passed over the stranger's face.

"In the name of Alfonso Ridalto," he said.

The old man procured a sheet of parchment and a pen, and wrote out the receipt in a trembling hand. When he had delivered it to the tenant of the haunted house he added slowly and with some hesitation:

"I will conduct thee thither and open the doors for thee. I keep the keys always about me. What a state it must be in since—"

He did not finish, but led the way out of the *posada.*

The serving-woman, Pepita, crossed herself as she passed the rash being who had rented the accursed house in the village of Las Cabañas.

Milagro silently led the way thither, his tenant following. In front of the haunted house was a garden or rather a copsewood of myrtle and pomegranate trees. The branches had sprouted here and there with the unrestrained but charming disorder produced by great confused masses of trees. The paths were so overgrown with long thick grass as to be indistinguishable; the walls were covered with yellow and white jasmine or clusters of roses; luxuriant vines formed, as it were, a lace-work, twining now upwards, now downwards, in a cascade of flowers and foliage, which had somewhat the effect of a moving curtain. This desolate house, upon which a seal of horror had been set by a long-past crime, had, nevertheless, its own charm and its own beauty. Ridalto, as the traveller had called himself to Milagro, could not help rejoicing at the thought that the superstition of the country folk would transform this dwelling into a hermitage. When the door was opened he found that the interior was in perfect accord with the exterior. The bars once taken from the window, Ridalto beheld great massive pieces of furniture of an almost monumental character, carved in solid wood by Flemish artists, besides some costly cabinets in polished Indian woods, inlaid with amber or silver. Whilst Milagro was letting air and light into the long-disused apartments he seemed extremely nervous and agitated. The furniture was thickly covered with dust, and the tapestries hung here and there in tatters; the whole aspect of the place was at once grand and funereal. As Ridalto had judged from the exterior, the house was not very large. The vestibule, decorated with that imperishable stucco-work of which we have lost the secret, opened upon the drawing-room, into which Milagro led the stranger. A *retiro**

---

* Boudoir.

adorned with colored glass came next; the chairs were covered with Cordova leather like the hangings; one the panels was occupied by a painting of Roelas,* and oddly in keeping with the rest a faded bouquet displayed its dusty petals upon a table laden with books.

"Those were roses," said Milagro, " roses which I used to cultivate in the garden for her—"

On the other side of the vestibule was a room hung with brocaded tapestries of faded blue. A great bed occupied the centre of it; upon a console table, in large vases of Arabic pattern, dating from the time of the Moorish domination, were more withered flowers. The counterpane and a mat dragged out of its place were the only symptoms of a confusion which none had ever dared or desired to repair. On the floor were spots of a dark brown color, which time had been powerless to efface. Seeing these Ridalto remembered Pepita's story.

The old man stood motionless upon the threshold.

"The library is farther on," he said.

Ridalto followed him therein, and saw that on either side were shelves laden with innumerable volumes.

"I shall not be lonesome here," he thought.

Two or three other unimportant rooms and a garden yet more tangled than the one in front, completed this singular habitation.

"Thou dost not regret thy bargain?" said Milagro.

---

* Juan de las Roelas, a Spanish painter of the Andalusian school, who brought into his country the rich coloring of which he had learned the secret in the schools of Rome and Venice. Over the high altar of San Isidor is his largest work, The Death of the Archbishop of Seville. It covers the whole altar screen. It is divided into two parts, heaven and earth, and was the first of that style of composition afterwards common in that school. He lived 1558 to 1625.

" Nay, not at all," replied Ridalto.

" And," said the old man with considerable hesitation, " thou wilt permit me sometimes, though it be but rarely, for I shall not be importunate, to come hither."

" Yea, surely," said Ridalto with an effort to conquer the invincible repugnance with which Milagro inspired him.

" Thou wilt not live here alone ?" said the old man.

"Quite alone !" replied Ridalto.

" And thy errands ?"

" I shall do them myself."

" Thy meals ?"

" I will prepare them likewise."

" So! but if thou shouldst need assistance—perchance, a guide in Valencia, I know the town well; I was born there, I hope to die there. If thou hast need of me—"

" For information, yes."

" I am at thy service. In our country we often use the meaningless phrase, *A la disposicion de usted;* * it is a mere formula with no significance. But with me it is different. What little I can do I will do joyfully. If thou wert from Valencia perchance thou wouldst reject my advances; but as thou art from Grenada—"

" Canst thou procure me clay, marble, a chisel ?"

" To-morrow. I will send thee these things by an un-happy man who has lately come out of the *presidio.*" †

Ridalto made an involuntary gesture, the import of which Milagro fully seized.

" He is an honest fellow, this José," said he, " he was unfortunate. What wouldst thou ? He underwent his punishment; there is naught to be said against him."

---

* At your disposition, or at your service.
† Jail, prison.

By a sudden revulsion of feeling, Ridalto said:

"I will be grateful to thee if thou sendest him hither."

The old man then took leave with new protestations of devotion.

Next day, thanks to the zeal of José whose worth Milagro had not exaggerated, the haunted house considerably improved its appearance. A few nails repaired the tapestries, the dust disappeared from the furniture, the light penetrated the rooms through wide-opened windows, and even the tangled foliage of the gardens was reduced to something like order.

The largest room was transformed into a studio with easels, tools, clay, and other artist's materials, and Ridalto was soon at work. He rose at dawn and chisel in hand worked nearly all day. He attempted nothing on a large scale, whether it was from distrust of himself or because he found the disposing of statuettes more convenient. He created exquisite groups, wherein the Virgin Mother held her dying Son upon her knees, saints in an ecstacy of prayer, or martyrs undergoing torment. The inspiration of Ridalto seemed full of deep piety and ardent mysticism. His works showed him to be one who prayed much and who had suffered much. The creations of artists or authors are not altogether the children of their imagination, the heart has as large a share in their inspiration as the intellect. Our passions have as much influence upon our works as our genius, and are often their chief sources of inspiration.

But who could guess what deep wellspring of sorrow flowed through Ridalto's silent and desolate soul? As he had declared to Milagro, he lived alone. Occupied with his work, absorbed in his own memories, he sufficed to himself. He had not even curiosity enough to visit the town which lay near to the village of Las Cabañas. He went from his dwelling to Grao but no farther. Sometimes as he watched the vessels dancing upon the blue waves, he asked himself if he might not find happiness in going far, far away to those new worlds which for two centuries had belonged to Spain, and there live forgetful of men and forgotten by them. He sometimes wrote, and José while keeping him informed of the departure of messengers for Madrid, sometimes brought him letters.

Three months had passed since Ridalto set foot in the village of Las Cabañas. He often saw old Milagro pass the window, stop an instant before the garden gate, hesitate as if he would fain have entered the house, and, withheld by some indefinable feeling of mingled shyness and grief, go slowly on his way.

One morning as Ridalto was busy painting, according to the custom of the time, and with the delicacy of a miniature, a wooden statue he had just completed, he saw Milagro as usual pass the window. A feeling of compassion suddenly sprung up within him for this forsaken old man.

"After all," said he, "the law acquitted him of the crime for which he was imprisoned. Therefore we should regard him as innocent, and to act as if we thought him otherwise is cruelty. If any one has a right to condemn him and shun his society, surely it is not I, it is not I."

And opening the door he called Milagro.

The ice was broken.

Thenceforth Milagro came every day to spend a few moments at least in the haunted house. He admired Ridalto's talent. Like most Spaniards, he had more than a tolerable knowledge of art, and Ridalto began to find in his conversation a repose from his incessant labors. The old man pointed out to him the means by

which he might dispose of his statuettes to enlightened
and generous men.   In course of time Ridalto achieved
great success.   He could have made double the sum if
he had not with strange moroseness declined all private
relations with merchants, traders, or connoisseurs, and
so gained the reputation of being unsociable and misan-
thropic.

As a rest from carving, he procured canvases and
painted interiors which were not realistic but real, or
saints, virgins, and martyrs of incomparable beauty, and
to which there was but one drawback, a certain resemblance amongst them all.   They were surely similar in
kind, these earthly creatures, raised by faith to Heaven.

The most sincere admirers of Ridalto's paintings declared, that while possessed of a great fertility in composition the artist had this defect, that he had chosen
one type of womanhood, to which he made all others
subservient.   But this slight drawback did not prevent
his works from bringing a good price.   The winter
passed slowly.   In the evenings around the *brasero,** before the blaze of the olive nuts, Ridalto and Milagro sat,
often in profound silence; both were self-contained and
full of some absorbing memory.   But though they spoke
little they found a curious sort of relief in each other's
society.   Never had Milagro asked Ridalto a single
question as to his past; never did Ridalto seek to raise
the veil which had fallen upon Milagro's memories.

When the fine weather came the artist, weary perhaps
of Grao, determined at length to traverse the long avenue
of ancient trees which separated it from Valencia.

Truly, beholding the magnificent country which surrounds this town, one acknowledges with what justice

---

* Brazier or grate.

poets have so enthusiastically celebrated this rich and luxuriant Huerta; the marvellous climate and the beauty so full of a subtle charm which belongs to Valencia, and is only equalled by the Vega of Grenada.

Lucio Siculo calls it "the miracle of nature," Piralta the "terrestrial Paradise," and Mariana* "the Elysian Fields." In truth, there could be nothing more exquisite than this town, which retains all the grandeur of a large city, though shut in by high walls with eight monumental gates. Its narrow and somewhat irregular streets seem, as it were, a network, surrounding the great wonder of Valencia, its cathedral.

Ridalto was too true an artist not to admire this monument raised upon the ruins of an ancient mosque. To efface all recollection of the Arabic architecture with its pagan grace, the Gothic predominated in the new structure. The different epochs at which improvements had been made left their traces upon the monument, where each addition bears a different date. Ridalto prostrated himself before the altar with deep fervor. The Christian for the time being overcame the artist curious as to antique remains. However, when he had prayed, he rose and admired the magnificence of the altar of serpentine marble, with ornamentations of solid gold.

The paintings of the high altar, and those in the lateral chapels, were all by well-known artists. Ridalto examined them each with real admiration, which reached its culminating point when he entered the sacristy and beheld there one of Murillo's finest efforts.

The sacristan then opened the relic closet and showed Ridalto some of the most precious relics in Spain: the shirt of the infant Jesus; the comb of His mother; the

---

* All three Spanish poets and writers.

chalice which our Saviour used at the Last Supper; and the skeleton of one of the Holy Innocents.

Ridalto remained in mournful meditation for some moments before these holy things. When he left the cathedral he was calmed and consoled.

Next day he described his journey to Milagro, and the impression it had made upon him.

" Didst thou enter the chapel of San Salvador?" asked Milagro.

" No," said the artist.

" Thou wert wrong. In that church is the *camarin* containing a Christ more than life size, the head of which is truly grand. What would perchance strike thee as less artistic, is the abundant brown hair and the thick beard covering the chest."

" What is the origin of this statue?" asked Ridalto.

" There is no certainty as to its origin," said Milagro; 'but I will repeat what the sacristan told me: Somewhere about 1250 some ships brought this curious work of art to Grao. An altar of solid silver was erected for it at Valencia, and upon this was placed the statue, between two candlesticks of the same precious metal. The beard, which is an object of admiration to all the faithful, has grown since the Christ received the homage of the people of San Salvador."

" I must visit the chapel," said Ridalto, smiling, "though I confess that the hair and beard, added by Spanish taste to religious statues, seem to me objectionable enough."

" Yes, thou art right," said Milagro. " But what wouldst thou? All artists cannot endow their works with the admirable sentiment which distinguishes thine; if they do not strike near the mark, they strike hard. And, after all, the faith which makes the people kneel before such statues is none the less agreeable to God. In fact its simplicity gives it new value."

Gradually Ridalto became accustomed to the society of old Milagro; each felt that the other had a secret, but each respected the other's sorrow. Sometimes the painter revolted at thought of the relations existing between Milagro and himself, but he always ended by proving himself in the wrong, saying:

"If he came not here, who would enter this house?"

It is certain that, owing to the great success with which the works of Ridalto had met, it would have been easy for him to make any new connections he wished at Valencia; but to the advances which had been made to him he responded with so much coldness that his warmest admirers considered him morose and unsociable.

One summer evening, which was more sultry even than the most sultry days of Spain, a storm of unusual violence burst over the village of Las Cabañas. The heavens, overcast by thick clouds, were rent asunder by streaks of jagged lightning; the rumblings of thunder struck terror into the hearts of the people; the waves upon the shore, usually so blue and peaceful, rushed mountain high upon the bank, dashing the vessels together, and putting seamen exposed to their fury in imminent peril of death. It would seem as if some terrible cataclysm was about to annihilate this corner of the earth. Flashes of lightning succeeded each other uninterruptedly; dull rumblings were heard in the neighboring Sierras; the people prayed shut up in their houses, and the chapel of Grao was crowded with suppliants sending up vows to the Madonna.

As the storm began Milagro was on the point of leaving Ridalto; the latter would not, however, permit that his visitor should depart in weather so dangerous, and

he insisted on him remaining to share his modest repast.
José, the hapless José, the former inmate of the *presidio*,
had given so many proofs of attachment to Ridalto, that
he had at last taken him into his service.

The poor lad was not naturally bad; in a moment of
anger he had struck his adversary with a knife which he
held in his hand. José was cast into prison. Fortunately
for him his \late adversary did not die, and his resentment having abated, he at once asked for José, first a
mitigation of sentence, and finally a full pardon through
the intervention of influential gentlemen in whose service
he was. His generosity and perseverance were rewarded,
and José was set at liberty, and was free to choose an
honest life.

José was well pleased with his new master, Ridalto,
and often repeated that he would never leave him unless
to marry Merced, the sister of him whom he had so
nearly killed. José did everything himself at the haunted
house, and from the order reigning there it might be
supposed that there were three servants to do the work.

Milagro, after a faint attempt at refusal, accepted the
artist's hospitality. He seemed at once glad and frightened at the prospect of remaining in that house. Was
it the storm which made him so nervous and excitable ?
His countenance reflected its every terrible phase, each
passing over his face with the rapidity of lightning. The
electricity in the air had evidently affected his nerves;
the veins of his forehead swelled, his eyes shone with a
dull fire, or sometimes grew so dim that it would seem
their light was extinguished forever. Now he was silent
for long intervals, or again he discoursed with astonish-
ing volubility, as if afraid of his own thoughts.

The meal was short, yet Milagro, to keep up his flag-
ging courage, emptied a whole flagon of Alicante.

Far from abating, the storm seemed to redouble its fury. Ridalto was about to call for lights when Milagro begged him to desist.

"For me the shadow," he said; "the shadow for me."

And throwing himself into an arm-chair he shuddered at every peal of thunder and every flash of lightning.

Meanwhile Ridalto seemed wrapped in some gloomy thought.

"Thou art praying, art thou not?" asked Milagro suddenly.

"I pray for consolation."

"I cannot pray; I cannot pray," cried Milagro with a groan.

"Wherefore canst thou not pray?" asked Ridalto.

The old man shook his head.

"God would not, He could not hear me," he said moodily.

"Ah," said Ridalto, "even through the tumult of this storm He hears a child's voice."

"No," said Milagro, with a certain desolate persistency. "When I have tried to call upon Him, my voice, full of tears as it was, was always drowned by a noise, a slight noise. Hearest thou it not?" he added, with growing horror. "It is faint; faint. Drops falling one by one upon the floor. Hearken; and dost thou not perceive a strange odor in this room?"

"It is the sulphurous vapor in the atmosphere," said Ridalto.

"Nay, nay; not that. But a vague, sickening, enervating smell—the odor of blood; blood ever flowing."

"Hush, hush," cried Ridalto; "thy words are terrible."

"They are within me; they stifle me; they choke me. Ah, how the lightning burns my eyes! Dost thou not see by its glare a figure advancing towards us?"

"No, no! thou art crazed, Milagro; these hallucinations proceed from the storm. Be calm; kneel and pray if thou art suffering or in terror, but yield not thyself to these phantoms of thy imagination."

"This imagination is called conscience," said Milagro. "I would speak, and I must speak, even though thou drivest me hence. Yet this secret should die with me forever, forever; and be known only to hell, which urged me to the crime."

Milagro appeared to have lost all control of himself; his every movement showed a mind whose equilibrium was upset.

"Just such a storm was raging," he said; "the thunder roared with the same fury on the night of the murder, the night of blood. I was intoxicated with rage; the knife was beside me; it gleamed in the darkness by the glare of the lightning. I know not what *she* said; it must have been something terrible, for my reason deserted me. I sprung upon her like a wild beast, and struck her. Ever since I hear the blood dropping from her wound, as it dropped then, and made that ugly stain, which all the water in the sea can not wash out."

When he had made this fearful revelation Milagro threw himself upon the ground and knocked his head repeatedly against the spot stained with blood. He remained a long time motionless. A clap of thunder more violent than any yet shook the haunted house to its foundations; the lightning struck one of the trees of the garden, while a cry of agony from Milagro redoubled the horror of the scene.

Ridalto ran to raise the old man, and found that he had fainted. Then, taking him in his arms, he laid him upon the bed. The storm seemed now to have somewhat abated its fury; the peals of thunder began to die away

in the distance ; the waves grew almost still ; and a great
calm succeeded the late tumult of the elements.

For more than an hour Ridalto sought in vain to rouse
Milagro to consciousness. He was just becoming seriously alarmed when the old man sighed deeply and
opened his bewildered eyes. He looked feebly around
him, and raising himself upon his elbow, said :

"I have spoken ; I have spoken."

For a moment the artist thought of denying that he
had, and thus leaving the old man in more complete
security, but his frankness of character forbade such
prevarication, and he contented himself with saying :

"What import the delirious ravings caused by that
terrible storm ? Besides, I was alone with thee."

"Ah !" cried Milagro, passing his hands through his
hair, which was standing upright with horror, "there are
moments when I am tempted to appear before my judges
and say, 'Ye did acquit me of the crime with which I
was charged. I was cunning enough to divert suspicion
from myself by procuring a false *alibi*. My craft stood
me in good stead against your strength, patience, and
justice. Ye gave me my liberty. Well, take it back. I
do not want it. I confess. I prefer the *presidio* with its
garb of infamy and its strangling collar of iron to the
life which I lead.' The multitude, more clear-sighted
than the judges, did not acquit me ; they condemned
me, and drove me from amongst them. At the galleys I
could converse, at least, with criminals. Here, no man
will take my hand, no child will greet me. My very
contact seems to leave a stain.' "

"Hapless man," cried Ridalto.

"I have said that I am often tempted to give myself
up, but when it comes to the point I draw back. Thou
art free to do it. I will not deny thy charge. I will

even thank thee for having rendered me this melancholy service. The weight that is upon my heart must be thrown off. I must speak and cry out, 'I have shed blood.'"

"Sleep in peace to-night within the haunted house," said Ridalto gravely; "to-morrow we shall consult as to what is best."

The artist remained for a long time at the old man's side, even when a restless sleep had closed his eyes. He felt the deepest compassion for him, and the motion of his lips showed that he was praying.

Next morning the heavens, swept the night previous by the wings of the storm, shone out again in all their beauty. Ridalto went into the old man's room.

"Wilt thou not arise?" he said, gently.

"Yes," said Milagro ; "to leave Las Cabañas."

"We will go together," said the artist.

"Together?" repeated Milagro with a shudder, "and whither?"

"To Valencia."

The old man shuddered again, but repeated with a sort of despairing resignation,

"To Valencia."

After a light breakfast they both set out from the haunted house, and through the avenue which led from Grao to one of the eight gates of the city.

When they had entered the town Ridalto laid his hand upon his companion's shoulder and exclaimed :

"Thou saidst to me once that I should visit San Salvador. Wilt thou guide me thither?"

"Yes," replied Milagro in surprise.

After passing through many intricate windings the two men found themselves at a church-door.

"Here is San Salvador," said Milagro.

"Let us go in," said Ridalto.

After a hasty genuflection the artist began to examine the architecture of the church with critical attention ; but, despite his interest in what he saw, his mind seemed deeply occupied by some more urgent matter.

At length he perceived an old priest coming down one of the aisles of the church. He went hastily towards him.

"Father," said he, "I have brought thee a soul to save."

The priest looked kindly at him and said, pointing to the confessional :

"Its salvation is at hand."

In an instant the priest was seated in the confessional.

In Spain the confessionals are quite unlike those of France and Belgium. The priest alone is hidden from the eyes of the multitude by a curtain. The penitent, kneeling upon the ground, makes his confession in presence, so to say, of the curious spectators. His fear or his contrition is evident to all. This mode of confessing detracts perhaps somewhat from the solemnity of that sublime mystery enacted between priest and penitent ; but at least it proves that men rise superior to human respect in conforming themselves to the holy law which brings the penitent to the feet of God's minister.

The priest, once seated, hid his face in his hands, and recollecting himself, asked of Heaven the grace and unction necessary for his sacred ministry. Meanwhile Ridalto seized Milagro by the hand and said, urging him forward with gentle force :

"Thou wouldst a tribunal to judge thee, a man to hear thee. Go, the priest is there to console and absolve thee."

Milagro turned deadly pale ; he staggered and leaned

against one of the pillars for support, but at length, with Ridalto's help, he fell upon his knees before the priest and began to sob out his story.

Meanwhile Ridalto prayed devoutly.

After some time Milagro reappeared. A complete change had taken place in him. His eyes were no longer wild, but had an humble and resigned expression. His brow was calm, and the agitation habitual to his face had disappeared. He brought Ridalto into the chapel of the miraculous statue, and there, wringing his hands as if he would break them, cried:

"Thou hast saved me, in this world and the next."

When they were outside the church Ridalto said:

"Art thou now willing to inhabit the haunted house?"

"With thee?"

"With me."

"But I am a pariah, an outcast."

"Thou art a man upon whom has fallen the purifying blood of Christ," said Ridalto; "thou art my brother."

Milagro wiped away his tears and went home with Ridalto to the village of Las Cabañas.

CHAPTER XI.

THE SECRET BETRAYED.

THE dwelling of Señor Aguidas was one of the most delightful in Valencia. The *patio** formed a perfect flower-garden; fountains playing constantly kept the atmosphere deliciously cool and fresh, and streams proceeding thence under the shrubbery produced a moisture which showed itself here and there in the form of light mists, rising above the white-blossomed orange trees or purple-flowering pomegranates.

The *patio*, with its marble pillars and mosaics of that peculiar brilliancy, the secret of which is lost in our day, contained many works of art of the rarest value, some dating from the time of the Moorish dominion, others brought at great cost from Italy, and others again the masterpieces of those who were then making Spain the greatest artistic country.   Low seats, divans covered with Cordova leather, separated the pillars or pedestals, each surmounted by busts, gigantic vases, or graceful statues.

All the principal people of Valencia, distinguished strangers, or travelling artists, made it a point to visit the dwelling of the Count Aguidas. He received in princely fashion, and his entertainments were renowned for their magnificence.

His wife was a handsome and elegant woman, whose decided love for dress did not exclude a cultivated taste.

---

* A sort of interior courtyard, usually paved with marble. It has a temporary cover for the daytime, which is withdrawn at night.

She had no children, and being herself possessed of a considerable fortune, encouraged her husband in his desire to increase the love of the beautiful in his own country, and to worthily represent at Valencia the nobility of Spain so renowned in France and in Flanders for its munificence.

Upon the particular evening of which we speak, an unusual number of guests were assembled in the count's drawing-rooms and corridors. Some of them stood grouped together in the *patio*, listening to a musician playing Andalusian airs; others, dispersed through the rooms, admired the splendor of their appointments, or passed the time in animated conversation.

"But, my friend," said a young man to his host, "thou didst promise us a surprise to-night."

"Did I ever break my word?"

"Never."

"Be assured, then, that I shall not fail now."

"Tell us at least what is the nature of this surprise."

"I will."

"Speak! speak!" cried a dozen voices.

"Well, I have simply discovered a great man."

"In Valencia?" asked the Marquis Juaréz.

"Yes, or rather in the village of Las Cabañas."

"Who is he?"

"One of the first artists of Spain."

A murmur of incredulity arose among the group. But Count Aguidas only smiled confidently, and said:

"I repeat what I have said, this man is one of the greatest artists of Spain."

"Count," said the Marquis Juaréz, "such testimony from thee is a brevet of genius."

"Like all who make an important discovery, I find myself singularly doubtful of the result," said Aguidas.

" To find in a man, so modest that he dreads the fame which his works necessarily win, varied knowledge combined with the rarest inspiration, is something so marvellous that I never heard the like. Presently I shall call upon you to confirm me in my judgment, or to combat it, if ye think me the dupe of my own admiration."

" What is this man's name?"

" Ridalto."

" A name quite unknown."

" Where doth he abide?" asked the marquis.

" In a dwelling which any person in Valencia would refuse to inhabit—the haunted house."

A shudder passed through the group surrounding Aguidas, for all present remembered the terrible drama enacted there.

" Probably this Ridalto is unaware of what took place in that house."

" The more probable since he is said to be on friendly terms with Milagro."

" But," said the marquis, " thou hast not told us how thou didst discover this strange being."

" One day I was passing Abraham's shop," said Aguidas, " and though I care not to cross the threshold—for I much misdoubt me that this dealer remaineth in his heart attached to the faith of his fathers, and hath but abjured to save his life—I paused an instant to look at an antique of Arabic device, when a statue of wood attracted my attention. Carved with exquisite grace, and painted with rare perfection, it really united, in an equal degree, perfection of form and power of conception. It was small, and yet it had about it a style usually seen in much larger works. I was so charmed with it that I entered Abraham's shop and bought it at his own price, asking the old Jew the name of the artist.

"He showed me upon the base the name of Ridalto, and declared that he knew nothing more, adding, however, that if I wished he could discover the artist's whereabouts.

"In a fortnight I returned to the Jew. This time he led me to a picture, and showed me beneath it the same name as upon the statue. The drawing of this picture, a Holy Family, was worthy of Raphael; a soft light color, marvellously fresh, showed off the drawing to advantage. I was amazed, and merely said to Abraham:

"'Send me this picture.'

"He bowed in that cringing fashion peculiar to the sons of Jacob, and said with a smile:

"'I have some information which may be agreeable to your lordship; Ridalto inhabits the haunted house.'

"'I thank thee,' said I, 'and shall proceed thither to-morrow.'

"'If it be to visit Ridalto,' said the Jew, 'your excellency will waste your time. He receives no one.'

"'But an artist cannot live in perpetual solitude.'

"'Yet that is what he does.'

"'Thou knowest him?'

"'Nay, not at all.'

"'How then dost thou hold dealings with him?'

"'I never see him,' he replied. 'Old Milagro brings his works hither, and names the price thereof. As he is not the proprietor, I am forced to accept the terms he offers. I must admit that Ridalto is usually moderate enough in his demands. If, instead of bearing as he does an obscure name, he had attained celebrity, his pictures and statues would be of double value.'

"'Ha! ha! seest thou, Abraham,' said I, laughing, 'I

would fain be this great man's Mæcenas. In six months' time I will have all his works in my gallery, and will give a ball to make them known to the public. Next day orders will pour in upon the mysterious dweller of the haunted house.'

"I kept my word; all that proceeded from Ridalto's chisel or brush I purchased. They are here, and it is to judge of them that I have invited you here to-night."

The curiosity of the guests was redoubled. Not only were they to see the admirable pictures and statues of this unknown artist, but to find, perchance, some clue to the mystery which enshrouded the mysterious stranger of Las Cabañas. In a short time their curiosity was gratified. The doors of the gallery were thrown wide, and a flood of light fell upon the *patio* below. The guests now thronged that portion of the gallery where, placed in the most favorable lights, statues and pictures shone like diamonds in rich settings. The Count Aguidas had not miscalculated his *protégé's* success; there was a unanimous cry of admiration from the assembly, and all enlarged upon the exquisite grace of the figures, the brilliancy of the coloring and the variety of conception.

Whilst the throng of cavaliers and ladies pressed around the statues and canvases, enthusiastically admiring these prodigies of scientific workmanship and rare taste, a lackey informed their host that a stranger desired the honor of waiting upon him, at once, if it were agreeable to him.

"Didst learn his name?" asked Aguidas.

"Yea, your excellency, the stranger bade me name him Estaban Murillo."

Count Aguidas uttered an exclamation of joy.

"Murillo in Valencia!" he cried; "Murillo in my house! What good fortune!"

With an eagerness which greatly enhanced the grace
and cordiality of his welcome to the stranger, Aguidas
went in search of him.

Estaban Murillo was young and handsome; his black
eyes, through all their brilliancy and vivacity, had a rare
depth and earnestness in them.   His high, broad forehead was shown in all its beauty and amplitude, for his
long artist's locks fell over his shoulders in graceful disorder.   His mouth was thin and delicate, and surmounted
by small moustachios; a beard, in the fashion of the period,
completed the beauty of his face.   He wore a sombre-
colored doublet slashed with violet velvet, and a heavy
chain of gold, presented to him by Philip IV.

He told the count that he had come to Valencia that
very morning, for the purpose of superintending the
hanging of one of his pictures in the Cathedral, and that
hearing of the ball at the Aguidas palace, he had taken
the opportunity to make the acquaintance of so generous
a patron of art whose galleries were said to contain rare
marvels.

The count's reception of him was all that Murillo
could have desired.   Scarcely had his name become
known to the guests when the artist found himself surrounded by men the most eminent, by titles or office, and
women the most elegant, all curious to see the author of
those wonderful creations which carry up our minds to
Heaven.   After the first excitement consequent upon
Murillo's arrival was over Aguidas said:

" Be good enough to look at these works, statues and
pictures, and, without observing the signature, to give me
thy opinion as to their value."

Murillo slowly examined the statuettes each in turn.
As he looked his eyes glowed with enthusiasm, and he
was heard to murmur ever and anon:

"How beautiful! How beautiful!"

At length, stopping before a "Dead Christ wept over by an Angel," * he said:

"Behold a work which shall never be surpassed by any one!"

"So my praise was not exaggerated," said Aguidas.

"Thy admiration could never have reached the level of their deserts," said Murillo; "no praise is too great for the perfect genius of the man who has erected the most magnificent *retablos* in Spain, sculptured marvellous statues in wood or marble, and painted Virgins that would make infidels believe."

"Thou knowest then this Ridalto?" said the count.

"Señor," cried Murillo, "whatever be the name upon the base of these works, they are from the chisel and brush of Alonso Cano."

"Alonso Cano!" cried Aguidas, "art sure?"

"Sure," replied Murillo. "God seldom gives the gift of a twofold genius to man."

Just then a man austerely clad in black approached Murillo. His countenance was stern, his gestures few, his voice cold and cutting.

"According to thee, then, these works are by Alonso Cano?" he said.

Murillo looked at the man who addressed him, and as he did so remembered his fellow artist's critical situation. He saw that his imprudent words might bring new persecution upon Alonso. The name of Ridalto no doubt concealed the identity of the hapless artist, who had fled from Madrid terrified by the awful accusation brought against him. He felt a lively remorse for what he had

---

* One of Alonso Cano's most celebrated works, which he left to the Museum of Granada.

done.   He cast a look of distress at the count, as if asking his help.

"No doubt," said the latter, with a presence of mind
which much reassured Murillo, "thou findest something
of his style in these works, but an intelligent pupil easily
acquires some of the touches of his master.   Therefore,
while recognizing considerable ability in these productions, I would hesitate to ascribe them to a man who,
once the favorite of Philip IV., was led, most probably
by a terrible grief, to an untimely death."

" Thou art informed that Cano is dead," said the man
in black, who seemed to attach great importance to
Murillo's opinion as to the merit of the unknown artist,
and to compare his verdict with the preceding revelations of Aguidas.

" I have heard nothing certain thereupon," said Murillo, "but the sorrow which overpowered that most hapless of artists at the death of his wife no doubt ended
in madness."

"Thou dost then believe in his innocence?" said the
man in black.

"In common with all the artists of Madrid, Señor, I
most certainly do," said Murillo.

" That is, indeed, generous," said the other, "but justice was evidently not of the same opinion when it accused him of one of the greatest of crimes."

"I was evidently mistaken, count," said Murillo, addressing Aguidas, "as thou sayest, this Ridalto has in
all probability studied under Cano, either at Seville or
Granada, and has succeeded in imitating his master to
an extent which could deceive even the eyes of an
artist."

The count appeared to coincide with this opinion, and
all the guests made it a point to share it likewise.

Nevertheless, the incident threw a damper upon the festivities. The man in black, who had seemed so interested
in hearing Murillo's opinion, left the gallery muttering
to himself.

When he had gone the count became curiously oppressed with a sense of impending misfortune.

"Señor," said Murillo, with undisguised agitation,
" where does this Ridalto dwell ?"

" Near Grao, in the village of the Cabins. I know
wherefore thou dost ask. Thou art, of course, convinced
of the identity of this mysterious personage with Alonso
Cano. Neither thou nor I are executioners."

"Ah !" cried Murillo, " I would be forever dishonored
if Alonso Cano were arrested through my imprudent
words."

" Those words were spoken in my house," said Aguidas,
" and I would fail in the duty of hospitality, so sacred to
a Spaniard, did I not aid thee in saving one who, through
our means, is in peril. I now comprehend his misan-
thropy and desire for solitude. If he be recognized he
is lost. Yet neither thou nor I can upon any pretext
whatsoever obtain admittance to the haunted house.
But one man in Valencia enters there, yes, and I believe
he is now an inmate of the house. Speak to Milagro,
tell him thy name, and God take the rest in His charge."

The count thrust a purse of gold into the artist's
hand.

"Spare no expense," said he; "one of my lackeys will
bring thee to the spot. Thou hast all night to take such
precautions as are needful. Lorenzo Tarifa will wait
till to-morrow to mature his plans for obtaining possession of Alonso Cano. The law, however hasty in its action, is clogged by many formalities. A Spaniard arrested at hazard and through an error caused by the over-

zeal of a judge can bring such a storm about the ears of his accuser that even the bravest are afraid. Tarifa must consult his colleagues, and it will be late in the morning when his myrmidons surround Milagro's accursed house."

"But," objected Murillo, "the city gates will be closed."

"Thou art right," said the count; "we must wait; only we must strive at least to gain upon Tarifa in speed. I will accompany thee that I may lend thee my aid."

Murillo and the Count Aguidas set out together. The dawn was whitening the east; in an hour the city's gates would open. Aguidas had, at first, some idea of trying the power of gold upon the guardian of the Gate of the Sea, so as to induce him to open it quicker; but if he had any hope of bribing the man it was soon dispelled; a dozen soldiers lined the way awaiting the regular hour for the opening of the gate. At sight of them Aguidas shuddered. The thought at once struck him that Alonso Cano's arrest would be more speedy than he had supposed, and that Tarifa evidently preferred erring through excess of zeal to failing in the capture of the accused. At length the gates rolled upon their hinges, and the soldiers dividing into two ranks went down the long avenue towards Grao.

"God be praised!" cried Aguidas, "a chance yet remains."

"What is that?" asked Murillo, anxiously.

"The soldiers are going by the avenue; there is a shorter way which we can take."

And the count pointed to a rugged and uneven path. They were soon traversing it. Upon one side were plantations of maize, so high as to form a wall, on the other an olive grove, which offered shelter in case of an alarm.

Both hurried on, wondering, silently, if it were possible for them to make an entrance into Milagro's garden before the soldiers arrived there.   They dared not speak, so full were they of mutual doubt and apprehension. The count merely said to the artist :

"Three horses will be at the foot of the avenue in less than half an hour."

At last they came to Milagro's garden, to which there was no entrance at the back.   The two men regarded the high wall, lowered in some places by the ravages of time and neglect.

"We must scale it," said Murillo tranquilly; "leave that to me, Count.   In this adventure we must divide the risks.   Thou wilt await Alonso here, and guide him to where the horses are in readiness.   I have a plan in my mind.   I am young and active; I shall be at the top of that wall in one moment.   In another my friend Alonso will be with thee."

Murillo began the ascent of the wall with the agility of a mountaineer.   Once at the top he looked down, and was glad to see that some old framework for vines, though rickety and crumbling, would assist his descent. He was soon in the garden.   He advanced to the door, opened it hastily, and came face to face with José, who was silently, as usual, going about his tasks.   The servant would have opposed his entrance, but Murillo said with an accent of convincing sincerity :

"The safety of thy master is at stake."

José bowed and pointed to the apartment of the artist known in Valencia as Ridalto.

Without an instant's hesitation, without even pausing to consider how terrified his old companion of the studio would be at sight of him, Murillo rushed into the room. It was empty, but, passing on to the next, the windows of which opened upon the sea, he saw a man seated at an easel, painting with all the ardor of inspiration. Murillo rushed over and caught him in his arms.

"Alonso!" he cried; "dear Alonso!"

Hearing himself thus addressed the man grew deadly pale.

"Hush!" said he; "hush!"

Then looking around distrustfully he said:

"How didst thou get in?"

"Through the garden. I scaled the wall."

"Thou comest then to save me," said Alonso, "for Murillo could not be a traitor."

"I come, indeed, to save thee," said Murillo; "thou art in instant danger."

"Who has betrayed me?" cried Alonso in a despairing tone.

"Thyself, misguided man," cried Murillo. "Didst thou not know that such talent as thine must reveal thy identity? To think otherwise was folly; for as a painter or sculptor thou must be Alonso Cano. Yesterday evening, in the gallery of the Count Aguidas, thy name was mentioned. Among gentlemen it would have mattered little; to request their silence would have been sufficient. But Judge Tarifa was there, and was determined to play the zealous magistrate. Before noon thou wilt be arrested; nay, perchance, in an hour."

"In an hour!" cried Cano, in horror.

Murillo opened the window and looked out. He saw the soldiers a little distance off advancing towards the house. He seized Alonso by the hand, crying:

"Fly, without an instant's delay. Pause not to look back. On the other side of yonder wall Count Aguidas awaits thee; he has horses in readiness, close at hand."

"But thou?" asked Cano.

"I will remain here."

"Dear and generous friend," said Alonso, "thy conduct proves that thou dost believe me innocent."

"I believe thee the noblest and most unfortunate of men," cried Murillo, impulsively clasping Alonso in his arms.

Just then they heard the measured tread of soldiers coming up the garden walk. An imploring look from Murillo resolved Cano's doubts. He sprung out into the back garden, just as the chief of the detachment raised the knocker of the door. José's frightened face was thrust into the studio.

"Thou mayest open!" said Murillo, calmly.

And whilst the trembling servant prepared to obey, the pupil of Pacheco, taking the palette of colors in his hand, sat down before the easel, and began to paint, with the rapidity and precision of touch peculiar to him, the figure sketched by Alonso Cano. The leader of the party hastily entered the studio and approached the artist.

"I arrest thee," he said, laying his hand upon Murillo's shoulder.

The latter turned and looked at him with a careless smile.

"So I see," he remarked. "Nevertheless I would be glad to know wherefore."

"That gratification will shortly be given thee," replied the other.

"Wouldst take me at once to prison?"

"Nay, we await here the Señor Tarifa."

"Good," said Murillo, "meantime I can continue to paint?"

"If thou wilt."

Murillo carelessly nodded his thanks to the soldier, and went on with the work he had begun. It was a

" Dead Christ," in the expression of which was extraordinary power and pathos. The figure of the Saviour was already painted by Alonso, with his wonderful inspiration; the face of the angel was merely sketched; this, Murillo hoped to finish before the arrival of Señor Tarifa. An hour passed. Old Milagro, uncertain as to what was going on, was a prey to the most cruel anxiety. He had seen Alonso fly, he knew that the house was full of soldiers, and perceived in a vague way that Alonso's safety depended upon the handsome young man who sat tranquilly painting in the studio.

José, by Murillo's orders, brought the soldiers some flagons of Spanish wine; they drank this readily enough, without, however, relaxing their vigilance. Tarifa's joy was great. He hoped, at one blow, to win a double triumph. Milagro's case might be brought up again, thanks to the presence of Alonso Cano in his house.

Aguidas and Murillo had been wise not to lose any time. Lorenzo Tarifa was not one to sleep over a plan once formed. Instead of going quietly home on leaving Aguidas's dwelling, he had sought out one of his colleagues, and made known his suspicions as to the identity of the mysterious tenant of the haunted house. The other judge agreed with him that it was best to make the arrest as soon as possible, and to procure, before day, the necessary authority. The signature of the Marquis de Miranda was indispensable, but the marquis was still at the ball, and would not be home before dawn, so that Tarifa could only wait patiently. By sunrise, however, he had in his possession a warrant for the arrest of a man of suspicious origin and habits, inhabiting a house of ill repute owned by Milagro.

Tarifa did not lose a minute in sending officers to surround Milagro's house, whilst he himself went to secure the presence of another magistrate for the purpose of establishing Alonso's identity. Tarifa, believing that he held fortune and advancement in his hand, did not let the grass grow under his feet. Accompanied by two eminent magistrates of Valencia, he proceeded towards Grao, after having, by an additional precaution, commanded some mounted soldiers to follow him at a little distance.

Just as the soldiers had finished the last flagon of wine, and while José was still watching the garden wall, over which Alonso had passed, Tarifa and his two companions appeared at the door and entered unannounced. José recognized one of them as the judge who had pronounced sentence upon him at his trial, and an involuntary smile crossed his lips.

He was not sorry to see this judge, who had been more than severe to him, about to commit himself to the arrest of an innocent man. He was, moreover, prepared to enjoy his surprise and vexation when he learned that he whom he sought had escaped.

Tarifa's air of triumphant self-importance was indescribable. He had so ridiculed the judge at Madrid, who, when he was in the very act of taking the murderer of Mercedes to prison, had found in his stead a peaceful guitar player, whose face was radiant with joy and triumph at the escape of the real criminal.

He took no pains to conceal his delight under that air of stern devotion to duty usually assumed by magistrates on such occasions. His joy shone out in every feature of his face, and in every curve of his short and portly figure. With a gesture of ineffable self-complacency he waved his companions aside, that he might enter first, and have the honor of laying his hand upon the shoulder of a wretch already doomed to the darkest dungeon in Valencia.

José was in the vestibule. Tarifa asked him:

"This house belongs to Milagro ?"

"Yes, your excellency."

"Where is he just now ?"

"In his own room."

"Has he a strange tenant ?"

"Yes, Señor, a painter."

"Observe !" said Tarifa, turning to his colleagues.

They bowed with a deference which ill concealed a certain jealousy.

"And this painter ?"

"Is now at work in his studio."

Tarifa made a step forward.

"Shall I inform him of your visit, Señor ?"

"The law may enter unannounced," said Tarifa sententiously.

So saying he pushed open the studio door and entered hastily. The other magistrates followed closing the door, and Tarifa passed round the easel, that he might be face to face with his victim.

Perceiving them Murillo rose with that rare, habitual courtesy which made him the equal of the first gentlemen in Spain, and motioned them to seats.

"It is not necessary," said Tarifa, rudely, "we shall not remain here long."

"Come ye to purchase a picture?" said Murillo, with perfect ease; "if so, I regret to inform your excellency that the work ordered by his most Catholic majesty, as well as by the various convents of Spain, will not permit me to undertake any farther commissions this year."

"We are not here to talk of pictures," said Tarifa, "but of a matter which may well cause thee to lay aside this air of levity which thou seemest to affect, and which will have its full weight upon our judgment."

"An air of levity!" repeated Murillo; "I confess that my mood is by no means sober, and thou thyself, Señor Tarifa, appeared to me of more jovial mien last evening."

"Last evening!" repeated the judge.

"Even so, at the Count Aguidas's ball, where I had the honor of meeting thee."

"I was there," said Tarifa, "which is but another proof that justice watches everywhere and always. It might be supposed that the magistrate sought his own pleasure in such a scene; whereas he was but accomplishing his duty. Thou must follow us."

Murillo laid down his pencil and palette upon the table, and looking steadily at the magistrate, said:

"Whatever my respect for the law and its representatives, I cannot permit any one—any one, hearest thou, Señor, to address me in so loud a tone of voice, and with covered head."

So saying Murillo, by a slight gesture, knocked off Tarifa's hat.

"Wretch!" cried he, "wretch! But the guards are there, and thou wilt answer for thine insolence. Thou dost seek to impose upon us; we know thy name, and the motive which has led thee to conceal thyself here."

"My name is not one of which I have any cause to be ashamed," said Murillo, "and as to my partiality for this house its situation fully justifies it. Thou dost speak of guards and of arrest; thou hast called me a wretch. Beware, in thy turn, Señor Tarifa, that I use not against thee the influence which I possess at court."

"We shall soon see how much thine influence will avail thee," cried the enraged Tarifa.

He opened the door, and at a signal six of the soldiers whom he had left in the vestibule entered the studio. An indignant flush mounted to the artist's face.

"Have a care what thou dost!" he cried; "if thou dost value thy place and thy reputation do not venture to arrest me, Señor Tarifa; for I swear that in less than a month thou wilt lose thy situation if one of these men so much as lay a finger upon me."

Tarifa shrugged his shoulders.

"Thou wilt sing a different tune shortly, my young popinjay," said he.

Murillo was at first tempted to defend himself, but he reflected that such a struggle would be degrading, and that it was better to undergo this momentary mortification, so as to make his own case stronger against Tarifa, and to render the judge's defeat doubly humiliating.

The artist's hands were quickly fettered. Tarifa then sat down, leaving the artist standing, and said rudely:

"Thy name?"

"Thou shouldst have commenced by that," said the painter, laughing.

"Justice proceeds according to its own good pleasure," said Tarifa.

"In truth," said the artist, "but not at all according to mine."

"Thy name?" repeated Tarifa, stamping his foot.

"Thou dost not know it, Señor," said the artist, "when it is known to all Spain. Behold the worthlessness of human glory. One dreams he is famous, and in Valencia, a town renowned for its artistic tastes, a man finds thee handling the brush and painting in full daylight the face of yonder angel, and he asks thy name."

A sound was heard in the vestibule; the studio door opened slowly, revealing the Count Aguidas.

The painter uttered an exclamation of delight.

"Count Aguidas," he cried, "thou, my lord, couldst never have been mistaken; and looking at the face which I have just painted, would have said at once that my name was—"

"Estaban Murillo," said Aguidas, advancing towards him.

He only then observed the fetters upon the artist's wrists.

"What is going on here?" he said sternly, addressing Tarifa. "Thou hast arrested Murillo, the painter to the King, and who shares the royal favor with Velasquez."

"This man has deceived thee, my Lord Aguidas," said Tarifa; "a zealous and clear-sighted magistrate is not so easily misled. Dost thou not remember the means of which this wretch made use at Madrid to escape from the hands of the law?"

"For whom dost thou take him?" asked Aguidas.

"For Alonso Cano, the murderer of his wife."

Murillo burst into a merry laugh.

"I am indeed distressed," he said, "that these fetters, with which thou hast been kind enough to adorn me, prevent me producing from the pocket of my doublet letters of credit from the King."

"Naught else will satisfy me," cried Tarifa; "and I will—"

Murillo waved him backwards.

"Touch me not," he said; "when the law descends as thou hast done to the level of *sbirri* * I feel so great a repugnance towards it that I am humiliated by its very touch. Count Aguidas will do me the favor of bringing forth my papers."

---

* Bailiffs or constables.

Aguidas put his hands into the pockets of Murillo's velvet doublet and brought forth great sheets of parchment sealed with the royal seal.   Tarifa took them, terror already taking the place of his late bravado.

"Murillo! Estaban Murillo! painter to the King! It is indeed he; it is the royal writing, the seal.   But then—'

"Thou art a fool!" cried Murillo; "and what I have promised I will do."

"What hast thou promised?"

"To deprive thee of thy place."

"But Cano, this Alonso Cano was here.   Thou didst not inhabit this house yesterday."

The little door communicating with that of Milagro suddenly was flung open, and two soldiers entered.

"The criminal has fled," they cried.   "He scaled the wall; but four of our men are in pursuit."

Count Aguidas turned pale.   Tarifa glanced triumphantly at Murillo, saying:

"The game is not yet ended, Señor Murillo, and if I win it, the worse for thee.   To assist in the escape of a prisoner is a crime expressly provided for by the law."

Tarifa rushed out into the garden, while Murillo, Aguidas, and three soldiers remained in the studio.

CHAPTER XII.

BETWEEN TWO FIRES.

BEFORE Alonso Cano consented to scale the wall he cried out to Aguidas:

"Dost thou not think it would be better to remain here and protect Murillo?"

"Nay," said the count, "Murillo is of those who protect themselves. Were I to leave thee now thou mightest not find the horses which await us, and we would all perchance be compromised, and our cause lost."

"As thou wilt," said Alonso; "let us go. Promise me only that thou wilt leave me as soon as I am in safety, which will be when I get on horseback."

"I promise," said Aguidas.

Just as Alonso had climbed to the summit of the wall he saw at the window of a neighboring house a black, woolly head, and a face of a singularly repulsive character. The curious and threatening expression upon the man's face showed him to be animated by anything but friendly sentiments. Cano's face grew troubled when he caught this piercing glance, and yielding to a momentary terror he jumped into the road. He uttered a cry of pain as he reached the ground, and quickly put his hand to his wounded foot. When Cano had taken this dangerous leap the Count Aguidas rushed over to him and Cano exclaimed:

"We are observed, and will be betrayed."

"There may yet be time for us to escape," replied Aguidas. "We will reach the place where the horses are

in waiting before this Tricordo, whom I know by reputation, has given us up. Canst thou walk?"

"I must walk or be taken," said Alonso; "I must
walk."

He rose and took a few steps, but the pain was so intense that it forced a groan from him. Then leaning
against the trunk of an olive tree he said, in a tone of
despondency:

"Perchance it is better to stay here. I am weary of
this perpetual mystery. What has occurred to-day seems
fatal and inexorable. Wherefore seek to escape a misfortune which follows me inevitably?"

"Thou shalt not," said Aguidas; "thou shalt not. All
my life would I reproach myself that, so far from having
been of service to thee, my admiration was the cause of
thy ruin. Thou must fly, Alonso; fly again, fly always,
till—"

"Till I die of despair," said the artist.

"Till thine innocence is made fully manifest."

"Will God ever permit that?" asked Alonso in a tone
of discouragement.

"He will, be assured."

"Moreover, where am I to go?" said Alonso wearily.
"It would seem that God wills my punishment, and I had
better resign myself to it at once; sooner or later I shall
be dragged before the bar of justice. If I have hitherto sought to elude its pursuit, it is because I awaited
the result of Miguel's endeavors. Miguel is my heroic
pupil, who is now in Naples watching the movements of
one whom he and I have reason to suspect of the crime
with which I am charged. Alas, many months have
passed, and Miguel has been unable to find any proofs.
Who knows if the truth will ever be made manifest?
His devotion may be in vain. Let me then appear be-

fore accusing justice; thou knowest that I can appeal thence to God."

"I know, too, that there is no power which can bring a man once dead to life again. I know that men are easily deceived, and that Tarifa seeks thee with the same eagerness now that Rosalés did before. · Thy wound will not permit thee to walk. I will leave thee for an instant, to return with the horses. Make no objection; I desire it."

Aguidas clasped Cano's hand in both his own as he spoke.

"Do as thou wilt," said Cano, with more resignation than joy in his tone.

The count rushed off leaving Alonso at the foot of the olive tree. When Aguidas was gone the repulsive face which we have described appeared again at the window. The piercing eyes looked out upon the road, then the grinning visage disappeared, and the window was closed.

No sooner did Tricordo discover that one of the men had disappeared than he ran down the stairs. He was a small, thin, dark individual, with legs too short for his body and a waist too long. His bristling head resembled that of a wolf, and there was a certain ferocity in his red gums and sharp-pointed teeth. He suspected at once that there was some mystery afoot. A man does not leave a house of which he is merely a peaceful tenant in such an unusual manner. Besides Milagro's connection with him seemed to justify all manner of suspicions; at least he must be a thief, and a thief seeking to escape from justice.

To give up such a person to the law seemed to Tricordo an occupation the more attractive that it was often lucrative. The magistrates always testified their gratitude to Tricordo in a substantial manner, and this time he resolved to deserve their appreciation.

Creeping cautiously along by the hedge which sepa-rated his own garden from the stony road, where Alonso awaited the count's return, Tricordo stationed himself behind the last group of shrubs which separated him from the path.

He was scarcely two hundred paces from Alonso.

He thought at first of approaching him, but on reflec-tion paused. Evidently, according to Tricordo's logic, a man who jumps from a high wall instead of going honestly out the door must needs be a thief. But, ad-mitting that this hypothesis was just, there was nothing to prevent this malefactor, abandoned by his accomplice for a cause which Tricordo could not guess, from having a finely-tempered sword about him, which might be plunged into the breast of any man who was curious enough to attempt to question him upon his name and means of living.

All things considered, Tricordo thought it more pru-dent to turn his attention to Milagro's house, and dis-cover whatsoever of unusual might be going on there. Once he caught sight of the uniform of the soldiers he was reassured as to his own safety and the result of his information. He therefore approached one of the soldiers and said:

"Thou art seeking some game for the *garote*." *

"It may be so," answered the soldier, "but that con-cerns Judge Tarifa, who at this moment is examining the prisoner."

"Where, in the room ?" said Tricordo.

---

* Strangling by means of an iron collar; the mode of capital punish-ment in Spain.

"As thou mayest see by passing in front of the window."

"But then," asked Tricordo, "canst tell me who are the two men who have just scaled the garden-wall, and escaped on to the road?"

"Two men leaped into the road?"

"Yes, a moment ago."

"Thou art sure they came out of the garden?"

"My window opens thereupon."

"*Caramba!*" cried the soldier, "the *alferes* must know of this."

The soldier approached his commander and repeated what Tricordo had told him. The officer at once knocked at the door of the studio. It was at the very moment when Tarifa had read the King's letters, proving that the man whom he had arrested was Estaban Murillo.

"We have been imposed upon, Señor," said the officer, "but, by the Virgin del Pilar, we shall have our revenge. Whilst thou art questioning this man, the one we are in search of has scaled the wall with his accomplice. By the intervention of Providence he hurt himself in falling, so that his capture will be easy."

"To horse! to horse!" cried Tarifa to the officer, "and bring back this man, living or dead."

Tricordo now advanced with an awkward salute.

"I dare to make known to your lordship," he said, "that it was I who called the attention of the soldiers to the prisoner's escape."

"Thou?" said Count Aguidas. "I shall remember thee again."

"Thy name?" said the judge.

"Tricordo, at thy service."

"Lead my men, Tricordo, and a hundred ducats reward if thou bringest back Alonso Cano alive."

"How much if he be dead?" said the informer cyni-
cally.

"The half."

"Rest assured he shall be brought unharmed."

Four horsemen, ready to pursue the unfortunate if he
had escaped, and six on foot, followed Tricordo, whither
he led the way.

"I left him at the foot of the olive tree," said Tricordo
to the soldiers.

But they and the spy looked in vain under the olive
tree. The coast was clear. In the distance they perceived a horseman going at full gallop.

"It is he!" cried Tricordo; "it is he."

The foot-soldiers saw at once that their interference
was useless, but the four others, well mounted, and
knowing that their prey was before them, put spurs to
their horses.

"And I," cried Tricordo, "I want to win the money."

Without waiting for an answer, he sprung upon the
crupper of one of the horses with an agility little to be
expected from so miserable a pigmy.

The man whom they pursued had still a considerable
start of them. It was indeed Alonso Cano.

Whilst Tricordo was observing their movements Count
Aguidas rushed off to where the horses were awaiting
him. He mounted his own, and his groom brought another for Alonso, just as Tricordo began his revelations
to the soldiers. Rapidly as it was decided upon to pursue the fugitive, Alonso, aided by the count and his
groom, had even more rapidly mounted his horse. Once
in the saddle he whispered to Aguidas:

"Stay with Murillo, give thyself no farther concern
about me. Thanks to thee I have a horse and gold.

And it please Heaven in less than an hour I shall be beyond the reach of my enemies."

"*Vaga con Dios*," said the count, wringing Alonso's
hand. "Wilt accept the escort of my groom?"

"His livery might be recognized: it is better that I go
alone," replied Alonso.

"Return home, then, Piquillo," said the count to his
groom.

Then, fixing his eyes upon Alonso, as the latter steadied
himself in the saddle, he cried:

"God grant that we meet again under happier circumstances."

Then they all three separated; the groom to return
home; Aguidas to re-enter Milagro's house; and Cano to
ride straight before him, where chance should lead, or
rather towards the shelter provided for him by Providence.

The artist had gone but a short distance when he
heard shouts and the whinnying of horses. He turned
his head and saw an officer, who with four men was evidently giving him chase. Alonso urged on his horse by
whip and spur, and the noble animal, one of the best in
Aguidas's stables, which were renowned through Valencia, sped on at a furious rate.

The rapidity with which Alonso went stimulated the
zeal of the soldiers, who were besides urged to enthusiasm by Tricordo.

"Faster, my friends, faster!" cried he; "we must
catch that wretched murderer and conspirator. He killed
his wife and tried to dethrone the King. Judge Tarifa
promised me a hundred ducats to bring him back alive.
Help me to gain this money and I will not be ungrateful.
I will scatter the reals cheerfully among good comrades
like you. Quicker! go quicker!"

And the horses were spurred and urged on to their utmost. Alonso was nearly hidden from their sight by a very whirlpool of dust. They soon reached the avenue leading to Valencia, but, instead of passing straight through it, Cano turned to the right and gained the open country. Unfortunately it was but a flat surface, whereon there was no possible shelter. Without perceptibly slackening his pace Alonso's horse, accustomed to more gentle management, began to rebel against the tight rein kept upon him, and to show mutinous symptoms. The soldiers, on the other hand, gained upon the fugitive, and whenever he turned his head to calculate the distance between them he perceived with horror that it was constantly diminishing. He saw that there was a crisis approaching. Flight was not enough; there would be a struggle. Alonso looked hastily around him, and observed at length a ruined hut, of which but two walls remaining formed a sort of right angle covered with thatch. It was certainly not a place of safety, but at least it gave Alonso a last chance in case he had to defend himself.

A few moments before he had given way to discouragement, and talked of giving up that terrible game which he must inevitably lose; but, by one of those apparent contradictions of the human mind, he was now seized with a perfect passion for the struggle. Strong in the justice of his cause and his own innocence, he was determined neither to lose his liberty nor sacrifice his life. The struggle was forced upon him, he accepted it. At that period, and especially in chivalric Spain, the time of judicial duels and the " Judgment of God " was not yet so remote but that the idea of the Almighty interfering in behalf of the innocent naturally occurred to the mind of the unfortunate. Hence Alonso hastily invoked the justice of God, and begged of Mercedes to intercede for him; he reached the ruined hut at a single bound, and placed himself in the extreme angle which it formed; protected thus on both sides he drew his sword and awaited his pursuers.

The officer was the first to come up with him.

"Yield thyself," he said; "I give thee my word that thou shalt not be molested."

"I am innocent," said Alonso. "I will not attack you, because you are in the King's service, but I will defend myself."

"Alonso Cano," said the *alferez*, "do not increase the danger of thy situation, which is already perilous."

"Thou thinkest to cast my name in my face as an insult and a reproach," said the artist; "thou art mistaken. I am strong in my innocence."

"There are four of us," said the officer.

"Five," said Tricordo angrily.

"Were ye a hundred I defy you," said Cano.

At a sign from the *alferez* the soldiers advanced and made an attempt to surround Cano. As he had said, he was determined not to attack, but to remain simply upon the defensive. However, as the contest was four to one, he needed all his skill in fencing to enable him to keep off the four swords drawn against him. Alonso's sword clashed with each in turn; it whistled, gleamed, and cut the air like a living flame. It did its work unweariedly, seeming to cover Alonso like a great shield.

The soldiers sought each in turn to strike Alonso in the head, neck, or chest; he parried each attack and evaded every thrust. Strangest of all, he did not feel any fatigue. This unequal, desperate battle seemed to increase rather than diminish his strength; the soldiers first gave signs of weariness. Hitherto Tricordo had contented himself with surveying the struggle. He had given chase to Cano, and would have mingled in the thickest of the fight, did he not fear that in the confusion of thrusts and counter-thrusts he might have received some injury.   For if Tricordo's master-passion was ava-rice, it did not exclude all care for his self-preservation. However, he remembered the hundred ducats, and, de-termined to win them, he thought of an ingenious mode of accomplishing his object.   Gliding under the horses' feet, he passed round to the other side of the hut.   A heap of stones assisted him in reaching that part of the roof over Alonso's head.   This sloping bit of thatch was still resting upon the walls.   Having examined the structure carefully, Tricordo drew a tinder-box and some matches from his pocket, and struck a light.   He then seized a handful of thatch and with it formed a torch. When it blazed he threw it upon the roof, and watched with ferocious joy the progress of the flame.

In another moment Alonso Cano would be dislodged from the protecting angle of the wall.   Once driven thence, the four soldiers could quickly seize upon him, even if each were obliged to inflict a wound in so doing.

The heat and the odor of burning straw warned Alon-so of his danger, and, raising his head, he saw the roof on fire above him.   Aware of his peril, Alonso felt that he must put an end to the struggle.   Another incident also forced him into taking the offensive.   While looking upward to see whence the smoke proceeded, a soldier had wounded him in the arm with his lance, so that the blood began to flow freely.   The pain caused by his wound and the fear of the new danger which threatened him from overhead made him abandon the defensive.   He returned every thrust.   A second time he was wounded in the side by his adversaries.   Then his horse, upon whom some sparks had fallen, made a bound forward.   Two of the soldiers profited by this movement to get in behind Alonso, and in their turn shelter themselves against the wall. They thought they were sure of victory, when all at once a cry was heard.

The burning roof had fallen upon the two soldiers, thrown to the ground by a plunge of their horses. Behind Alonso was now a living furnace; before him two naked swords. The swords seemed the less formidable. He rushed forward, his sword outstretched, in such manner as to protect himself without aiming at any one. A soldier, in the act of rushing at him, fell upon the point of the sword, which was buried in him up to the hilt.

Alonso drew out the reeking weapon with a cry of horror.

" Wouldst thou thy life ?" he asked the remaining soldier.

" I would avenge my officer and my comrades," answered he.

" Alas! they served an evil cause," said Alonso. " God refused them His protection."

The soldier and the artist rushed upon each other, and Cano would certainly have had the advantage, but that Tricordo, seeing that his late plan had failed, and that there was no hope of bringing Alonso a prisoner before Tarifa, resolved, at all events, to render him incapable of farther resistance. He picked up the dead officer's sword and struck Alonso's horse in the flank. The animal threw up its head and fell, carrying its rider with him. Tricordo had made one mistake, however; he had miscalculated the distance; the horse fell upon him. The wretch uttered a cry of agony, which proved that he was seriously injured. Seeing Alonso upon the ground, his adversary determined to finish him. It must not be forgotten that

Alonso had hurt his foot in leaping from Milagro's garden-wall. While on horseback, supported by his good steed, he was able to maintain the struggle, but, on foot and unable to stand, he would inevitably have been overcome. Instead of seizing the hilt of his sword he grasped it by the point. To stun his enemy seemed his only chance of escape. Just as the soldier dealt a blow at him Alonso struck him with tremendous violence upon the head, and sent him rolling into the dust.

He was free and alone.

Of his enemies two had perished in the flames lit by Tricordo; another was dead upon the blood-stained ground beside him. Tricordo was pitifully crying for help.

Cano dragged himself over to the dead officer's horse. With the utmost difficulty he mounted it, seized his bloody sword, wiped it, and restored it to his belt. Then he rode away from a spot the aspect of which filled him with indescribable horror.

Whither was he going? He knew not. He felt the necessity for flying, still flying, always flying. He might meet peasants or other wayfarers upon the road. When Tarifa saw that his four soldiers were not coming back he would no doubt send others in pursuit of him.

Alonso put spurs to his horse; the good beast went off at a gallop, its mane flying to the wind, its jaws covered with foam. Suddenly Alonso saw the spire of a church arising from a grove of ancient trees.

Many of the monasteries still retained the right of sanctuary, the grandest and most noble with which the middle ages endowed churches and cloisters.

Once at a convent Alonso was saved. He hurried on. In the high wall which protected the gardens—without, however, obscuring the tree-tops—was a large, broad gateway.   Over this entrance was the legend, "*Porta Cæli.*"

"Yes, it is, indeed, the gate of Heaven," cried Alonso.

Raising the heavy knocker, he let it fall with such violence that the timbers shook.

CHAPTER XIII.

THE CARTHUSIAN MONASTERY.

NOTHING could be more peaceful than this great house of prayer, which has now disappeared, but was then known by the sweet name of *Porta Cæli*. Those who crossed its threshold left behind them the crushing burden of ambition and human sorrows. They threw off the yoke of their passions to live in the holy liberty of obedience. They renounced perishable and transitory goods for the treasures of holy poverty.

No tumult of the world came hither, save echoes perchance of its disasters or its shipwrecks, which made these peaceful dwellers of the cloister find an added sweetness in their solitude and their austerities. The moral and mental sufferings of those whom the world calls happy is the best lesson that can be given to the men of the cloister, and the most indisputable proof that they have chosen the better part.

The enclosure of the convent contained the cloisters and the monastery; behind the gardens were broad waste lands, which the Carthusian monks had cultivated and rendered fruitful. When they were not at prayer they labored, tilling the earth that it might bring forth the grain and vegetables necessary for their own support and for their poor.

When Alonso Cano, wounded, knocked at the gate of the convent the monks had just finished their prayer, and were going from the cloister to the refectory.

The brother porter hastily answered the knock. Only the unfortunate came to the monastery gates. And whether they were needy in pocket or in mind, they must receive succor.

When Brother Eugenio perceived a cavalier, wounded and bloody, he uttered an exclamation of pity and astonishment.

"What wouldst thou?" he said.

"Hospitality," answered Alonso.

"Enter, my brother," said Eugenio.

"But," said Alonso, "I am unable even to alight from my horse, so painful are my wounds."

The brother then took him in his arms and brought him into a little room which served as a porter's lodge.

"And thy steed?" said Brother Eugenio.

"It doth not belong to me. Let it go free; its instinct will surely bring it back to its master's stable."

The brother then attached the bridle to the saddle, and, as Alonso had foreseen, the steed, after sniffing the air several times, turned and took the road towards Valencia.

"My brother," said the religious, "the fathers are now in the refectory. Awaiting their return wilt thou accept a slight collation, or shall I bring thither at once our good Superior?"

"I will wait," said Alonso in a faint voice.

"Let me at least staunch thy wounds."

"They are not dangerous; concern thyself not with them, good brother," said Alonso.

Brother Eugenio nevertheless insisted upon removing Alonso's torn and stained doublet. He washed the wound, and Alonso felt the greatest relief.

He was, however, growing very feverish. While the struggle lasted he had scarcely felt the pain in his foot; but now that the ardor of battle was over his artificial strength gave way, and he suffered excruciating agony, which was greatly augmented by his mental suffering.

Brother Eugenio saw that he was shivering, and moreover growing rapidly delirious; he went for the Superior and told him all that had occurred.

"Brother," said Father Eusebio, "the unfortunate cannot wait; thou shouldst have informed me at once."

And hurrying down with the holy eagerness of charity, the Superior was soon at Alonso Cano's side.

Certainly the appearance of the traveller was far from prepossessing. His hands were stained with blood; his sword, reddened to the hilt, proved that it had rendered him ominous service; his face pale, his eyes wild and feverish, his aspect fierce, made him resemble rather a criminal pursued for a crime than an innocent man seeking refuge beneath the wings of charity.

Father Eusebio regarded him with angelic sweetness.

"We will keep thee," he said.

"Thou wilt really permit me to remain?"

"Yes, my brother."

"And if justice demands me?"

"It has no right to enter here," replied the monk.

Alonso's face showed his great relief. Aided on either side by the two religious, he succeeded in reaching the room assigned him.

It was a small, whitewashed apartment; a crucifix hung upon the wall. Its furniture consisted of a bed, some chairs, a table, and a book. Entering there Alonso felt himself in another world. Once in bed the Father Infirmarian came to examine his wounds. He dressed them, carefully bandaged his foot, and prescribed perfect rest. Then he departed, making the sign of the cross over the patient before leaving the room. A young novice was commissioned to watch over him day and night.

Alonso's clothes were thrown upon a chair near the bed; the sight of the blood upon them affected him painfully, and he murmured in a troubled voice:

"Take them away; take away all that recalls—"

He did not finish, but turned his face to the wall, while the novice removed the clothing and begged one of the lay brothers to wash the blood-stains from them, and to clean the sword carefully. Alonso was almost asleep when a tumult of voices and the sound of horses' feet aroused him from his stupor.

He sat up in bed and cried out in terror:

"They are seeking me! shall I be given up?"

"My brother," replied the young novice, "we would all perish rather than betray the guest of God."

Alonso's head fell back upon the pillow, and he muttered feverishly:

"So much blood; so much blood."

The unhappy man was not mistaken.

On sending soldiers to overtake and capture the fugitive who had escaped by Milagro's garden-wall, Tarifa was convinced that he would at last obtain possession of the real Alonso Cano. But, despite his confidence in the sagacity of the spy Tricordo and the zeal of the soldiers and the *alferez* who commanded them, he could not yet feel certain that he had won the game.

Turning to Murillo with a manner half stern, half respectful, he said:

"It is not for me precisely to define, nor yet to condemn, the part thou hast played in this matter, Señor Estaban Murillo. The King himself must decide whether one of his painters, howsoever high in favor, may arrogate to himself the right of making a mockery of the law, and to mislead it playing an unworthy comedy in which my Lord Aguidas himself was not ashamed to take part.

Thou art convinced that thou hast won the battle. I think otherwise. Four men are in pursuit of the fugitive. I will myself set out with still more. Either I shall lose my place, or Alonso Cano—"

"His head, sir magistrate," said Murillo with bitter irony. "I admit that the game is unequal, first in regard to the stakes, and second in the means employed. I would give ten judges' places for Alonso Cano's right hand. And as for the means employed, surely a dozen soldiers sent in pursuit of one poor wounded fugitive seems to me but sorry justice."

"Have a care how thou insultest the law!" cried Tarifa.

"Have a care thyself, Señor Tarifa," said Murillo, "for judges who in the pursuit of a criminal seek rather their personal advancement than the interests of justice, are not worthy of the office they hold."

"Is that a personal affront?" asked Tarifa.

"It is anything you like," said Murillo contemptuously; "but I need have no anxiety; men of your temper do not fight."

"The duties of their office forbid," said Tarifa.

"And their own cowardice prevents," said Murillo.

Count Aguidas now advanced to Tarifa.

"I beg of you to remember, Señor," he said, coldly, "that Estaban Murillo is my guest, and that whatever befalls I am the protector of him whom thou dost persecute."

"Ah!" cried Tarifa in a rage, "ye would both protect him?"

"And God be our aid," added Murillo.

After which the count and the artist went out together, and the judge mounted his horse.

"We will go in search of your comrades," he said to the soldiers.

In point of fact but a comparatively short time had elapsed between the moment when Alonso leaped from the wall and that in which Tarifa himself set out in pursuit. Alonso's flight and his victory over his pursuers had occupied but a brief space. Hence it followed that if the late tenant of the haunted house had been taken alive, Tarifa would certainly have met both prisoner and escort before very long.

He saw no signs of them, however, and he was beginning to fear that as Alonso had been mounted on one of Aguidas's swiftest coursers he had given his pursuers a long chase. When he had passed through the long avenue of trees and come out upon the open plain, he suddenly perceived a group of peasants surrounding the smoking ruins of a hut. Surely something unusual must have transpired there. Tarifa rode over and made his way through the curious crowd. An angry exclamation burst from his lips when he beheld the spectacle there presented to his eyes. He had not a thought of pity for the two soldiers dead beneath the smoking ruins, nor yet for those who still lived and were suffering from their wounds. All this was of little consequence to him. But what really touched him deeply was that he did not see the body of the fugitive among the corpses.

Some passing laborers had turned aside to render what assistance they could to the wounded. The soldier who had fallen upon the sword was dying, the other was vainly seeking to staunch his wound with a rag in order to stop the flow of blood. Tricordo, whose leg was broken, was uttering shrill cries of pain.

To extricate this wretched being the laborers had lifted aside the body of Alonso's horse. Tarifa, catching sight of Tricordo, cried out:

"Miserable spy, behold thy work: four men killed and justice set at naught."

"Ah, Señor," said Tricordo in a plaintive voice, "is it my fault? He is not a man, but a devil. I conceived such a plan to ensnare him. I set the roof on fire to roast the murderer before bringing him to thee. That was a stroke of genius. But, unhappily, the roof, instead of falling on the villain fell upon the soldiers. The idea was none the less ingenious, and yet your lordship has no pity for me. His cursed horse broke my leg when I was carrying out a marvellous inspiration. I pierced him with a lance so that he might throw his rider."

"What became of the rider?" cried Tarifa.

"He fled, most illustrious lord, he fled," whined Tricordo; "and had the indelicacy to deprive me thus of the hundred ducats with which your excellency would have deigned to gratify me. *Sancta Virgen!* how I suffer. Your excellency should pay me two hundred instead of one hundred ducats. Ah, my poor leg, my poor leg!"

"Have done with thy groaning," said Tarifa, "and try to answer."

"I am suffering so much. *Sancta Virgen!* My lord, I am suffering."

"We will have time to pity thee when we have found the wretch in whose capture thou art interested."

"Yes, to the extent of a hundred ducats. A hundred ducats, most illustrious lord."

"In what direction went he?"

Tricordo groaned.

"Despite my sufferings I would do my duty," said Tricordo; "it was impossible for me to stir, but I nevertheless kept my eyes open. The fugitive from the haunted house, my lord, after having disposed of the soldiers and reduced me to my present state, mounted another horse, to which he gave spurs and rode off."

"In what direction?"

"Straight before him."

"Then," said the judge, "the rest is easy. He is wounded and cannot go far."

"But," said Tricordo, "there are people ill disposed enough towards justice, and uncharitable enough to lose me my hundred ducats, who may offer him hospitality."

"We shall search houses, villages, and towns," cried the judge.

"Wilt thou pay me a hundred ducats if I give thee a clue?" said Tricordo, his eyes glowing at the thought.

"I will give thee the *garote* and thou art silent," said the judge; "for what is to prove that all this is not part of the comedy, and that thou art not the accomplice of that Murillo and Count Aguidas?"

"On my life, by my baptism. Ah! *Sancta Virgen*, I betray thee? I will prove my sincerity to your lordship. The Carthusian monastery of *Porta Cœli* is upon thy way, seek there. That is the advice I give thee."

Without taking time to answer Tricordo, Tarifa cried out to the soldiers:

"To the monastery of *Porta Cœli*. And ye, worthy laborers, carry the wounded to Valencia, including this wretch whose groans are greater than his injuries. Come to me to-morrow, and I will compensate you for time lost."

Tarifa rode on hastily, and in an hour perceived the white walls of the convent. He raised the knocker with an agitated hand. Brother Eugenio, as calm and peaceful as was his wont, opened the gate.

"Brother," said Tarifa, in a voice which he softened as

much as possible, " did a wounded traveller enter the monastery about an hour ago?"

"Several travellers have asked hospitality of us," replied the porter.

" This one would not easily be confounded with the rest. He had just sustained a combat, which must have left traces upon his clothing."

" Your excellency will deign to excuse me," said the brother; "my duty is to open the gates to those who knock, but our holy rule forbids me to break silence, save in cases of absolute necessity."

" There can be no necessity greater than that of aiding justice in its work," said Tarifa.

"I am but an humble lay brother," said the porter, " thou wilt therefore permit me to place the will of my superiors above that of men, howsoever powerful they may be."

"Inform the Superior, then, that Judge Tarifa desires to hold speech with him."

" I pray thee enter this room," said the brother mildly, "and I will make known thy arrival to him."

Tarifa alone entered the monastery; he left his horse with the soldiers outside the wall.

Impressed with the gravity of the situation, Brother Eugenio proceeded with unusual speed to the cell of his Superior. Having heard what the porter had to say Father Eusebio assembled all the monks as quickly as possible. He took his abbot's mitre and cross and went down-stairs followed by the other religious. At the door of the cloisters he bade them wait.

" Keep here," he said, "these insignia of my office; I would not wear them in appearing before Judge Tarifa for the first time. If Heliodorus attempts to enter the temple of the Lord it will then be time to display, not the pomp which encircles us but the majesty of those powers which Heaven itself has bestowed upon us."

Father Eusebio entered the room alone.

"Reverend father," said Tarifa, in a tone of ill-restrained impatience, "thou hast received into thy convent this morning a wretch—"

"A great many poor wretches, my son; thou speakest truly," said the abbot.

"When I say a wretch I mean a criminal, guilty at first of the blood of his wife, but now, pursued for that crime, he has aggravated the horror thereof by murdering the soldiers sent by me to apprehend him ?"

The monk made no answer to this harangue.

"Dost thou not comprehend what I desire of thee, father ?" asked Tarifa.

"That we should pray for him ?" said Father Eusebio. ' Ah, doubt not that our supplications shall go up asking Heaven to have mercy upon him and give him the grace of repentance if he be guilty, or permit his innocence to be made manifest if innocent he be."

"It is to decide that point that justice would fain obtain possession of Alonso Cano."

The abbot, with his hands folded in his sleeves, and his head bent, listened without looking at Tarifa.

"Wilt thou give up this man to us ?" asked the judge.

"My son," said the Superior, "this house contains many disciples, but not one Judas."

"Dost forget that I speak in the name of the law ?"

"Dost thou forget that I represent Christian charity ?"

"It is thy duty to give up this criminal."

"It is my duty to save the unfortunate."

"I requested it as a favor," said Tarifa; "I now demand it."

The Superior raised his head and looked Tarifa steadily in the face.

"Does that mean that thou wilt make use of force?"

"I will make use of it," said the judge. "I have soldiers without, and at a sign from me—"

"Make that sign if thou darest, my son," said the monk.

Tarifa rushed out of the room. At a signal from the Superior a brother opened the outer door, whilst Eusebio rejoined his brethren. He put on his mitre and took his abbot's cross in his hands, giving a sealed parchment to one of the monks.

"Thou wilt read it when required," he said.

Tarifa went out to the soldiers.

"The criminal is there," he said; "ye must search the monastery."

The soldiers remained an instant irresolute, but finally crossed the threshold, and stood within the vestibule. At the same moment the doors flew open and disclosed Father Eusebio in all his peaceful majesty.

"Dost expect to impose upon me by thy processions of monks?" said Tarifa. "I desire to enter, and I will."

The abbot stretched out the ivory cross in his hand till it touched Tarifa's doublet and said :

"Wait!"

Then turning to his secretary he gave the order:

"Read, brother!"

The secretary read aloud in a slow and distinct voice an ordinance of King Ferdinand of holy memory granting the right of sanctuary to the Carthusian monastery of *Porta Cœli*, and authorizing the Church to strike with its thunders whosoever should, in defiance of this royal ordinance, attempt to cross the threshold of the convent in pursuit of a criminal.

"Come one step farther," said the monk, imperiously addressing Tarifa, "and by virtue of the powers which I hold from the Holy See I excommunicate thee."

Tarifa turned pale, but advanced one step.

Father Eusebio, however, addressing the soldiers, said:

"As for you, my children, I will give you my blessing."

The soldiers knelt, and Tarifa alone remained standing

The doors of the cloister were closed, and the judge said, looking contemptuously at the soldiers, who arose after making the sign of the cross,

"Cowards! ye have deserted me."

"The service of God before the service of the King!" answered they.

The homeward ride from the monastery of *Porta Cæli* was a very silent one. Tarifa had lost the game. He knew well that Aguidas would use all his influence against him. The adventure of the haunted house would be represented as a foolish and chimerical fancy of his. He had counted upon the capture of Alonso Cano as a ladder to fortune, and this ladder had precipitated him to his ruin.

"Oh," thought he with rage, "henceforth I will seek him not only for justice's sake but to gratify my own hatred of him."

He dismissed the soldiers and shut himself up in his house in a state bordering upon frenzy. The next day the episode of the haunted house was the common topic. Murillo and Aguidas represented it as a ridiculous escapade, for which Tarifa alone was responsible. In a few days the luckless magistrate, baffled, jeered at, and stung to the quick by the ridicule cast upon him, resigned his office at Valencia, and secretly set out for Madrid.

Whilst Murillo superintended the hanging of his pic-

ture; whilst Aguidas rejoiced at Cano's safety, which
was partly owing to his efforts; whilst Tricordo slowly
recovered and retarded his progress by frequent bursts
of rage, Cano was regaining in the monastery of *Porta
Cæli* health of body and peace of mind.

The fever which had been brought on by his wounds
and the various emotions of that terrible day on which,
after having defeated his pursuers he had so narrowly
escaped falling into the hands of a sacrilegious judge,
lasted a week. Delirium had ensued, and from his ravings Father Eusebio, who, with the novice Pablo, often
kept long watches beside Alonso's bed, became fully
convinced of the innocence of the artist, and the unjust
persecution of which he had been a victim.

"Father," said the novice to his Superior once when
they had watched Alonso during one of those terrible
crises in which it almost seemed that he must die, "I
confess to thee, in all humility, that I have sometimes
been tempted to ask whether beyond these walls, within
which I have grown up and hope to die, there may not
be what men call happiness. I bethought myself of
warriors, famous by their exploits, and whose swords
have won crowns for kings; of the glory of those who
make their thoughts, as it were, living, and who endow
the creatures of their imagination with immortality, such
as Lope de Vega and Calderon."

"Lope de Vega became a monk, my son." said the
Superior.

"Then I dreamed of even more marvellous feats than
these. I fancied myself struggling against the ignorance
of some and the ill-will of others, the storms of heaven
and ocean tempests, pushing on a frail barque till I discovered a new world with which I endowed my country."

"Christopher Columbus was a martyr. my son."

"In a word, taking them by turns, soldier, admiral, dramatic poet, I envied all who had made themselves a name before men."

"Perchance thou hast heard the name of Alonso Cano?" said the abbot again.

"Yes, my father; encircled with an aureola which was all but heavenly I know that he painted angels and saints, and found in the fervor of his prayers marvellous types which he reproduced upon our altars to the edification of the faithful."

"Poor boy!" murmured the Superior.

"Thou dost condemn me, father?"

"Nay, my son, I scarce can blame thee. Such thoughts, such leanings towards the world are temptations which all of us must undergo, whatsoever our age, or whatsoever the penances we impose upon ourselves. Anthony experienced in the wilderness a horror of the struggle in which he was engaged against the spirit of darkness. Jerome in the deserts remembered the feasts of pagan Rome. Temptation is but a trial, my son, and proves our vocation. Blessed are the tempted if they close their ears against the false, alluring voices."

"Thanks be to our Saviour Jesus," said Pablo, "and to the merciful Virgin; but though I have often experienced such thoughts they have never led me for a moment to so far as to dream of leaving this holy house."

This conversation took place at the window of Cano's cell. The latter was sleeping. While the two religious talked they could see afar the delightful fields of Valencia, intersected by flowering *huertas*, overtopped by the forest-covered hill, and near a portion of the monastery garden, with its regular beds of grass or immortelles, from which uprose simple white crosses

All at once the patient started up.

"Help!" he cried, "help! They are pursuing me. Oh help! Do not let this judge take me. I am innocent! God of justice, Thou knowest I am innocent! Give me my brushes. I saw the Madonna in my dreams. I want to paint her as she appeared to me, with her blue dress, her circlet of gold, and her heavenly look. No! no! not canvas. I want a block of wood or marble. I want a chisel. I would fain make a statue of a monk. Who better than I can render the austerity of the sons of St. Francis, their ascetic faces, upon which heavenly visions are reflected? Canvas! marble! I want to be at work, and if I die I want them to know."

Father Eusebio approached the bedside rapidly and laid a finger upon his lips. Pablo listened, pale and breathless, his hands crossed upon his breast.

"What matters it? What matters it, father?" said the wounded man in a more gentle voice; "I may well tell my name, though it is now but the name of an unfortunate."

Then turning to the novice he said:

"Pray for him who was Alonso Cano."

The novice uttered a cry of surprise and fell upon his knees. What! one of those whose fortune and fame he had almost envied was there stricken, pursued by calumny, tracked by justice, stretched upon a monk's pallet, hovering between death and madness. There was a lesson for youth! Pablo approached Alonso and seized his hand.

"Thou wilt get well," he said; "thou art better already. Already thou couldst stand upon thy wounded leg. Thy fever will pass away under our care, and soon—"

The sick man rose upon his couch.

"Wilt thou drive me hence once I am cured?"

"My son," replied the Superior, "we drive no one hence; but the unfortunate who come to our door are numerous and the house is small."

Cano closed his eyes and fell back.

"Lord!" said he, "here are we well."

And gently he fell asleep.

In two days more he was up; at the end of a week he was able to walk in the gardens. Sometimes he left their cool shade for the modest enclosure where the sons of *Porta Cœli* lay at rest. One evening after the office the Superior vainly sought Alonso in his cell; not finding him in the chapel or the cloisters he went out into the gardens, calling him softly by name. As he passed on into the graveyard he discovered him hard by a grave dug in advance for the first of the brothers whom the Lord should call to Himself.

"I fear," said Eusebio to him, "that thou wilt fatigue thyself; dost thou not think of coming in ?"

"I was thinking of death, father," said he.

"Is it because human courage has failed thee ?"

"Nay, it is rather that divine strength is urging me."

"Thou wouldst wish then—"

"To remain in this hospitable house forever."

"Strangers pass on and do not tarry here."

"What if I were to ask permission to remain, accepting in advance thy holy rule and promising to be the docile son of Saint Bruno?"

"Hast thou thought of it long, my son ?'

"Since I have known thee, father."

The old man seized the painter's hand.

"God has brought thee, my son," said he, "desolate stricken, hunted, to the monastery gates, and thou art grateful to the Samaritans who have saved thee. But between this sentiment and a vocation there is a wide difference."

"What can I expect from the world?" cried Cano. "It took me, young, ardent, and celebrated, the favorite of a king, in whose presence I sat with covered head, like the grandees of Spain, and it cast me, covered with wounds and infamy, upon the roadside, whence thou didst pick me up. The world! To win rank, a name, and that ephemeral thing they call renown, I have watched and labored unceasingly. I desired that applause which accompanies one in public places, that thrill which greets thee from a multitude. I yearned for the acclamations of the populace hailing my work, and when the people prostrated themselves before my *sargas* or my pictures at the feast of *Corpus Christi*, I was fairly intoxicated with enthusiasm, youth, and vigor. A king called me his friend, Spain saluted me with the proud title of the Iberian Michael Angelo. I did more than dream of glory, I held its palm branch in my hands, and wore its wreaths upon my brow. One drop of blood washed out that glory, those dreams, that renown; the great artist was deemed a murderer; judges pursued him in whose studio Philip IV. had so lately sat. I was forced to fly from hatred and calumny. It was horrible, father, to see men who had a motive for my ruin, and whose personal advancement depended on my imprisonment, hunting me like hounds. Can I therefore regret anything in a world which has thrown blood and dirt in my face? Can I wish to return among men from whom I have received such cruel injuries?"

"The severity of thy trial leads thee to exaggerate," said the Superior; "all whom thou hast known could not have been thus false and cowardly."

"Nay, thou art right, father. Miguel, my heroic pupil,

has devoted himself to the triumph of my cause, but Miguel is very young and all his devotion has been so far in vain. His companions to the last moment protected Alonso Cano. Murillo, the brave and chivalrous Murillo, saved me from Tarifa's hands as before Miguel from those of Rosalés. But I am weary of defending my liberty; take it, I will yield it to thy holy rule."

Father Eusebio seemed to be reflecting deeply.

" Misfortune alone has brought thee here," he said at length. " Ill health has impoverished thy blood and diminished the ardor of thy nature. Who knows but that health may bring back thy youth, and that a few months passed in this house will convince thee that thou art destined to live in the world. Were I to consult my own heart and the interests of our house I would say to thee, Remain. I would give thee this garb of poverty, which would make thee forever our brother. But a secret instinct warns me that thou wilt leave us. Let me then unite the prudence of a director with the affection of a father. Remain with us as long as thou findest the place to thy taste, and if ever these walls seem to thee too narrow remember that thou leavest here friends whose heart and arms are ever open to thee."

Alonso made no reply. He felt that there was wisdom in what Father Eusebio said.

In fact gratitude and enthusiasm had an extraordinary influence upon his impressionable nature, and his first impulse which led him to rush into the cloister might be one that he would regret. He spoke unreflectingly. Just then the fervor of his soul was in unison with the inclination of his heart. Whilst highly approving of what Father Eusebio said, he was still convinced that he would never desire to leave this ark of refuge where he found the repose after which he had aspired in vain. He believed himself forever done with dreams of worldly honor and with ardent aspirations. Sorrow had purified him. The atmosphere of the cloister had poured a salutary dew upon his arid heart. He had absorbed this new and hidden life, so full of a secret charm, known only to those who have experienced its delights. He had fallen asleep, so to say, in this place of infinite peace, and the chanting of the psalmody and the full chords of the organ transported him farther and farther into another world.

He thanked Father Eusebio, and, insisting upon the sincerity of his vocation, declared that time would strengthen instead of weakening it.

"I accept the probation," said he; "how long will it last?"

"Two years," said Father Eusebio.

"And meanwhile thou wilt permit me to wear the garb of my brethren?"

"I will permit it if thou findest consolation therein."

"Yes," replied Alonso Cano eagerly, "it will seem to me that thenceforward I am utterly dead to a world which has misunderstood, forsaken, and insulted me, and to which I should blush to be bound by any ties of perishable ambition."

Father Eusebio raised his hand to give Alonso his blessing, but something like a melancholy and incredulous smile played over his pale lips.

CHAPTER XIV.

THE STATUE OF ST. FRANCIS.

THE days glided by for Alonso Cano in the Carthusian monastery like the ripples upon a peaceful river flowing towards the sea.   The river loses itself in the ocean, and the soul moves on to the infinity of the eternal.

Alonso submitted readily and of his own accord to the holy rules, the full severity of which Father Eusebio did not yet impose upon him.   He found repose after his work in prayer; or, having joined in the magnificent psalms of the office, he returned to his cell and sought to reproduce upon canvas the figures of patriarchs, prophets, or sibyls.   His soul seemed to expand under this holy influence, and his mind to gain new inspirations. Sorrow had crushed that once indomitable spirit; faith was now gradually restoring it.   Alonso felt himself to be in a haven of safety, and asked but one favor of God: that he might never leave it.

He was universally beloved in the community.   The secret of his dramatic entrance there had not transpired. The accusation of murder under which he lay was not known to any except Father Eusebio and Pablo.   The rest knew not for what reason Tarifa had demanded him; though had they known it they would not have shown less indulgence towards him.

Charity alone inspires such perfect compassion. Human kindness never suffices for certain misfortunes, or for certain repentance.   The sight of the cross enables us to bear all burdens, our own, and those of our brethren.

Alonso Cano's life was then as tranquil as that of the Carthusians; he rose with them for matins, went to the choir, assisted at Mass, and, shutting himself up in his studio, passed the great part of the day there.

Even his talent seemed to have undergone a transformation. Hitherto he had painted his saints and martyrs with a sort of factitious inspiration; but now the constant presence of men vowed to the practice of austerities and to holy poverty, living upon the earth indeed, but letting their souls forever soar into the glories of Paradise, gave him a wider conception of certain secrets of expression, certain truthfulness of attitude, so that he touched the emaciated faces of his hermits with a light whi ch art alone could never supply.

The more Christian he became the more firmly he walked in that road upon which he had hitherto but tottered, the more intimately did he learn the secret of true greatness, of sublime works, and of heavenly inspirations.

Instead of reading the poets he studied the lives of the saints. He had never understood before to what heights divine love can raise souls. The first time he read the verses of St. Francis of Assisium he felt a strange tumult in his soul. It was a revelation. These divine flowers left within him a perfume which was never to die away. He read and reread them till he knew them by heart.

His conversation was full of this new and beautiful character thus revealed to him. He sought to penetrate more and more the mystery of charity which had filled that soul, so ardent that it found not enough scope in man, but extended even to nature, and embraced it in a close embrace of mingled admiration and ecstacy. He read eagerly and with deep emotion those legends

which show us the gentle St. Francis preaching to a ferocious wolf of charity towards lambs, or giving advice,
full of a simple poetry, to grasshoppers, and taming one
of these charming insects till it made its home in a fig
tree hard by the convent, where it hummed its little
nooutide song.

Alonso was never weary of admiring the tender compassion of the saint who, not having wherewith to purchase an innocent lamb from the butcher, begged till he
had procured the ransom of the unoffending creature,
and confided it to the religious of St. Claire.

But it was especially in his long walks through the
cloisters or when meditating in his cell that he felt the
full sense of that sublime poetry which gushed from the
heart of Francis of Assisium, rather like a flame than
like a thought.

Those admirable lines, " Love hath cast me into a furnace," awoke such an echo within Cano's artist soul and
exercised so powerful an influence upon him that he was
ready to accept all the austerities of the cloister, provided
only he could remain therein forever. For a whole
month he worked in his studio in the deepest recollection, permitting none of the monks, not even Father
Eusebio, to cross its threshold. The work upon which he
was then engaged was of his soul rather than of his genius.
Like Fra Bartholomeo and Angelico da Fiesole, he knelt
before working, till his work seemed but a continuation
of his prayer.

He felt that he could not express his own conception
of what should be the expression upon the face of that
little figure he was at work upon. Yet never was inspiration truer and more heartfelt placed at the service of a
noble idea.

One morning the artist knocked at Father Eusebio's cell.

"Thou didst promise me," he said, "that some day thou wouldst permit me to wear the habit of thy Order, unworthy though I be of so great a grace. I know not why I have a feeling that the work I have just completed will obtain me this longed-for happiness."

"Thou art then sure of thy vocation, Alonso?"

"Yes," replied the sculptor.

"No tie binds thee to the world?"

"None."

"Well, if, as thou sayest, I should this very day experience a sentiment of pious joy at sight of thy statue just completed, I promise thee that to-morrow thou shalt take the habit of a novice."

"How much longer will it be before I am professed?" asked Alonso.

"Six months," replied Father Eusebio.

Alonso then bent his head for the monk's blessing.

After their repast of black bread and vegetables stewed in water, which was the ordinary fare of the Carthusians, the abbot and the other religious repaired to Alonso's studio.

Cano, remembering the art with which he had of old, in his house at Madrid, arranged his pictures and statues, hung one end of his cell with black the better to throw out his work.

While waiting for the monks, whose rule and habit he was soon to adopt, he threw a light veil over the finished statue; and, his heart full of emotion and his eyes wet with tears, he awaited their arrival. Meanwhile he looked out from the high, narrow casement to where, far below, among shrubs and flowers, crosses marked the graves of those who slept in the peace of God.

Father Eusebio at last opened the cell door and entered, followed by the monks and novices.

When all had taken their places Alonso threw off the veil which concealed his work, and showed a medium-sized statue of painted wood. It was the figure of St. Francis of Assisium, chiselled with the perfection of art. Never had artist rendered in fashion more admirable and more complete the union of prayer and asceticism upon a human face.

There was nothing studied in the attitude of the saint, and the stiffness in the lines of the figure only threw into stronger relief the divine inspiration resplendent upon the face. The robe fell in straight heavy folds over the sandalled feet; this habit of serge was confined at the waist by a rope. The hands were folded in the ample sleeves, and the hood framed the face, which was actually living. There was fire in the ecstatic gaze fixed upon Heaven; there was a breath upon those lips, whence seemed to arise hymns which were an echo of Paradise. An intense, supernatural life vivified that pale face; no aureola surrounded the head, yet a beatific crown seemed to hover above him who was deemed worthy to bear in his hands, feet, and side the sacred Stigmata of Christ.

Nothing in antique art, nothing among the myriads of exquisite creations which marked the two preceding centuries, was comparable to this statue of St. Francis of Assisium, as it came forth marvellous and complete from the most Christian of inspirations.

Father Eusebio could not restrain a cry of admiration

"It is beautiful," he said, "truly beautiful."

"I had many models," said Alonso.

"But no one sat for this statue."

"You all unconsciously sat for it, father," said Alonso; "the atmosphere which surrounds me raised me, en-

tranced me, carried me out of myself. I caught the secret of that wonderfully peaceful attitude when I saw,
motionless in their prayerful recollection, monks whose
eyes were raised with that same ardor to Heaven. Never
in my worldly existence could I have conceived or rendered what here I have found and interpreted almost
without effort."

Father Eusebio turned to his brethren.

"For some time," said he, "the author of this work
has sought admittance to our holy Order. My paternal
affection is now at length in accord with my admiration. Still I ask all of you to advise me. Should we accept him as a new member of the community of *Porta
Cæli ?*"

"His artistic renown is only equalled by his reputation
for piety," said one father.

"Let him be our brother," said another, "his genius
and his faith are alike shown in this work."

Pablo, the young novice, advanced timidly.

"Father Eusebio," said he, "beg of him to teach us
the secret of his art, that one day we may reproduce in
immortal stone the marvellous epic of the life of St.
Bruno."

The monks surrounded Alonso, manifesting for him so
fraternal an affection, so enthusiastic a welcome, that it
brought tears of emotion to the eyes of one who, stricken
by the world, received consolation and relief which was
almost triumphant from those who had given up earth
for Heaven.

Only one religious was silent. He was an old man,
nearly a century old. He had been blind for twenty
years. A young novice who was deputed to watch over
him guided him through the cloisters or along the garden
paths. He had come with his brethren into Alonso's stu-

dio, and hearing their applause of the work, desired in his turn to examine and appreciate it.

"Lead me," he said to his young conductor, "over to the statue. Though unable to see it I can by feeling appreciate it somewhat, and I shall then enjoy with the rest of you the pleasure of admiring a beautiful work which is truly Christian."

The novice brought the blind monk to the pedestal upon which rested the statue of St. Francis, and the old man feeling it carefully slowly drew his fingers over every line of it. When he touched the ecstatic countenance of the patron of Assisium his own face at first showed only deep thought, then a real joy.

"It is beautiful," said he; "more than that, it is sublime."

Alonso knelt before the old man.

"Bless me," he said, "and since thy brethren in religion have deigned to accept me as an humble postulant do thou likewise lend me thy voice."

The old monk let his hands rest upon Alonso's bowed head and seemed to be wrapped in fervent prayer. His eyelids drooped over the sightless eyes, his lips moving, he called down upon the man prostrated before him the light of the spirit of consolation.

Absorbed in himself, the blind monk appeared to hold communion with a being invisible to all others. Instead of addressing the artist in affectionate words, which would seem called forth by his late appeal, the old man appeared filled with a species of terror. The expression of his face changed. A deep sadness overspread it. Its usual calm, especially when in prayer, gave place to something like horror. With an almost mechanical movement he passed his hands over the hair, shoulders, and arms of Alonso, and when he spoke it was in a tone such as prophets might have used when making known irreparable misfortunes.

"Not yet," cried he, "not yet. Wait, my son, until the last wave of bitterness has passed over thy head. All thy tears and anguish have not yet paid the penalty which God exacts of thee. Privileged soul, thou shalt mount the last steps of thy Calvary."

Alonso Cano shuddered at the touch of the monk, whose hand now rested heavily upon his shoulder.

"I understand," continued the old man; "it seems to thee that thy trial has already been greater than that which Heaven usually inflicts upon men. Thou wert great, thou art cast down; thou wert happy, and thy happiness was snatched from thee. Thou art poorer than Job, more afflicted than Tobias. Tears have dried thy eyes and withered up thy heart, so that it could only revive beneath the dew of the Cross, and yet it is not enough. Before the indissoluble vows bind thee, before we have recited over thee the prayers for the dead, before the name of a new elect of Heaven has replaced that once famous among men, thou shalt suffer—thou shalt suffer more. Blood! ah, Lord, so much blood! fetters and irons, torture for these limbs! Mercy, Lord, mercy for him! Or, if Thine adorable decrees must be carried out, give Thy hapless creature at least the strength to adore Thee in his martyrdom."

"My God! my God!" murmured Alonso, terrified; "thou who with thy sightless eyes seest farther than this world, tell me, Must I one day leave this house?"

"Thou shalt leave it!" said the monk.

"Before pronouncing my vows?"

"Yea, before."

"Shall I never belong to the Lord?"

"Yes," replied the old man, "but the wheat must be

threshed, the grape be trodden in the press. If thou comest forth victorious from thy latest trial, if thou bearest the last wound of thy martyrdom, then only shalt thou win thy robe of serge. The gold must pass through the crucible."

" Then," said Alonso, " thou wouldst reject me ?"

" Arise," said the monk, " arise !"

The artist obeyed, and the old man, taking him in his arms, said :

" My son I my son! I shall see thee again before I die !"

Two great tears fell from his sightless eyes, and Alonso sobbed in his arms. The memory of his past sorrows, which for some months had seemed to slumber in his heart, now re-awoke with terrible distinctness. The predictions of the blind monk touched him deeply. He could not help believing his terrible words, and it seemed to him that when the time of trial came he should lack the necessary courage for it. The Superior himself appeared painfully impressed, and the monks who, a moment before, rejoiced at counting Alonso among their number, were oppressed with a dark foreboding.

Nevertheless, Father Eusebio said to the artist:

" If thou dost persist in thy demand, thou wilt take the habit in a month."

" Be thou blessed for these words !" answered Alonso, touching the hem of the monk's robe with his lips.

The Carthusians quitted the studio one by one, and the blind monk was the last to press Alonso's hand.

" The trial will be hard !" he said, " but thou shalt come forth triumphant."

The artist was alone. It seemed to him that in that short interval everything around him had changed. The prophetic voice of the old monk sent him back to the

midst of his calamities. He had supposed himself in
port, and the storm was about to rage more furiously
than ever. He had not the courage to go to the chapel
with his brethren in whose chanting he had joined so
heartily the day before. He remained for hours motionless, his arms resting upon his window-sill.

Thence he could see great portions of the road leading
to Valencia, and by leaning out could follow the dusty
path, making an abrupt turn, and ending at the ruined
hut which had been the scene of his combat with the
soldiers of Tarifa and his miserable spy.

As he thus gazed out of the window he perceived a
horseman coming at full speed in the direction of the
monastery. Neither his figure nor his face was distin-
guishable. An ample cloak hid the one and a broad hat
concealed the other, yet a thrill passed through Alonso
as if between him and that mysterious horseman there
existed an invisible link.

Still under the influence of the blind Carthusian's prophecy, the slightest incident seemed to have some bearing on his life. Had there been some question of life or
death for him in the greater or less speed of the advancing traveller Alonso could not have watched him with
greater anxiety.

When at a short distance from the monastery the
horseman paused and cast a rapid glance about him, as
if studying the aspect of the convent and its high walls,
and comparing it with some description which had been
given him. Apparently satisfied with his scrutiny the
traveller urged on his horse, and Alonso perceived with
growing uneasiness that he rode to the gate of *Porta
Cæli.*

He knocked twice, the gate rolled back upon its
hinges, and the stranger entered the holy precincts.

Alonso closed his window and, scarcely knowing why, fell upon his knees, while his clasped hands rested against the pedestal which upheld the statue of St. Francis.

In a few moments the cell door opened, and the traveller stood upon the threshold.   He cast aside his hat and mantle with a hasty gesture, and Alonso recognizing him, gave a cry of mingled hope and joy.

"Miguel !" he cried, "Miguel !"

"Did I not tell thee that I would return, master?" said Miguel.

"To Spain, certainly, but here—"

"I undertook a task, which I pursued."

"Noble boy !" cried Alonso, "thou hast sacrificed thyself for a most miserable man."

"Do not say that, master! do not say that!" cried Miguel; "never was there a more consoling part to play than mine, despite all the difficulties which I had to encounter.   And behold how the Lord hath protected me, for am I not once more in Spain?"

"I believed thee still at Naples, busy with the pursuit of a wretch whose name would soil my lips."

"Yes, master! I have been for nearly two years the evil genius of Lello Lelli.   Following him like his shadow I went from tavern to tavern, my eyes never left him.   Even in the common and public life I was always at his side, masked like a conspirator, armed like a brigand.   Such a life as I have led for the past two years!   How far removed from this adventurous existence seemed the studious times of old.   However, I did not lose my time.   My portfolio is fairly swelling with notes, and I have made innumerable sketches, which I may use some day if, like Frank Floris, I paint hell or the fallen angels.   Thou mayest suppose, master, that Lello Lelli was not to be met in the best circles of

Neapolitan society. I was not mistaken in him. I found him at the head of a score or so of rascals, the best of whom would not be worth the cord that strangled him. They use the stiletto for the benefit of Ribera who still reigns over his school, less like a master than a tyrant. I passed many a night around a table covered with bottles, while Lello drank to intoxication."

"And," said Alonso, "did the wretch never betray himself?"

"No," said Miguel, "and yet I discovered a terrible clue."

"Speak! speak!" said Alonso, seizing Miguel's hand.

"One evening," began Miguel, "in a tavern, full of revellers, sailors, painters of a low class, and other such, a dispute arose for a very trifling cause. The question was, whether the hair of the Venetians, of that artificial red so appreciated amongst them, offered to the painter of contrasts as fine lights and shades as hair of a natural hue. Some contended that the reflection was the same, others upheld the contrary. When Lelli's opinion was asked he smiled, and said with a peculiar expression:

"'I never saw really beautiful hair except in Spain.'

"This led to a fresh dispute, each one maintaining his point, till Lelli, pushed to the wall, pulled out of his pocket a little scent-bag, whence he drew forth a tress of blue-black hair. O master, master! thy lost wife alone had hair of that peculiar hue and of that marvellous length. When the other young men advanced to look at it I advanced with the rest. I wore a velvet mask, so that Lelli could not recognize me.

"I touched the tress, and withdrawing my hand with a horror which was not at all feigned, I said:

"'That hair belonged to a dead person.'

"Lelli shuddered visibly. Then fixing upon him my

eyes, which seemed to glare through the holes in my mask, I continued:

"'To a woman who was murdered!'

"There was a cry of terror from the spectators.

"'He is a sorcerer!' said one.

"'He is the devil!' said another.

"'One thing is certain,' said Lelli, putting his hand to his belt, 'that I consider his words an insult.'

"'I did not say that thou wert the murderer,' said I. 'But I draw my sword in turn.'"

"Go on," said Alonso feebly.

"Ah! that time, master," said Miguel, "thou wert not there to prevent the duel, and hadst thou been present I doubt, spite of the respect which I bear thee, whether thine influence would have been powerful enough to restrain me. For my anger at that moment led me to do an act of justice."

Alonso turned deadly pale as Miguel resumed.

"We were face to face, both armed, both glaring at each other with eyes of fire; threats were upon our lips, and yet, with a sort of prudence which neither of us could have defined, we hesitated to utter them. I felt oddly reluctant to cry out to Lelli, Thou art the man! Perhaps, he would have been stricken like David when the prophet Nathan reproached him with his double crime. Lelli, on the other hand, seemed full of impatience to know what hidden mystery lay beneath my words. He dared not ask, and it appeared to him the simplest course to kill me, and thus secure my silence in case I had any suspicions. Admitting that I spoke at hazard, a life more or less weighed so little upon his mind that he would have had no scruple in adding me to the list of his victims. For my part I had no desire to kill him. What I wanted was to have his life in my

power, at the point of my dagger, my foot at his throat.
To kill him in a duel, pierce him through and leave him
lying speechless and senseless upon the pavement would
be of little avail.   Wouldst thou not still have remained
under an accusation which is slow torture to thee?   It
was plain then that I must vanquish him.   However, I
gave him a last chance.

"'Wilt thou,' I asked, 'give up to me that tress of
black hair, which is of such an extraordinary length that
it cannot be real?'

"'I never will!' he answered.

"'Art thou afraid?' I asked.

"'Of what?' said he arrogantly.

"'Come,' said I, 'on leaving Spain I travelled through
France, and in France they are fond of sorcerers.   I
admit that it is not right.   What they do is damnable,
and there is so much deviltry mixed up with it that the
tribunals have great reason to concern themselves about
the infamous means employed by these people to gain
occult knowledge.   But, evil or not, such a science exists;
the compact which they make with Satan gives them a
power the price of which is their salvation, and this power
they wield in this world, till the law chastises them by torments and hell drags them into its gulf.   Now in Paris,
whilst I lived there, I knew a man versed in the secrets of
witchcraft.   He had learned these secrets from his mother
who had been duly convicted of magic and burned as a
witch on the Place de Grève.   He declared to a friend of
mine who was curious about such matters, of which I
must confess I have the greatest dread—that it sufficed
for him to obtain a lock of hair belonging to any person
living or dead, and that he could tell his whole life and
history.   The vital fluid still remains, he said, in the
capillary tissues after the person to whom the hair be-

longed has ceased to exist.   I know not why that tress
of blue-black hair inspires me with such an eager, mor-
bid curiosity.   Give it to me, then, that I may satisfy
this fancy, or know that I will pierce thy heart with the
point of my sword to snatch it from thee.'

"Lello Lelli returned the little bag to his doublet, and
said:

"'On guard!'

"I raised the sword as if to salute some one.

"'I call upon thee, Mercedes,' I said gravely.

"I had scarcely time to cross swords with him.   Lello
made a thrust, and had I not leaped backwards I would
have been pierced through and through.   Thou mayest
suppose that after such preliminaries the combat was
necessarily mortal.   What I had said to Lello was true
in all respects.   I fought for Mercedes, for that dead
lady who took thy honor with her into the tomb.   I
begged her to be my aid since my cause was sacred.   I
regarded myself rather as an executioner than as a
duelist.   It seemed to me that the Almighty must grant
me the life of a wretch whose confession could exonerate
thee.   A circle had formed around us.   There was a
vague impression among the spectators that there was
something more in the affair than the apparently futile
matter of a lock of hair.   I felt myself endowed with an
almost superhuman strength.   After this first surprise
I returned Lelli's thrusts with equal address and much
greater coolness.   His mode of attack was like that of a
bandit.   He rushed upon me like a tiger and ground his
teeth like a hyena.   His sword gleamed like lightning.
I was apparently calm despite my secret anxiety.   A moment's hesitation and I was lost.   My eyes were riveted
upon him.   Anger had mounted to his brain and crim-
soned his face.   He had that feeling which is always

dangerous for a duelist, that he was eager to end matters.

"Most of those present honored me with their evident sympathy; perhaps they felt that I was avenging many an injury.

"Gradually the circle of spectators had however widened. Some of the new-comers did not seem like the usual *habitués* of the tavern. The glances which they cast upon me were not reassuring. I guessed that Lelli had both friends and accomplices among them.

"All at once Lelli by a hasty movement let the little bag fall. I sprang forward, and whilst I set my foot upon that tress of hair, which to my mind was proof sufficient to convict him, my arm seemed to grow preternaturally long, and I pierced Lelli's doublet with the point of my sword. I drew it away red. Lelli fell upon the floor. The new-comers, whose lowering looks I had remarked, surrounded me in a threatening fashion. The witnesses to the quarrel prepared to take my part, while the landlord and his serving people bore away the wounded man, in whom no one seemed to have any interest. The opposing parties were hastily looking to their arms, when all at once happily there was a cry of 'Police!'

"It needed nothing more; in an instant the room was empty. I then hastened to Lelli's bedside. A monk had preceded me there. There was foam upon Lelli's lips, he seemed scarcely breathing, and the death rattle was heard in his throat.

"The monk looked at me severely.

"'This is no place for thee,' he said.

"'I crave thy pardon,' said I, 'but I would know—'

"'If he pardons thee?'

"'No. He is not of those who pardon or who forget.
I want to hear if he will confess—'

"'What?'

"'His crime!'

"'That is the secret of God, my son.'

"'And the secret of death,' said I.

"'Thou would'st then—'

"'Remain here.'

"'Till he is cured?'

"'Ay, or till he expires.'

"'What if the sight of thee by nourishing his wrath
should prevent him from repenting?'

"'He cannot repent without confessing.'

"'What?'

"'A crime, I tell thee, a crime for which another is in
danger and in exile.'

"'Thou hast proofs then of this man's guilt?'

"'I have one already.'

"I showed him the tress of hair, and added:

"'His delirium may supply others, and thou wilt hear
them with me.'

"The old monk rose.

"'I swear before God,' said he, 'that henceforth I consider myself this man's confessor. My heart and soul as
a priest are open to his avowals and to his dying confidence. Hence I adjure thee to quit his bedside.'

"'Father,' I said, 'thou dost forget the hapless man
who is waiting and suffering.'

"The old man returned to his prayers, and I sat down
close by Lelli's bed.

"His face was of a livid paleness, his eyes were closed.
Sometimes his lips moved, and a sound came through
them which I took to be 'Mercedes.'

"The monk never ceased praying a moment, seeking to

snatch from hell that deeply stained soul, and watching over his earthly tenement, whilst I kept guard for the sake of justice."

"Ah, what devotion, what devotion!" cried Alonso.

The young man respectfully pressed his master's hand.

"It was but discharging my debt of gratitude," said he.

"What next?" said Alonso.

"Twenty days passed thus," continued Miguel, "and during those twenty days the monk struggled to save the body from death and the soul from damnation of a wretch whom I longed to deliver into the hands of the law. And when Lelli opened his eyes and saw me beside him with the monk he smiled ironically, knowing that his secret was well guarded. As soon as he could rise he left the inn. I had learned nothing new; I had only obtained this solitary clue."

As he spoke Miguel drew from his pocket the little bag.

Alonso Cano took it with a trembling and convulsive hand. He had scarcely courage to open it and display a tress of hair of a black like the bluish wing of a swallow. He put it to his lips, crying out through tears, "Mercedes, Mercedes!"

After a short pause, he asked:

"Art thou certain thou hast found no other proof?"

"I believe more firmly than ever that the criminal will not go unpunished, master."

"Wherefore?"

"Lello Lelli arrived in Spain a month since."

"He has dared to reappear?"

"There is no one, as thou knowest, to accuse him openly; besides he is now protected by one who is all-powerful with Philip IV."

" Who is that ?"

" Ribera."

" Lo Spagnoletto at Madrid ?"

" And high in favor," said Miguel.

Alonso's head fell upon his breast.

" Thou wilt be alone, all alone," said he slowly to Miguel, "in thy struggle against two wretches whom Judge Rosalés will uphold; alone in unmasking Lelli, alone in laying such a snare for him as even the most wary sometimes fall into. And this wretch, who could assassinate a defenceless woman, will not fail to attempt a second crime upon thee."

" It is because I feel my weakness," said Miguel, " that I came here, master. I will not depart without thee."

" What, thou wouldst—"

" That thou dost return with me."

" But I am accused, placed under the ban of the law ! If I am arrested before thou hast found proof of my innocence, I am lost."

" Thou shalt not be arrested.   Thou hast friends !"

" The unfortunate have no friends."

" Alonso Cano has many," said Miguel, " and amongst them the most devoted, as well as the most powerful of us all, offers thee an asylum in his house."

" Rafaël Sanguineto ?"

" Thou hast guessed it, master."

" But such imprudence is almost madness. A magistrate."

" The less reason to fear ! Who would seek thee under the roof of the *regidor* ?"

" No, no, it cannot be, Miguel; persecution would follow me even there."

" It has found thee even here!"

" Judge Tarifa was powerless to cross the threshold of this house to snatch me hence."

" Tarifa is now in correspondence with Rosalés. Thou didst make seven pictures here which by their perfection betrayed thee, as thy works in the gallery of the Count Aguidas denounced thee before. Believe me thy danger is as great near Valencia as it was at Madrid. Thou and I will see each other every day; we will concert our plans; we will make truth triumph, and the wretch who has blighted thy life will expiate his misdeeds by torture. Thy innocence once proved, thou wilt be once more the great Alonso Cano. Philip IV. will compensate thee for thy long probation; the prestige of thy misfortunes will enhance that of thy genius, and the Michael Angelo of Spain, an object of universal admiration, will forget all that to-day he believes it impossible to forget."

Alonso began to pace his cell with rapid strides.

" Oh noble and valiant heart !" he said, " thou art right. It is Providence who brings Lelli back to the theatre of his crime. Only at Madrid is it possible for me to complete thy work and prove to all that the tears shed over my dead Mercedes were not hypocritical tears. Oh, to traverse again and be able to hold up my head in those streets which have erstwhile seen me so proud and happy, on terms of intimacy with the proudest grandees of Spain who were my friends, hearing from the King the assurance of his friendship! Oh, to recover a portion at least of the goods snatched from me by Lelli. Ah, what a victory it would be!"

" Let us win it together, master!" cried Miguel.

Alonso Cano did not answer; his eyes fell upon the statue of St. Francis, sculptured with so much inspiration, and so enthusiastically admired a few hours before by the monks of *Porta Cæli*.

He remembered how he had begged of Father Eusebio permission to remain in the solitude and peace of the monastery. Now when he was about to abandon that cell in which he had known holy resignation, fervor in prayer, and the consolations of faith, he felt a strange perturbation in his soul. No doubt he was profoundly touched by the thought of being cleared of the crime which had sullied his reputation; but the idea of seeming ungrateful to those who had received him, the apprehensions which had before seized him of being thrust back into the furnace, made him shrink from the ordeal.

"No," he said, "I have suffered too much. I will stay here."

A moment before the cell-door had opened to admit Father Eusebio, who stood silently upon the threshold.

"Go," said he, "go my son; the struggle is beyond thy strength. Besides, remember the words of the saintly old man who this morning declared that the hour of rest in God had not yet come for thee. Thy soul is too disturbed, thy mind too full of resentment, for thee yet to offer it to God; the victim struggles under the sacrificial knife, and to enter here thou must be in advance a corpse."

"Father! father!" cried Alonso.

"If it be the will of God that thou shouldst consecrate thy life and thy talents to His service, He will prepare the means necessary to bring about this result. However thou mayest decide remember that thou hast friends here who will pray for thee every day."

Alonso made a last feeble effort at resistance, but it was indeed a feeble one.

Father Eusebio was right. Alonso, attracted, captivated, by the sweetness of the monastic life, was not yet ready to accept it entirely. He would willingly have ·

practised its austerities, but he shrank from certain sacrifices that he had to make.

Father Eusebio had, however, to use all his influence and even authority to induce Alonso to depart with Miguel. It was finally decided that both should leave at nightfall. Miguel retained his cavalier costume and Alonso passed for his groom.

Miguel had left horses in waiting at an inn near Valencia, and when night came Alonso with tearful eyes quitted the friendly shelter of *Porta Cœli*.

Just as he was leaving the old blind monk stretched out his hands to him.

"Thou wilt come back," said he; "thou wilt return to the ark, stricken, crushed by sorrow, and so bent beneath the weight of thy cross that thou wilt lack the strength to rise. Yes, thou wilt return, but next time to depart no more; for then shalt thou judge of the things of earth from such a height that thou wilt desire to contemplate thenceforth only the things of Heaven."

CHAPTER XV.

THE FEAST OF CORPUS CHRISTI.

IT was the day of the Christian and Spanish festival, by excellence, when all the pomp of earth is displayed to honor the divinity of Jesus, hidden under mystic veils Nothing, even in France, can give any idea of these so- lemnities in the noble city of Madrid, especially at an epoch when faith flourished like a gorgeous flower which shed its perfume over a whole people. It was not only the altar that was resplendent with the fire of the diamonds enriching the Remonstrance; it was not only the altar that sparkled with its golden chandeliers and its ostensoriums, or the *retablos* with their carved figures that gleamed and glowed in the light of innumerable tapers. The portals were almost as magnificent as the chancel; the streets, hung with costly draperies, were as sumptuous as the ca- thedral. Here and there upon the line of the procession pictures by celebrated painters awaited at once the bless- ing of the priest and the acclamations of the populace. Immense canvases called *sargas* unrolled their holy epics and their mystic symbols upon the flag-decorated houses. The people thronged the streets while waiting to enter the church. The balconies were filled by crowds of de- vout, attentive worshippers elegantly attired, less from love of display than to do honor to the festival. The flower-beds stripped of their contents filled vases and baskets with their luxuriant gleanings.

The bells rang out in grand accord; processional crosses of silver, abbatial crosses, banners of convents, confraternities, and civic corporations were displayed high in air. Afar could be seen carved and gilded reliquaries to be devoutly borne on the shoulders of Levites or young men of the town. Statues of saints richly attired were carried upon litters. Madonnas in robes of brocade shone in the sunshine; the natural hair fastened upon their head was crowned with a diadem towards which each lady contributed a diamond. And shining down upon the multitudes of superbly dressed men and women with their veils of rare lace, upon reliquaries, upon the gilded or painted figures, some of solid gold, upon silken embroidered banners, upon streets strewn with rushes and roses from the royal gardens, was the brilliant, joyous, fervid sun of Spain.

There was unusual stir and bustle in the dwelling of Rafaël Sanguineto. The exterior decoration of the house was just completed. The *miradors*, hung in purple silk, permitted the ladies to look out upon the procession from behind their shelter. In a high chamber fitted up as a studio sat the host and his guest, Alonso Cano.

"Never will I permit such an act of folly on thy part," said Sanguineto; "for the six months during which thou hast been in Madrid thou hast had patience and courage enough to conceal thyself from all eyes. This prudence has had its reward; none suspects thy presence here, and with Miguel thou canst follow every detail of the search which is being made in thy behalf."

"No," said Alonso, "I am not free enough."

"Thou seest Miguel each day."

"True, but thou wilt not permit me to accompany him."

"Hear me," said Sanguineto, "if thou takest but a single step in the street thou art lost."

"Ah!" said Alonso, "this captivity oppresses me. To

know that I am in Madrid and but a few paces from the house wherein I dwelt with Mercedes, and yet that I dare not cross the threshold of that home where I experienced all the sweetness of love and gratified pride; to see from this window the palace of the King and be afraid even to approach it; above all, to hear the bells of the cathedral ring, and be unable to mingle with the pious throng who follow the *Corpus Christi*, and bow down to receive the blessing of the priest."

" Thou hast still another motive, Alonso."

" I admit it. I have exhibited a picture around which it would seem a crowd will gather. How ofte, the multitude have applauded my works displayed upon the cathedral steps. For a long time I have practiced my art like a criminal, hiding my productions away in obscure galleries, and burying them in monasteries. Weil, to-day my canvas is displayed living and luminous; the multitude will see it, hail it as of yore, and I shall not be there to enjoy my triumph."

" Go not thither, Alonso; one gesture, one exclamation might betray thee."

" I will be still, Sanguineto, I will be still."

" Thou canst not answer for thyself, and I half regret having allowed the exhibition of this work at all."

" There is no name to it."

" It is the touch of the master and not the letters of his name which makes him known to the populace."

" Oh I beg of thee," said Alonso imploringly, " do not oppose me thus. Thou dost not know what it is to be a fugitive, weary and worn, threatened on all sides. I need air and liberty. I feel that the tumult of an active, joyous multitude will expand my heart and soul. Remember how long I have been deprived of such festivals, of

religious pomp, of solemnities of all kinds. Are they
not to play an *auto** of Calderon ?"

"Yes," said Sanguineto.

"And wouldst thou keep me here shut up in the house
whilst a multitude thrilling with enthusiasm are applauding the work of our first dramatic genius? Calderon, who was my friend, has produced a new piece, and
shall I not be there to applaud it, and from my hidden
corner enjoy it with all my heart? Such deprivation is
more than I can bear. Knowest thou the name of this
new piece, Sanguineto ?"

"The 'Devotion to the Cross.' "

"I must and will see this sacramental play. It seems
to me that the soul of Spain lives in these productions,
which all literature envies us, and which none has yet
imitated. Calderon having once been a soldier retains
in his works the fiery ardor of the warrior struggling for
his master. His faith raises him above this world of
ours. He looks down upon this earth which he has de-
spised, but above his head is always a glimpse of Heaven,
where angels are singing; a mystical rose half opened, a
sun of justice and of love shining upon groups of the elect.
I shall see the 'Devotion to the Cross,' Sanguineto, and
without peril to myself."

"How ?"

"Lend me a penitent's dress."

Sanguineto shook his head.

"Why dost thou hesitate?" said Alonso; "the city of
Madrid will soon be full of penitents, gray, black, white,
red, blue, or purple, all so enshrouded by their habits
and hidden by their cowls that a father could not recognize his own son. Thanks to this costume, which casts a

---

* *Auto*, a sort of religious drama.

sort of monastic shadow over such numbers of men, I can conceal myself in the crowd. I should be wearing the Carthusian habit; instead I will assume a penitent's dress."

"Alonso," repeated Sanguineto in a troubled voice, "by yielding to thee I make myself the accomplice of thy imprudence. God is my witness that I do not fear for myself; and howsoever dearly I might have to pay for the hospitality I offer thee, would still hold myself honored that thou didst accept it. But canst thou answer for thyself? Mayest thou not come face to face with Rosalés, who accuses thee, and Lello Lelli, who would desire nothing better than thy condemnation?"

"Whatever may befall," said Alonso, "I promise to keep possession of my faculties."

Sanguineto exhausted every argument: Cano refuted them with more passion than logic, and the *regidor* at length yielded to his friend's entreaties and provided him with the gray dress of a penitent. Miguel appeared soon after.

"What news?" asked Alonso.

"I´ have discovered Ribera's motive in coming to Madrid."

"What is that motive?"

"It entails the ruin of Don John of Austria."

"Ribera is then busying himself with affairs of state, and comes here as an ambassador."

"Lo Spagnoletto could not govern his own household. In his foolish pride he was honored by the attentions of a prince, and now comes to denounce him to the King, and so avenge his daughter."

"In that case," said Alonso, "Don John of Austria may well fear for his life. Lello Lelli and others such will offer their sinister services."

The young man suddenly perceived the penitent's robe thrown upon a chair. His face clouded.

"Master," said he, "thou didst promise never to leave this house."

"For this one day, Miguel, for less than a day!"

"It is still too much, far too much."

"Oh my friend, my child, I am stifling in the solitude to which I have been condemned for four years past. I feel the need of being once more amongst men. I am convinced that the seeing of this procession will be of incalculable benefit to me. When I kneel to receive the blessing of the priest, it will be like a new baptism."

"Let me at least go with thee!" said Miguel.

"Yes, my friend, joyfully!"

The sound of bells, pealing out loudly and joyously, fell upon the air; from afar came the chanting of litanies and snatches of hymns. Alonso threw on his penitent's robe with feverish haste, and prepared to set out.

This dress was not a monastic habit, but a sort of religious livery. Those who wore it practiced works of charity during the year. Some took care of the sick, others buried the dead; there was, one might say, a confraternity of penitents, answering to every affliction of body or soul. These men in Spain, Italy, and Southern France devoted themselves each to a special sorrow. The color of their robe distinguished them one from the other on occasions of ceremony; the cowl which almost completely covered their faces, but which could be thrown back at pleasure, made them all resemble spectres.

Miguel and Alonso, in his garb of gray, went out of the regidor's house. At the very first step which he took in the decorated streets, strewn with flowers, gay with banners, Alonso felt himself transported back to the days of his youth. The blood coursed freely through his veins, a new fire burned in his eyes.

He observed the *sargas* displayed for the feast, and whose greater or less success was to have so important a bearing upon the life of the young artists who had painted them. He breathed again the perfume of roses, jasmine, and of incense; he was wonder-stricken and stirred, as if he beheld all the pomp of the procession for the first time. His heart, crushed as it was by his afflictions, shared in the tumultuous joy of the populace.

Each people must be judged in its own surroundings, under its own sky, and without regard to its neighbors. The originality of each nation is composed of divers elements. In Spain, we find but two predominating sentiments: complete, absolute, almost excessive, chivalrous honor and faith. Not a hesitating faith, mingled with many other sentiments, hidden, so to say, in the depths of the soul, but a robust, ardent, enthusiastic belief. A faith which delights in public manifestations, which places the crucifix not only upon the altar, but at every cross-road, and in every thoroughfare. A domestic faith, if such an expression can be used, which unites that sentiment with every action of life, and makes it apparent even in its very costume and language; which mingles with its pleasures, and creates for its grandest celebrations a class of dramas unique in literature, called sacramental *autos.*

Certainly Calderon's new piece, the " Devotion to the Cross," was not the least attraction of the day. This representation served, so to say, as the prologue to the pious ceremony of the procession. Having heard the recital of the wonders which Heaven ceases not to operate in favor of those who honor the sacred sign of the

Redemption, Christians were necessarily led to invoke it with redoubled fervor.

Calderon, who gave up the sword for the service of the altar; Calderon, the most poetic of the galaxy of dramatists, who gave to Spain Lope de Vega and Alarçon, from whom Corneille borrowed his *Menteur*, had the power, in a greater degree than any one else, of raising faith to enthusiasm. His genius hovered in all its brilliancy over each of his conceptions. The undercurrent of a noble and generous passion ran through every scene of his dramas. Honor displayed there al' its Castilian pride, and punctiliousness and faith led men to martyrdom.

The *autos* of Calderon and Lope de Vega cannot in any sense be compared to the *mysteries* represented in France a century or two before. These *mysteries* were but poor and feeble attempts at that which in Spain found its full perfection.

Spain has not borrowed anything from other nations. Living her own life, rich in an inexhaustible mine of genius and inspiration, she reached, almost at once, perfection in various arts. But the generous spark which then vivified her was suffered to languish, and she was condemned to see it die out for want of food; hence, without transition, she fell from the pinnacle she had attained into the gulf of oblivion.

Everything seemed to bloom at once in that wonderful country. While Miguel Cervantes related with subtle irony the adventures of the last Knight of Spain, " The Tisserand of Segovia," the " Secret Offence," and " Secret Vengeance," all magnificent dramas, the beauty of which has never been surpassed, drew crowds to the theatre. Whilst Cervantes' book was read, and the dramas of Calderon were being performed, Murillo was painting his Madonnas, Zurbaran reproducing his austere monks, Ribera representing the martyrdom of saints with flashes of genius that resembled rage, and Velasquez, the friend of the King, was planning the downfall of Olivaréz, Marquis de San Lucar, while painting his marvellous portraits and scenes of common life.

The "Devotion to the Cross" was performed upon a stage erected in the open air. There was no hall which could have contained that ardent, enthusiastic, eager multitude. The public squares scarcely sufficed; there was a dense, suffocating throng. Sometimes a cry arose from the crowd: some one had fainted, and there was no way of getting him or her out. However powerful their lungs, the actors certainly could not hope to make themselves heard by that immense assemblage; but they could see the gorgeous scenery and behold those wonderful sword-thrusts which made them thrill with joy or terror. Their sympathies were keenly excited by the heroes of the piece, who were, perhaps, neither saints nor even just men, and whose final conversion exalted the power of the crucifix which Calderon desired to make manifest.

At length the curtain rolled away, the people gave a cry of joy, and applauded vociferously! They thus showed their appreciation in advance, with perfect confidence in the author's powers. They were sure of being at once entertained and edified.

The part played by Eusebius of the Cross, the hero of the drama, is far from being exemplary; but, abandoned at the foot of Calvary, he makes the cross his exclusive devotion, and whenever he is tempted to anger or any other excess the temptation thenceforth disappears before the sign of the cross. It is through this devotion in the crucifix that, despite his faults and crimes, Eusebius merits the grace when dying of receiving absolution

from the priest; to this adorable sign of our redemption Julia owes the inspiration which, at the moment
when her life is threatened, makes her cry out:

"Divine Cross, save me! I swear to live and die in
penance!"

Then the multitude cry out with one voice:

"A miracle! A great miracle!"

And, according to custom, the principal actor in the
drama appears, and bowing to the audience, says:

"So ends the wonderful comedy of Devotion to the
Cross. May the author be happy, and do you pardon
him his faults."

Then there was an indescribable tumult of applause. No
other *auto* had met with such success. It was not alone
admiration, but a sort of frenzy, that seized upon the multitude; the spectators felt themselves raised to the same
heights as the dramatist. If, according to Raphael's
beautiful expression, "to understand is to equal," all
that pious throng assembled to applaud this *auto* of the
priest Calderon were elevated by the power of his
genius, and felt its influence in an extraordinary degree.

Miguel and Alonso Cano were both deeply touched by
this magnificent spectacle.

The last bursts of applause were followed by the first
sound of the hymns: the procession was coming out of
the cathedral. The tumult was all of a sudden hushed
into profound recollection. The people devoutly followed the cross, towards which their devotion was
stimulated by the late performance.

The procession passed slowly and majestically along
the adjacent streets and squares. All heads were bowed
before the ostensorium, and all knees were bent upon the
pavement. After the clergy and religious came the
penitents of the various confraternities. Then the multi-

tude, an ever-increasing multitude, followed the Madonnas, the images of saints, the miraculous crucifix, and the royally decorated reliquaries.

None but the Spaniards or Italians understand that holy exaltation. Where they put faith we seek to put reason; to their enthusiasm we offer our skepticism.

The Voltairean spirit, which passed over France like an icy wind, and the rationalism which led some of its finest minds astray, has found an echo elsewhere. But in Spain faith has undergone no transformation; beyond the Pyrenees belief is still as fervent as ever.

In every quarter of the town the same pomp was displayed. It was only when the procession had re-entered the church, that the crowd gathering about the cathedral ventured to give its opinion upon the works of art exhibited upon the steps or in its immediate vicinity.

All the great artists of Madrid were represented there. Many of them had sent pictures, with their names attached; others more modest, or more curious to know the general opinion, uninfluenced by the artist's fame, omitted sending their names with their works, preferring to hear them criticised or applauded by the multitude.

Lo Spagnoletto delighted in this opportunity of comparing the progress of his compatriots and of discovering what rank was assigned him among contemporary artists. Proud of his success, as well as of his appearance, he passed through the streets of Madrid, followed by a crowd of curious observers.

Like his pupils he ostentatiously wore a magnificent costume, the splendor and the brilliant tints of which contrasted strongly with the sombre black doublets of the Spaniards. Occasionally a dark cloud overshadowed his face; whether it was that he observed a canvas worthy to compete with, or even surpass the finest of his own, or that the remembrance of Don John crossed his mind.

Beside him was Lello Lelli who, with his hand upon the hilt of his sword, and with more than his usual bravado, seemed less like a person who kept the feast religiously than like one who would fain have disturbed its solemnity by engaging in a brawl.

He had lost none of that vein of satire which we remember to have seen him display in the studio of Alonso Cano; but this satire had become still more bitter. He not only wounded the pride of those with whom he spoke, but he managed to reach the most vulnerable point in every heart. His only pleasure was in getting up a quarrel or pursuing some scheme of revenge. A time comes in some lives when salvation is not indeed impossible—for salvation can never be impossible as long as the standard of the cross is raised over the world, and the Holy Sacrifice is celebrated upon our altars—but very doubtful. Evil has so taken possession of these natures that good cannot find entrance there. Thought is so vitiated in its source that the conception of a noble action cannot enter their mind. Whosoever abandons the practice of virtue forgets at length that virtue exists.

After his return to Naples Lelli had completely given himself up to evil ways. He spent his nights in the lowest taverns, and, unless when some nocturnal adventure required that his head should be cool and his hand steady, he usually drank to intoxication, and was often carried home dead drunk. He lowered his prices for brawls and murders, as if any one would have done him a favor by requiring such services of him. His expression had become more fierce and restless, the lines around

his mouth more bitter.   And when in his fits of drun-
kenness he lost control of himself, strange words often
escaped his lips.   But he spoke before men whose own
heads were at stake, and usually when Lelli came to
himself a neighbor merely remarked to him that he had
better take care to drink only among comrades.   Pushing
and jostling Lelli had forced his way into the front row of
those who were examining the works of art upon the cathedral steps.   Stopping before a medium-sized picture
representing the Virgin and Child he uttered an exclamation of surprise.

"It is she!" he cried in a troubled voice, " it is she."

He fixed his haggard gaze full of a sudden terror upon
the head of the Madonna, finding only in the features
the memory of a woman whom he had seen stretched
upon a bed covered with wounds.

Near the picture stood a man wearing the gray robe
of a penitent.   His gaze never wandered from Lelli, his
eyes seemed to burn through the holes in his capuchin,
and he trembled with some deep emotion.

The praises of this picture were rung on all sides;
people spoke of the beauty of this composition, its simplicity of conception, the dignity in the attitude of the
Virgin, and the divine loveliness of the Infant Jesus.

"His name!   His name!" cried the enthusiastic spectators.

Magnificent offers accompanied the applause.   They
cried out that Spain possessed another master, and be-
sought the author of the work to make himself known.
A monk offered him the decoration of the refectory of
his convent; a great lord begged him to adorn his gallery.   It was a fever, a frenzy, of enthusiasm.

The penitent in gray was silent, but at each cry of

admiration a thrill passed through him and he unconsciously drew himself up.

Lello had remarked the demeanor of the man. Hatred,
like sympathy, is rarely deceived in its object. Without
knowing why, Lelli felt that under the penitent's hood
and robe he had an enemy. Besides, as he attentively
examined the man disguised by his costume, singular
suspicions darted across his mind. His eyes wandered
back and forth from the magnificent painting to the
mysterious person who stood beside it. What had struck
him at first and elicited his cry of surprise was the
strange resemblance between the dark Madonna of the
picture and the face of a woman whom he had good reason to remember.

A sudden and unexpected test might put the life and
honor of a man in his power. He mounted the highest
step which separated him from the picture, and, casting
glances of rage and hatred around him, said to the crowd
who were risking the danger of suffocation to behold the
work which had been the great success of the day:

"You would know the name of him who painted this
picture ?"

" Yes, yes," cried innumerable voices.

"You shall know it later," said Lelli with a disagreeable laugh. "Let me imitate Calderon and Lope de
Vega when they write a drama. They so dispose their
effects as to astound by an unexpected *dénouement*, and
that is wherefore you did during the representation of the
auto of our inimitable author so loudly applaud when
Julia, lost, threatened by her father's dagger, embraced
the saving cross."

"Most certainly!"

"Speak! speak!"

"Tell us the name of this painter."

Such were a few of the exclamations that arose from the crowd. Whilst Lelli kept them thus breathless with curiosity and impatience Miguel seized the gray penitent by his flowing robe.

" Come," said he, " come !"

" No," said Alonso, " I will remain."

" My instinct warns me that thou art in danger."

" I have braved dangers as great," replied Alonso.

" I implore thee!   Lelli even now suspects."

" I must see and hear," said Alonso.

Lelli went on addressing the crowd:

" You find this Madonna very beautiful, do ye not? And in truth she is lovely and perfect.   The expression of the face, the grace of the contour, are painted and rendered most wonderfully.   You see only a Virgin worthy of your homage; I find a strange and fatal resemblance.   Far from inspiring me with veneration she causes me a secret horror.   Instead of reproducing the features of the Mother of God they remind me of a victim."

" A victim ?" repeated a score of voices.

" Yes, a victim whom you all knew; she was brutally murdered.   Her features, stamped upon this canvas by memory and remorse, should tell you the name of her assassin.   The woman was called Mercedes, and the painter Alonso Cano."

There was a universal cry from the listeners.   At the same time Lelli let his hand fall heavily upon the shoulder of the penitent.   Alonso felt that he was lost.

" Throw back that cowl," said Lelli, making a movement as if to snatch it off.

But Miguel, dagger in hand, leaped forward.

" Back, sacrilegious wretch!" he cried, "this man is clad in the livery of Christ, which is sacred to all! I appeal to the Catholic people of Spain."

"Yes, yes," cried the crowd, applauding.

Miguel seized Alonso by the arm.

"Not a word nor a sign," said he; "enough imprudence for one day."

He dragged him forward through that multitude, which still pressed round the steps of the cathedral.

Then Lelli struck his forehead, saying in a low voice:

"I have seen enough; but we shall meet again Alonso Cano."

CHAPTER XVI.

THE CHAMBER OF DEATH.

MIGUEL dragged his companion after him through the crowd. Whether it was respect for the habit of the penitent which he wore, or pity for one whose crime had never been proven, the people seemed to lend themselves as much as possible to the escape of the two friends. Pushed, jostled, forced out of their way a hundred times and regaining it with the greatest difficulty, obliged to traverse innumerable lanes and by-ways, they believed that Lello Lelli must have lost all trace of them.

But the Italian was not a man to lose sight of his prey. He had followed their flight at a convenient distance. Alonso's costume enabled him to keep his eye upon them, while remaining himself a few paces behind, till a crowd of gray, black, and white penitents pouring out upon a square confused him, and when the long train had disappeared Miguel and his friend were no more to be seen. Lello was then about a hundred paces from the *regidor's* house. His rage was almost uncontrollable. A moment before he had believed his vengeance certain, now it had escaped him.

He thought of going into Sanguineto's house and apprising him of Alonso Cano's presence in Madrid. But in sober reality what could he affirm?

Positively nothing.

One of the pictures upon the steps of the cathedràl had reminded him of Mercedes, but that might be merely a chance resemblance. A man concealed by a penitent's dress had seemed to take an extraordinary interest in the judgment of the people upon a work; and in this work Lello Lelli believed he could trace the touch, the drawing, the execution of Alonso Cano. Such suppositions would weigh but little in the balance of justice, or at least the justice exercised by the *regidor*. The latter could not act without an order, and Gaspardo del Roca would not give it on mere chance. Besides, where to find this mysterious penitent?

"The first thing is to find Miguel," thought Lello; "after that we shall see what is to be done. Miguel probably frequents the artists' quarter; I will go thither in the evenings, and by keeping eyes and ears open I shall be sure to discover him."

While pursuing this train of thought Lelli's eyes strayed mechanically around him; they fixed themselves unconsciously upon the *regidor's* house; he uttered an exclamation:

"It is he!" he said; "I am sure it is he."

Then, drawing his sombrero over his eyes, he quitted the spot, even more hastily than he had approached it. Instead of going to Gaspardo del Roca he went to Rosalés.

Meanwhile the *regidor* was deeply distressed.

"I told thee," said he in a voice of extreme agitation, "it was an imprudence, a terrible imprudence. Thou shouldst not have gone out on any pretence whatsoever. Miguel alone should have been left to act. He is clever, intelligent, and devoted; he would probably have found some means of ensnaring this Lelli and making him confess his crime. Thou seest now how the situation has changed. Thy deadly enemy suspects thy presence. He will make it known and bring about thy ruin, which is more certain this time because the law has a double account to settle with thee, that of thy imputed crime in the first place, that of thy escape in the second."

"Oh, I confess I was wrong," said Alonso Cano; "I ask thy pardon, Rafaël, for having exposed thee through my fault to anxieties which I might well have spared thee. But if thou couldst know what it was for a miserable outlaw like me to feel that he still lived amongst men, to behold that enthusiastic multitude whose outbursts of admiration for art followed upon their manifestations of faith. Whilst I heard them applaud my work I forgot that I was exiled, outlawed, that the sword of justice was hanging over me, and that if I did not succeed in making known the real criminal it must inevitably fall upon me. I forgot everything but that I had once lived proud and happy amongst the privileged of fate; an echo from the past came to me across the bygone years and the cruel sufferings endured."

"I understand all that," said the *regidor*, pressing his friend's hand affectionately, "I do not blame thee, but hatred is ingenious and persevering. Lelli will not fail to discover thy hiding-place."

"Thou wilt be compromised," cried Cano.

"Oh, think not of that," said the *regidor*. "I have a right to be less suspicious than Rosalés, and I am merely exercising this right."

"As a man thou art free to exercise it," said Alonso; but as a magistrate—"

"Well," said Sanguineto quietly, "I shall lose my place, that is all."

"I shall not expose thee to that," replied Alonso.

"I always accept the responsibility of my acts, and the obligations of friendship," said Sanguineto.

"I know," said Alonso. "thou art most generous."

Turning to Miguel he added:

"I will go."

The young man sadly averted his head.

"I deem it indispensable for thy safety," he went on.

"Whither wilt thou go?" said Sanguinto.

"I shall return to the asylum which I should never have quitted."

"To *Porta Cæli!*"

"Yes, and this time I will pronounce my vows."

"And I," cried Miguel, "will remain in Madrid to carry on thy work, master."

"My boy," said Alonso, "once I have taken the vow of humility believe that I shall not disturb myself farther about the opinions of men."

Sanguineto made a violent effort to control his emotion but without success. He threw himself into Alonso's arms and wept.

"Señor Rafaël," said Miguel, "I shall begin the preparations for departure at once. A carriage will be here at nightfall. I myself shall accompany and protect my master."

Alonso, paler than ever, turned towards the young man. He took one of Miguel's hands and one of Sanguineto's; his troubled look passed from one to the other; some struggle was going on within him. He seemed afraid to speak, and yet some secret emotion was burdening his heart. At length he said, addressing these two friends, upon whom he knew he could depend to the last hour of his life:

"I said that I would go, and I will!"

"When?" asked Miguel.

"This very night," said Alonso.

"Thou art more courageous than I had dared to hope," said Sanguineto.

"I go, but on one condition."

"What is that ?" asked Miguel.

"Condition is not the proper word, dear boy," said Alonso, "for what condition could I put to thy devotion ? I should have said that I have but one wish remaining, a wish that is so ardent and intense that it consumes my very heart, and the accomplishment of which, far from increasing my sorrow, would, I am sure, mitigate it."

"Speak! speak!" cried the *regidor*.

"Well!" said Alonso, in a voice broken by emotion, "I would see once more the house wherein I dwelt in Madrid."

"That fatal house!" cried Miguel, with horror.

"Yes!" replied Alonso, "I want to return thither, if it be but for an hour, hoping, perchance, to seize the shadow of happiness forever lost. Ye cannot comprehend this unconquerable attraction towards a place where at first all seemed to smile upon me, and where I afterwards endured the most terrible suffering that the heart of man can conceive. Since I left that truly fatal house the longing has never left me to revisit it. I want to see the studio, peopled with my works; the living tokens of a fame, stained with dishonor; the *salons*, the *patio*, where my private life was spent; the room wherein I saw Mercedes wounded, dead."

"Master, I implore thee," said Miguel, "renounce this desire, the gratification of which may have terrible consequences; let us depart at once, without hesitation, without even pausing to look backwards."

"No," said Alonso, "I have not the courage. Even if Lelli suspects my presence in Madrid, he has doubts of which I must reap the benefit. He will use every endeavor, I admit, but before he has arrived at any result I shall have fled forever. Admitting even that they suspected Sanguineto of remaining my friend, who would

dare to search fo. Alonso Cano in the house of the *regidor ?*
It would be the last in Madrid that they would enter.
Lelli did not recognize me in my penitent's dress; we
have escaped most happily; as far as he is concerned we
have nothing to fear for the present."

" Yet I do fear!" said Miguel.

"I still have the key of the house," Alonso replied,
" and will steal in there to-night like a thief, seek the
cherished memories of other times, and when I have wept
over the ruins of my happiness, I will return to the path
of exile."

" I will not permit such imprudence," said Sanguineto.

"If thou dost refuse me this," said Alonso, "I will
abandon all idea of flight, quit thy house so as not to
compromise thee, conceal myself in the most wretched
posada of Madrid, and remain there till I am dragged
thence by the law.   But whilst I retain my liberty I will
go each night to that fatal house, that it may be the
witness of my last hours."

Sanguineto and Miguel looked at each other, and the
regidor asked in a trembling voice:

" Thou wilt do what thou hast just said ?"

." Yes!" answered Alonso.

" May Heaven forbid!" added Sanguineto.

" Ay, and help me, despite what thou callest my
folly."

" Yes," replied the *regidor*.

" Miguel," said Alonso, " procure me a carriage; when
all is ready wait for me in it, within ten paces of my
house."

" I promise!" said the young man.

" Thou wilt find gold and weapons of defence in the
carriage," said the *regidor*.

" To thank thee would be but to humiliate thee, Rafaël," said Alonso; "what thou dost for me I would have done for thee."

Miguel took his cloak.

" I will go to secure a post-chaise," said he, " ten paces from thy house, at ten o'clock!"

" It will be needless to apprise me," said Alonso. " I will keep watch!"

Miguel then went out. He did not perceive that a man was shadowing him, and following his every movement with the greatest persistency. When he reached the inn-court, where he was to procure horses, the spy concealed himself against the wall, while Miguel entering made his arrangements, paying generously without bargaining.

" Be tranquil, Señor," said the master of the *posada*, " punctuality is but the least of my virtues. At a quarter to ten the carriage will be ready for thee; it is thine as well as the horses, since thou hast so liberally paid for them like a noble *caballero*."

Miguel departed much relieved in mind.

Scarcely was he gone when the spy came out from his hiding-place.

" Torre," said he to the innkeeper, " knowest thou this sign ?"

" Too well!" said Torre, with signs of evident perturbation.

" Thou wilt obey without reserve ?"

" Without any reserve, *Sancta Virgen*."

" Another carriage at the hour agreed upon, only five minutes in advance."

" Yes," replied Torre, trembling more and more. " But my conscience may be easy as to the price received for this carriage ?"

" Thou mayest keep it as payment for the service thou
wilt render to a good cause."

" I will keep it!" said Torre with a sigh of relief.

Miguel, somewhat reassured by the success with which
he had met, returned to Sanguineto's house.   The *regidor*
and his friend were having a last interview, in which the
latter· made a sort of moral testament, bequeathing to
him the better part of his soul.

" I have undergone my last trial," said he.   " I made an
effort to resume my place in the world, and the first man
who arose before me was an enemy.   Yonder, in the
quiet of the Carthusian monastery, I sometimes felt a
lurking regret for lost joys.   When I saw Miguel my
whole heart went out to him; Miguel was just then the
embodiment of a glorious past, art, the adulation of my
kind, the friendship of the King.   That noble youth, who
has pledged his life to clear his master from suspicion,
personified both past and future.   Heaven, no doubt,
willed that I should try my vocation in a more certain
manner, before permitting me to make my vows.   I
yielded to the temptation of winning back a portion of
what I had lost, and I came.   I return to the monastery
voluntarily, Sanguineto, to leave it no more.   Thou shalt
keep, in memory of me, the picture exposed upon the
cathedral steps to-day, and which I believe to be not unworthy of what was called my genius."

Alonso ceased speaking; the *regidor*, overcome by
emotion, could only press the hand of his friend.

Night came on rapidly.   The artist folded Sanguineto
in a close embrace.

" I shall never see thee again," said he; " but my most
fervent and heartfelt blessings be upon thee!"   With that
they separated.   Alonso soon found himself alone in the
streets of Madrid.

All day long they had presented a scene of tumult and animation; now they seemed unnaturally still. The dwellings and hostelries were filled to overflowing. The evening meal was unusually prolonged. The fatigue of the dáy seemed to increase the appetite. There was a careless and unrestrained gayety, an expansiveness and general atmosphere of good cheer, which are almost un-known elsewhere.

Absorbed in his thoughts Alonso proceeded towards his former dwelling. No one had crossed its threshold since the day when Mercedes had been borne thence upon her bier to her grave in the cemetery, and the artist had been taken to prison, under Rosalés' guard-ianship.

Alonso's key turned readily in the lock. He entered, closed the door softly, as if he feared to break in upon the stillness, and hastily lighting one of the waxen ta-pers which remained in the bronze candelabra of the vestibule, looked by its flickering light at the objects which surrounded him.

The statues in the studio seemed like so many ghosts; the grand *retablo* still resembled a chapel peopled with angels and saints. The great gilt frames, tarnished and obscured by dust, made dimly luminous spots amongst the shadows falling from above. This apartment, which had been as brilliant as the hall of a palace, was now as mournful as a grave. Upon the easel stood the unfin-ished portrait of Philip IV. In a single day the artist had fallen from the summit of his grandeur to an abyss of misery. Alonso turned away his eyes from this can-vas with its so real sketch, and remained long absorbed in a painful reverie.

"Ah, nothingness of human glory," he cried out "must we spend our lives in striving to realize the promises with which thou dost lure us on, and which thou leavest ever unfulfilled?"

He left the studio and slowly went up the stairs. As he ascended his step grew heavier and his head bent lower and lower.

The first apartment through which he passed was a dining-room, decorated with superb carvings in wood and panels of those marvellous *faïences* with which the Moors decorated Spain, without, however, revealing the secret of their brilliant colors and the formation of their enamels.

How often had friends met around that hospitable table! How many times they had drunk Cano's health and happiness, or greeted his latest artistic triumph! Mercedes' place was still indicated by her high chair covered with Cordova leather. Seated at that table Alonso was wont, when the fatigues of his long, laborious day were over, to tell his wife of visits received and of new commissions for pictures, to impart to her some fresh success, and to place at her disposal sums of money which, though perhaps extravagant for his means, proved his indulgence towards his young and childish wife. Upon the side-table, laden with massive silverware, was a special cup which Mercedes always used, and a costly flagon which she herself had filled with rose-water. He quickly averted his head and passed into the next room.

It was that in which he had sat with Mercedes for the last time. The guitar she had then used still lay upon a little ebony table, inlaid with ivory. Its ribbon trailed upon the carpet. A little bouquet of flowers Mercedes had worn lay in dust upon the table.

Mercedes' sleeping-room was still farther on. Alonso paused upon the threshold. He drew aside the draperies, and before going in placed the wax-light which he held in a candlestick. Owing to the confusion which had accompanied the tragic events there were still traces of disorder in the room. The empty jewel-cases were still open upon the dressing-table. The ivory crucifix placed at the foot of the bed remained to remind him of the last prayers which had been said there. A robe of *lampas*,* thrown upon a chair, touched the ground and, falling in heavy folds, had something the effect of a kneeling figure. The bed, covered with its counterpane of silk, was as mournful as a catafalque. Alonso threw himself into an arm-chair facing it, and abandoned himself to all the bitterness of retrospection. He brought vividly before his mind Mercedes, as he had seen her for the last time, pale with the awful pallor of death, and covered with wounds. He closed his eyes and, lost in sorrowful meditation, reflected upon the transitoriness of human love, as he had before pondered upon the bitterness of human friendship and fortune.

He was right when he told Rafaël Sanguineto that in that deserted house, where he had known so many joys, he would bid a final *adieu* to the world which had deceived, wounded, and crushed him. He experienced the terrible sensation of a man who, going down alive into a tomb, undergoes all the various transformations of death. As a man, he was to leave there the last remnants of earthly passion; as a Christian, he was to go thence with a soul completely regenerated. The hours and moments flew by; the hapless artist, absorbed in his dreams, his prayer, and his sorrow, scarcely perceived their rapid flight. The bell of the neighboring convent, which was wont to regulate the hours of labor for the pupils of the studio, rang out upon the night with a dis-

* A heavy stuff.

tinctness which seemed ominous to Alonso. Having counted its strokes, he rose.

"Farewell to life," he said. "Farewell to the world. I now return to *Porta Cæli.*"

He pressed his pale lips to the crucifix and took the candle, in order to make his way from the room and downstairs. But the candle, which was almost entirely consumed, gave forth a wavering, uncertain light, flickered, leaped up, and suddenly went out.

The artist groped his way to the stairs, went slowly down, opened the door, and looked out into the street. It was almost completely deserted. At a few paces from the house stood a carriage.

"Miguel is punctual," thought the painter.

He approached it, opened the door, and entered. Scarcely was he seated when he felt his hand pressed with extraordinary fervor, a whistle was given as a signal to the driver, and the carriage set off at full gallop. Almost at the same moment a second carriage took the place of the first, within a few paces of the artist's house, and a man who seemed young walked up and down, keeping watch, and giving frequent signs of impatience, in front of the dwelling which had returned to its former darkness and silence. The carriage in which Alonso sat drove through the streets with reckless haste. Streets and squares succeeded each other; but the artist could not obtain a single word from his companion, who sat mute and motionless in the corner of the carriage.

A vague mistrust crossed the painter's mind.

"A word," said he, "a word for pity's sake, Miguel."

There was no answer.

The artist leaned out of the window, and by the light of a lamp burning before an image of Mary he fancied he saw a huge, dark building arise before him like a terrible phantom.

His fears had not time to shape themselves. The carriage stopped, but no one came to open the door when the artist would have alighted. The great gate leading to the edifice rolled upon its hinges, and the carriage passed on to the inner court.

"Betrayed!" cried Alonso, in a voice of utter desolation, "betrayed!"

Both doors of the carriage were now flung open, the courtyard was suddenly lit up, and a rough voice cried out:

"Alight!"

Alonso leaped to the ground. Then, looking round him with mingled fear and horror, he exclaimed:

"The prison!   The prison!"

Rosalés had taken his revenge.

CHAPTER XVII.

TORTURE.

THE cell was one of the darkest in the prison of Madrid; neither light nor air could penetrate it; it was not only a dungeon, but a black hole, a foul pit. A full-grown man could neither stand nor lie down in it. Its unfortunate inmate was obliged to remain crouched together, deprived at once of all movement, and of even a breath of air. No sound could reach this den. Hollowed out at the extremity of a species of funnel, it was isolated from all the other cells. It was, as it were, the lowest pit of a human hell. When the jailer opened the door, once a day, he could at first distinguish nothing in the profound darkness. The reflection of his lantern at length penetrated the corner of the cell, where he could vaguely discern a human form chained motionless to the damp floor.

The prisoner, who in the first days of his arrest had begged permission to hold some communication with his judges, understanding at length the uselessness of his entreaties, had ceased speaking entirely; he never by a word broke the silence enjoined by the rule, and might have feared himself that he had lost the power of speech, were it not that, whenever he found himself alone, he broke forth into lamentations, or recited fervent prayers.

God alone knew the full extent of his trial, and the depth of his despair. God surely used this sorrow as a means of sanctifying his soul. The jailer, at first surprised at the captive's docility, began to wonder whether this apparent resignation did not conceal some deadly resolve.

Lest he might put an end to his misfortunes by suicide, they had fettered his hands and feet. A ring encircling both his hands was affixed to an iron belt. His ankles, encircled after the same fashion, supported heavy chains, fastened to a hook in the belt.

When the feeble glimmer of light from Piquillo the jailer's lantern fell upon the face of the prisoner, the beholder was filled with a painful emotion at sight of that grand and noble forehead, the seat of a lofty intellect, lined by suffering, and prematurely furrowed by deep wrinkles. In every line of that countenance was suffering tempered by resignation.

He had prayed and suffered in this cell for four months, when one day he heard an unusual noise, as of footsteps descending the stairs to his cell. He knew it was some one for him, as those stairs led nowhere else. Then, full of lofty courage, he summoned to his aid that dignity which had been saved by faith from the universal shipwreck; he raised himself upon the handful of straw which served him at once for a seat and a bed, and waited.

It was not one person but several persons who had come to visit him in the cell. The clanking of swords and the subdued murmur of voices resounded through the vaulted arches. The captive had to collect all the energy of his soul to sustain a combat which became every day more difficult and desperate.

The grated door opened. The light of three lanterns cast their red glare into the cell; half a score of soldiers ranged themselves without, facing the prisoner, and two men in black entered. One was Rosalés, the other an assessor to take down the prisoner's deposition.

When he beheld the judge, whom he had too much cause to regard as his persecutor, Alonso's eyes flashed fire; he made an effort, as if to release his hands from the fetters, but, feeling the uselessness of all demonstration, waited in silence the communication which the magistrate might have to make.

"Alonso Cano," said Rosalés, "hast thou yet resolved to make the confession which justice has vainly demanded of thee for four months past?"

"I can only renew my protestations of innocence," replied the artist, with an energy which could scarcely have been expected from his wasted frame.

"What will this criminal stubbornness avail thee?" demanded Rosalés. "Everything condemns thee, from the circumstances preceding the murder of thy wife Mercedes, to thy flight."

"I did not flee from justice, but sought to escape from those who would have been my murderers," said Alonso.

Rosalés resumed, without appearing to notice this remark:

"By a fatal law, the source of which must be sought no doubt in remorse, every criminal comes back to the scene of his crime. A strange but inevitable attraction draws him there where he shed blood. It would seem that avenging angels force him thus to the theatre of the murder, that the Lord may avenge the victim. The history of almost all murderers proves the truth of this theory. The workings of remorse are not only within the criminal's soul, but show themselves besides in exterior actions. He is compelled to take nature as a witness of his crime, or he avows it to irrational beings, or, as in thy case, he seeks to retrace the bloody footsteps of the tragedy whereof he was the hero."

"I am innocent!" repeated Cano, mildly.

"If thou wert innocent, wouldst thou have fled from the tribunal of justice ?"

" I left it to Providence to unmask the real criminal."

" Such was the agitation occasioned by remorse that, lest thou mightest have to blush before a worthy friend and confidant, thou didst choose at Valencia Milagro, who was likewise accused of having murdered his wife."

" It was chance alone which made me an inmate of his house," said Alonso. "When, in a moment of painful excitement, he told me of the terrible suspicion which had blighted his life, I felt that I had no right to cast him off since I too had sustained a similar misfortune. I knew not but that Milagro might have been falsely accused, as I was myself."

"Wherefore didst thou leave Valencia ?" pursued Rosalés; " hitherto thou hast assigned no reason."

" I could at need part with my liberty, but not with the pursuit of my art. Besides, I had to live, and my brush and chisel enabled me to obtain a livelihood. My name was discovered by what they call my genius; a too zealous judge, eager for his own advancement, at once ambitious and hypocritical, would have preyed upon me with the fury of a wild beast, and I fled."

"Whither didst thou then retire ?"

" To the Carthusian monastery of *Porta Cæli !*"

" Thou wert in safety there," said Rosalés, " thy talent no doubt endeared thee to the monks. What motive led thee to return to Madrid ?"

" The urgent one of seeking to trace—"

" Who ?"

" The murderer of Mercedes."

" Thou dost then persist in accusing Lello Lelli ?"

" I do."

"What interest could he have in committing such a crime ?"

"A double interest: he wanted to obtain possession of my wife's diamonds, which were renowned, and to revenge himself upon me."

"So much blood for so trifling a cause ?"

"Lelli is an Italian."

"If anything could aggravate the gravity of thy situation," said Rosalés, "it is the animosity with which thou dost accuse a young man whose only offence was that of drawing a sword in thy studio. We must in truth add, of course, that it touched thee deeply, recalling the death of the hapless Sebastian Llano y Valdez."

At this recollection Cano trembled in every limb.

"That was indeed murder," said he.

"Thou saidst thou wert seeking to prove Lelli's guilt," said Rosalés. "How could that be when thou didst never leave Sanguineto's house ?"

"Miguel was seeking for me."

"Miguel has been arrested !" said Rosalés.

"Arrested ?" cried Alonso, "he, the noblest and most generous of men !"

"Arrested on suspicion of having a second time plotted thy escape," said Rosalés.

"My noble and hapless Miguel," cried Alonso.

After a moment of painful thought, he asked:

"And my friend Rafaël ?"

"The *regidor* is also in prison !"

"I am fatal to all who love me," cried Alonso.

"There is but one means of setting them both at liberty," said Rosalés.

"What is that? Oh, tell me, tell me."

"Confessing thy crime," said Rosalés.

"I told thee I was innocent !" cried Alonso.

"All criminals protest the same," said Rosales; "if thou wert innocent thou wouldst prove it by accounting for thy absence on the night of the 14th of June."

"I cannot as yet."

"Is there then a certain fixed period at which this revelation may be made ?"

"There is !" replied Alonso.

"What is it ?" asked Rosalés.

"The hour which sees the downfall of my benefactor

"The Count d'Olivarez ?"

"Yes, my lord judge, but my gratitude towards him is both deep and sincere. I cannot wish that that hour should approach."

"Hearken to me," said Rosalés; "for the past four months thou hast undergone examination after examination, and thou hast never yet contradicted thyself nor varied in thy tissue of well-concocted falsehood. Thou art suffering here, no doubt, from these fetters upon thy hands and feet, the dampness of this cell, and thy insufficient food, but thou still hast hope that thou mayest be forgotten."

"Not so, Rosalés," said Alonso; "the other judges might forget, but I know thou wilt always remember."

A sudden flush overspread Rosalés' sallow countenance.

"The clemency of the King, supported by the protector whose name thou didst this moment mention, has hitherto protected thee. But the Count d'Olivarez can in future protect no one. Convicted of secret negotiations with the house of Braganza, of having amassed a fortune at the expense of the people, and betrayed the master who had treated him as a friend, he has fled from Spain to escape the final punishment."

"Can this be true ?" cried Alonso.

"So thou art free to speak," said Rosalés.

"I do not believe thee," said Alonso.

"To-morrow thou wilt have proof of what I say."

"Then I will speak!" said Alonso. "I will say that, urged by a most solemn obligation, I spent that terrible night in a wretched house in Madrid, with two young creatures whom I felt in conscience bound to assist and to save."

"Their names?" said Rosalés.

"Thou dost forget, Señor, that I have no proof of the disgrace of the Count d'Olivarez, Marquis di San Lucar."

He added with touching sadness:

"And even when I have told thee all, thou wilt refuse to believe it."

"Thou canst, no doubt, support thy statements by evidence?"

"Nay, I have no proofs."

"Thou deemest the law harsh and cruel," said Rosalés, "but hearken to the advice I give thee, Alonso Cano; confess thy crime, and the clemency of the King will mitigate the severity of thy sentence as far as possible. Nay, he may even grant thee an absolute pardon. But remember that I now offer thee a final chance; if thou dost now refuse to confess, if the assessor appointed to take thy deposition does not record a complete and formal avowal of thy crime, thou wilt be questioned no longer by men."

"By whom, then?" asked Alonso.

"By instruments of torture."

Alonso groaned. He had long dreaded this terrible announcement. He dreaded it, for however brave one may be, he shrinks affrighted from red-hot irons, bloody pincers, the rack and thumb-screws. There are instinctive terrors which affright the body. The muscles quiver, the nerves are strained, and imagination shows all the coming tortures which are already felt by anticipation.

" Thou didst never dream that such an hour would come for thee, Alonso Cano," hissed Rosalés.

" On the contrary, I was prepared for it," said Alonso in a firm and courageous voice; " for four months past my existence here has been one long torture; thou art going to add a more excruciating one. I only ask of our Lord the grace to endure it patiently, for love of Him."

Rosalés was right when he said that Olivarez had hitherto used all his influence with the King to protect Alonso, despite the eager demands of the judges, who were anxious to finish what threatened to be an interminable case. Philip, who had refused to believe Herrera capable of counterfeiting when he marked the perfection of a ·picture just completed by him, could not believe that Alonso Cano had murdered his wife when he saw his marvellous Madonna exposed upon the cathedral steps. Such fervent inspiration, so peaceful a vision of Heaven as were there depicted, could never have been allied with the instincts of a murderer. The hand which had produced the figure of the " Dead Christ wept over by an angel," could never have grasped the dagger of an assassin. Alonso's genius remained his best defence. Hence, against all the demands of the judges, and the requisitions of the court, Philip IV. had been his indefatigable protector. Olivarez too had upheld his cause with the devotion of a brother. But when the minister, the favorite, whose government had discredited Philip with the people, was forever fallen in his sovereign's estimation; when he found the Marquis de San Lucar as ungrateful as he had been powerful, the King began to regard with equal disfavor all who had served the former favorite, or received kindness from him.

Rosalés, seizing what he thought a favorable moment to deprive Alonso of a life already so miserable, was no sooner informed of the downfall of Olivarez, than he hastened to the King to request an order empowering him to bring the trial to a close.

"Is it not finished yet?" asked the King.

"Nay, the Count d'Olivarez protected him, sire," said Rosalés.

The King frowned.

"Thou hast no positive proof against this artist?" he asked.

"None!"

"Acquit him then."

"There is a form to be gone through with."

"Go through with it then," said Philip briefly, "and let me hear no more of this matter."

"It shall be done according to your majesty's good pleasure," said Rosalés, "but it still requires one thing."

"What is that?"

"Thy signature."

The King cast his eyes over the document.

"Torture!" cried he, "torture!"

"It is the law!" said Rosalés coldly.

"Not that, ah, not that!" cried the King; "is there no other means?"

"They have all failed, sire!"

"Since then he denies it," said the King, in an agitated voice, "and proofs are wanting, set him free."

"And with him all the wretches who fill the dungeons of the prison, and like this Cano deny their guilt."

"Set free thieves and brigands?" cried the King.

"If your majesty would liberate murderers, why not?" said Rosalés.

"But it would be too horrible," said the King; "a man

whose hand I have touched in friendship, a great artist whose pictures decorate our churches, and whose statues are the crowning glory of Spanish art! I cannot and will not sign it."

Rosalés bowed with affected submission.

"May I then announce that your majesty has given orders for the release of all the prisoners?" said he.

"No, Rosalés, no. In truth this terrible responsibility weighs upon me. To be too indulgent towards criminals is as bad as being unrelenting towards the unfortunate. Let us remember that Don Pedro's title to glory was that he called himself the Executioner. Rosalés if thou canst not mitigate this law, of which I curse the severity, spare Alonso as much as possible. I will send my own confessor to him, and if he must, indeed, suffer that he may be led to confess his crime, I absolutely forbid thee, hearest thou, to touch his right hand, that hand which I have pressed, and which has created immortal works."

Philip covered his face with his hands, and groaned aloud. When he looked up Rosalés was gone, taking with him an order that Alonso should be put to the torture. The judge, who had thus his revenge in his hand, did not lose a single instant; he feared that the King might revoke the order, or that Gaspardo del Roca might make some effort to save the artist from the horrors that awaited him.

Did Rosalés believe him guilty? The secret remained between God and himself; but he was resolved in any case that, innocent or guilty, Alonso should come out of that ordeal mutilated in body or sullied in honor.

At this awful announcement which Rosalés made, with a coldness that but ill concealed a cruel joy, Alonso summoned to his aid the courage that is born of innocence. He rose from the ground, drew himself proudly up, and fixing his eyes upon Rosalés with an expression which made the latter quail, said:

"I am ready."

" Rosalés made a sign to the torch-bearers to proceed, and in another moment Alonso, accompanied by the jailer, passed up the staircase leading from his cell to other subterranean dungeons. As we have before hinted, Alonso's cell was in the very bowels of the earth, so that he could go up a hundred steps, at least, before reaching the ground level.

Two large rooms facing each other opened at the head of the second stairs. The jailer threw open the one upon the left, and the soldiers thrust Alonso in. No sooner had Rosalés and his assessor crossed the threshold than they were lost in a deep obscurity. At first Alonso could distinguish nothing. He only felt that he was in a large room. Accustomed as he had been for so long a time to the cramped existence of his cell, he knew at once, from the circulation of the air, that the room was large, high, and vaulted. The torches of the soldiers scarcely shed a flickering light therein; men clad in leather seized upon him, and the soldiers withdrew.

Alonso shuddered with horror.

The soldiers at least were men, but he was conscious that those who now surrounded him were executioners. He heard Rosalés' voice close by, and yet, even on turn-ing his head, could not distinguish him.

Soon a red glare was reflected upon the ground at the artist's feet, and he saw that the room was divided into two by a large black curtain. From behind this curtain came the red light. All at once the curtain was with-drawn, and Alonso had the feeling that one has on sud-denly beholding a conflagration.

At the end of the second half of the chamber of torture

Alonso saw a glowing furnace, beside which two men, fantastic in the red light, were busy heating pincers and bars of iron upon the live coals.

Close by a hideous, deformed being was filling casks of water, and two gigantic figures were arranging the thumb-screws and the rack.

The walls were hung with strange instruments, vague in form and terribly mysterious as to their use.

Seated at a table, upon which were two iron candle-sticks, Rosalés and the assessor preserved their ordinary impassibility. They gave Alonso time to observe all the ominous objects which filled this subterranean apart-ment. When the judge felt that Alonso was sufficiently impressed by his awful surroundings, he said to one of the men:

"Remove the prisoner's fetters."

Alonso sat down on a bench, while they successively removed his irons and wristlets. He stretched his pain-ful limbs, and, despite his courage, could not repress a shudder at the thought that in another moment iron, wood, and fire must combine to torture him.

"Alonso Cano," asked Rosalés, "hast thou reflected, and art thou now willing to confess the execrable crime for which thou must answer to God and man?"

"I am innocent!" said Alonso.

"An humble confession is a step towards repentance," resumed Rosalés. "Thy judges may be merciful; the King may pardon thee."

"I am innocent!" repeated Alonso.

"Then prepare to suffer a most painful ordeal in thy body."

"I accept it as a martyrdom. Jesus too was innocent when He was delivered into the hands of His execu-tioners."

Perceiving a great crucifix hanging upon the bare wall, he cried out with thrilling fervor:

"I appeal to Thee. I am no longer a man, but a worm, a wretch; soon to be made an object of pity and disgust. Here, at Thy feet, I disavow in advance whatsoever rash words torture may wring from me. I am innocent, but Thou knowest human weakness. If I come forth victorious from this trial, I vow to consecrate myself to Thee forever, to fly from a world which has deceived, betrayed, and tortured me, and to give myself to Thee in poverty and penitence."

Even the executioners silently permitted this solemn invocation.

The assessor went on writing, and Rosalés said to him:

"What art thou writing?"

"This prayer of Alonso Cano!"

"Efface it," said Rosalés; "it is my wish."

The judge then turned to the men who stood near the rack, saying:

"Do your work."

Alonso was seized and laid upon the rack, where there was a special torment for every limb. Each of his legs and his left arm were affixed to boards by solid pieces of leather. One of the executioners then seized a mallet and a wedge, and placing the wedge between the boards, drove it in with a single blow.

"Wilt thou confess?" said Rosalés.

"I am innocent," said Alonso; "my blood be upon thee."

"The second wedge," said the judge coldly.

The second wedge was thrust in and a groan was forced from Alonso's lips.

"My God!" he murmured, but that was all.

Rosalés trembled with rage.

"The third wedge," he said.

A physician approached and felt Alonso's pulse.

He was filled with the deepest pity for the sufferer, for he felt instinctively that the judge aimed rather at gratifying some private spite than at discovering the truth.

"The prisoner is very weak," he said.

"The sound of his voice has enough life in it that he may well endure a third trial," said Rosalés, "and have a care, doctor, that an excessive compassion for criminals may not cast suspicion upon thyself."

At a sign from Rosalés the executioner took the third wedge. Alonso lay with closed eyes. His limbs seemed disjointed, bruised, and broken; his heart was beating wildly; he thought it must leap out of his bosom.

When the third wedge was driven in it wrung a cry of agony from his blanched lips.

"Wilt thou confess?" cried Rosalés.

"God is my witness, I am innocent," said Alonso. "I beg of Him in His mercy to take me. This is not torture, but death."

"Wretched assassin!" cried Rosalés, "thou must confess thy crime."

And rising he called out to the men who stood beside the furnace:

"The pincers! the red-hot pincers!"

At that very moment a clamor was heard without on the stairs. The clanking of swords against the pavement was mingled with a confused murmur, above which could be heard an imperious voice shouting:

"An order from the King! An order from the King!"

And a younger voice crying:

"Alonso! Alonso my master!"

In this latter Alonso recognized that of Miguel.

Before Rosalés had recovered from his surprise, before the executioners had finished unbinding Alonso's limbs, Gaspardo del Roca and Miguel rushed into the torture-chamber.

"What would you?" cried Rosalés, turning deadly pale.

"We would snatch thy victim from thee, wretch. Dost know this seal and signature? The King—"

"Pardons him?" asked Rosalés.

"Nay, renders him justice," said Del Roca.

Meanwhile Miguel took his hapless master in his arms and laid him on a mattress.

"My master! my venerated master!" said he, kneeling beside him, "thou art saved! Spain will rise *en masse* to testify her admiration and regret. I have never doubted thine innocence; the King and court are now convinced of it."

"Who has worked this miracle?"

"The sister of Sebastian Llano y Valdez."

"She is in Madrid?"

"Since this morning. Seeking thee, inquiring thy whereabouts, she learned all. Then hastening to Señor del Roca she made known to him the plot formed by her husband and a number of other young nobles against the Count d'Olivarez, and with it all thy generosity and self-sacrifice. Gaspardo did not lose a moment in hastening to the King, who signed at once the order for thy release. Unhappily this man's hatred has got the start of us, against all law, all custom, all demands of justice. But thou shalt be avenged, master, and the disgrace of Rosalés—"

"Speak not of vengeance," said Alonso, "I have suf

fered so much that I have learned how to forgive. Should I die from the effects of this terrible ordeal it will be in peace, reconciled with men, and full of confidence in the mercy of God."

But Gaspardo del Roca had positive orders.

"In what cell was Alonso Cano confined?" he asked the jailer.

"In the lowest, my lord judge," said the jailer.

"The lowest, the smallest, the vilest, no doubt," said the judge.

"Those were my orders," said the jailer, pointing to Rosalés.

"Henceforth thou wilt obey mine," said Gaspardo. "Take this man, this dishonest judge, to the cell of Alonso Cano."

And before the martyr stretched upon the mattress had time to beg pardon for his persecutor the soldiers had dragged Rosalés from the torture-chamber.

CHAPTER XVIII.

The King's Present.

THE studio of Alonso Cano was once more open to the public. It had recovered its pristine grandeur and that air of sublimity which made it the most remarkable room in Madrid, and unsurpassed as an artistic centre save, perchance, by the gorgeous *salon* of Velasquez, which was in the King's own palace.

The affectionate zeal of his old servants had restored everything to its former order. The pictures were again displayed in the most favorable lights, and the rays of the sun came down once more through the glass over-head and gilded as of yore the countless works of art which filled the room.

To console Alonso for his sufferings by permitting him the more quickly to gaze upon the glorious works of his own hand, a bed had been arranged for him at one end of the studio. It was, in fact, rather a heap of silken cushions and soft warm rugs than a bed; a fine netting protected him during the night, and in the day draperies veiled the light from his wasted face.

No sooner had Gaspardo and the devoted Miguel, act-ing upon the King's orders, released Cano and cast Rosa-lés into the same dungeon to which he had consigned his victim, than a physician was brought to give every possible attention to Alonso. It was the same who had manifested such great compassion for Cano, and who would fain have mitigated the horrors of his torture. He

now did all that zeal and science united could do to heal
the cruel wounds in Cano's legs and arms.

The wounds were washed with aromatic spirits; the
wounded limbs were kept by splints in their normal position, while bandages prevented him from moving them.
Nature and time alone could fully restore them. The
bones had to reknit and the flesh to heal. There was no
reason to despair of ultimate recovery, and Vego, this
learned physician, promised Alonso that he would give
him back the use of his legs and his left arm.

After all this had been done Gaspardo and Miguel carried him in their arms to a room higher up in the prison,
till his own house should be rendered habitable, and he
himself gain needed rest before undergoing the fatigue
of removal.

A litter was prepared for that purpose. As the news
of these events had spread through the town every one
of any importance in Madrid came to ask for tidings of
the unfortunate. The whole city seemed to feel that it
owed some reparation to a man of genius who had been
so cruelly maltreated in body and tormented in mind.

Hence, when the great doors of the prison were thrown
open and the litter upon which Alonso was carried came
into view, cries of pity and enthusiasm arose from the
crowd. It was a perfect ovation to the hapless artist;
sobs mingled with wishes for a long and happy life; the
women snatched pinks and pomegranate blossoms from
their hair and threw them upon the litter. Miguel's devotion was fully applauded, and people cordially wished
the *garote* to Rosalés as a punishment for his hate.

Meanwhile Alonso, pale and motionless, his eyes alone
gleaming out from the corpse-like pallor of his face, experienced the only consolation which this world could
give him, that of being surrounded by all the honest

people of the capital, where, upon that day, he was more truly King than the King himself.

A group of Alonso's pupils followed their master. Conspicuous among them were Bartholomeo Roman and Pedro Castello, with all the others who had gloried in studying under Cano's direction.

Lello Lelli alone was absent, and it was whispered with disgust and horror that at that very time he was drinking in a low tavern, and prophesying that Alonso Cano could never survive the injuries he had received.

When the artist reached his own door every head was uncovered. The bell of the neighboring convent rang out with a joyful sound, and it seemed to the people that its brazen tongue invited them to pray for him who had so nearly lost his life at the hands of the executioners.

All hearts and minds joined in one fervent prayer to Heaven, and during this brief instant of devout recollection Alonso Cano was borne across the threshold of his dwelling.

Miguel had taken charge of everything. Juana, Mercedes' old nurse, had returned to the house of mourning, and received her master kneeling. Alonso was soon laid upon the bed in the studio. The angelic patience with which he endured months of suffering provoked general admiration. He spent whole hours conversing with priests and monks. Amongst others, one day, the Abbot of *Porta Cæli* was announced.

"I knew I should see thee again," said Alonso.

His visit seemed to leave Alonso calmer and happier than he had been yet.

Every day Alonso received his friends. Velasquez was one of the most assiduous, and his beautiful wife, the daughter of the venerable Pacheco, always accompanied her husband. Seeing her so full of life and happiness, so proud of her beauty and her costumes, Alonso remembered his poor Mercedes, who had so envied the brocade robes and jewelled necklaces that bedecked the wife of the King's favorite.

Philip himself sent every day for news of the artist, but he never came during all the time of Alonso's convalescence. Perchance his sorrow and regret were too great to allow him to see Alonso upon his bed of pain. But as soon as the painter was up and able to use his brush the King sent to ask him to continue the portrait begun on the ill-omened day of Mercedes' murder. Alonso replied gently:

" Tell the King I am at his orders."

Just as before, when the royal carriage stopped at Alonso's door, the pupils ranged themselves in the vestibule. Leaning upon Miguel's arm, Alonso Cano slowly advanced to meet his royal master. At sight of him the King could not conceal his deep emotion.

He scarcely recognized in that pale, emaciated spectre the man whom he had known in all the fire of youth and enthusiasm, robust in body, powerful in mind, greeting hope with smiles, and finding in the applause of men a solace for secret sorrow.

Alonso advanced, and, with the same respect as of yore, bowed and made a feeble effort to bend the knee. The effort was a failure and wrung from him a cry of pain. The King turned paler even than the artist. He seemed to be preserving his composure only by a mighty effort. He had come with the intention of ignoring the past. He feared to awaken painful memories in the bosom of Alonso, and to do him an injury perhaps by the effect of such retrospection upon an organization so enfeebled.

Philip approached the portrait, which still remained

sketched upon the easel, in the same position where
Alonso had placed it four years before.

"Art thou strong enough to complete this work?" said
the King.

The artist smiled with a sadness in which there was a
touch of gentle irony.

"My right hand," he said, "has never lost its power.
I have been only six months idle."

The sitting was long. Philip made every possible effort to banish the sadness from Alonso's face. He constantly referred to the future, which he pictured to the
artist more glorious than his wildest dream had ever
imaged it. In every word a promise lay concealed. It
was plain that his sovereign was anxious to repair Alonso's wrongs, and to console him in his sorrows. The latter scarcely seemed to understand the counsels of the
King or to hear his flattering encouragement. It would
seem that his soul had passed into a calmer sphere than
this, and that he no longer deigned to bring it down from
celestial heights to mingle with those who still suffered
or still enthusiastically rejoiced at perishable goods and
fleeting happiness.

There was not only a wonderful calm upon Alonso's
face, but a species of interior joy that illumined it with
its tranquil reflection.

Philip IV. regarded the artist with astonishment. He
had expected to find a man wearing his sorrow like a
mantle, and awaiting, as it were, the apologies of his
sovereign. On the contrary, he met with a being simple
and gentle, far more humble than of old, and whose
countenance was marked with the peace of those for
whom earth is but a ladder to Heaven.

On the other hand, Alonso had lost nothing of his artistic power; a melancholy grace added an indefinable

charm to all he did. Unconsciously he changed the character of his prince's face. Certain shadows softened it, and it bore the prophetic sadness of future sorrows. And when the King expressed his astonishment at the progress made by Alonso in a single sitting the artist calmly replied:

"Of yore, sire, I painted with my mind; now I paint with my soul."

At nightfall Philip rose to go. He said to the artist:

"Hast thou nothing to ask of me?"

"Many things," said Alonso, "since thou dost permit me to speak."

"Not only I permit thee, but I promise beforehand."

"Then thou wilt sign Rosalés' pardon?"

"A wretch who pursued thee with his hatred!"

"He believed himself acting in the interests of justice."

"Undeceive thyself. Gaspardo del Roca told me all," said the King. "Rosalés had been a suitor for Doña Mercedes; he hated thee as his successful rival."

"Then God grant him mercy, as fully as I pardon him," said Alonso.

"Thou dost still make this request?"

"I desire it more ardently than ever," said Alonso.

"Thy virtue is too great," said the King.

"Your majesty will deign to admit that it is strictly in accordance with the law?"

"Be it so then," said the King. "Rosalés is free!"

"I thank your majesty most humbly."

"Is that all?"

"Miguel did more for me than if he were my own son," said Alonso· "deign then to grant him a share in thy royal favor, and give him an opportunity to display his talent.

"He shall decorate a hall of the palace."

"Your majesty overpowers me."

"And yet I can see that thou art not yet satisfied?"

"I admit it."

"What more can I do for thee?"

"Your majesty knows my history, and under what circumstances I quitted Granada—"

"Alonso, I implore thee, do not dwell upon these memories."

"On the contrary, I owe it to myself and others to keep them ever present to my mind. When Sebastian Llano y Valdez fell beneath my sword his sister was left doubly orphaned. She since wedded a brave young lord, who, out of an extravagant care for the welfare of Spain and a passionate devotion to his King, became involved in a conspiracy against the Count d'Olivarez."

"Speak not of him," cried Philip, in a tone of severity.

"Yet I remember and must continue to remember him," said Alonso firmly. "To him, who has ruined himself by ambition, I owe the honor of having been presented to your majesty. I know nothing of the Marquis di San Lucar but his misfortune, and I still have my debt of gratitude towards him. The husband of Inez Llano hated the favorite, and conspired for his downfall. He lost, in the service of his royal master, his modest fortune and his peace of mind."

"Wouldst thou for him a place in my household?"

"Ah, sire!"

"It is given. To-morrow he may appear at the palace."

Alonso bowed respectfully.

"And thou?" said the King.

"I have need of nothing!"

"Is that resentment?" asked the King.

" It is discretion!"

" Let me then anticipate thy wishes."

" They are so moderate, sire, thou couldst never guess them."

" I will try," said Philip graciously.

He extended his hand, which Alonso kissed, and turning upon the threshold, said:

" Till to-morrow !"

Philip came every day for a week to the studio. The portrait was finished. Never had artist completed a finer piece of work. He rejoiced, but took not the slightest pride in it. He seemed every day to grow more detached from the things of earth; however, he thanked the King warmly when he heard that Rosalés was released, and that Inez was happy with her husband, to whom the King had vouchsafed his special protection. It was evident that Alonso was guarding some secret. His resolution was, indeed, taken—a resolution born of solitude and silence. All his leisure time was spent in the practice of good works, or in visiting convents or miraculous shrines.

Every one whom he met in the streets saluted him with the deepest respect. Many regarded him as a saint, and saw around his head the aureola of much sorrow heroically endured.

The wretched dwellings of the unfortunate knew him far better than the palaces of the great. His name, mentioned with enthusiasm by the one, was humbly and devoutly blessed by the other.

The portrait of the King only wanted a few of those touches which give the final charm and perfection to a picture. Cano knew that the King was to sit for the last time in his studio. He felt more than an artist's joy at the completion of the work; his heart was relieved of a great weight. It was like the breaking of a chain which left him wholly free.

On the morning of the day upon which the King's portrait was to be finished the Abbot of *Porta Cæli* paid Alonso a long visit.

"I beg of thee," said Alonso, eagerly, "to grant me my request, and at once."

"We will talk of that later," said the monk.

Then, leaving Alonso's room, he went down with him to the studio.

Soon after the King arrived. The monk saluted him humbly, and would have retired.

"Remain, good father, remain," cried Philip gently. "I who am Cano's friend can understand how dear he is to thee."

During the sitting the King took pleasure in hearing Father Eusebio talk of Alonso's stay at *Porta Cæli*. The monk was loud in his praises of the wonderful statue of St. Francis of Assisium, which he declared was a masterpiece of carving in wood.

"I will go thither to see it, as we go upon pilgrimages," said the King, "and meantime I will send thee a lamp of gold for the sanctuary."

Shortly after Alonso laid down his brush and palette upon the table and said:

"Sire, the artist has done his utmost."

"It is another masterpiece, Alonso," cried the King. "It remains to pay thee for it."

"Ah, sire," said Alonso.

"Alonso Cano, Count di Porta Cœli," said the King.

"That title—" cried the painter.

"Is henceforth thine," said the King.

Then taking a golden order from his neck the King said:

"Accept it for my sake."

Alonso took it trembling; but did not fasten it to his doublet.

The King advanced and said:

"Put on thy hat, Count di Porta Cœli; thou art a grandee of Spain."

And the King handed Alonso documents to which were affixed the royal seal. The courtiers and great nobles, whom the King had invited to be present that day, now filled the studio. They looked at each other in amazement. Never had they seen an instance of a favor at once so sudden and complete. The unmerited sufferings of the artist justified all that the King had done for him, and several of the nobles advanced to congratulate Alonso.

But before they could reach him the Abbot Eusebio came out of the shadow into which he had retired. He advanced slowly to Alonso Cano, and presented him with divers objects.

"Here," said he, "are the scapular worn by the sons of St. Bruno, their wooden rosary, and the cord which encircles their waist."

"Father!" cried Alonso, "father!"

Upon either side of the table were the monk and the King. The patent of nobility and the golden collar of its proudest order were side by side with the scapular and girdle of the monk. The artist never hesitated. He gently pushed aside the King's present, and with pious respect raised the livery of the Sons of St. Bruno to his lips.

"What wouldst thou do?" asked Philip.

"Bid farewell to the world, sire."

"Thou, my painter, my _protégé_, my friend?"

"I am now but the friend of God, sire."

"Ah, thou hast not pardoned me!" cried Philip.

"That would be indeed unworthy of a Christian, much less of a religious," said Alonso. "Do thou pardon me, sire, that I must refuse favors the full value of which I comprehend. My gratitude will only end with my life; from the depth of the cloister wherein my remaining years will be spent, I shall constantly ask of God the ever-increasing prosperity of Spain and the happiness of my sovereign."

"But if thou shouldst regret one day, Alonso?"

"Ah, sire, what have I to regret? Thy favor? Thou wilt grant it to the poor monk, who will paint as long as strength and inspiration are given him. Believe not that this is a sudden impulse. For six months past I have waited to pronounce my vows; it is two years since I first asked for the holy habit. At the moment when I was being put to the torture I vowed to consecrate myself to the service of the Lord if I were saved from polluting my lips by a base falsehood."

Philip, deeply moved, took Alonso's hand.

"Thou wilt pray for me," he said.

After they had all gone Alonso brought Miguel into Mercedes' room.

"As thou hast henceforth obeyed me," he said, "swear that thou wilt now conform thyself to my desires."

"I swear, master," said Miguel.

"Then, my dear boy, thou must never leave this house, which is now thine."

"Mine, master!"

"I have no other heirs, and I wish to dispose of all my goods before making a vow of poverty. Thou wilt keep old Juana always in thy service. It is sweet to believe that nothing will be disturbed here. Sometimes thou wilt think of thy master, who sincerely loved thee. No word of thanks, my Miguel, we can never be quits. Come to these arms that I may embrace thee as a son, and bless thee in saying farewell forever."

"Farewell, but we must meet again."

"Yes, I was wrong, Miguel. It is rather, until we meet again in eternity."

CHAPTER XIX.

THE GAMBLERS.

THE dwelling of Señor Diego Fuentés y Marivedas y Fontanillos was nothing more nor less than a gambling house. He had, indeed, striven to adorn it with high-sounding names, and conceal it under a veil of honor, as a rogue hides a face known to the police under a carnival mask. A gambling house it remained to all intents and purposes; and when certain young men of Madrid, who had not only golden ducats but *maravédis* to spare, yet sought to increase their store by the chances of fortune, they always turned their thoughts towards the dwelling of Fuentés.

To each new-comer Fuentés related the story of his misfortunes. The cause thereof varied with each revolution. He always explained his penury, which was the child of vice and prodigality, by the pretence of a conspiracy in which he had been mixed up in his own despite; a desperate and persistent struggle against some man in power. Fuentés had chosen this special rôle, and perpetuated himself in the character of the victim of a political intrigue. The King remained on the throne, it is true, but he was too loyal a subject of the sovereign of the two Spains to dream of overthrowing him, so he always fell back upon favorites. The long-expected fall of Olivarez gave new scope to his imagination, and from the moment it occurred Fuentés declared to all who had patience to listen, that the ruin of the ambitious minister had cost him his fortune, and that his ducats had fallen into the gulf opened by the misfortunes of the former favorite.

Once Olivarez had left Spain Fuentés expatiated upon the many details of his respectful and devoted friendship for the minister. The latter had been his foster-brother, and Fuentés, who had followed him in his gradual ascent, had likewise fallen with him into the depths of the pit.

Most of the old *habitués* of the place knew what to think of these stories, but unsophisticated strangers were always deceived by them. Moreover, Fuentés was specially gifted by nature for the part he had assumed. There was a certain loftiness in the general expression of the face, a candor and openness in the smile, which more than counterbalanced the low forehead and unprepossessing chin.

Notwithstanding the complacency with which Fuentés lent his house for cards or other games of chance, he never made any money. His doublet gave hints of long service; his linen had often a yellowish tinge, which was made the subject of many a rude joke.

"Why," he would exclaim, "I possess seven hundred and thirty linen shirts, so that each one's turn comes but rarely. They grow yellow from want of use. It is an *embarras de richesse*, nothing else !"

Diego Fuentés had among his furniture an old chest for clothes, which was always easy to lift, and whose emptiness might have told many a tale of Diego's resources had it been gifted with speech.

But if his guests jeered at him, they had nevertheless an odd sort of friendship for him. He had certain qualities which helped to counterbalance his defects; his patience was marvellous, and his readiness to oblige proverbial. When he possessed anything, which was very seldom, indeed, he was always ready to share it with others. He would have made any sacrifice to serve a friend, and he dignified with this title all who frequented his house. He drank merrily of the wine provided by others, and always kept his wits about him, even when intoxicated.

Like all good Spaniards he played the guitar and castanets, and his thin, threadbare voice had a certain melody in it.

Fuentés threw open what he pompously called his drawing-rooms to all *hidalgoes* who honored him with their company. They indemnified him for fuel and lights in the winter evenings, and when the stakes were high often gave him an additional gratuity. His profits might have been considerable had he not played on his own account, for whatever money came into his hands he always lost, and was often obliged to have recourse to the generosity of some friend, or, at least, of one of his guests, who said to him so constantly, with that inimitable accent which would be Gascon were it not Spanish:

" *A la disposicion de usted.*" *

He borrowed, and always forgot to pay.

A large number of men usually assembled every evening at Fuentés' house. There were medical students, pupils of celebrated artists, and generally some strangers. The noise in the lower room opening upon the *patio* was something diabolical, and frequently the *alguazils* were obliged to call to order the knots of young men who surrounded the gaming-tables.

It sometimes happened that the games were interrupted in order to empty some flagons of old wine. This usually ended in an orgy, and if all the guests did

---

* At your service.

not reach home safely it was because they slept in the *patio*.

Upon his arrival at Madrid, in the train of Lo Spagno-letto, Lello Lelli, who had few acquaintances in the town, managed to gain admittance to Diego Fuentés'. He never failed to appear there in the evenings. His caustic wit often displeased the frequenters of the place, but he was free at treating to wine or sherbet, and seemed to have plenty of gold in his pouch, so he was tolerated.

Not that Lelli had grown rich; his pencil brought him in less money than ever; and if he earned some ducats at Naples by his trade of bully it was an utterly unprofitable one at Madrid. Ribera, intent upon the ruin of the young prince whose downfall he was seek-ing to compass, left Lelli free to dispose of his time as he liked. He went about all day, and spent every night in the dwelling of Fuentés.

He was always the first to arrive, told Diego all the news of the day, what the King had done, at what of-fices the Queen had assisted, what drama Calderon was engaged upon, and how the portable altars were to be decorated for the next religious procession.

As there were no newspapers in those days Lelli sup-plied their place. Politics, topics of the day, or literary matters, he discussed, if not with any degree of superi-ority, at least with that same ease which had once made the grave Alonso Cano himself take pleasure in his so-ciety. Having exhausted his bulletin, he usually chose his place at the table and carefully marked it.

Lelli had all the superstition of the ignorant Italians, and was full of almost childish terrors. Having decided upon his place, he took a chair and placed it at the table. Upon this chair he laid a horseshoe of pink coral, mounted in gold, to drive away all evil influences from him. This done he assisted Diego in arranging the various objects required for the games—cards, dice, chess, or markers—holding each in his hand for a time, as if this contact could impart a special virtue to them. The snares being thus laid, he stationed himself in the embrasure of a window, and awaited the game.

The supper was early in those days, for the police regulations obliged peasants and citizens to retire almost with the sun. The guard arrested all who were out in defiance of this rule. Hence the play commenced at a very seasonable hour in Fuentés' house. The rooms opening upon the *patio* were enabled to keep a light long after hours; and when it was too late to go home the gamblers threw themselves on the tables or on the floor and slept till morning.

Diego made much of Lelli. Through him new game was brought to the house every day. Lelli himself, as was evident, did not often lose, for his purse was usually full. Perchance some of those whom he had led into this dangerous way cursed him, once his influence had ceased; but for a week at least each remained under the charm, and if they broke with Lelli, it was only when their money had completely given out.

"Certainly," said Fuentés to him one evening, "thou hast done wonders towards increasing the number of my customers, but thou hast failed in one quarter: thou hast brought neither the pupils of Velasquez nor those who once studied with Alonso Cano."

"Patience!" said Lelli; "have patience."

"Thou hast often repeated that word to me," said Diego, "but I begin to think that there are souls over which the devil has no power; and honest young men who will never come here."

Lelli burst out laughing.

"Take no wager upon that, Fuentés," he said.

"Why?"

"Thou wilt lose."

"Thinkest thou that Miguel will come?"

"Yes, Miguel himself."

"Dost thou not fear to meet him?"

"Wherefore should I fear?"

"I know not, save that he hath maltreated thee before."

"In words," said Lelli.

"Didst thou not answer him?"

"I never answer insults by insults," said Lelli.

"How, then?"

"With this!" said Lelli, pointing to his stiletto.

"Have a care! It would need but a word—"

"Which no one would dare to speak!"

"Or an act!"

"I will beware of all imprudence."

"Miguel has a poor opinion of thee."

"Yet he will come, I tell thee."

"To-day?"

"No; to-morrow."

"Why wouldst thou bring him here?"

"He is rich," said Lelli; "the King, in memory of his friend and master, Alonso Cano, loads him with favors. He has given him the decoration of a hall in the palace, and the *sargas* for the next procession. In a year's time he will bear the title of painter to the King. Oh, I did not set the bait of gambling for him; he would not bite. A young merchant who does business in the Indies has arranged to meet him here, promising to give him a large order for pictures. Now when one has

tasted the forbidden fruit one generally desires to finish
it."

"Who dost thou bring me to-night?"

"The young Francesco, and this merchant who is to
lure Miguel here to-morrow."

A snatch of a song was just then heard in the street
without, and the conspirators made a sign to each other
to be silent.

A young man entered. He could not have been more
than sixteen; his hair was of that peculiar red in vogue
at that period, and which was lent by artificial means
if the hair were naturally dark. This youth, already
worn out by late hours, seemed scarcely able to bear the
burden of mere existence, and dropped into a large arm-
chair.

"Heaven! but I am bored, Fuentés," said he, "always and everywhere! At thy house less than elsewhere, I admit, but even here I am not sure of finding
amusement. It is a change of scene, that is all. Even
that is something, but not enough. There are poor
people who find existence a blessing, and rich people,
too; but I yawn my life away. I have travelled, and
travel wearied me infinitely. Dinners or banquets interfere with my digestion. Gambling rouses me, not
exactly to enjoyment, but to something like interest, and
I devote myself thereto and throw myself into it, simply
to forget."

"But thy father has a large fortune which thou wilt
one day inherit."

"To be sure; but my father is only fifty."

Even Fuentés shuddered at this precocious cynicism.

"I thought that thou wert ruined by yesterday's vein
of ill luck?" said Lelli.

"So I was, most completely; and yet—'

He drew out his purse and clinked it, it was full of gold.

"Thy father came to thine aid, then?"

"Not he! he wants me to go to India."

"Thou didst borrow?"

"Nay; my friends are spendthrifts like myself."

"Then," said Lelli, "I do not understand."

"My mother has diamonds!" said Francesco.

"She sold them for thee?"

"She is too much under my father's control to do that!"

"Then, whence this gold?"

"I thought thou hadst wit enough to guess."

"Thou sayest that thy mother did not sell her diamonds?"

"No; but I pledged them for her."

"Without telling her?"

"Naturally."

"Should she discover?"

"I may win to-night."

"But if thou dost not win?"

"If I lose—"

He paused and continued:

"If I lose I will do something desperate !"

"Seest thou?" said Lelli, laughing; "this Francesco becomes tragic."

The door opened again, and two other men appeared. Both were grave and pale, with the traces of many cares upon their worn faces. One was an honest man whom the dishonesty of a friend had ruined. Some payments coming due on the morrow, and knowing that he would then be dishonored, he had come to seek at the gambling-table a last desperate resource.

The other was the head of a family reduced to utter

poverty, and, unable to provide for the wants of his numerous family, come to find bread for his children in this cursed haunt.

The men had known each other in happier days, and, meeting under such melancholy circumstances, had confided their desperate situation each to the other. The merchant advised his friend to stake his little all upon the chances of the dice.

The room became gradually full. Young and old, gentlemen and citizens, thronged the *apio* and the *salons*. The merchant from the Indies who was to order pictures from Miguel promptly put in an appearance. The gold clinked in his pockets, and he looked round upon the assemblage with all the assurance of wealth. The play commenced. Scarcely had they taken their places at the table when each one's countenance assumed a different aspect. A deep anguish appeared upon some faces. Their nostrils dilated; their eyes grew fixed; their trembling lips moved only to utter incoherent words, or appeals to the deity of chance, who was to show himself favorable or unfavorable. The chess-players established themselves in a little room apart, while the rest kept possession of the great drawing-room.

The East Indian merchant and the *blasé* youth were the two principal players at dice. Each threw a purse of gold upon the table, and the dice were thrown with marvellous rapidity. So far neither won. The young merchant, with flaming cheeks, and an expression almost of fury, leaned forward with flashing eyes, that he might the more quickly observe his adversary's throw. Francesco, on the contrary, was deadly pale; spite of his perversity the evil deed he had done awakened a latent remorse in his heart. If he had fallen so low he wished at least to gain some return from the passion

that had brought him there. Moreover, he was anxious
to redeem his mother's diamonds. He played with a
sort of desperation, mingled with outbursts of rage or
impatience. Though he had boasted to Lelli of what he
had done, and seemed indifferent as to the consequences,
he felt that he could not meet his mother's eyes if he
had to go home without redeeming the diamonds. Lelli
furtively observed him. The young merchant, playing
with considerable eagerness, had himself more under
control. But chance, upon which Francesco had depended, chance which he had pursued for so many
months, and never caught, far from smiling on him
now, seemed at first to fly farther than ever. He lost
throw after throw till but one piece of gold remained.
Not wishing to risk it on a single throw he changed it
for smaller coin. He won, doubled his winnings, and
won again. He was not cool enough to play with discretion; the demon of avarice, the fever of gain, drove
him to madness.

The young merchant lost his purse of gold, his diamond finger rings, and the buckle of his cap. And as
the merchant lost, the youth saw money being heaped
up around him. He now possessed such a pile of gold
that it seemed as if he could scarcely count it. His face
beamed; he spoke with great volubility, and challenged
all the unsuccessful players.

"I offer," said he, "to play against each of you in
turn."

"Even against me ?" said Lelli.

"And wherefore not, Señor !"

"I bring bad luck."

"Bah!" said the youth, "that is a superstition of thy
country."

"Thou dost not believe it ?"

"Not in the least."

"Let us play, then," said Lelli.

"I am ready," replied Francesco.

Lelli threw first; he had six; his adversary three.

They were playing for a ducat.

"I defy thee to struggle against my luck!" said the youth, confident in his late success.

"Luck varies," said Lelli, shaking the dice.

His adversary bent forward eagerly.

"Five!" cried he; "I can surely beat that!"

But he threw four.

"Let us play for four ducats," said Lelli.

"Agreed; and I throw five."

But Lelli won again. From that time forth the lad lost without interruption. He saw the pile of money which he had so quickly won disappearing even more rapidly.

The blood flew to his head, his eyes grew red, his hands trembled like those of an old man. Once Lelli stopped and said with a mixture of pity and contempt: "Let us stop now; thou still hast enough to redeem thy jewels."

"No! no!" cried the other; "I must play, and go on playing."

"As thou wilt," said Lelli, throwing the dice.

"Lost! I have lost again!" cried the youth, enraged. He looked at what remained of his gold, weighed it in his hand, and said:

"I risk all!"

"I hold the play!" said Lelli.

The young merchant leaned over Lelli's shoulder, the better to watch the play, and most of those present in the house that night formed a circle around the two gamblers. Francesco was deadly pale. Lelli seemed certain of victory.

"Play," said he.

His adversary played.

"Six!" cried he.

Lelli threw the same number. The spectators were breathless. The youth took the dice-box.

"Five!" said he, triumphantly.

"Six," said Lelli, calmly.

The young man pressed his hands to his forehead, and a light almost of insanity shone in his eyes. Lelli did not seem at all vain of his luck, and appeared perfectly willing to continue should any other adversary present himself. He even remarked, courteously enough:

"I am at the service of any one who would like to play against me."

"To-morrow, perchance," said the merchant; "not to-night. The surest way to lose at these games is to be too persistent."

Lelli slipped three pieces of gold into Fuentés' hand, and shortly after went out. He was walking quickly homewards when, before he had time to anticipate the attack, or seek means of defence, he gave a cry, and fell face downwards on the ground. A dark figure, which had followed him from Fuentés' house, had stabbed him between the shoulders with a dagger. By a hasty movement the assassin snatched the pouch which contained the gambler's gold, and disappeared down an adjoining street.

The cry given by Lelli when falling was:

"Confession!"

This is the despairing cry usual in Spain or Spanish Flanders when a sword thrust or dagger stroke threatens the life of a man. Earth crumbling from beneath the feet of him, thus slain, he calls upon his murderer not to close heaven against him. But this time the murderer had fled; and Lelli terrified, lying helpless in that deserted street, and rapidly losing blood from his terrible wound, raised himself, and repeated the cry:

"Confession ! confession !"

The desolate cry penetrated a room, still lighted, in an adjoining house, and the window was opened. Here might be help; and Lelli, whose eyes were already obscured by a film, perceived a man leaning out of the window to see what was going on in the street be'ow.

CHAPTER XX.

THE MONK'S PARDON.

THE man who had opened the window in the neighboring house, now closed it quickly when the wretched Lelli gave his second cry of distress. He hurried down stairs and called to a lackey who was sleeping in a room below:

"Lights, Tote, lights."

Tote soon lit a torch, and when the vestibule was thus illumined, the lackey, by his master's orders, opened the street door, and both rushed out to where, lying upon the pavement, was the follower of Lo Spagnoletto.

The master of the house carefully raised the head of the wounded man, while Tote took him by the feet.

"Señor Miguel," said the servant, "what wouldst thou do with this hapless man?"

"Bring him into my house," said Miguel.

"What! a vagrant, perhaps, a wretch, a—"

"Wounded man who needs our care," said Miguel.

The servant said no more, and helped his master to carry Lelli in. As they passed through the vestibule, the light of the torch fell full upon the man's face.

"Lello Lelli!" cried Miguel.

"Thou knowest him?" asked the domestic.

"Ay, I know him," said Miguel hoarsely. "I know him as a being who was the instrument of a double crime and a double misfortune."

"Thou art trembling, master," said Tote, "If the sight

of this man is so repulsive to thee, we can put him back
where we got him. Besides, I think he is dead."

A groan from Lelli proved that he was still alive.

"No," said Miguel, making a violent effort to overcome his repugnance. "We will do what is necessary
for him. He is still breathing, and it would be wrong
to leave him lying on the pavement. Besides, Heaven
may reward our charitable action by wringing the truth
from these cold lips. Let us hasten to carry him up,
Tote; he is failing fast; and remember he asked for a
priest."

The torch lighted the staircase enough for them to
make their way up, and, besides, a lamp burning in
Miguel's room threw out a bright light from the open
door.

The two men carried Lelli carefully, and reaching the
ante-chamber, laid him upon a divan. Neither dared to
draw out the dagger from the wound, until a surgeon
was brought, so that it was necessary to place Lelli face
downwards among the cushions. The wretch moaned
incessantly, and seemed to be suffering terribly.

"Get a bed ready!" said Miguel.

Tote was about to draw aside the curtains from the
young artist's bed, when the latter seized his arm abruptly, and said:

"Not there! not there! but facing it."

A portable bed was quickly rolled over facing Miguel's,
and upon this Lelli was laid.

"Now, Tote, go for the doctor; wake him and bring
him hither. Meanwhile, I will prepare all that is necessary. As soon as thou hast sent a physician, go and
bring a monk to hear this man's confession."

"I will go, Señor Miguel, I will go," said Tote.

The young painter approached the couch whereon

Lelli lay, and stood looking down upon him with singular intensity.

"Providence," he murmured, "how strange are thy decrees. It was ordained that this man should be stricken in front of this house, should be borne over this threshold, whence he was dismissed, and which he crossed again to do his work of death. O my God, grant him repentance for the evil he has done, and let the truth escape from his lips!"

Miguel then began to busy himself in preparing all that the physician might require in dressing the wound, and this done, impatiently awaited his arrival.

He had not long to wait, and heard the step upon the stairs almost as soon as he had completed his preparations. The artist brought him at once to the bedside.

"Where was he found?" asked the doctor.

"In the street."

"Dost know him?"

"Yes!" said Miguel in a suppressed voice.

"Thou didst well, my dear boy, to leave the dagger in the wound. A hemorrhage seems inevitable, but I may avert it."

The doctor then knelt upon the bed, and with a hasty movement drew the steel from the wound. Lelli uttered a piercing shriek.

"A terrible incision," said the physician, "a difficult wound to heal. If, however, the blade be not poisoned, there may be hope. We must undress him. It would be impossible to take his clothing off, so we must cut it."

Lelli's doublet being cut off him, and his shoulders bared, the doctor found it easier to stanch the wound. He had to bring the bandages across Lelli's chest to keep them firm. When all was done, Miguel gave Lelli some Madeira wine, which revived him.

"Lie neither upon thy back nor chest," said the doctor; "keep always upon thy side, and avoid any sudden movement which may bring on hemorrhage."

"I am lost!" said Lelli.

"There is but little hope!" replied the physician.

Lelli's teeth chattered in affright.

"There is nothing to be done until to-morrow, my friend," continued the physician, addressing Miguel.

"If any unexpected change should take place—"

"Thou wilt send for me."

The doctor pressed Miguel's hand, saying:

"I have had proof of thy goodness of heart before now."

The doctor then went out, and Miguel was left alone with Lelli. In order to keep the light from the patient's eyes, Miguel had turned the lamp very low.

The light in the room was consequently dim. During the dressing of the wound, Miguel had kept as much as possible out of sight, lest Lelli should recognize him. Hence, the wretch had no suspicion that he owed this generous care to the man with whom he had a few years before fought a duel. As is usual with people who are suffering, Lelli kept his eyes closed most of the time. It would seem that when exterior objects no longer strike upon our view, we enter more into ourselves. Thus, Lelli thought of that terrible hour when the unfathomable mysteries of an eternity of justice should be unveiled to him.

He remembered himself at Rome as a child, noisy, violent, harsh with his mother, playing with children of his own age, whose greatest delight was to torment some unoffending creature, or insult some old man. He recalled—oh, how the memory came back to him—his good but weakly indulgent mother, who reproved him gently for a fault, when she should have taken a rod to chastise him. Alas! she dearly expiated a fault which arose from her very goodness of heart. One day, in seeking to force money from the poor woman, whom Lelli had gradually reduced to indigence, he raised his hand as if to strike her. She would not yield, and the blow fell. She did not cry out, nor call for help; she did not even curse him; but Lelli fled, and she never saw him again.

At the age of twenty, he arrived in Naples, where he frequented the lowest haunts, and attached himself to the service of Ribera with a facility which showed a natural perversity. God alone knew the truth as to the bloody tragedy of which Domenichino * was the victim.

As certain animals are irritated by the sight of blood, or by anything of a red color, so Lelli was readily disposed to murder and crime of all sorts. Everything seemed good to him from which he could derive any profit. He had a special tariff for his misdeeds, so much for killing an adversary in a duel, so much for ridding a man of some deadly enemy, so much for ruining a reputation. When he had used the sword and dagger to some purpose in one town, he went to another to continue his course of evil. When this phase of his life came before his mind, Lelli, seized with an awful horror of himself, uttered a cry of agony. Miguel approached the bed. Lelli's eyes were closed: he was, as it were, looking into himself. His memory had transported him to Madrid, where he was a stranger, and which was a new theatre of crime for the gambler and the bully.

---

* Domenichino died before reaching Rome after his sojourn in Naples, and a strong suspicion prevailed that he had been poisoned by a faction at the head of which was Ribera.

He remembered Alonso Cano's benevolent welcome,
his easy life in the studio, amongst the other young men.
This time he had had a chance of repentance, an opportunity to redeem himself.   Virtue and happiness seemed
the atmosphere of the house.   For a time his soul had
been impregnated with it, but evil had so gangrened his
heart, that a cure was impossible.   Hatred soon killed
the germs of good that were unfolding in Lelli's mind.
All at once, he fancied himself in Cano's studio crossing
swords with Miguel—Miguel, for whose sake he had been
dismissed.   And his old vindictiveness surviving his
bodily strength, he murmured:

" Miguel, I will be revenged !"

Miguel heard the words, and still keeping in the shadow, said slowly:

" For what wilt thou be revenged ?"

The sound of his voice, which Lelli at once recognized,
agitated him deeply.   Yet he thought it was a fancy, and
after a feeble attempt to turn in the direction of the
voice, murmured:

"I find him everywhere—him and her !"

Then memory, which was now accompanied with poig-
nant remorse, showed him Mercedes, so merry and so
childish, and who had never either wounded or humiliated him.   First he saw her in her robe of rich brocade,
embroidered in gold, then—

Then he rose upon his elbow, and gazing out before
him, saw a vision truly terrible.   The curtains which
enveloped the great bed, just in front of him, were drawn
aside, and he recognized, by the pale light of the lamp,
Mercedes, her face distorted with horror, her neck and
breast showing deep wounds, her hands covered with
blood.   Thus had he seen her one terrible night, a night
which he could never forget.   Had she come back in his

dying hour, to terrify him with a vision of his crime ? Where was he ? With a fearful effort, he raised himself to a sitting posture, looked round him wildly, in the bewilderment of an unspeakable terror.

He recognized the room now. Every detail of it was familiar, and the bed facing him, the bed in which he had beheld a murdered woman, was one not easily forgotten.

The name of Mercedes rose to his lips.

"Help !" he cried, "help !"

Miguel advanced, but this time confronting Lelli.

"What wouldst thou, Lello Lelli ?" he asked.

Lelli recognized him immediately.

"What revenge art thou going to take ?" said he at once, recovering his composure.

"I have taken it already," said Miguel.

"Yet thou didst not murder me," said Lelli; "it was Francesco, to punish me for having won his money at dice."

"Knowest thou no other vengeance than the spilling of blood ?" asked Miguel.

"No !" said Lelli fiercely.

"I know of a better one," said Miguel.

"What is that ?"

"To return good for evil."

"That is why thou didst pick me up, and bring me here ?"

"Yes."

"Where am I ?"

"In my house."

"Yet it is the same !"

"It was Alonso Cano's !"

"Take me away from here !" said Lelli with feverish

violence. "Take me away! Since thou canst pardon render me that last service."

"I know wherefore thou wouldst go," said Miguel.

"No," said Lelli; "thou dost not, thou canst not know."

"Must I then tell thee?"

"But thou canst not."

"Thou seest *her* here," said Miguel. "Thou seest *her* as upon the night when thou didst leave her for dead, taking with thee *her* diamonds."

"Take me away!" cried Lelli. "These are but hideous fancies; this is but a spectre that pursues me. When I leave this house the bloody phantom will vanish."

"Didst thou not ask for a priest?"

"I shall be dead when he comes, and damned before he can hear my confession."

Just then steps were heard upon the stairs, and Miguel opened the door. Upon the threshold was a monk in his habit of serge. The cowl concealed his face, and his hands were folded in his sleeves.

"Thou didst send for a priest," he said; "I am here."

The tones of the voice went to Miguel's heart. He would fain have caught sight of the face, but the monk held down his head so that recognition was impossible. Miguel pointed to the bed, upon which lay the wounded man, whose gaze was still fixed upon the phantom within the curtains. Miguel drew them together, and when Lelli glanced in that direction again they fell in regular, heavy folds. A sigh of relief escaped him.

The monk, regarding him a moment with a tranquillity which, perhaps, concealed some violent emotion, said in a voice softened by the divine unction of charity:

"I am ready to hear thee, my brother."

Then a strange revulsion took place in Lelli's soul

He had cried out "Confession!" in falling upon the pavement, and the confession which he had to make, all at once caused him such a feeling of horror that he stretched out his arms as if to repulse the monk. A man, on the point of undergoing a dangerous operation, shrinks thus from it, through fear of the pain which is to bring about his salvation.

"My brother," said the monk, "God will soon call thee before His tribunal. Thou wilt have to render an account to Him of evil desires, and criminal acts to which these desires have led; of the good thou hast omitted to do, and the evil thou hast done!"

Lelli sighed deeply.

"Thou hast had," said the monk, "courage to commit many sins—it may be crimes—and thou hast not resolution to avow them. Yet who am I?. The unworthy servant of Him whom thou mayest indeed fear, unless thou takest care to appease His justice."

Lelli was still silent.

"Thou dost not know the man who is hidden by this cowl and robe of serge, and did he know thee, the secrets thou mayest confide to him are guaranteed by his own salvation. What canst thou then fear? Art thou ashamed of him? Yet each day he humbles himself before his God. Art thou unwilling to submit to the justice of God? In an hour hence He will demand of thee an inexorable account of every word and thought. Speak as though thou wert alone, and striking thy breast before the Lord, ask Him to apply the merits of His passion to thy soul, and to pardon thee."

"Pardon!" cried Lelli. "Dost thou believe that God will pardon all crimes?"

"All!" said the monk gravely.

"But if the criminal, blinded by cupidity and the thirst

for gold, had robbed a friend of all that he possessed, and having robbed him, found himself at the hour of death totally unable to make restitution?"

"The Lord will be content with the sincerity of his repentance."

"And the man whom he has robbed?"

"The servant is not greater than the master," said the monk.

"So much for material goods," said the penitent, with an effort; "but if there was question of a life, that most precious of all possessions, and which man is unable to restore, once he has taken it?"

"Those who are with God, pardon after His example," said the monk.

"But suppose," continued Lelli, "that a man had stricken a feeble, defenceless creature—a woman—which is a double crime; that, this murder committed, he fled, letting suspicion fall upon an innocent man; that this innocent man was proscribed, condemned, put to the torture, from which he escaped alive almost by a miracle. Dost believe that there can be pardon for crimes like this?"

"I believe so, firmly," said the monk.

"What? Can the blood of the Saviour wash a soul so deeply stained?"

"It would suffice to wash away the sins and the crimes of generations past and future!"

"Hear me," said Lelli. "A moment since I suffered from a terrible hallucination; the form of my victim arose before me. In the shadows of this room the bloody figure of Mercedes appeared to me."

"Mercedes!" repeated the monk, in a voice faint as an echo.

Lelli continued in an abrupt way.

"If thou couldst but know how I hated Alonso Cano! Wherefore, when he had loaded me with benefits? It was because I was at once jealous and ungrateful. I hated him as the serpent might hate the generous lion. His reputation, his glory, his wealth seemed to me so many thefts committed to my prejudice. I detested not only Alonso Cano, but all who were connected with him in any way—his wife, who seemed to have an instinctive terror of me; his pupils, who left my poor talent as a copyist so far behind. When Alonso Cano drove me away, I wished to leave him shame and sorrow as my legacy. Having ostensibly left the house, I returned at night by means of a key which I had kept. The master was absent; his wife, for some childish reason, in tears. There was some talk of a ball, and of a hasty departure I had often enough seen Mercedes' diamonds to appreciate their full value. I resolved not to leave Spain till I took them with me. Having reached the little room which I had formerly occupied, and in which no one now knew of my presence, I waited till the house was perfectly still. Then I came out and stole into Mercedes' room. She seemed to be asleep. I snatched up the jewels, which lay upon the table, and was about to fly with my spoils, when Mercedes suddenly awoke, recognized me, and screamed aloud. I feared she might be overheard, and rushed over, bidding her be silent. She threatened to rouse the house. I took my dagger!"

The monk stifled a sob, and Lelli, absorbed in the memory of that terrible scene, went on:

"I struck her blindly, recklessly, madly, till my hands were red with her blood, till I felt that the body was lifeless beneath my stiletto, and the breath gone from the lips which I violently compressed."

A foam gathered upon the wretch's lips as he spoke.

"I killed Mercedes !   I killed Mercedes !" he cried.

After a moment's pause he asked:

"Is there pardon for me ?"

"If thou dost repent."

"Oh, that is not all !" said Lelli: "I threw the terrible suspicion of this crime upon another, upon the husband of Mercedes !"

"What next ?" said the monk, calmly.

"When, by some imprudence, he fell into the hands of the law," said Lelli, "he was put to the torture and suf-fered excruciating agony."

"That was his martyrdom !" said the monk.

"Ah !" cried Lelli, "that crime was even more horrible than the first. After having stricken my benefactor in his affections, I attacked him in his honor, his unsullied reputation, and even in his person, which I would have killed. Can God pardon that ?"

"He only wishes to pardon thee," said the monk.

"I will then finish my confession," said Lelli.

He told of his youth, up to the time of his arrival in Madrid; of what he had done during his first journey to Naples, and the events which had followed his return to Spain. He spoke of the evening at Fuentés' house, and the revenge of Francesco, whom he had robbed by cheat-ing at play.

"Dost thou repent of these sins ?" said the monk.

"I know not whether I repent," said Lelli, "but I be-lieve and I am afraid."

"Of eternal punishments ?" asked the monk.

"Yes !" said Lelli.

"Brother," said the monk, "through the merits of thy Saviour, Jesus, this fear must lead thee to repentance. When the absolution of the priest falls upon thee, thy soul will be purified. But that thou mayest offer more to thy Lord than a sentiment so feeble and imperfect, try to find another motive for thy sorrow. Remember the mercy of the divine Saviour of men, and the miracles of His bounty, so that thou mayest come to repent of thy sins, not only because divine justice reserves for them a punishment proportioned to their magnitude, but because in sullying thus thy soul, thou hast tarnished a pure mirror which contained the reflection of God, profaned the treasures of His grace, and trampled His sacred redemption under foot. Forget everything at this supreme moment but the crucifix which I hold to thy lips. Repent of thy sins for the love of Jesus Christ; not only will they be remitted, but thou mayest hope for the eternal felicity granted to repentant sinners, as well as to the just."

So saying, the monk drew a crucifix from his girdle and held it to Lelli's lips.

"Father! father!" murmured the wretch, "I believe that God will pardon me, but oh that the man whom I have injured, and delivered up to torture, were here to forgive me. Bring him, I implore thee. I would arise from my dying bed to cast myself at his feet. I would cry out, 'Mercy! mercy!'"

"Strike thy breast, thou who hast sinned," said the monk, with superhuman authority. Lelli obeyed, shuddering.

In a voice of thrilling power, the monk then raised his hand.

"*Absolvo te,*" he began, "I absolve thee."

Whilst his right hand made the sacred sign, his left unfastened the hood of his capuchin, and showed to the astonished eyes of Lello Lelli the transfigured face of Alonso Cano.

"Thou !" cried Lelli, "thou ! and hast thou the power to absolve ?"

"I am a priest !" said Cano, "with the power to absolve thee ! I pardon thee from my heart, and I thank our Lord Jesus Christ that He hath made me the instrument of His mercy."

"Pardon ! oh, pardon !" murmured Lelli; "I am dying."

Miguel rushed forward and seized him in his arms, while Alonso Cano fell upon his knees. All night long the two men kept watch beside the mortal remains of Mercedes' murderer. After having attended to the burial, Alonso returned to Granada, where obedience called him; but by a special privilege granted to his incomparable genius, he inhabited till his death a studio which was fitted up for him in the Great Tower.

The Michael Angelo of Spain was buried in 1676, under the chancel of the cathedral of Granada.

THE END.

STANDARD CATHOLIC BOOKS

PUBLISHED BY

BENZIGER BROTHERS,

CINCINNATI:	NEW YORK:	CHICAGO:
343 MAIN ST.	36 AND 38 BARCLAY ST.	211-213 MADISON ST.

DOCTRINE, INSTRUCTION, DEVOTION.

ABANDONMENT; or, Absolute Surrender of Self to Divine Providence. Rev.
J. P. CAUSSADE, S.J. *net*, 0 40

ADORATION OF THE BLESSED SACRAMENT. TESNIERE. Cloth, *net*, 1 25

ANECDOTES AND EXAMPLES ILLUSTRATING THE CATHOLIC CATE-
CHISM. Selected and Arranged by Rev. FRANCIS SPIRAGO, Professor of
Theology. Supplemented, Adapted to the Baltimore Catechism, and Edited
by Rev. JAMES J. BAXTER, D.D. *net*, 1 50

APOSTLES' CREED, THE. Rev. M. MÜLLER, C.SS.R. *net*, 1 10

ART OF PROFITING BY OUR FAULTS. Rev. J. TISSOT. *net*, 0 40

BEGINNINGS OF CHRISTIANITY. By Very Rev. THOMAS J. SHAHAN, S.T.D.
J.U.L., Professor of Church History in the Catholic University of Washington.
  net, 2 00

BIBLE HISTORY. 0 50

BIBLE HISTORY, PRACTICAL EXPLANATION AND APPLICATION OF.
Rev. J. J. NASH. *net*, 1 50

BIBLE, THE HOLY. 1 00

BOOK OF THE PROFESSED
Vol. I. *net*, 0 75
Vol. II. *net*, 0 60
Vol. III. *net*, 0 60

BOYS' AND GIRLS' MISSION BOOK. By the Redemptorist Fathers. 0 40

CATECHISM EXPLAINED, THE. SPIRAGO-CLARKE. *net*, 2 50

CATHOLIC BELIEF. FAA DI BRUNO.
Paper, 0 25; 100 copies, 15 00
Cloth, 0 50; 25 copies, 7 50

CATHOLIC CEREMONIES and Explanation of the Ecclesiastical Year. ABBE
DURAND.
Paper, 0 30; 25 copies, 4 50
Cloth, 0 60; 25 copies, 9 00

CATHOLIC PRACTICE AT CHURCH AND AT HOME. Rev. ALEX. L. A.
KLAUDER.
Paper, 0 30; 25 copies, 4 50
Cloth, 0 60; 25 copies, 9 00

CATHOLIC TEACHING FOR CHILDREN. WINIFRIDE WRAY. 0 40

CATHOLIC WORSHIP. Rev. R. BRENNAN, LL.D.
Paper, 0 15; 100 copies, 10 00
Cloth, 0 25; 100 copies, 17 00

CEREMONIAL FOR ALTAR BOYS. By Rev. MATTHEW BRITT, O.S.B., 0 35

CHARACTERISTICS OF TRUE DEVOTION. Rev. N. GROU, S.J. *net*, 0 75

CHARITY THE ORIGIN OF EVERY BLESSING. 0 60

FIRST COMMUNICANT'S MANUAL.   o 50
    100 copies,   25 00
FLOWERS OF THE PASSION. Thoughts of St. Paul of the Cross. By
    Rev. Louis Th. de Jesus-Agonisant.   o 50
FOLLOWING OF CHRIST. Thomas à Kempis.
    With Reflections,   o 50
    Without Reflections,   o 45
    Edition de luxe,   1 25
FOUR LAST THINGS, THE: Death, Judgment, Heaven, Hell. Meditations.
    Father M. v. Cochem. Cloth,   o 75
GARLAND OF PRAYER. With Nuptial Mass. Leather.   o 90
GENERAL CONFESSION MADE EASY. Rev. A. Konings, C.SS.R.
    Flexible. o 15; 100 copies,   10 00
GENERAL PRINCIPLES OF THE RELIGIOUS LIFE. Verheyen, O.S.B.
    net, o 30
GLORIES OF DIVINE GRACE. Dr. M. J. Scheeben.   net, 1 50
GLORIES OF MARY. St. Alphonsus de Liguori. 2 vols.,   net, 2 50
    Popular ed. 1 vol.,   1 25
GOD THE TEACHER OF MANKIND. Müller. 9 vols.   Per set, net, 9 50
GOFFINE'S DEVOUT INSTRUCTIONS. 140 Illustrations.   1 00
    25 copies,   17 50
GOLDEN SANDS. Little Counsels for the Sanctification and Happiness of
    Daily Life.
    Third Series,   o 50
    Fourth Series,   o 50
    Fifth Series,   o 50
GRACE AND THE SACRAMENTS. By Rev. M. Müller, C.SS.R. net, 1 25
GREAT MEANS OF SALVATION AND OF PERFECTION. St. Alphon-
    sus de Liguori.   net, 1 25
GREAT SUPPER OF GOD, THE. A Treatise on Weekly Communion. By
    Rev. S. Coube, S.J. Edited by Rev. F. X. Brady, S.J.   net, 1 00
GREETINGS TO THE CHRIST-CHILD, a Collection of Poems for the Young.
    Illustrated.   o 60
GUIDE TO CONFESSION AND COMMUNION.   o 60
HANDBOOK OF THE CHRISTIAN RELIGION. By Rev. W. Wilmers, S.J.
    net, 1 50
HARMONY OF THE RELIGIOUS LIFE. Rev. H. J. Heuser.   net, 1 25
HELP FOR THE POOR SOULS IN PURGATORY. Prayers and Devotions in
    aid of the Suffering Souls.   o 50
HELPS TO A SPIRITUAL LIFE. From the German of Rev. Jos. Schneider,
    S.J. With Additions by Rev. Ferreol Girardey, C.SS.R.   net, 1 25
HIDDEN TREASURE: The Value and Excellence of the Holy Mass. By
    St. Leonard of Port Maurice.   o 50
HISTORY OF THE MASS. By Rev. J. O'Brien.   net, 1 25
HOLY EUCHARIST. By St. Alphonsus de Liguori. The Sacrifice, the
    Sacrament, and the Sacred Heart of Jesus Christ. Novena to the Holy Ghost.
    net, 1 25
HOLY MASS. By Rev. M. Müller, C.SS.R.   net, 1 25
HOLY MASS. By St. Alphonsus de Liguori.   net, 1 25
HOW TO COMFORT THE SICK. Rev. Jos. A. Krebs, C.SS.R.   net, 1 00
HOW TO MAKE THE MISSION. By a Dominican Father. Paper, o 10;
    per 100,   5 00
ILLUSTRATED PRAYER-BOOK FOR CHILDREN.   o 25
IMITATION OF CHRIST. See "Following of Christ."
IMITATION OF THE BLESSED VIRGIN MARY. Translated by Mrs. A.
    R. Bennett-Gladstone.
    Plain Edition,   o 50
    Edition de luxe,   1 50
IMITATION OF THE SACRED HEART. By Rev. F. Arnoudt, S.J. Entirely
    new, reset edition.   1 25

3

IMMACULATE CONCEPTION, THE. By Rev. A. A. Lambing, LL.D. o 35
INCARNATION, BIRTH, AND INFANCY OF JESUS CHRIST; or, the
    Mysteries of Faith. By St. Alphonsus de Liguori. *net*, 1 25
INDULGENCES, A PRACTICAL GUIDE TO. Rev. P. M. Bernad, O.M.I.
    o 75
IN HEAVEN WE KNOW OUR OWN. By Père Blot, S.J. o 60
INSTRUCTIONS AND PRAYERS FOR THE CATHOLIC FATHER.
    Right Rev. Dr. A. Egger. o 60
INSTRUCTIONS AND PRAYERS FOR THE CATHOLIC MOTHER.
    Right Rev. Dr. A. Egger. o 60
INSTRUCTIONS AND PRAYERS FOR CATHOLIC YOUTH. o 60
INSTRUCTIONS FOR FIRST COMMUNICANTS. By Rev. Dr. J. Schmitt.
    net, o 50
INSTRUCTIONS ON THE COMMANDMENTS OF GOD and the Sacraments
    of the Church. By St. Alphonsus de Liguori.
    Paper, o 25; 25 copies, 3 75
    Cloth, o 40; 25 copies, 6 00
INTERIOR OF JESUS AND MARY. Grou. 2 vols., *net*, 2 00
INTRODUCTION TO A DEVOUT LIFE. By St. Francis de Sales.
    Cloth, o 50
LETTERS OF ST. ALPHONSUS DE LIGUORI. 4 vols., each vol., *net*, 1 25
LETTERS OF ST. ALPHONSUS LIGUORI and General Alphabetical Index
    to St. Alphonsus' Works. *net*, 1 25
LITTLE ALTAR BOY'S MANUAL. o 25
LITTLE BOOK OF SUPERIORS. *net*, o 60
LITTLE CHILD OF MARY. A Small Prayer-book. o 35
LITTLE MANUAL OF ST. ANTHONY. Lasance. o 25
LITTLE MANUAL OF ST. JOSEPH. Lings. o 25
LITTLE MONTH OF MAY. By Ella McMahon. Flexible, o 25
LITTLE MONTH OF THE SOULS IN PURGATORY. o 25
LITTLE OFFICE OF THE IMMACULATE CONCEPTION. o.05; per 100, 2 50
LITTLE PICTORIAL LIVES OF THE SAINTS. New cheap edition. 1 00
LIVES OF THE SAINTS. With Reflections for Every Day of the Year.
    Large size, 1 50
LIVING CHURCH OF THE LIVING GOD. Coppens. o.10; per 100, 6 00
MANUAL OF THE HOLY EUCHARIST. Conferences on the Blessed Sacra-
    ment and Eucharistic Devotions. By Rev. F. X. Lasance. o 75
MANUAL OF THE HOLY FAMILY. o 60
MANUAL OF THE HOLY NAME. o 50
MANUAL OF THE SACRED HEART, NEW. o 50
MANUAL OF THE SODALITY OF THE BLESSED VIRGIN. o 50
MANUAL OF ST. ANTHONY, LITTLE. Lasance. o 25
MANUAL OF ST. ANTHONY, NEW. o 60
MANUAL OF ST. JOSEPH, LITTLE. Lings. o 25
MARIÆ COROLLA. Poems by Father Edmund of the Heart of Mary, C.P.
    Cloth, 1 25
MASS DEVOTIONS AND READINGS ON THE MASS. By Rev. F. X. Lasance.
    o 75
MAY DEVOTIONS, NEW. Rev. Augustine Wirth, O.S.B. *net*, 1 00
MEANS OF GRACE. By Rev. Richard Brennan, LL.D. 2 50
MEDITATIONS FOR ALL THE DAYS OF THE YEAR. By Rev. M. Hamon,
    S.S. 5 vols., *net*, 5 00
MEDITATIONS FOR EVERY DAY IN THE YEAR. Baxter. *net*, 1 25
MEDITATIONS FOR EVERY DAY IN THE YEAR. Rev. B. Vercruysse,
    S.J. 2 vols., *net*, 2 75
MEDITATIONS FOR RETREATS. St. Francis de Sales. Cloth, *net*, o 75
MEDITATIONS ON THE FOUR LAST THINGS. Father M. v. Cochem.
    o 75

MEDITATIONS ON THE LAST WORDS FROM THE CROSS. Father CHARLE. PERRAUD. *net*, 0 50

MEDITATIONS ON THE LIFE, THE TEACHINGS, AND THE PASSION OF JESUS CHRIST. ILG-CLARKE. 2 vols., *net*, 3 50

MEDITATIONS ON THE MONTH OF OUR LADY. 0 75

MEDITATIONS ON THE PASSION OF OUR LORD. 0 40

METHOD OF CHRISTIAN DOCTRINE, SPIRAGO'S. Edited by Right Rev. S. G. MESSMER. *net*, 1 50

MIDDLE AGES, THE: Sketches and Fragments. By Very Rev. THOMAS J. SHAHAN, S.T.D., J.U.L. *net*, 2 00

MISCELLANY. Historical Sketch of the Congregation of the Most Holy Redeemer. Rules and Constitutions of the Congregation of the Most Holy Redeemer. Instructions on the Religious State. By St. ALPHONSUS DE LIGUORI. *net*, 1 25

MISSION BOOK FOR THE MARRIED. Very Rev. F. GIRARDEY, C.SS.R. 0 50

MISSION BOOK FOR THE SINGLE. Very Rev. F. GIRARDEY, C.SS.R. 0 50

MISSION BOOK OF THE REDEMPTORIST FATHERS. A Manual of Instructions and Prayers to Preserve the Fruits of the Mission. Drawn chiefly from the Works of St. ALPHONSUS LIGUORI. 0 50

MOMENTS BEFORE THE TABERNACLE. Rev. MATTHEW RUSSELL, S.J. *net*, 0 40

MONTH, NEW, OF THE HOLY ANGELS. St. FRANCIS DE SALES. 0 25

MONTH, NEW, OF THE SACRED HEART. St. FRANCIS DE SALES. 0 25

MONTH OF MAY; a Series of Meditations on the Mysteries of the Life of the Blessed Virgin. By F. DEBUSSI, S.J. 0 50

MONTH OF THE SOULS IN PURGATORY, The Little "Golden Sands." 0 25

MORAL BRIEFS. By the Rev. JOHN H. STAPLETON. *net*, 1 25

MOST HOLY SACRAMENT. Rev. Dr. Jos. KELLER. 0 75

MY FIRST COMMUNION, the Happiest Day of My Life. BRENNAN. 0 75

MY LITTLE PRAYER-BOOK. Illustrated. 0 12

NEW MAY DEVOTIONS. WIRTH. *net*, 1 00

NEW MONTH OF THE HOLY ANGELS. 0 25

NEW MONTH OF THE SACRED HEART 0 25

NEW SUNDAY-SCHOOL COMPANION. 0 25

NEW TESTAMENT. Cheap Edition.
32mo, flexible cloth, *net*, 0 15
32mo, lambskin, limp, round corners, gilt edges, *net*, 0 70

NEW TESTAMENT. Illustrated Edition.
16mo, printed in two colors, with 100 full-page illustrations *net*, 0 60
16mo, American Seal, limp, solid gold edges, *net*, 1 25

NEW TESTAMENT. India Paper Edition.
American Seal, limp, round corners, gilt edges, *net*, 0 90
Persian Calf, limp, round corners, gilt edges, *net*, 1 10
Morocco, limp, round corners, gold edges, gold roll inside, *net*, 1 25

NEW TESTAMENT. Large Print Edition.
12mo, large, *net*, 0 75
12mo, American Seal, limp, gold edges, *net*, 1 50

NEW TESTAMENT STUDIES. By Right Rev. Mgr. THOMAS J. CONATY, D.D. 12mo, 0 60

OFFICE, COMPLETE, OF HOLY WEEK. 0 50

ON THE ROAD TO ROME. By W. RICHARDS. *net*, 0 50

OUR FAVORITE DEVOTIONS. By Very Rev. Dean A. A. LINGS. 0 75

OUR FAVORITE NOVENAS. Very Rev. Dean A. A. LINGS. 0 75

OUR LADY OF GOOD COUNSEL IN GENAZZANO. Mgr. GEO. F. DILLON, D.D. 0 75

6

VISITS TO JESUS IN THE TABERNACLE. Hours and Half Hours of Adora-
tion before the Blessed Sacrament. With a Novena to the Holy Ghost and
Devotions for Mass, Holy Communion etc. Rev. F. X. LASANCE. 1 25
VISITS TO THE MOST HOLY SACRAMENT and to the Blessed Virgin Mary.
By St. ALPHONSUS DE LIGUORI. 0 50
VOCATIONS EXPLAINED: Matrimony, Virginity, The Religious State, and the
Priesthood. By a Vincentian Father. 0.10; 100 copies, 6 00
WAY OF INTERIOR PEACE. By Rev. Father DE LEHEN, S.J. *net*, 1 25
WAY OF SALVATION AND PERFECTION. Meditations, Pious Reflections,
Spiritual Treatises. St. ALPHONSUS DE LIGUORI. *net*, 1 25
WAY OF THE CROSS. Paper, 0.05; 100 copies, 2 50
WHAT THE CHURCH TEACHES. An Answer to Earnest Inquirers. By
Rev. EDWIN DRURY, Missionary Priest. Paper, 0.30; 25 copies, 4 50
Cloth, 0.60; 25 copies, 9 00

JUVENILES.

ADVENTURES OF A CASKET.	0 45
ADVENTURES OF A FRENCH CAPTAIN.	0 45
AN ADVENTURE WITH THE APACHES. By GABRIEL FERRY.	0 45
ANTHONY. A Tale of the Time of Charles II. of England.	0 45
ARMORER OF SOLINGEN. By WILLIAM HERCHENBACH.	0 40
AS TRUE AS GOLD. MANNIX.	0 45
BERKLEYS, THE. WIGHT.	0 45
BERTHA; or, Consequences of a Fault.	0 45
BEST FOOT FORWARD. By Father FINN.	0 85
BETTER PART.	0 45
BISTOURI. By A. MELANDRI.	0 45
BLACK LADY AND ROBIN RED BREAST. By CANON SCHMID.	0 25
BLANCHE DE MARSILLY.	0 45
BLISSYLVANIA POST-OFFICE. By MARION AMES TAGGART.	0 45
BOB O'LINK. WAGGAMAN.	0 45
BOYS IN THE BLOCK. By MAURICE F. EGAN.	0 25
BRIC-A-BRAC DEALER.	0 45
BUNT AND BILL. CLARA MULHOLLAND.	0 45
BUZZER'S CHRISTMAS. By MARY T. WAGGAMAN.	0 25
BY BRANSCOME RIVER. By MARION AMES TAGGART.	0 45
CAKE AND THE EASTER EGGS. By CANON SCHMID.	0 25
CANARY BIRD. By CANON SCHMID.	0 40
CAPTAIN ROUGEMONT.	0 45
CARROLL DARE. By MARY T. WAGGAMAN.	1 25
CASSILDA; or, the Moorish Princess.	0 45
CATHOLIC HOME LIBRARY. 10 vols., each,	0 45
CLAUDE LIGHTFOOT; or, How the Problem was solved. By Father FINN.	0 85
COLLEGE BOY, A. By ANTHONY YORKE. Cloth,	0 85
CONVERSATION ON HOME EDUCATION.	0 45
COPUS, REV., J.E., S.J.:	
HARRY RUSSELL.	0 85
SHADOWS LIFTED.	0 85
ST. CUTHBERT'S.	0 85
DIMPLING'S SUCCESS. By CLARA MULHOLLAND.	0 45
EPISODES OF THE PARIS COMMUNE. An Account of the Religious Perse-
cution.	0 45
ETHELRED PRESTON, or the Adventures of a Newcomer. By Father FINN.	0 85
EVERY-DAY GIRL, AN. By MARY C. CROWLEY.	0 45
FATAL DIAMONDS. By E. C. DONNELLY.	0 25

8

9

LINKED LIVES. A Novel. By Lady Gertrude Douglas.   1 50
MARCELLA GRACE. A Novel. By Rosa Mulholland. Illustrated Edition.
                                                                      1 25
MISS ERIN. A Novel. By M. E. Francis.   1 25
MONK'S PARDON, THE. A Historical Novel of the Time of Philip IV. of
    Spain. By Raoul de Navery.   1 25
MR. BILLY BUTTONS. A Novel. By Walter Lecky.   1 25
OUTLAW OF CAMARGUE, THE. A Novel. By A. de Lamothe.   1 25
PASSING SHADOWS. A Novel. By Anthony Yorke.   1 25
PÈRE MONNIER'S WARD. A Novel. By Walter Lecky.   1 25
PILKINGTON HEIR, THE. A Novel. By Anna T. Sadlier.   1 25
PRODIGAL'S DAUGHTER, THE. By Lelia Hardin Bugg.   1 00
RED INN OF ST. LYPHAR, THE. A Romance of La Vendée. By Anna
    T. Sadlier.   1 25
ROMANCE OF A PLAYWRIGHT. By Vte. Henri de Bornier.   1 00
ROUND TABLE OF THE REPRESENTATIVE AMERICAN CATHOLIC
    NOVELISTS. Complete Stories, with Biographies, Portraits, etc.   1 50
ROUND TABLE OF THE REPRESENTATIVE FRENCH CATHOLIC NOV-
    ELISTS. Complete Stories, with Biographies, Portraits, etc.   1 50
ROUND TABLE OF THE REPRESENTATIVE GERMAN CATHOLIC NOV-
    ELISTS. Illustrated.   1 50
ROUND TABLE OF THE REPRESENTATIVE IRISH AND ENGLISH
    CATHOLIC NOVELISTS. Complete Stories, Biographies, Portraits, etc.
    Cloth,   1 50
RULER OF THE KINGDOM, THE. And other Phases of Life and Character.
    By Grace Keon.   1 25
THAT MAN'S DAUGHTER. By Henry M. Ross.   1 25
TRANSPLANTING OF TESSIE, THE. By Mary T. Waggaman.   0 60
TRUE STORY OF MASTER GERARD, THE. By Anna T. Sadlier.   1 25
UNRAVELING OF A TANGLE, THE. A Novel. By Marion A. Taggart.   1 25
VOCATION OF EDWARD CONWAY. A Novel. By Maurice F. Egan.   1 25
WOMAN OF FORTUNE, A. By Christian Reid.   1 25
WORLD WELL LOST. By Esther Robertson.   0 75

LIVES AND HISTORIES.

AUTOBIOGRAPHY OF ST. IGNATIUS LOYOLA. Edited by Rev. J. F. X.
    O'Conor. Cloth,   net, 1 25
BIBLE STORIES FOR LITTLE CHILDREN. Paper, 0 10; Cloth,   0 20
CHURCH HISTORY. Businger.   0 75
HISTORIOGRAPHIA ECCLESIASTICA quam Historiæ seriam Solidamque
    Operam Navantibus, Accommodavit Guil. Stang, D.D.   net, 1 00
HISTORY OF THE CATHOLIC CHURCH. Brueck. 2 vols.,   net, 3 00
HISTORY OF THE CATHOLIC CHURCH. By John Gilmary Shea, LL.D.
                                                               1 50
HISTORY OF THE PROTESTANT REFORMATION IN ENGLAND AND
    IRELAND. By Wm. Cobbett. Cloth,   net, 0 75
LETTERS OF ST. ALPHONSUS LIGUORI. By Rev. Eugene Grimm, C.SS.R.
    Centenary Edition. 5 vols., each,   net, 1 25
LIFE AND LIFE-WORK OF MOTHER THEODORE GUÉRIN Foundress of
    the Sisters of Providence at St.-Mary-of-the-Woods, Vigo County, Indiana.
                                                               net, 2 00
LIFE OF CHRIST. Illustrated. By Father M. v. Cochem.   1 25
LIFE OF FR. FRANCIS POILVACHE, C.SS.R. Paper,   net, 0 20
LIFE OF MOST REV. JOHN HUGHES. Brann.   net, 0 75
LIFE OF MOTHER FONTBONNE, Foundress of the Sisters of St. Joseph of
    Lyons. By Abbé Rivaux. Cloth,   net, 1 25

LIFE OF SISTER ANNE KATHERINE EMMERICH, of the Order of St. Augustine. By Rev. THOMAS WEGENER, O.S.A. *net*, 1 50
LIFE OF ST. ANTHONY. WARD. Illustrated. 0 75
LIFE OF ST. CATHARINE OF SIENNA. By EDWARD L. AYME, M.D. 1 00
LIFE OF ST. CLARE OF MONTEFALCO. LOCKE, O.S.A. *net*, 0 75
LIFE OF MLLE. LE GRAS. *net*, 1 25
LIFE OF ST. CHANTAL. BOUGAUD. 2 vols. *net*, 4 00
LIFE OF THE BLESSED VIRGIN. Illustrated. By Rev. B. ROHNER, O.S.B. 1 25
LITTLE LIVES OF SAINTS FOR CHILDREN. BERTHOLD. Ill. Cloth, 0 75
LITTLE PICTORIAL LIVES OF THE SAINTS. New, cheap edition, 1 00
LIVES OF THE SAINTS, With Reflections and Prayers for Every Day. 1 50
OUR LADY OF GOOD COUNSEL IN GENAZZANO. A History of that Ancient Sanctuary. By ANNE R. BENNETT-GLADSTONE. 0 75
OUTLINES OF JEWISH HISTORY, From Abraham to Our Lord. Rev. F. E. GIGOT, S.S. *net*, 1 50
OUTLINES OF NEW TESTAMENT HISTORY. By Rev. F. E. GIGOT, S.S. Cloth, *net*, 1 50
PICTORIAL LIVES OF THE SAINTS. Cloth, 2 50
REMINISCENCES OF RT. REV. EDGAR P. WADHAMS, D.D., First Bishop of Ogdensburg. By Rev. C. A. WALWORTH. *net*, 1 00
ST. ANTHONY, THE SAINT OF THE WHOLE WORLD. Rev. THOMAS F. WARD. Cloth, 0 75
STORY OF JESUS. Illustrated. 0 60
STORY OF THE DIVINE CHILD. By Very Rev. Dean A. A. LINGS. 0 75
VICTORIES OF THE MARTYRS. By St. ALPHONSUS DE LIGUORI. *net*, 1 25
VISIT TO EUROPE AND THE HOLY LAND. By Rev. H. FAIRBANKS. 1 50

THEOLOGY, LITURGY, SERMONS, SCIENCE, AND PHILOSOPHY.

ABRIDGED SERMONS, for All Sundays of the Year. By St. ALPHONSUS DE LIGUORI. Centenary Edition. GRIMM, C.SS.R. *net*, 1 25
BLESSED SACRAMENT, SERMONS ON THE. Especially for the Forty Hours' Adoration. By Rev. J. B. SCHEURER, D.D. Edited by Rev. F. X. LASANCE. *net*, 1 50
BREVE COMPENDIUM THEOLOGIAE DOGMATICAE ET MORALIS una cum aliquibus Notionibus Theologiae Canonicae Liturgiae, Pastoralis et Mysticae, ac Philosophiae Christianae. BERTHIER. *net*, 2 50
CHILDREN OF MARY, SERMONS FOR THE. From the Italian of Rev. F. CALLERIO. Edited by Rev. R. F. CLARKE, S.J. *net*, 1 50
CHILDREN'S MASSES, SERMONS FOR. FRASSINETTI-LINGS. *net*, 1 50
CHRISTIAN APOLOGETICS: A Defense of the Catholic Faith. By Rev. W. DEVIVIER, S.J. Edited by the Rt. Rev. S. G. MESSMER, D.D., D.C.L., Bishop of Green Bay. *net*, 1 75
CHRISTIAN PHILOSOPHY. A Treatise on the Human Soul. By Rev. J. T. DRISCOLL, S.T.L. *net*, 1 50
CHRISTIAN PHILOSOPHY: God. DRISCOLL. *net*, 1 25
CHRIST IN TYPE AND PROPHECY. Rev. A. J. MAAS, S.J., Professor of Oriental Languages in Woodstock College. 2 vols., *net*, 4 00
CHURCH ANNOUNCEMENT BOOK. *net*, 0 25
CHURCH TREASURER'S PEW. Collection and Receipt Book. *net*, 1 00
COMPENDIUM JURIS CANONICI, ad usum Cleri et Seminariorum hujus Regionis accommodatum. *net*, 2 00
COMPENDIUM JURIS REGULARIUM. Edidit P. AUGUSTINUS BACHOFEN, O.S.B. *net*, 2 50

COMPENDIUM SACRAE LITURGIAE JUXTA RITUM ROMANUM UNA cum Appendice de jure Ecclesiastico Particulari in America Foederata Sept. vigente scripsit P. INNOCENTIUS WAPELHORST, O.S.F. Editio sexta emendatior. *net*, 2 50

COMPENDIUM THEOLOGIAE DOGMATICAE ET MORALIS. BERTHIER. *net*, 2 50

CONFESSIONAL, THE. By the Right Rev. A. ROEGGL, D.D. *net*, 1 00

DE PHILOSOPHIA MORALI PRAELECTIONES quas in Collegio Georgiopolitano Soc. Jesu, Anno 1889-90 Habuit P. NICOLAUS RUSSO. Editio altera. *net*, 2 00

ECCLESIASTICAL DICTIONARY. By Rev. JOHN THEIN. *net*, 5 00

ELEMENTS OF ECCLESIASTICAL LAW. By Rev. S. B. SMITH D.D.
ECCLESIASTICAL PERSONS. *net*, 2 50
ECCLESIASTICAL PUNISHMENTS. *net*, 2 50
ECCLESIASTICAL TRIALS. *net*, 2 50

ENCYCLICAL LETTERS OF POPE LEO XIII., THE GREAT. Translated from approved sources. With Preface by Rev. JOHN J. WYNNE, S.J. *net*, 2 00

FUNERAL SERMONS. By Rev. AUG. WIRTH, O.S.B. 2 vols., *net*, 2 00

GENERAL INTRODUCTION TO THE STUDY OF HOLY SCRIPTURES. By Rev. FRANCIS E. GIGOT, S.S. Cloth, *net*, 2 50

GOD KNOWABLE AND KNOWN. By Rev. MAURICE RONAYNE, S.J. *net*, 1 25

GOOD CHRISTIAN, THE. Rev. J. ALLEN, D.D. 2 vols. *net*, 5 00

HISTORY OF THE MASS AND ITS CEREMONIES IN THE EASTERN AND WESTERN CHURCH. By Rev. JOHN O'BRIEN. *net*, 1 25

HUNOLT'S SERMONS. 12 vols., *net*, 25 00

HUNOLT'S SHORT SERMONS. 5 vols., *net*, 10 00

INTRODUCTION TO THE STUDY OF THE HOLY SCRIPTURES. GIGOT. *net*, 1 50

INTRODUCTION TO THE STUDY OF THE OLD TESTAMENT. Vol. I. GIGOT. *net*, 1 50

JESUS LIVING IN THE PRIEST. MILLET-BYRNE. *net*, 2 00

LAST THINGS, SERMONS ON THE FOUR. HUNOLT. Translated by Rev. JOHN ALLEN, D.D. 2 vols., *net*, 5 00

LENTEN SERMONS. Edited by AUGUSTINE WIRTH, O.S.B. *net*, 2 00

LIBER STATUS ANIMARUM; or, Parish Census Book. *Pocket Edition*, *net*, 0.25; half leather, *net*, 2 00

MORAL PRINCIPLES AND MEDICAL PRACTICE, THE BASIS OF MEDICAL JURISPRUDENCE. By Rev. CHARLES COPPENS, S.J., Professor of Medical Jurisprudence in the John A. Creighton Medical College, Omaha, Neb.; Author of Text-books in Metaphysics, Ethics, etc. *net*, 1 50

NATURAL LAW AND LEGAL PRACTICE. HOLAIND, S.J. *net*, 1 75

NEW AND OLD SERMONS. A Repertory of Catholic Pulpit Eloquence. Edited by Rev. AUGUSTINE WIRTH, O.S.B. 8 vols., *net*, 16 00

OUTLINES OF DOGMATIC THEOLOGY. By Rev. SYLVESTER JOS. HUNTER, S.J. 3 vols., *net*, 4 50

OUTLINES OF JEWISH HISTORY, from Abraham to Our Lord. By Rev. FRANCIS E. GIGOT, S.S. *net*, 1 50

OUTLINES OF NEW TESTAMENT HISTORY. GIGOT. Cloth, *net*, 1 50

PASTORAL THEOLOGY. By Rev. WM. STANG, D.D. *net*, 1 50

PENANCE, SERMONS ON. By Rev. FRANCIS HUNOLT, S.J. Translated by Rev. JOHN ALLEN. 2 vols., *net*, 5 00

PENITENT CHRISTIAN, THE. Sermons. By Rev. F. HUNOLT. Translated by Rev. JOHN ALLEN, D.D. 2 vols., *net*, 5 00

PEW-RENT RECEIPT BOOK. *net*, 1 00

PHILOSOPHIA, DE, MORALI. RUSSO. *net*, 2 00

POLITICAL AND MORAL ESSAYS. RICKABY, S.J. *net*, 1 50

PRAXIS SYNODALIS. Manuale Synodi Diocesanae ac Provincialis Celebrandae. *net*, 0 60

13

REGISTRUM BAPTISMORUM. *net*, 3 50

REGISTRUM MATRIMONIORUM. *net*, 3 50

RELATION OF EXPERIMENTAL PSYCHOLOGY TO PHILOSOPHY. Mgr. DE MERCIER. *net*, 0 35

RITUALE COMPENDIOSUM seu Ordo Administrandi quaedam Sacramenta et alia Officia Ecclesiastica Rite Peragendi ex Rituali Romano, novissime edito desumptas. *net*, 0 90

ROSARY, SERMONS ON THE MOST HOLY. FRINGS. *net*, 1 00

SACRED HEART, SIX SERMONS ON DEVOTION TO THE. By Rev. Dr. E. BIERBAUM. *net*, 0 60

SANCTUARY BOYS' ILLUSTRATED MANUAL. Embracing the Ceremonies of the Inferior Ministers at Low Mass, High Mass, Solemn High Mass, Vespers, Asperges, Benediction of the Blessed Sacrament and Absolution for the Dead. By Rev. J. A. McCALLEN, S.S. *net*, 0 50

SERMON MANUSCRIPT BOOK. *net*, 2 00

SERMONS, ABRIDGED, FOR SUNDAYS. LIGUORI. *net*, 1 25

SERMONS FOR CHILDREN OF MARY. CALLERIO. *net*, 1 50

SERMONS FOR CHILDREN'S MASSES. FRASSINETTI-LINGS. *net*, 1 50

SERMONS FOR THE SUNDAYS AND CHIEF FESTIVALS OF THE ECCLESIASTICAL YEAR. With Two Courses of Lenten Sermons and a Triduum for the Forty Hours. By Rev. J. POTTGEISSER, S.J. 2 vols. *net*, 2 50

SERMONS FROM THE LATINS. BAXTER. *net*, 2 00

SERMONS, FUNERAL. WIRTH. 2 vols., *net*, 2 00

SERMONS, HUNOLT'S. 12 vols., *net*, 25 00

SERMONS, HUNOLT'S SHORT. 5 vols. *net*, 10 00

SERMONS, LENTEN. WIRTH. *net*, 2 00

SERMONS, NEW AND OLD. WIRTH. 8 vols., *net*, 16 00

SERMONS ON DEVOTION TO THE SACRED HEART. BIERBAUM. *net*, 0 75

SERMONS ON OUR LORD, THE BLESSED VIRGIN, AND THE SAINTS. HUNOLT. 2 vols., *net*, 5 00

SERMONS ON PENANCE. HUNOLT. 2 vols., *net*, 5 00

SERMONS ON THE BLESSED SACRAMENT. SCHEURER-LASANCE. *net*, 1 50

SERMONS ON THE CHRISTIAN VIRTUES. By Rev. F. HUNOLT, S.J. Translated by Rev. JOHN ALLEN. 2 vols. *net*, 5 00

SERMONS ON THE DIFFERENT STATES OF LIFE. By Rev. F. HUNOLT, S.J. Translated by Rev. JOHN ALLEN. 2 vols. *net*, 5 00

SERMONS ON THE FOUR LAST THINGS. HUNOLT. 2 vols., *net*, 5 00

SERMONS ON THE ROSARY. FRINGS. *net*, 1 00

SERMONS ON THE SEVEN DEADLY SINS. By Rev. F. HUNOLT, S.J. 2 vols. Translated by Rev. JOHN ALLEN, D.D. *net*, 5 00

SERMONS ON THE STATES OF LIFE. HUNOLT. 2 vols., *net*, 5 00

SHORT SERMONS. By Rev. F. HUNOLT, S.J. 5 vols., 10 00

SHORT SERMONS FOR LOW MASSES. SCHOUPPE, S.J. *net*, 1 25

SOCIALISM EXPOSED AND REFUTED. CATHREIN. *net*, 1 00

SPECIAL INTRODUCTION TO THE STUDY OF THE OLD TESTAMENT. Part I. The Historical Books. By Rev. FRANCIS E. GIGOT, S.S. *net*, 1 50

SYNOPSIS THEOLOGIAE DOGMATICAE AD MENTEM S. THOMAE AQUINATIS hodiernis moribus accommodata, auctore AD. TANQUEREY, S.S. 3 vols., *net*, 5 25

SYNOPSIS THEOLOGIAE MORALIS ET PASTORALIS. 2 vols. TANQUEREY. *net*, 3 50

THEOLOGIA DOGMATICA SPECIALIS. TANQUEREY. 2 vols., *net*, 3 50

THEOLOGIA FUNDAMENTALIS. TANQUEREY. *net*, 1 75

VIEWS OF DANTE. By E. L. RIVARD, C.S.V. *net*, 1 25

MISCELLANEOUS.

A GENTLEMAN. By M. F. EGAN, LL.D.   0 75

A LADY. Manners and Social Usages. By LELIA HARDIN BUGG.   0 75

BENZIGER'S MAGAZINE. The Popular Catholic Family Magazine. Subscription per year.   2 00

BONE RULES; or, Skeleton of English Grammar. By Rev. J. B. TABB, A.M.   0 50

CANTATA CATHOLICA. By B. H. F. HELLEBUSCH.   *net*, 2 00

CATHOLIC HOME ANNUAL. Stories by Best Writers.   0 25

CORRECT THINGS FOR CATHOLICS, THE. By LELIA HARDIN BUGG. 0 75

ELOCUTION CLASS. A Simplification of the Laws and Principles of Expression. By ELEANOR O'GRADY.   *net*, 0 50

EVE OF THE REFORMATION, THE. An Historical Essay on the Religious, Literary, and Social Condition of Christendom, with Special Reference to Germany and England, from the Beginning of the Latter Half of the Fifteenth Century to the Outbreak of the Religious Revolt. By the Rev. WM. STANG. Paper,   *net*, 0 25

GUIDE FOR SACRISTANS and Others Having Charge of the Altar and Sanctuary. By a Member of an Altar Society.   *net*, 0 75

HYMN-BOOK OF SUNDAY-SCHOOL COMPANION.   0 35

HOW TO GET ON. By Rev. BERNARD FEENEY.   1 00

LITTLE FOLKS' ANNUAL. 0.10; per 100,   7 50

READINGS AND RECITATIONS FOR JUNIORS. O'GRADY.   . *net*, 0 50

SELECT RECITATIONS FOR CATHOLIC SCHOOLS AND ACADEMIES. By ELEANOR O'GRADY.   1 00

STATISTICS CONCERNING EDUCATION IN THE PHILIPPINES. HEDGES.   0 10

SURSUM CORDA. Hymns. Cloth, 0.25; per 100,   15 00
Paper, 0.15; per 100,   10 00

SURSUM CORDA. With English and German Text.   0 45

PRAYER-BOOKS.
> Benziger Brothers publish the most complete line of prayer-books in this country, embracing
>> PRAYER-BOOKS FOR CHILDREN.
>> PRAYER-BOOKS FOR FIRST COMMUNICANTS.
>> PRAYER-BOOKS FOR SPECIAL DEVOTIONS.
>> PRAYER-BOOKS FOR GENERAL USE.
>
> Catalogue will be sent free on application.

SCHOOL BOOKS.
> Benziger Brothers' school text-books are considered to be the finest published. They embrace
>> NEW CENTURY CATHOLIC READERS. Illustrations in Colors.
>> CATHOLIC NATURAL READERS.
>> CATECHISMS.
>> HISTORY.
>> GRAMMARS.
>> SPELLERS.
>> ELOCUTION.
>> CHARTS.

www.ingramcontent.com/pod-product-compliance
Lightning Source LLC
Chambersburg PA
CBHW060519030726
47498CB00004B/997